THE FOLLOWING

Harshada Pathare

Anecdote
Publishing House

Anecdote
Publishing House

Anecdote Publishing House
E-35-A, E Block, Gali No. 2, Ganesh Nagar,
Pandav Nagar Complex, Delhi - 110092

Published by Anecdote Publishing House

First Edition 2023

ISBN: 9788195251841

MRP: ₹ 299.00

Book Promoted and Marketed by Champ Readers Pvt. Ltd.
Edited by Harshada Pathare
Layout and Cover by Anecdote
Printed by Thomson Press, India

Contents

This book is dedicated to my Grandfather

Shri. Prabhakar Shivram Pathare

After his demise, I learned, the story of my maternal grandfather, my strongest blood connection; my love for literature along with my creativity, abilities, and optimism largely came from him.

Preface

Kalki Agastya is content with her common life, common happy life. She is in her early twenties, earning by freelancing, and living in a 2BHK flat with her mother in the busy metropolis of Mumbai. All the ordinary thoughts, common lifestyle, and simple things mark the philosophy of her life except for her indecisive high-profile boyfriend. As of now, nothing in her life seems like a challenge than calm her boyfriend's angry mood to a better in-control mood. This is the main reason why her mother does not approve their relationship.

She is her mother's wings, the very wings that forced and inspired her to fly against the storms. Had it not been for Kalki, her mother would have been caged in an abusive and loveless marriage. Growing up, she has seen her mother as strong and sad, a calm in the chaos, an ocean in turbulence, hope in the azure sky, a wisdom found in the library, and God in every sense. Her life revolves around her mother, her prolific boyfriend and her gigs making it a perfect universe to live in.

However, one line that is certain, eventually, something would pull her common life apart.

The dead are not dead. They are howling out their countless stories while wandering around aimlessly in the dark. Ghosts have a unique approach inspired by their intellectual level at the time of death. Many believe that an exorcism acts as a fire extinguisher of sorts - that the targeted ghost is snuffed out, but remember, a ghost is born of its own free will, and no one can force one to vacate. Compelled by visceral longing and purposeful blindness, we make our own Ouija boards and call upon ghosts at midnight. We believe that we have created communication lines to the other side and have de-energized the ghostly power in our surroundings.

However, what happens when the communication lines are hijacked by the spirit world and they attempt to contact her for a mission. How far can she go from these paranormal experiences? What is the real identity of the girl besides being her mother's daughter? Is there an escape route to it? Is Kalki ready to surpass her limits and know the real purpose of her existence? Is she willing to take up that role or willing to weave her ordinary craft?

Kalki has started seeing ghosts, paranormal occurrences and is freaking out trying to make sense. From saints to soothsayers, she is approaching all but not getting any answers until she rests her foot on the mystic land of Kashi.

MAIN CHARACTERS

- Kalki Agastya – Female protagonist
- Meera Agastya – Kalki's mom, lecturer in a college, separated from her abusive husband
- Abheer Suryavanshi – Eldest son of a real estate typhoon, Kalki's current boyfriend
- Karthik Dev – Orphan – an ex-student of Meera Agastya – and Kalki's future lover in the upcoming chapters

CHAPTER ONE

I AM NOT ALONE

In the world of digitalization, socialization of the media is sprouting as a strong medium to recreate social experiences. Everyone desires to have large number of followers but what happens when you come to know that your followers are not fake, cyberbullies, criminals but DEAD PEOPLE...GHOSTS.

I could feel the gaze of multiple eyes watching me closely. Metaphysical beings were not only watching me but transmitting their massive spiritual energies in my direction. The reason was still unknown. From the boundaries of two worlds demarcated by the rules of the cosmos, I knew someone lighter than venerated marble was strolling in the nocturnal light, whispering deep melodies—inaudible but heard by the soul. Following me like a shadow.

“Who are you? Why do you follow me? What do you want from me?” My questions would echo back to me, sometimes in a mocking tone.

I browsed Google, reading about invisible dark forces, ghosts, and spirits following you. Would it be like a vampire as in Twilight or some magic world like Harry Potter? Did I have a connection to the demons or was there some mystery about my previous incarnation that needed to be discovered?

Considering the importance of elderly advice on such topics, I secretly shared these happenings with my grandmother, in the hope to find a solution. She gave a list of recommendations that consisted of superstitions, hearsay, and her own devised formulas—like reciting Hanuman Chalisa, visiting temples every day, not washing hair at night, avoiding meat and beer, detoxing during a full moon, and keeping a distance from my boyfriend, as a female ghost could possess my body to have a night of romance with him. Grandma broke my trust when she shared these things with my mother. The result of this was a ban on watching all sorts of horror and supernatural series. Mom emphasized that I should focus on positive energy and thoughts to overcome such dark phases. Her commands had no other say at home. I started obeying her words. Soon, I was seen praying, chanting mantras, planting plants, and watching mythological shows with a devotional face.

My horoscope revolved around the best astrologers insisting on in-depth analysis and a powerful solution to stop the effects of negativity. Some of the remedies were Kaal-Sarp yoga, puja (worship), the havan ritual at temples, and gemstones or donations as prescribed in Lal Kitaab. Mom was entertaining all of these ideas, and seeing this, I had no alternative but to tell her I'd been fooling her to seek her attention. It was a joke to get time from her busy schedule. I could convince Grandma to forget. But mom was smarter and couldn't be convinced.

"I know my sincere and studious daughter. Does she even know the meaning of prank?" I overheard her arguments with Grandma and walked away.

It was a dark, beautiful night, stormy and loaded with violent gushes of wind, distracting the silence. Rain fell in torrents while lightning illuminated the dark rooms. I was feeling like a sailor lost in a wide ocean without any compass, just looking up at the sky to guide me. As I thought about it, I was soaked through with sweat and tears.

"Is this real or a hallucination?" I asked my best friend, my table lamp, and waited for an answer. The table lamp was my age-old friend, having been around since my school days, and we talked about everything. Sometimes, the power of attention received by small things transforms them into something very significant.

Suddenly, the lamp flashed . . . blink . . . blink . . . as if communicating some answer to me.

"What?" I yelled in a soft muffle.

"Is it true? Someone is following me?"

There was no reply to this question. As if someone had placed a gun on his back, my best friend had become non-responsive.

Thinking and thinking, I fell asleep. At midnight, I wanted to drink water but didn't dare to open my eyes. Finally, my parched throat made my eyes open. I looked up to my room in disbelief.

Some numbers were reflected on the walls—maybe eight or nine—make me think someone was there in the room. I had little bookish knowledge of physics, but nothing I knew was in line with the current scenario. I closed my eyes tight and started chanting Hanuman Chalisa. I felt as if some apparitions would appear to my left or right or front or back, but I didn't have the guts to see whatever it was in its true form.

A low, indistinct voice echoed and bounced off before reaching me. I remained perched on the bed, imagining monstrous specters. The darkness around me continued to fade as faint sunlight penetrated the windows.

Not knowing when I lay down on the bed, I continued to toss and yank from one side to the other, trying to drift back to sleep. Finally, I got up, determined not to talk about this to anyone and worry them further. I didn't want to worry my mom further; she had already suffered a lot. At least till now, I had no proof to the presence of any invisible force.

After having omelet sandwiches and orange juice in breakfast, I decided to go to the gym and do a rigorous workout as a mental detox. The best thing about being a freelance content writer was that I didn't have to stick to any office schedule, though my working hours extended beyond daylight and even ate up Sundays. I loved the freedom of choice, and I loved leveraging my creative expertise for my passion. All it takes is a simple idea and tons of courage.

Gyming is a hodgepodge of pain and pleasure. A firm body, defined structure, tight abs, and sleek shoulders are the best assets any woman can get from a regular workout. Exercise not only enhances your whole body but also keeps you energetic. Skipping the warm-ups, I leaped directly to the power moves to shift my focus. After a vigorous squat press session, push-ups, jumps, upper body exercises, and leg exercises, I continued running on the treadmill, ignoring the trainer and other gym friends.

Drenched in sweat and mental impurities, I was tempted to jump into a sweltering steam bath to soothe my senses.

I entered the hot, wood-scented steam room, ready to towel off but suddenly stopped. The steam room was staring at me, making me sweat faster than usual. I felt something creeping around me. I stepped back . . . but was stepping back the only solution? How long and how many times should I step back? I resolved to face it, once and for all. I made up my mind not to get frightened but to continue the steamy ritual. A steamy scented bath was a heavenly luxury, and I continued to immerse myself in it greedily and gratefully.

Afterward, I walked away with refined radiance and peace of mind. Due to my ongoing garboil, I stopped interacting with the people, but right now, nothing mattered more to me than the present.

After reaching home, I opened the fridge to quench my post-workout dehydration. I added a spoonful of honey and a slice of lemon to my glass of water, stirring it and thinking that the paranormal episode would soon end.

Just then, my phone rang. It was Mom, so I picked up the call.

"Hi, dear. Are you working now or can you go to the mall to buy some groceries? I'll SMS the grocery list."

"Look, Mom. I'm tired and highly worked. Why don't you order groceries online; they'll be delivered at the doorstep and make our lives much easier."

"Okay, dear. I have a lecture now. I'll keep on calling you in between. Love you, baby," she said with an unseen smile and ended the conversation.

I headed back to my room. It seemed that mom aimed to do a hundred things at once. She had charged my laptop, rearranged my wardrobe, refilled the air purifier, and done a basic clean-up of my work desk. The rest was good, but I didn't like that my work desk being touched in my absence. This rule even applied to my mom also. Please keep a distance from my home office.

I turned off my MacBook's charger and took out the EarPods from the case, playing Zen music to bring in positive vibes. Breathing calmly, I lay on the bed as the loving ambiance cradled me, welcoming sleep.

Still, half-asleep, half-awake, I tossed on my belly to drift into REM sleep and release the hormone of darkness—melatonin.

Something exceptional happened. A tactile yet mystical experience that will stay forever in my brain.

A puff of air blew over my body and through my hair. The effect of soothing comfort and an unfamiliar caress engulfed my empty veins in ecstasy. Locked in the depths of the mind, I performed a mid-air loop in the light spectrum of amplitude.

"Kalki, Kalki." I could hear our maid was trying to wake me up.

My body was far away, sleeping in a peaceful atmosphere. Listening to her voice, I had to throttle that sense of peace to return. Slowly, I opened my eyes and started reconnecting the dots. "What?" I asked in a soft tone, trying to weave the correlations between tangible and intangible.

"Should I bring lunch to your room?" she asked and waited for an answer.

Vaishali had been working with us for more than two decades. She was our trusted confidante and had been with us through ups and downs. Mom counted on her opinions, and Vaishali was part of our home life. Her husband, Raghav, was a workman in a manufacturing company and earned an average salary. He was a decent man with a helpful nature and allowed Vaishali to work, as it was her personal choice. The major chunk of Raghav's salary was allocated to their mortgage, medical expenses, and life insurance premiums. Vaishali's income was solely spent on her children's educational expenses.

"Kalki." A slight squeeze jolted me from my thoughts.

"I'm not hungry. Please leave me alone," I pleaded in a merciful tone.

"Are you okay?" She got more inquisitive and spoke in a softer tone.

"I'm very tired and need some rest." I had quickly substituted the truth with a lie.

"What else will happen with such food habits?" She started grumbling about my lifestyle. "You are just nestled in your room with work all day. Go out for fresh air. Take a holiday, and visit some hill station. Why will you not listen to me?" she continued until I interrupted her with a spooky line.

"Have you ever seen any ghosts?" I asked in a frightened tone.

Hearing the word ghost, the pupils of her black eyes widened like saucers, and her mouth dropped open. After a moment of deadly silence, she said in a tone of fear and confusion, "In our village, there is an old peepal tree. It is believed that on every new moon, ghosts and ghouls sit on the branches of the trees to possess the body of anyone who sits in its shade. Villagers avoid going near the tree on such days . . ."

She succeeded in convincing me that ghosts exist with her folklore legends. We had a long exchange of stories and facts that forced me to believe that the invisible forces behind me really could be ghosts—maybe like in The Sixth Sense or something. One way or another, I was locked into something mysterious. It didn't occur to me that it was already night.

The first rule of success for any entrepreneur is good and prompt communication, and the second is to keep upgrading your knowledge, skills, and abilities. I have always focused on these tenants and established a good reputation for myself in the market. In my college days, I started writing reviews as a tool to improve my writing skills. Suddenly, I received my first paid gig to write content for a product website, and from that point, my journey began. Even before I tossed my graduation cap and walked across the stage with a big degree in hand, my freelancing was no more than a side hustle. My freelancing had progressed with a list of myriad clients and sleepless nights with gigs and exams. Though mom wanted me to focus only on my studies, I convinced her that freelancing was giving me practical exposure to the creative market. By the time, I was out of college, my name was already under the brand spotlight.

I walked into mom's room, remembering how she had created her own unique image from the experiences that had broken her into hundreds of isolated fragments. It was my presence in her life that sparked her desire to live. Still, the shadows of her pain and sufferings were cast all over the surface. Her stillness and courage were piecing every together to weave a part of her legacy.

"Mom, I want to speak with you," I said, trying to distract her attention. Surrounded by a stack of volcanic books, she was skimming the pages of an academic tome, analyzing an unknown topic.

"I'm not here to speak with you, not the walls," I loudly exclaimed to see how she'd reply.

She gave a sarcastic smile and pushed the book aside. "Thank God, you're not here for walls. Even they would have collapsed listening to your gibber-jabber." She brushed her fingers through my hair.

I sat down on her bed and leaned on her pillow. "I'm sleeping here, and you're telling me real ghost stories."

"You want to listen to ghost stories?" she chuckled as I nodded mischievously.

"Yes," I said, my voice carrying through the room.

"Were Vaishali's ghost stories not enough for the day?" she asked, glancing into my eyes.

How could Vaishali do this to me? I thought. She's a real gossip-monger passing out every bit and piece to mom.

"Kalki, listen to what I'm saying," said in a firm voice.

We stared at each other. I knew we are heading to a not-so-calm discussion. A series of lectures, loaded with quotations from Bhagavat Geeta and anecdotes of great lives—everything to make me agreeable to her point of view.

I lay on the bed as she sat beside me, touching my forehead. It made me feel better.

She said, "No talks or lectures. Let's have a friendly chat. This is a real happening on our maternal side of the family. My aunt (Mausi) would often tell us stories about how she had the psychic powers to speak with ghosts."

"Speak with ghosts? Mom, this is impossible according to quantum physics. How can a body of matter and a soul composed of light communicate?" I was really puzzled.

"Science explains rationality, not a mystery. If there is positive energy, then there is negative energy also. Look at the sky; you will see a full moon and a dark moon; there is a combination of black and white to complete the symmetrical configuration of nature. Generations have passed ghost stories—the fear of evil—to others, and we will continue to do so. Ghosts are embedded in our minds, and few people have certified the presence with their stories of paranormal activities, exorcism, and other horror tales. The body and soul are a whole composition after death. The body and soul get separated, and the soul exists on a separate metaphysical plane—a different dimension altogether." She smiled and continued to stroke my hair.

"Mom, what is the proof that your aunt really spoke with ghosts?" I raised my eyebrow.

"Proof?" she sounded amazed. "Baby that was a different culture existing at a different time in a different environment. The earlier ecosystem was filled with affection, compassion, and trust, where everyone adjusted and accommodated to live in harmony. In the jungles of concrete, there was a river of love that flowed to quench the thirst of thirsty travelers. People had a lot of respect for words, and trust was the foundation of every relationship. My aunt was a child-widow and had a position of utmost respect in society. She was awake before the gleaming rays of the morning sun would pass through her window. Many other ladies would participate in her devotional puja, mantra chanting, and recitation of Vedas and Satsang. People in society looked upon her for blessings and guidance. She had the power to communicate with ghosts in the dark. Once, when a senior person, Joshi, died of a sudden heart attack, her widow approached my aunt for help. It is said that the ghost of Joshi informed her of the secret place where he had hidden property papers, cash, and other valuable deposits. After this episode, the aunt had become something of a legend.

There was a silence, and I realized that it was all getting too complex. I started making assumptions, linking all of these paranormal arrests to genetic coding. Mom switched off the lights, creating total darkness in the room and my mind, too. The breeze wafted through the room; mom continued to brush my hair till sleep subdued me once again.

In the middle of the gloomy night, I woke up with some instinct. I spun my head around to look in every direction. The clock struck 3 a.m., meaning the demons were now free. The witching hour was enough to scare me. Strong winds rattled the window panes; mom was sound asleep. I snuggled down under the cozy blanket to be safe from the demonic power. But curiosity forced me to peep out from my blanket. I stared at the bedroom door, which had been left open.

I was staring at the bold red lumbar door when there was an explosive sound—like cannon fire rumbling across the sky. After a moment, my attention went back to the door. I sighed in disbelief as fear spilled through the pores of my body. Grandma was standing beside the door in a slouching posture and staring at me with languid eyes. She was different; there was a glimmer of an evil soul inside her.

Did grandma come home? I wondered. Why is she behaving so weirdly? I looked at her for some sort of reciprocation.

And suddenly . . .

Something had pinned me down. I felt a force on top of me—something that had halted my every movement. I couldn't move or yell or even wink. I was awake yet in sleep. My eyes were fixed on the figure as its face became clearer upon approach. I was unable to stretch out my hand to wake up my mom. My whole body was paralyzed by its stare.

But God made mothers because he couldn't be everywhere. Suddenly, my mom's hand fell upon me, and in a fraction of a second, the trance was broken. I was free.

I woke her up with my shouts and cries and started narrating the entire episode to her. She thought it was a result of our supernatural thoughts and tried to pacify me with scientific theories.

"Kalki, it's okay. This happens to everyone; it's called sleep paralysis. It's nothing else. Stop linking it to evil and devils," Her words resonated in my mind like an ineluctable mantra.

"But . . . I saw grandma there. She was standing halfway behind the open door and staring at me. If you're not afraid, why do you not check?" I asked.

"Ok, let me check it out," she asserted.

"No, you're not leaving me alone here." I caught hold of her wrist.

"I need to check the house. Call me if you see anyone." She brushed my hand aside and went to inspect the home. She returned ten minutes later with relief on her face and cheeks shining with sweat. "There is no one in this room except for us two."

Mom consoled me. I pretended to be calm."

"Mom, why don't you call up Uncle and check if Grandma is okay?" I pleaded in a soft voice to which she made no reply.

I looked at her again, but this time, she reacted in a harsh voice. "Kalki, I have to go to work tomorrow. Let me sleep now."

Mom switched off the lights, signaling me to sleep quietly. With closed eyes, I thought of everything possible to keep myself safe. I recollected some TV soaps that mentioned an electromagnetic frequency detector and an EMF gauss meter.

**"The skies are dark blue with smell of oceans and trees,
Will these energies ruin peace of my life even today?"**

CHAPTER TWO

Reconnecting With Him

Mom laid breakfast on the dining table. "Kalki, come, sit down for breakfast. Let us have a talk." She crouched down and pulled me close to her chest. She looked at my slightly overloaded face. A silence loomed between us as we munched on some sandwiches and cornflakes.

"Do you want to pursue higher studies in some foreign university?" Mom wanted to get me back to being my usual self.

"I want to focus on starting my own creative agency soon. Mom, I will not accept any financial support from you. If there's any other thought, I'll let you know." I held her palm in my hand and reassured her with an expression of love and trust.

"Did you speak with Abheer? Are you two still together . . .?"

"Mom," I said in a stern voice.

"I need to know," she bounced back.

"Please try to understand, Mom. Love is about happiness, joy, and emotional stability. In this relationship, I am only the poem, and the poet, Abheer, is just an abstract emotion. Give us time to light up the spark that's ready to surge between us."

"Why should you devote so much energy to sustaining a relationship?" Mom questioned with a deepened frown.

"Is it you who is asking me this question?" I asked sarcastically.

"Yes, so you don't suffer the same fate," she interjected.

"Abheer is my boyfriend. We aren't even considering marriage at this point. We want to focus on our respective careers as of now. So, don't worry about it anymore," I replied nonchalantly before taking a sip of water.

"Please, don't end up being pushed in the wrong relationship," she said, raising her voice.

"Mom, look at the time. You're late for college. Please, be quick," I said, jamming her laptop and a few files into her bag, which she shouldered before kissing me goodbye and walking out, slamming the front door.

Grabbing my big cup of hot coffee, I walked to the balcony dressed in a red embroidered top and denim jeans. The view was so beautiful—a delicacy beyond measure. I looked up at the deep, azure sky with half-closed eyes. A patch of teal was adding double beauty to the sky-blue love. All shades and shapes of grey were racing across the horizon. We could hear the footsteps of black storm clouds drawing closer. The birches began to dance with joy, and birds soared back to the safety of their nests as the trees started whistling with partners calling them back home. The blending, foaming, and merging of nature were ongoing. A beautiful panoramic view, all for free in the best resolution.

"Love is much, much worse," I said to myself. "It's not going to be easy for me. If I want you forever, then I'll have to work on enriching it every day. Together, we need to make this relationship meaningful and satisfying." I mumbled and continued to sip coffee.

I vividly remembered our first meeting. He'd been sitting in his office cabin, looking around at some product prototypes when I entered, and suddenly, the world around us vanished. It was love at first sight—love at every sight—and we were in awe of each other.

Abheer was a product designer but, above all else, an art-lover. He spent most of his time wandering around, looking for consumer insights, product demand, and other research material. His job was to design and deliver delightful, seamless experiences to millions of people.

Design played a vital role in his job. It's through a perfect design that the team comes to focus on the right problems, crafting holistic products. Their role needs them to closely work with some of the best engineers and marketing champs. Design is an art—a peer to everyone. Believe it or not, every job in this world has some degree of art involved in it.

The melodies of our meetings continued to play in my mind like an endless song of a sailor. His smile . . . there was something in it that I couldn't look away from. His sight made my heart crash against my rib cage, breaking into a thousand pieces. I had never guessed this meeting would be more about love than a freelance content assignment. The one glance. Layers of staring. Everything was suspended in the air. A tide of longing. First-drawn sketches and the bracing of lips upon lips. Nothing on this earth matters more than an amorous embrace.

As mentioned in The Little Book of Big Management Theories, after the forming stage, we enter into the storming mode. If life was good at work, he brought positive vibes on our dates; or else, everything was about his job issues and deadlines. Initially, I loved to motivate him—enable him to change his outlook, look at problems from different perspectives, and appreciate his hard work. But slowly, he placed more complaints on the table. His estranged relationship with his father, non-selection for a higher post, and his younger brother's increasing dominance in the family business. I tried to give him a glimpse of a bigger world—a calmer one, endowed with gratitude and full of abundance. But Abheer had narrowed down everything—even our relationship.

Seeing my work as a freelancer infuriated Abheer. He made a mental comparison of our jobs and aired remarks like, "It's difficult to work here. I feel like I'm entering a warzone daily. I haven't seen the twilight sky for a decade. You're your own boss—no pleasing or buttering. Working or not, only you will only check your performance." The gravity of his comments was aggravating.

"Oh, Abheer, how can I explain to you the constraints and challenges of working as a freelancer? Sample presentations to acquire a gig, no fixed pay, no mentoring, contract-signing, project cancellations, feedback, competition, no paid holiday, and worst of all—we compete with all of the workers in the worldwide gig, not just your 4–5 colleagues in a well.

Abheer's father, Mr. Suryavanshi, was a well-known real estate developer in Mumbai; he'd started his business from scratch and wrote his exceptional success story. Abheer's younger bro, Kabeer, was very much inspired by his father's entrepreneurial guts and joined the family business after completing his studies. Kabeer now represented the second generation of his father's sprawling empire. Ambitious, political, and focused, he was hell-bent on making it extraordinary.

Abheer followed his mother's footsteps. From his mother, he inherited a love for art, virtue, and truthfulness. He had a disdain for his father's business, which I respected, supporting Abheer in his decision not to enter the family business.

His father seemed to have been deeply hurt by Abheer's attitude and behavior. This was the sole reason for his refusal to fund Abheer's business ideas. Even Abheer's mother couldn't change his father's mind. Gradually, Abheer's mother made him the nominee of her three prime residential properties, and his 5% share in the profits continued.

There wasn't much interaction between Abheer and Kabeer—only mutual recognition and respect. But Kabeer was a staunch follower of his father, making Abheer feel insecure at times. As he had said, Abheer felt suffocated and irritated at home, what with all the business talk and constant planning. Every time he returned home, he felt he was heading toward a place devoid of peace. Abheer believed that—other than his other—he had no one at all in his life. He just wanted to move out but remained there, thinking of his mother.

Pared- down to his barest essence, he was imperfectly perfect to me. Without flaws, the perfect aspects of our lives become dull and colorless. The Japanese philosophy, Wabi-Sabi, explicates how real beauty lies in simplicity, imperfection, and transience of things in nature.

There are a hundred things I dislike about Abheer . . . and a billion more reasons to love him. Seeing the plentiful rain falling outside, I wished to be struck again by the lightning of his love. I walked back inside the house and picked up my cell phone to call him. Just then, my ringtone sounded, and my caller ID flashed on the display screen.

"Think of the devil; the devil is here," I murmured, tapping on the green button to accept the call. "Hello," I answered in a soft voice.

"Do you wish to continue missing me like this forever?" Abheer said.

I remained quiet for a long minute. "Abheer, trust me, I was about to call you today."

"It's been more than a month since we last spoke," he quickly replied.

"How's everything, Abheer? Your work? Your family members?"

He didn't reply to my questions, but his silence spoke volumes.

After a while, I said, "You're a designer; you know how to create better solutions with an empathetic view toward consumers. You incorporate sustainability in products, so why is your own life an exception? Abheer Suryavanshi, redesign yourself." My motivating words threaded into him. Silence loomed.

"I want to start my own product design consultancy or innovation consultancy, but what if I fail?" he argued.

"Are you succeeding now?" I shot back.

"I can't forget how dad's business suffered because of my decisions," he said in a soft voice.

On graduating, he joined his father's business as a business acquisition manager. When his father had gone abroad for some business, Abheer had made a few decisions and implemented them without even consulting the seniors or his father. There was some dramatic shift in the market scenario, and the organization suffered heavy losses in income and assets.

The Suryavanshi developers had to strive for years to mitigate the loss and re-establish the topmost position in the real estate market. Abheer had resigned, though no one blamed him directly. And though it had been a brief stint in the organization, his mind still drifted back to the repercussions, wounding his spirit.

"Baby steps, Abheer," I exclaimed in a positive tone. "Start taking small gigs, and then you can evaluate the response and results compared to your current job. You'll need to invest a lot to create your brand. Take some help from your dad's employees for marketing and promotion."

He listened to me without making a sound. In a calm voice, he responded, "Let's meet in the coming week. We can have a discussion and also spend some quality time together."

"Ok, dear." I nodded, feeling really glad to see him after a month's absence.

After talking with Abheer, I looked around the home with cheerful, beaming eyes that seemed to say, "Here is my prince! He's back."

Just then, the doorbell rang. I opened the door with a delighted face. Vaishali entered and, looking at my expression, asked me the reason for my happiness. I blinked my eyes and she understood the rest.

"Let me cook something nice for you today." She gently nudged my shoulder and went into the kitchen.

I was missing his presence so much that I couldn't help but look at the lovely pictures of our smiling faces—strolling the campus, sipping coffee at Starbucks, photos during the user research surveys performed on streets. I felt so close to him . . . as if we were under each other's skin. Deep down, he was like a sailor in distress, waiting for the wind to take his boat toward the shore. With each succeeding day, I longed for a tomorrow with him. There would be many more moments filled with chaos, mistakes, doubts, and prejudice but our love would thrive for ages.

I finished a sumptuous lunch cooked by Vaishali and moved to my home office to complete the content writing assignments. After the gig orders were complete, I searched for content and communication consulting jobs on Google.

I opened my brand app and jotted down the major things to be streamlined to start my own consultancy.

- Domain registration
- Website creation
- Social accounts and podcasts
- Guest posts on high-tier sites above DA70
- Business social media post creation and promotion
- Reviews and recommendations

I logged onto the GoDaddy website, checked the available domain names. Authorkalki.com was available, and I purchased it immediately.

Feeling very excited, I send a WhatsApp ping to mom:

'I purchased a domain address to start my website. Feeling awesome and then some.'

I got a slew of incoming SMS and WhatsApp messages on my phone, but I was waiting in anticipation for my mom's reply and ignored most of them.

I was chalking out my way ahead when there was a beeping sound. It was my mom's reply.

"Good step. I'm sending you the contact details of my ex-student. He's a good web developer. Speak with him and let me know."

I opened another message to save the new contact details, unaware that it wouldn't only be a contact saved in the sim card.

MR. KARTHIK KASHYAP

Mobile no - 9**** *****

To take a break from work, I called up my best friends, Nisha and Asma, to share our ups and downs in life. After college, we all split up, each going ahead on their own path but still connected to the core. Asma was busy writing dialogues for a script based on a true story. The shooting was ongoing in Delhi; she asked me to come there for a few days and be a part of the scripting team. Nisha's claim to fame was for writing advertising jingles—an interesting art, unventured by many.

Our trio had been known as "Charlie's Angels" in college. We genuinely loved and cared for each other, and even though, life was changing, we were always entertaining and enriching each other. We talked for a long about our professional plans, breakup blues, melodramatic moments, self-discovery, and our pending expedition to Mt. Everest.

We were so engrossed in the call that we didn't notice the passage of time. Mom entered my room to check me, as I didn't greet her when she returned from work. I waved and smiled at Mom, signaling that my call would end soon. But Mom knew the underlying definition of "end soon." Likely pondering what we are discussing for so long, she walked out of my room to have a bath and complete the night chores.

She reentered after an hour and asked, "Are you girls discussing apocalypse on the phone?"

"Mom . . ." I gave a little irritated exclamation.

My eyes met her piercing gaze, and I agreed to join her at the dining table in five minutes. She pushed my hair back, drew me closer, and slowly showered light kisses on my forehead. Squaring her shoulders, she said, "Food."

We hung up after saying goodbye, planning to meet for a movie next Sunday.

Mom had made an additional dessert for dinner as I had commenced my first step in my own creative entrepreneurial venture.

After dinner and doing the chores, I went into Mom's room. She was reading a few insurance brochures and checking figures on the calculator.

"Mom, what are you doing? Is this investment for a tax-deduction?" I asked, picking up a few brochures.

Glancing through her reading glasses, she said, "Kal, yes, partly for investment. I'm checking the reliable schemes affiliated with IDRA. Also, these will be good for you. I want to give you a secure financial future. All of these efforts are only for you, my baby."

"Not every future is secured by insurance and savings plans. I can't think of a future where you won't be here for me." My voice was like a sorrowful rain.

I lay on the bed and twisted to my other side to express my anger.

She came from behind and gently cuddled me. "I will always be with you. Trust me. Whether alive or dead—you will find me beside you."

Her words sunk deep into my mind as she covered me with a blanket.

"Good night, my love," she said in a smiling tone and switched off the lights.

But from that point forward, my nights wouldn't be the same.

There was no noise. Absolute silence everywhere. Stars appeared. The waning moon was visible through the window as it slowly rose in the pitch-black sky. The moon and I had a silent exchange going on. I closed my eyes, and my subconscious began dusting all sorts of unwanted thoughts.

I was in the deepest depths of sleep when something began to suffocate me. It was crushing me with its weight and had pinned to the bed, so I was unable to move my legs or even wiggle my little finger. I was completely paralyzed, but my mind was awake, calling out for help. This terrifying experience continued until Mom's feet gently hit me. What felt like an eternity of suffering was over in a few seconds. But it wasn't be stopped forever. I went to sleep again, my breathing regular . . . my body unpinned and free to move.

The squawking of birds woke me up. I continued to lie down on the bed, remembering yesterday night's incident. The noise of utensils, the delicious aroma of food cooking, and the humming of old melodies marked the beginning of Mom's day. I wanted to get up to avoid hearing mom's nagging, but the fear was still within me.

When Mom entered my room, I still had a question in mind about how to deal with a similar situation again. When you know you are powerless, then waiting is the best solution. Living with the question is easier than hunting for the unknown answer.

"Hey, baby," Mom said, pushing aside the curtains. "Come on. Get ready. You're late for breakfast. It's 7.30 a.m., and I need to leave for college soon."

"Mom, come here. Do you know what happened yesterday night?" I said in a trembling voice full of fear.

Mom came over and sat on the edge of the bed while I tried to open up. "I was asleep when someone pinned me to the bed and immobilized me for a long time. It was so horrifying. Even my eyes were closed. I couldn't see anyone or understand what was hap—"

"Sleep paralysis," she intercepted. "This mysterious phenomenon is witnessed by every human being at least once in a lifetime. Scientists have written specialized literature on this topic, linking it to stress and other hormonal imbalances. Even I have witnessed the process—post-marriage, during pre-pregnancy, and post-pregnancy. Connecting with the scientific point of view, those were the times when I had experienced high stress in life because of your father. Finally, when we separated, though there were challenges in life, having you in my arms, I had peace of mind. The doctors recommend hypnosis, antidepressants, and serotonin, but the results were insignificant.

"So, Daughter, chill and be cool. I'll give you a nice head massage before bed tonight." Saying so, she led me to the dining table where breakfast was laid out.

"There's so much to talk about, Mom. Tell me more," I said as we sat at the dining table for a breakfast of idli, chutney, poha, and hot ginger tea.

"Different people have different perspectives. Religion says it is a demon sitting upon your chest . . . or a dead person venting their anger . . . or a dark figure lying with you. I already told you the scientific story of it.

Irrespective of your country, religion, race, or any other parameter, this happens to everyone. It is a worldwide phenomenon. The Japanese call it kanashibari; Egyptians call it a Jinn attack, where demons come to kill sleeping people; Brazilian folklore refers to it as pisadeira, where a crone with long fingernails hangs on the roof and tramples the chest of people sleeping on their stomach." She paused for a moment.

"How do you know so much about it?" I asked eagerly

"Research. When it happened to me, I started searching out

books in the library and browsing the Internet," she said smilingly.

"Is it dangerous, Mom?" I asked with a hint of fear.

"In Hmong culture, sleep paralysis is responsible for most nocturnal deaths. Some even believe it to be an alien abduction. Some experience it as hypnagogic hallucinations, which occur at the onset of sleep, or hypnopompic, while subconsciously waking up from sleep. Now, it's also termed narcolepsy, and 90% of the world population suffer from this disease," she replied with a smile on her face.

"Mom, you're a genius. You rock." I was blown away by her intelligence and applauded her with a joyous cry.

"For more, you can confer with Google, but I have to rush now. Finish your breakfast and keep messaging me." She gave me a goodbye kiss and disappeared fast. I could still feel the warmth of her breath after she was gone.

I stretched out my body, took some deep and long breathes, watered the plants, and continued to loll around. Sometimes, it's good to be alone at home. You get the grand privilege of total privacy, and everyone needs to cherish that.

I was in the living room, watching something but not really the television. I held my iPhone and automatically, I was logged into Facebook, Instagram, Twitter, not really reading everything but subconsciously clicking like and retweet buttons. Suddenly, looking through one of the windows, I saw white cumulus clouds forming wispy designs in the infinite sky.

I went to take a bath and turned the faucets on to fill the tub. I sprinkled in bubble bath and lavender oil, then undressed to slid into the tub. I immersed myself in the steaming liquid and rested my head against the rim of the tub. I closed my eyes and relaxed as water covered my shoulders. With a feeling of comfort and pleasure, I continued to soak myself for a long time.

Drenched, I pulled myself out of the bath, letting all of my emotions drain with the water, and I wrapped up in a bath-suit. All dressed up in jeans and a V-sleeve T-shirt, I emerged as bright as sunshine.

I heard the ringtone of my phone and walked back into the living room. I pressed the accept button on the display screen and answered the call from Abheer. "Hello," I said in a charming voice to cast my spell on him. "How are you, my only?"

"Hey, Kalki. I'm fine. I want to share the good news with you," he said in a voice of perfect confidence.

"Is it a promotion or job change?" I made a mental guess, knowing he would never dare to quit a salaried job.

"Well, Kalki. I've been promoted to manager—international product design and development," he said in a joyful voice. On hearing that his efforts had paid off, I couldn't control myself from bursting out in tears of joy. Seeing his joy and excitement, I avoided bringing up the topic of sleep paralysis.

"Kalki, I really want to thank you for helping me with user research, presentation slides, and even giving me important tips on the user interface experience, people insights, and user research experience," he said in an obliged tone.

"Yes, I remember when you were working on a product, I suggested that you think about cost and after-sales features more than design and aesthetics.

"Kalki, I have communicated this news to you after my mom. I hope, this tells you how much I love you. This life will be what we make it. No matter how much I mess it up, I know you will always be there to reshape it again. I'm greedy for your love . . ." I could catch the fervor in his accent and the purity in his words. I felt equally impassioned in the glow of his generous emotions—like a flame on wax.

"Abheer, I love you too," I said, my voice blooming.

"Kalki, I'm deputed to an orientation program for one week.

The program is basically to acquaint me with my new role, responsibilities, processes, and on-the-job training. The entire program will be hectic, but if you're okay, we can meet on Sunday. Give me a chance, and I'll give you a better me—full of positivity, love, and happiness."

He sounded genuine. I was blinded in the light of his love. I could see stars shining in the broad daylight sky as we spoke of melding our flaws. We ended the call with lots of kisses and wishes, keeping the hugs for Sunday.

Mom's message notification popped up.

'Baby, Vaishali is on leave today. Try to do the laundry and vacuum the house. The rest, I will manage. I'll try to come early today."

I took a deep breath and mumbled, "Cons of working as a freelancer."

I walked over to the washing machine, hit the switch, and lifted the lid to fill the drum with clothes. I sprinkled in two heaps of powder, connected the water pipe, and dialed the washing machine. The drum began to rotate like a wheel as water flowed through the tubes. The rest required no effort at all. The program was set, and thankfully, it wasn't a very big load—Mom's nighties, my casual wear, and a night suit.

The vacuum cleaner was lying in the corner of the balcony. I dragged it to the front room, plugged it in, and switched on the power. I started running the machine in a straight line on the floor and carpet. After a smooth run on the floor, I hovered the long attachment with thick bristles on the curtains, sofa, and other furniture to remove the debris and dust. I continued running the machine up and down the hallway. The lavender fragrance inside the vacuum bag was disintegrating in the air, uplifting my cheerful disposition.

Suddenly, I felt that somebody was near to me. I peered around the corners of the living room and then looked at the passageway. At that moment, a ghostly figure at a distance of ten feet appeared before me. I was gobsmacked and shaking. Around and around, the mist began to whirl, forming an outline of the human body. My courage was withering away, seeing the unearthly identity get thicker and larger. The figure increased enormously until it was a true monstrosity. Watching this happen, I felt utterly powerless and numb.

As quickly as it had appeared, the cloud of particles lost its cohesion and disintegrated into the air. The mysterious figment had vanished completely. When I was sure the ghostly figure had gone, I stood beside the window of the living room to absorb what had happened. I could feel the whole house mocking me. I wanted to call Mom but tried to regain my balance. Why should I bother her with this stupidity?

I was almost scared to death. I stood there stiff like a statue, unable to move a muscle. Suddenly, I remembered grandma's words—the miraculous effect of chanting Hanuman Chalisa gives you protection from internal and external fears, enemies, ghosts, accidents . . . almost anything. Reflecting on the most popular remedy, I raced toward the remote of the smart TV and switched it on. I tapped into the world of YouTube TV and play the Hanuman Chalisa on continuous play mode. I increased the volume to make it sound like my inner roar.

After listening to the Hanuman Chalisa, I felt relentless valor within me, and I was empowered to crusade against the paranormal forces. As the muscles in my body came to life, I slowly moved about in the house, chanting the divine Chalisa. In a hurry, I took out the washed clothes from the machine and hung them on a drying rack. Then, I completed the job of cleaning and parked the vacuum cleaner at its usual spot.

In all this chaos, I didn't notice that it was 5 p.m. I cleaned my face with Aloe vera gel and applied strawberry lotion to my trembling skin. I switched on my laptop and read up on ghosts. After browsing for so long, I was feeling anxious again. There were tons and tons of data, facts, stories, and visuals that seem to obscure rather than clarify the topic. But, nowhere I couldn't find a concrete answer or an assured solution.

"Ectoplasm is mostly the residue of spirits or the manifestation of ghosts." I continued researching, curious to know more.

After browsing, I realized that it was a futile attempt. Mom was a good cook, and dinner was filled with nutritious and tasty dishes. An idea clicked to me: If I cook dinner, then Mom's time will be saved, then we can have a long discussion about the eco-misty force in the evening. The dishwasher is well-equipped to manage the after-dinner mess.

For a change of pace, I donned the apron and commenced—Mission Dinner.

"It's time to prepare rotis and green peas vegetable curry," I mumbled and chopped a few onions, tomatoes, potatoes, and pieces of coriander. Following the usual Marathi culinary style, a spicy vegetable gravy was ready in just fifteen minutes.

Then, I made a salad of beetroot, radish, onion, cucumber, and lettuce—full of vitamins. To increase the health benefits, I added olive oil, pomegranate juice, salt, and tulsi leaves. This would steal Mom's heart.

Mom returned home with a bag full of Alphonso mangoes. She had a quick shower and dressed up in a blue nightgown.

"I'll make something for dinner," she said, lovingly stroking my face before heading to the kitchen.

"Mom, everything is ready. I cooked dinner. You can reheat it. Also, the salad is a bonus for you."

Hearing this, she gave me a look of concern. "Is everything okay? Do you want something?" she probed, brow furrowing.

"Just love. Can't I do something for my mother," I said.

"Shut up, girl. Tell me, what do you want? Or what you have done?" She paused to hear my reply.

"Nothing, just to spend some quality time together," I said in a timid tone, withholding the main facts.

While having dinner, Mom talked about her childhood memories and continued the ghost talk. We finished our dinner, and Mom was soon cleaning up the kitchen. I went to the balcony to fill my eyes and senses with the powerful radiance of moonlight. I stood there for a really long while browsing the black and white scenery.

I felt the supple touch of wind in the strong voice of silence. Mom came up behind me and tenderly stroked my back.

"Mom," I said in a soft voice. "Can you see the combination of randomness and probability in this universe, or is this is my weird imagination?

"Daughter, these all are the sub-sets of the universe. Not everyone can decipher the profound truth of the higher universe. From the beginning of the universe till today, an infinite number of configurations are hidden from mankind. So, your thoughts can be a product of your imagination or awaken from a higher consciousness." She expressed her opinion and engulfed me in her warm embrace.

"Is it possible that I can see ghosts?" A gamut of emotions flooded my voice as I asked this question.

She held her breath for a moment. I drew closer to her. She took another breath—this one deeper.

"Kalki, the science of horoscope is based on certain mathematical equations, galactic energy codes, cosmic transits, and effects." She stopped to observe the magnificent moon.

"In the horoscope or Janam Kundli, we have a section called Ganas, which is divided into three sub-sets—Dev Gana, Manushya Gana, and Raksha Gana.

"Astrology states that people subject to Dev Gana—have sattavik energy imbued in them, so no ghost or no negative energy can haunt them.

"People falling under Rakshas Ganas have tamsik powers, and

it's said that ghosts, evil spirits, and ghouls do follow them, torture them and try to steal their energy, but the person can be more powerful than the unearthly spirits. Also, the sixth sense is very strong, and they have the capability to understand a negative presence first.

"Individuals grouped in Manushya Ganas have Rajasik powers and are troubled. They're susceptible to being possessed by paranormal powers or entities.

"However, this only possesses a fractional space in your horoscope, so don't make any inferences when it comes to this philosophy. Also, this cannot be accurate, and results can vary, depending on the moon affliction in the birth chart," she said and ran her fingers through my hair.

"Which bracket do I fall in?" I asked impatiently.

She firmed the look on her face and said, "If a person is born under a specific nakshatra, then he or she belongs to the corresponding ganas."

"Mom," I said in a firm voice. "Open up, please."

"People born under these nakshatras—Krittika, Ashlesha, Magha, Chitra, Vishakha, Jyeshtha, Moola, Dhanista, Satabhisha—are grouped in Raksha gana. Your lunar mansion is Ashlesha, so you're a member of this Gana. Be bold; it is in your destiny to see ghosts, but they cannot harm you. Remember, you are above them in energy and power."

"Mom, is this Gana bad or something because it is called Raksha Gana?" I asked, the concern visible on my face.

"No, this is just a classification, and it is a belief. There are exceptions everywhere. Do you know how many notable people are born under this nakshatra? Shree Ram, Lakshaman,

Shatrughan of the Ramayana, and even Mahatma Gandhi. So, please don't overthink. A person is analyzed on many more features and a horoscopic equation.

Her words brought relief to me. In a conversation, she pulled me from shadow to sunlight. If I'm destined for it, then there are only two options: survive with it or quit this life. The latter option, I could never do because my mom has raised me with her blood, sweat, and tears. Life is the most valuable gift one can give. I would never quit because of anyone in this world—even the Devil himself.

"It's getting pretty cold here. Kalki, let's go to the bedroom.

I followed her inside to get more food for thought. I lay on the bed and thought of the things Mom had spoken about.

Mom adjusted the thermostat settings, closed the bedroom door, and dimmed the lights. She walked into the darkness and laid down beside me.

"Mom," I said and cuddled in her arms. "Tell something more," I insisted, knowing that she was tired.

"I love your amber eyes, Kalki. They say eyes are the window to the soul. Our family Pandit always tells me "Your daughter's eyes are a rare gift. Not everyone has amber eyes. One in a thousand. She has some spiritual powers." She paused, looking into the golden light shining in my eyes.

"After listening to the Pandit, I really got interested and searched about amber eyes. It was a gift in the making for billions of years. Some complicated mutations occurred from the Stone Age that made this eye color possible. There was a mystery about eyes that would be unveiled in good time. It's bestowed on you by your nature, and of course, your father.

The only thing you inherited from him." She talked as both of us continued gazing at the ceiling.

"Mom, did he ever see a ghost?" I asked, biting my lip.

"Are you mad? Even if he saw a ghost, it would make no difference. Ghosts would know a demon stood before them. He never visited his newborn daughter in the hospital. I had dropped all expectations as a wife but when he showed similar behavior towards you, I made up my mind. Enough!" her voice got moist, and she turned her back to, ready to sleep. The silence lulled us into slumber.

My feet were cold, and my teeth started chattering. I opened up my eyes very slowly and saw a woman standing at the window, looking out at the night view. She was dressed in an emerald saree and red blouse. Though her face wasn't visible, her long and thick tresses were blowing high in the air. My gaze was fixed at her, and I heard her unsaid woes of despair and shrieking cries. I don't remember the next until my eyes opened remembering . . . remembering the incident.

"Mom," I yelled out loudly.

I screamed aloud.

Mom heard my voice and hurried toward me. She hugged me and loaded me with motherly kisses.

"What happened?" I asked in a voice full of fatigue.

"You were shaking with a fever the whole night—102 degrees. Thankfully, I got up at 4:30 a.m. to drink water and noticed your symptoms. You didn't even wake up to take medicine. I was applying saltwater patches to your forehead and Vicks VapoRub to your chest." Her tears began to flow.

"Mom, please," I said in a weak voice.

"It's my mistake. I fed all of these ghostly-ghastly things into your head. I'm such a fool. I'm sorry," she said, continuing to blame herself.

"Kalki, it's midnight. I'll get you some milk to drink. You need strength. Look, you've become so pale." She was about to go when I caught hold of her wrist.

We both stared at each other for a brief moment.

"It's not you." I pointed at the window and narrated the night's full episode to her. She was so stunned that she couldn't speak. She stayed rooted in place, thinking hard.

"Kalki, I can't leave you alone at home. Vaishali can't stay with us for twenty-four hours, and I can't quit my job due to monetary crunches. Even if I decided to teach in the coaching class, I would have to be there physically. The only option is to ask your grandma to stay with us."

"Better than a ghost," I said mockingly.

"Great, girl. Thank you. I will speak with your aunt and uncle immediately and ask them to make the arrangements. Also, I will speak with astrologers and pandits for some havan or pooja . . ."

"Mom," I interrupted. "Can I have a mouthwash rinse? Also, I want to drink a cup of coffee and sleep again."

"Do you need my help in the bathroom? I have taken leave today," Mom said in a concerned voice.

"I'll manage, Mom." I pulled myself together and sat up. Slowly, I walked toward the bathroom, rinsed my mouth, and washed my face, which made me feel a little better. I peeked through the bathroom door and asked Mom to get other clothes to wear. She was busy rearranging my bed so I could sleep once settled in.

"A minute, please." She went out of the room to get my regular wear from the drying rack. She returned and placed the set of clothes on the dressing table. I changed the lingerie and dressed up in a pink T-shirt and blue pajamas. Mom picked the dirty laundry spread on the floor and poured it into the basket for washing.

I took the pills, ate an egg sandwich, and sipped a cup of hot coffee.

Though I was afraid, weakness was sweeping over me.

"Mom." I lay down on the bed as she wrapped me in a blanket. "Be here; don't go anywhere," I said, and she agreed.

Mom sat at her desk next to my bed, clicking the laptop keys.

"Will this continue every night?" I asked Mom, and she said after a long pause, "Sometimes, we have to depend on divine intervention. I have no answers except unshakeable faith in my God. Now, close your eyes and rest."

"If I close my eyes, I'll see this darkness that conceals my happiness. I'm on the verge of nyctophobia. Please, don't let it happen," I pled in despair.

Mom listened and was listening to what I didn't express to her.

"If you become weak, then you're not my daughter. If you can face people who are worse than ghosts, then you can manage them. Fear is your only weakness. If you fear them, then you will never know, WHY YOU?" her voice sounded like steel.

"Mom . . ." The word goodnight hammered in my ear. Mom faked a smile on her wheatish face. I closed my eyelids, loading her face in my amber eyes.

I heard a lot of talking from outside that drove the sleep from my eyes. The voices belonged to Mom's relatives—her brother, his wife, and Grandma. I heard several words from the hodgepodge conversation of astrology, temples, and rituals—all jumbled up with the sounds of the TV.

Mom's brother, Harish, worked as a government officer and had a good reputation for working hard. His wife, Mithali, a homeworker, was engaged in raising their two sons, managing the household, and selling homemade snacks as party orders. Grandma and Mithali Mami's relations weren't very cordial, but the two had managed to adjust to each other over time. Mami found grandma to be very overbearing in nature. She must have been glad that grandma would be staying with us for the next 3–4 months.

I could hear the cranking of utensils in the kitchen that released aromatic vapors into the air.

"Mom," I called out. In a few minutes, all of them entered the room in a single file and squeezed onto the bed. Mama sat on the chair next to the bed.

"How are you feeling now?" Mithali Mami asked gently.

"Better." I smiled at her. She had always made an effort to bond with me.

"Take her for Kuldevi darshan—female goddess presiding over each family. For the last twenty years, she hasn't been to the temple; that's why all these things are happening. The Goddess must be angry. Go and do some pooja rituals." As usual, Grandma had opened her book of illogical reasoning. Mami and I exchanged smiles over her comments. Mom was listening, not able to decide anything. Mamaji nodded his head affirmatively at grandma's explanation. Only when Mithali Mami gave him a glare did he stop.

"Kuldevi is Kuldevi. She is the ultimate authority in your family. Our forefathers have been worshipping Kuldeva / Kuldevi and the same is expected to be done by us. Your marriage broke, but the child born from that marriage continues to be presided over by their Kuldevi." Her spiritual beliefs dominated the room.

To cool the atmosphere, Mamiji politely added, "Kuldevi Darshan may eliminate these issues. The blessings of Kuldevi will help you to live positively and destroy these negative happenings. Wearing a talisman from Kuldevi's Pooja will protect our Kalki." Her positive thoughts convinced Mom that I needed the blessings of my Kuldevi. I had no vivid memories of visiting Kuldevi temple.

"Kuldevi is Kuldevi—the prime deity of your family, worshipped by your ancestors. She is the primal divine source guarding and blessing your family. Your marriage broke, but the child born from that marriage continues to be looked over by their Kuldevi." Her spiritual philosophies stormed the room.

Mithali Mami acceded to her point. "I agree with Ma's opinion."

"Even the greatest of the great have bowed down before their Goddess. Remember our history; Chhatrapati Shivaji Maharaj received the divine sword from his Kuldevi, Goddess Tulja

Bhavani of Tuljapur. Even though he was busy establishing Swaraj, he worshipped her with full devotion and fulfilled all the rituals pertaining to her worship. Then, who are you? and why should your daughter suffer because of your ego?" Grandma's voice got loud and harsh, but Mom kept her cool. Seeing the bickering atmosphere, Mithali Mami suggested in a convincing tone, "Let Kalki rest. She has just woken up. You all can discuss outside. I'll get something for her to eat."

All of them dispersed from the room, giving me a glance of love and sympathy. Mom didn't look into my eyes. She never wanted to go back to the past—the birthplace of her suffering. Never. But she was my mother, and I know she would do anything to save me . . . even if that meant crossing into a raging inferno.

"My sculptor held me in, protective.
Living in her weather's golden glow,
I now have camped my trust and faith at her feet-divine."

CHAPTER THREE

A NEW INTRODUCTION

Grandma had settled down with us. She had a good reputation for being one of the best cooks and we benefitted from it a lot. But everything comes with a price. Every morning, my sleep got disturbed by her chanting, clanging bells, puja rituals, and singing bhajans.

"I now understood what Mamiji wanted to convey, but she never opened her mouth."

Grandma had set a few norms - cultural and disciplinary for me. I asked Mom, to intervene but she supported Grandma completely. According to Grandma, I had to start fasting on Monday, no hair-wash in the night, no work after 12 am at night, morning jogging or yoga, no skipping of lunch or dinner, no junk food except once in a month, visiting the temple every Saturday and reading one shloka of Bhagavad-Geeta every day. Grandma's rules were hitting me hard on my head and I felt the paranormal characters were friendlier than her.

"At least, they use to torture me in the night. This old lady is sucking me up day and night." I whimpered.

After imposing rules on me, and receiving Mom's support, Grandma started spying on me. She loved to listen to my phone calls, check my food habits, my online shopping, my credit card bills, straightening my room, and everything to steal away my privacy.

In short, I had become her new entertainment channel.

"I don't eavesdrop, just happened to stop by," she said in a mild voice when I caught her listening to my phone conversation with Abheer.

The moment, Mom came from work, we leaped to her, complaining about each other. She was a champion in maintaining her calm and listened to both of us.

"Your daughter is a night owl, she drinks five cups of coffee every day, and then the caffeine in her blood travels to her head and broadcasts hallucinations," Grandma's voiced out loud.

"Meera, discipline your daughter, today's generation is really hopeless," she continued bawling.

I was spinning around Mom. She quickly held me close by my waist and said, "Why do you trouble your grandma. Listen to her, you will learn from her experiences. She is so old, you should take good care of her and make her feel happy," she said in a gentle voice.

"Mom, you have no idea. She is worse than the ghosts. I am better off without her," I screamed.

"Ssssh..." Mom chided me. "Respect your Ghost, oh...sorry...I mean, Grandma," Mom said and we burst out laughing as she realized her mistake.

Though lost in the labyrinth of darkness, I would still need to focus on my work to earn income. Of course, I cannot depend on Mom for an allowance. Besides, it is very important for every individual to be financially independent.

Suddenly, I realized that my website task is pending, and creating it on my own will not be a so good option. I checked up mom's messages and found the website developer's contact number.

I took a deep breath and then dialed Karthik's number. A voice, heavy with a thoughtful and energetic accent, picked up the call on the fourth ring.

"Hello, Karthik here," he introduced himself.

"Hello, that was a quick intro," I said with a smile. "I am Kalki and my mom, Ms. Meera Agastya, gave me your reference contact for website designing."

"Yeah, yeah, I know. Meera mam spoke with me. Don't worry, Mam, we will make a brilliant website for your brand. I will discuss the user interface, designing features with you in detail soon. But first, tell me, are we working on a website or a brand website?" he said with a powerful throw.

I paused for a moment.

"Well, to be honest, Karthik, I didn't think so much. Actually, I am a freelance content writer. Till now, I have written content for more than twenty websites, products, and even sales copy. Last year, I graduated from college and started working as a content writer." I said in a serious tone.

"Mam, for a branded website, we will need an SEO friendly website tagline, logo design, brand message, and a color palette selected from a whole slew of shades. As you know, so many people are online every day hence we need to set consistency in our brand - like a blog post every week or month, quiz on social media, reviews, etc. You should come under the spotlight..." he concluded to sip water.

"Sounds great," I said amazed at his agility.

"Mam, these are all side-efforts. Your clients, their testimonials, links of sample work, unique proposition, and upcoming projects will get you the actual score - the main elements. " He waited for me to speak.

"It's a big challenge. I have not decided anything about the website structure or any of this branding stuff. I am sorry to say, that I am unprepared," I sounded apologetic.

"Well, well, you just need to provide me the content and social accounts for your website pages - About me, My blog, My team, Unique offerings, Clients, Reviews, Contact us." I jotted down quickly as he mentioned it.

"Karthik, I have only a LinkedIn account, rest are all personal accounts. Also, I work solo," I said, somewhat embarrassed.

"But the clients don't know you work solo. I can add two of my employees in your team for showcasing only. I will create your six professional social accounts, two official email accounts, and a website. You need to send me your website content and 6-7 profile pics in HD resolution. You can change the passwords later after everything is set," he waited for a few minutes to give me a chance to speak or revise anything.

"I will email you the website domain name. So, you can draft the work contract. It will be a website for a Content Writer,"

I spoke in an excited mood knowing something good is summing up.

"Mam, Content writer sounds good but not brilliant. We are creating a custom branded website, please widen your scope. A content writer has a limited scope, we can go limitless if we twist it to - Creative Consultant. What do you say?" he crackled triumphantly.

"Wait..." I interjected him. "Content consultant is better as of now. After 3-4 years, I can tune in as a Creative Consultant. I have just finished my grad and cannot be a creative consultant so soon. I need that kind of backing - qualification, experience, or brand." I gave a long sigh.

"Ok," he laughed off.

"Karthik, can you give me an approximation of the commercials?" I raised an eyebrow.

"The project includes - user interface designing in PSD files, website creation and maintenance, hosting charges, social accounts creation, on-page SEO setup, and profile highlight in search engines. I will share the detailed breakup at your email address," he asserted.

"Please, just an approx.," I insisted and waited for his reply.

"You can check in the market; the cost of UI designing is very high as it is specially designed for your website only. The price for UI designing is 10000/- per page but I will charge only Rs. 5000/- per page - Rs. 35000/- for UI designing and Rs. 35000/- for complete website setup, on-page SEO, hosting, 1-year maintenance, social account set-up, and all other minor tasks. This is the most economical deal, I have given to you because of Meera Mam." he paused to hear my reaction.

"Thanks for it, Karthik. But, is the UI designing an essential part of the website structure. You can use any premium WordPress theme and later when the business grows, we can plan a revamp?" I tried to sound wise but couldn't.

"Kalki, wait. Think over it. After 3-4 years, the UI designing price will double up as it is the latest trend in the website market. Today, it is 10K then it will be 20K without any discount. You can speak with Meera Mam. In fact, I explained everything to her. She shared your profile and I actually made this proposal for you. So, decide and let me know." He greeted me Good-night and ended the call.

I was browsing same-profile websites for reference when Mom entered in with a plate full of nicely diced jackfruits simmered with lime.

"Vitamin C, Baby," Mom pitched in.

She collapsed into the nearest recliner for a few minutes' rest. I changed the angle of my chair in front of her.

"It was a tiresome day. Thinking of new ways to stimulate students to learn financial accounts," she sighed looking at me.

"Was I not enough?" I giggled remembering how she would storm at me over finance, accounts, algebra, and geometry lessons.

"But you were good with other subjects and mainly, the right side of your brain is more dominant inducing you to think creatively. You are more of a creative thinking person than a logical thinker," she explained as I started eating the jackfruits pieces one by one.

“If you knew this, why were you so demanding with me?” I asked with a frown.

“I had to be demanding because the final score results matter not the cerebral graph sheet. I loved to see the tiny doodle drawings in your geometry notebooks. I knew you hated math but it is a high-powered tool of analysis that should be known. I had to take up the carrot-stick approach to encourage your improvements.” she slowed down recalling the past.

“Whatever, it worked well. I secured outstanding marks in my academics,” I complimented her efforts.

“Kalki, I know you dream of traveling to the beautiful cheeks of North India, expressive islands covered in blue rims, dense green countries like Bhutan, capturing the lustrous architectural splendor, and the Himalayan confluences. In the struggle to repay the home loan, household expenses, and investments, so of these things got sidelined. We visited a few places in our and other countries but it is not enough to give in to your wanderlust. You can join travel groups, and fulfill your dreams before you end up in the routine marriage and mom trap. I don’t want to see you as a beautiful, broken moon,” she chuckled.

“Oh, come on. You are my world, my heaven, and my inspiration. None of these beauties matter more than you to me. Be it shopping in a mall, a walk to the temple, or a stroll after dinner it is equivalent to visiting all these places. It is not only these places but the presence of your loved ones at these places that makes it a memoir.

I may join on a few trips with friends and travel groups like hiking, camping, sports, and water adventure but still, I am going to have a wider world view with you,” I said in a strong and confident voice.

She said nothing. But those are the times when she says everything.

In an attempt to break her thinking, I diverted the topic.

"Mom, I had a talk with Karthik. We discussed everything but the total project cost summing up to Rs. 70000/- and if we exclude UI designing then it can be around Rs. 35000/- only. What is your opinion?" I gave her a bewildered look.

"Look, this is a one-time investment project. The next website redesigning will be done after 7-8 years. Now, you need to attract clients and create your brand name, and you are not going to get it by Aladdin's magic lamp. Your website is the only connecting tool so, please do as said by Karthik. You can make part-payments - 10% advance, then 50% after project completion, and the remaining 50% after a month. I can speak with Karthik or else, I can help with 50% of the cost," Mom said in a thoughtful orientation.

"No, Mom. I will manage it. You need not invest."

"Wait...wait...I mean you can repay the money in EMIs or pay the electricity bill for the next six months.

"Thanks, Mom," I said sarcastically. "I thought you wanted to help."

"There is no free lunch, Baby," Mom remarked in a high-pitched tone.

"You have a good amount of confidence in Karthik," I said straightening my back and standing up for some time.

"Karthik's life resonates with the metamorphosis of life,

death, anguish, isolation, and depths." She brought out her flair for drama in telling stories. She knew the perfect timings for a pause, weighing down on the phrases, speaking in pieces, and absorbing the spirit of the story. These moments of closeness were the most treasured ones in our mother-daughter relationship.

I sat down before her. Full of curiosity, I placed my palms on her thighs and rested my chin upon it. Her downwards glance and my upwards peek intersected at the perfect point to create a portrait of storytelling. Her fingers slowly traced through my hair and stroked my back gently.

"He had brilliant academic, sports records and loved to sit on the deserted backbench, mostly alone. Most of the time, he would look out of the window. Sometimes, I alerted him, scolded him but there were no improvements. At one moment, I thought he must be a poet milking his creative juice from the beautiful greenery around and preferred ignoring him. But, I knew something was wrong when..." she paused for a minute to check her mobile beep and continued.

I entered the examination room as an exam invigilator and greeted all the faces wrapped with anxiety, tension, and confidence. Among the faces, was a known but unknown face without any emotions and it troubled me a bit. As the exam bell rang, I distributed the answer sheets and then question papers after the second bell. Some heads were staring at the question papers, some heads were bent down filling the answer sheets, and some heads were focused on me as to how to avoid my attention and cheat. The exam was in full swing. One student was just drawing on the question papers and had written some lines on the answer field. After an hour, I looked around to check each student, he was looking outside at the window. I tapped on his shoulder when he looked at me, his eyes were dark red and watery. His glance was wild and angry, his eyes caught mine for a few seconds. He handed over the almost blank answer sheet and walked out of the examination room. I watched to see him speed away to disappear.

Thousands of emotions, varied and intense passed through me at a lightning speed. I had decided to speak to this boy. Sometimes, I waited for the class to leave so that I could speak to him. But he was non-responsive. I was bitterly resolved to make him speak and made many attempts. He never responded or replied or reacted.

I was getting exhausted and decided to quit when he walked into my office. I made him sit and drink a glass of water. After a few minutes, he cried like a baby. I attempted to pacify his crying and succeeded but his grief was deeper. With a moist tone and hiccups, he narrated an accident that changed his existence and outlook.

"My parents died in a car crash when I was in ninth grade. I was tossed from one home to another by my relatives. Seeing this attitude, both grandparents took over my responsibility. I stayed at my maternal grandparent's home and my paternal grandfather made the financial provision by liquidating my parent's assets to support my future. Somewhere, in the warmth of my grandparents, I started finding solace and hope when destiny again snatched both of them from me. Now, I am living with my paternal grandfather, in the constant fear that even he will leave me and go." He tried to suppress his sobs but they cascaded out. I inspired him with some inspirational talks, stories of prominent historic personalities, spiritual talks, and offered him all the help possible from my end. But, all of this sounded mechanical, I couldn't heal him internally.

This boy doesn't require counselling, he needs to feel empowered to thrive. Hence, I employed another technique - A diamond cuts another diamond. I ignored him for a few days, and finally, he walked into my office to ask the reason. I ignored him and walked out of the office with a heavy heart. He got more curious and worried and continued to follow-up.

Finally, one day, I told him my story, the story of the survival of a woman. Though the pain is gone, the scars are a reminder of the war. How I took the risk of flying as staying perched on the branch was also full of danger. As a woman, I had to wear many defenses to shield myself from the vulturous eyes eager to pry upon. When the dumb thought landed in my mind to do something and bleed to death, I realized it's not my life anymore. A part growing inside me ripped apart to free me from the pain and weight of life. When the woman in me was replaced by the mother - I stood there wondering, dreaming, fearing, struggling but no more silent or still. Life unfolded with more challenges but living independently and fighting was easy than living in a bond filled with constant humiliation, suffering, hatred, and disrespect. Even, today, I am fighting and failing, but you know what do I pride on? ...I stepped out," My voice echoed in his mind sending tremors to his temporal lobes.

He listened with open ears and wet eyes. After that day, I observed a radical change in him. Finally, he was the boy I always wanted him to be – playful, happy and bold. He took interest in studies, sports, and life. The most beautiful discovery about him was his laughter...the music that played after a long interval.

Karthik requested me to help him with accounts and few subjects as his base was weak. After college, we met in the library where I taught him these subjects. You remember, at times, I would come late from the office - those times. Once, when his grandfather was ill, I visited him in the hospital and promised to take care of Karthik like a son. As they had incurred a lot of expenditure on heart surgery, that year I offered him financial assistance by paying his college fees and exam fees. You were in the eighth standard, and due to the additional expenses incurred for Karthik, I refused to buy your promised gift - 'The Premium Acoustic Guitar'. The refusal drove you on a long agitation, revolt, misbehaving, and creating a non-stop fuss that ended up with a hell of a good beating… I am sorry for that day, I had lost my patience," she said kissing me tenderly on my forehead.

"Mom," I said in an obedient, and loving accent, "Please, don't be sorry." She was overwhelmed hearing my kind words. After a soft silence, I added,

"Even now, you can give it," I said laughing, as she tilted towards me, squeezing and stroking my arm in the fun.

"I love your buoyancy, girl," she clutched me closer to her chest.

I jumped into the comfy bed for a deep and restful sleep. Mom was busy with her laptop, ferociously penning her opinion on a social change topic for a high-tier publication.

"Mom, any plan to gift me the guitar this month," I irked her.

"Kalki, do you want an action replay," she chided me.

I closed my eyes but the sound of hitting the laptop's keys was stomping inside my head. Soon, there was a dusting of darkness in front of my eyes. I could feel the gentle breeze as trees swayed in the pleasing pitch. I felt my chest move up and down but my body was pinned to the bed. The thoughts in my mind were slowly disappearing away. In the night, I become someone different.

The next moment, I was flying above my bed toward a white, soothing light. There's a lullaby played on the reed flute of the mad winds. I was swirling upwards in the air like a miniature tornado producing a storm around me. Everything was coal blank; I had no idea of what was happening around me. Before I could decode anything, a powerful force funneled me down toward the ground. The energy drove me at the speed of light from darkness to the dark world. I was in a new and unknown unearthly place. It was very vast but I could see only a stretch of it. I could see and hear orbs, shadowy outlines, and transparent figures wailing loud. Fragments disintegrating and merging up on their own like a robotic toy-piece. I continued to float here also in the alleys of darkness where dark, developing, dread spirits or ghosts hanged in a revengeful mood. My breathing was synchronized with the rhythm of the dark world. I could see some good spirits unable to open up or been tortured by vengeful souls or finding The Light.

As I floated in the ethereal darkness like a firefly glowing in the night, some apparitions circled me and bounced me up and down like a basketball. They wailed, spoke some words in their ghostly voice, and shrieked in a blasting volume. They came closer to me and said in a gurgling and indistinct voice, "WE ARE WAITING FOR YOU."

Their voice was piercing my eardrums and my body was trembling like a leaf. Suddenly, a violent and turbulent force tossed me back on the ground.

I was hearing the noises in my subconscious mind when I woke up with a jerk. When I looked at the watch to see the time, I noticed mom was still working on her documentary piece.

'Did I really fly or was it a weird dream?' I asked myself. There was no answer.

"Mom," I screamed in a single breath. She swirled her chair and rushed toward me.

"Kalki, are you okay. Why are you sweating? The AC is on, dear? Are you feeling okay?" Her questioning was on, but my mind was unfolding the visual manifestations just experienced. Seeing me shiver, she instinctively wrapped me in her embrace chanting the divine and energy-orientated 'Gayatri Mantra'. I was trying to analyze the inner meaning of the nightmare that had mercilessly tormented me.

'Somewhere between sleep and consciousness, darkness and light, sound and silence, I was desperately pleading for it all to stop.'

Mom pacified me in her arms, endeavoring to put me into a sound sleep. Gradually, I sank and didn't wake up till the squawking of crows awakened me. I stood upright and flinched the blanket to the bed. I headed toward the bathroom for a morning routine and then stood in front of the bathroom mirror crying in a deplorable manner.

After a long reserve, I swiped the tears from my cheeks and washed my face with apricot face wash. The face wash cleansed my skin from all kinds of grime and debris but couldn't remove the puffiness from my eyes.

'I didn't want to go before Mom with this face but if I did so she may get more worried.' Thinking so, I headed towards the kitchen. Mom had prepared the breakfast and Grandma was sitting in the living room listening to the morning news on television.

Mom was dressed in a deep purple color gown flowing into the lavender shade. She was looking perfectly comfortable, and I did not want to disrupt her mood.

"Mom, are you on leave today?" I asked with my head down deeply buried in the mobile phone.

She didn't answer me. I looked slightly up to see her face. She was looking at me. She met my gaze and held it.

"Kalki, today is Sunday. Kindly follow the family rule - No mobiles or laptops while having breakfast and dinner." She sterned her voice and extended her hand toward me.

I placed the mobile in hand. She inserted the passcode and scanned through the messages.

"Mom, this is not acceptable," I argued in a faint voice.

"What are you browsing on the mobile net," she asked with a concerned face.

"Mom, how can you? I understand checking messages, but not my browsing history. Am I not eligible for any privacy in this house?" I urged in a high pitch.

"I have not snatched away your freedom, Kalki. Did I come between your relationship with Abheer? Did I force you to take up a regular job? Did I ask you ever to show me your bank statements or any income statement? I just want to make sure that you are on a safe-track always. As a mother, I can definitely have some standard checks." she said defending her act.

"Fine," I exclaimed in a loud voice pushing away the breakfast plate.

"Now, this is what I hate. Kindly never disrespect food in this house," she stormed.

"Stop all these traditions and superstitions statements," I protested, I could see no reason why she was extending these verbal arguments.

"This is what I was telling you, Meera. Over pampering, now face the consequences," Grandma fanged between our heated conversation.

"Will you be quiet?" I uttered loud enough to reach Grandma's ears.

"Don't be rude. I hope you really don't want to make a bad situation worse." Mom gave me a deadly stare. "What are you browsing, answer me." She yelled loud enough for the world to hear.

"It is nothing harmful only Melatonin tablets for a deep sleep at night. Mom, it is totally safe and not like sleeping pills. It is dietary supplement recognized by medical science. You can research yourself." I lowered my head and spoke almost in fear. Mom seemed serene.

I tried to convince her further, "Melatonin is a sleep hormone, and it promotes healthy sleep and orients our circadian rhythm."

"It is a natural hormone produced by the pineal gland in darkness," Her sharp voice cut my resolve.

"Mom, I was just browsing... God swear I didn't purchase it. You can check my Amazon account," I almost broke into tears.

"Congrats on taking the first step," she said in sarcasm. Before I could say anything, she walked out of the dining room to her room and slammed the door so hard, it shook the window panes.

The food remained uneaten on my plate and hers. I was tired, drained, and had no appetite left for breakfast.

I murmured to myself, 'Maybe, a long soak would replace this hopelessness and tiresomeness into a vibrant and energetic version.'

I cleaned the mess lying on the dining table and entered the bathroom to clean my body and soul. I placed the steel lid on the drain of the bathtub and poured large amounts of bath salts into the hot water filling the tub. The water was getting anxious to immerse me in its delicious embrace and whisper smooth and slim poetry in my ears. Chewing over the moments, I shredded the clothes and sat in a reclined position resting my neck on the cool edge. Steam rose slowly from the water; I applied sandalwood scrub on my loofah and ran it all over my body. Lifting the hair from my neck, I twisted it into a bun and tied it at the top of my head. The invigorating smell of perfume, the freshness of the freshets, and the swirling of emotions enveloped me in a sanctuary of peace and self-love. I rinsed my hair with a mild herbal shampoo to remove oil and applied a hair conditioner to make my hair shinier and silky.

For ages, the power of the water element needs no introduction in any culture. Water is emotional, soothing, and feminine - nourishing, loving, and healing everyone's life on the earth. From our conception, the water element carries us from shore to shore with endless love and care showing us a way out always.

The sacred power and purity of water calmed my engulfed mind filling it with blue-green, tranquil vibes. I stepped out of the tub, tripped the plug, and drained the discolored water. I immediately wrapped a huge, blue towel around me and hurried back to the room. I wore blue color denim shorts and a grey color T-shirt with a red border. Then, sat down at the dressing table, singing my favorite song, and ran the blow-dryer over my wet hair. I combed my hair into a ponytail and put on a fresh coat of eyeliner.

The cell phone sounded with incoming WhatsApp messages from Abheer. I wanted to see him, talk with him, and tell him about my feelings but he was busy sending me naughty emoticons and sharing his new updates. Sometimes, I feel talking with him is talking only about him. I am just filling his emotional gaps sidelining my psychological cravings.

I sat down on the concrete floor, leaning against the wall, and placed the drawing book on my lap. In a deep trance, the ebony pencil moved across the paper to set a picture in motion. Drawing is a spiritual doorway that directs my alpha brain energies to find the natural rhythms of the mind. Like meditation connects us with the light within; drawing creates a sanctuary of stillness and mindfulness where I can retreat anytime to inner peace.

I was searching for something outside to push my inner boundaries. Mom entered the room, pulled a chair in front of me, and sat down as well. She eyed the drawing for a few seconds to see if I was sending out some secret message.

I put the gliding pencil on a brake and looked up at her, said softly,

"When the mind turns into a hotspot for worry and stress, then words don't make sense. Needless to say, for the last so many nights, I have not slept well. My mind is running in deep agony as every night I see bewildering and terrifying dreams of bones, apparitions, and shrieks. I have a fear that thick darkness is waiting to take me over. All these paranormal events, unknown manifestations, and scary horror have taken away my perfect life. I don't know the way out?" Tears falling from my eyes were watering the trees in the drawings.

Mom resumed her silence. I continued in a softer voice,

"I am not stressed, or overloaded, or imagining things. Also, I am not a hyperactive or attention-seeking person, so please don't take me to any counselor or psychologist. I was fine until these supernatural things punched me."

"Kalki, Science is not the only tool for finding out the truth. Religious faith is also equally powerful in expressing the true sense," she said confidently. "You mean the world to me; did you not feel like talking with me once? Do you really think I didn't notice your pain or the puffiness in your eyes? It doesn't matter if we have to travel to every temple - Kashi-Viswanath, Kamakhaya, Jagannath, Kali Mata, or Ajmer Dargah, any place that gives us an answer. But first, we will visit the Kuldevi temple at Kolhapur."

"Hmmm," I said and stroked a line on the drawing.

"Mom, I am sorry for all this chaos. Are you sure these visits will end our problem?" I narrowed my eyes.

"You are not a human being, but a spiritual being. The day you will realize your superpowers as a human being, experience the higher consciousness, and discover the eternal existence of the human soul that will be the time you will be born to battle out all these negative forces. The answer is within you," She placed her hand on my shoulder, leaning towards me.

"Get up know, Girl. It is 10 am and there is a surprise for you today," she said cheering me up with a tender hug.

"Mom, surprises don't excite me anymore. The creasing of the moon that ebbs the seas, cools the tender earth fevered with heat, and sings lullabies to every heart destroys my peace and calm. Nowadays, the word, 'Good-Night', makes me shiver thinking of what the night will do with me.

Mom stood quiet. Perhaps, she had run out of words. She said in a reassuring tone, "It's just started, have faith upon my God. Till then, your positive energy will be the befitting answer to these negative spirits. Girl, prove to me that you can be a fighter. Show me that you are my daughter. I fought with customs, stereotypes, bias attitudes, sexual harassment and you cannot face the dead?" Her iron determination ignited a spark of fearlessness inside me.

For the first time, I felt the nerve of strength to meet the force with force.

"Kalki, I am going to the Supermarket to buy some groceries. You can order something light for lunch. I will get something for myself on the way. Check with your grandma. Also, I have called Vaishali for some time today. She may come around 1 pm."

She walked to her room to get ready. I ordered Khichdi for grandma and a strong and super refreshing Tropical cold coffee for me. I plugged in the laptop charger and sat down to work on my gigs and the content of my website. I have a great capacity for work and once, having started I get deeply engrossed in it.

I turned toward the door at the sound of Mom's approaching footsteps. She walked toward me dressed in a maroon color pathani kurta and gold color churidar. The sunlight glinted off the 24K thick gold bracelet studded with diamond across her right wrist and a smartwatch festooned her left wrist.

"Feeling better?" she asked leaning toward me.

I touched the beautiful hand-carved sunflower pendant looming in her golden necklace chain. The shiny petals formed around the dark cabochon yellow sapphire diamond always amused me.

"You ordered something, right?" she again asked as I smoothly rubbed my finger across the sapphire.

She looked in my amber-gold eyes to find the answers. I continued to be quiet.

"I will be back in an hour," She pressed her palms on my shoulders.

"Mom, drive carefully. I will be okay," I said in a much calmer voice.

"Good," Mom said with a raised eyebrow. "Good, to hear that."

She said bye and left. I heard the door close and straighten up to finish my work. While browsing the internet, I felt as if someone was behind me. The weirdest thing there was no one.

While I was in this thought, I heard the doorbell ring, and the door open and close. About minutes later, Grandma came and kept the ordered cold coffee on the table.

"Ma, you got your order?" I asked while continuing typing.

"Yes, next time better not order Khichdi for me. I would like to have something tasty like pizza," she said that in a very sarcastic way.

I ripped opened the wrapper and sipping the coffee said, "I didn't know your teeth are so healthy and gums are so desperate to chew yeast?"

"Better than your teeth structured with a root canal and loaded with tooth fillings," she grumbled and walked away.

"She really hates me..." I said to myself darting the empty can in the dustbin. I missed the shot and the can roll away in the mid-passage outside the room.

"Continue, Continue," I heard Vaishali's voice as she scuttled to pick it up.

"Sorry, Vaishali Mausi," I gave her an unapologetic and she got soft. "I didn't hear the doorbell. When did you come?" I asked her out of curiosity.

"Spare key," she giggled.

The gigs were over and I started working on the website content. I heard the noise of the washing machine and the clatter of dishwashing. It is clear though the noise exceeded the threshold, but I preferred to keep the door open. After an hour, Mom returned from the supermarket. The watchman had volunteered to assist, he dropped the bags in three rounds and handed over the car key to mom. She thanked him and offered a tip of a hundred rupees. He smiled wide in gratitude as I closed the door.

Now, this is my favorite activity, unloading the stuff from the bags and placing it at their respective places. I kept the pallet load of milk and juice cartons in the refrigerator, fruits in the fruit bowl, vegetables on the cooling shelves, other grocery items, and spices on the kitchen platform. Vaishali was transferring the items into airtight containers to keep them fresh. I was checking if Mom brought my favorite protein cookies, cornflakes, and chocolates.

"Where is Mom?" I asked Vaishali.

"Mam is in the bathroom," she replied pulling out the home furnishing stuff from the bags. "Mam has told me to keep these items in the storage box," she picked it up and went in Mom's room.

"Kalki," Vaishali called me from behind after coming out of Mom's room.

"Mam has told you to wake her up at 4 pm sharp. She is taking a nap now. I am doing the preparations for today's dinner," she hurriedly to the kitchen.

I checked my watch. It was 2 pm, and a good time to play a video game on the desktop. I love to play games and ended up as someone's game. Grandma kept on bugging me for playing some dumb game.

"Why can't you help Vaishali or learn something from her?"

she kept on tweaking constantly.

Ignoring her jibes, I focused on the surroundings of my game and increased the volume of the speakers to the maximum extent. The underlying intention - to challenge Grandma. However, her old brains refused to be underpinned by my revolt and continued to crap at me.

"Can I not have peace in this house?" Mom came out, her eyes were red and swollen, her voice thick and angry. I muted the volume, tore my gaze from the screen, and looked at her.

"Tell that to your daughter. Instead of learning some culinary, craft, or knitting skills, she is well-engrossed in playing video games, and other nonsense," Grandma croaked louder.

"Will you be quiet, Mom. Let her do play, sing, or dance what is your problem? Will she be free to play such games later in her life? Let her enjoy as she wants. Don't you lecture me on how to raise my daughter? Instead of that introspect on how you could have supported your own daughter. Had it not been my father you would have convinced me to continue living in hell. Please, don't give lectures and don't weep now. Where were you when I was weeping for whole night?" Mom expressed out her unprocessed thought without any filters.

Grandma was crying, her sobs throbbing through the living room walls. In fact, in a few minutes, I found myself crying. Grandma spoke a few disjointed sentences but Mom paid no attention to her.

"Mom, it's my mistake. I stood have not revolted," I took the entire blame.

'Shut up, Kalki," Mom yelled back, "I know my mother, she is a total old school of thought. Should she not be supporting her granddaughter at this point rather than dampening her spirit."

It took a while for mom to cool down, "Go to your room, Kalki. I want to speak with my mother for some time." I obeyed her instruction and went back to my room.

I exploded in my room and ran to the window with a heavy heart and blazing eyes. I looked out, the outside world was brimming with gay and joy, but I was absorbed in the retake of a sad scene. I closed my eyes and listened intently, expecting to hear vitriol words and rash arguments, but there was a deadly silence. The air in the house was supposed to be infused and blown away in harrowing sound. I waited and turned down to sit at my work desk to tackle the task of opening, reading, and responding to the emails. But my mind was set on thinking about what was happening between mom and grandma.

My mind was too occupied trying to fit the puzzle pieces. In an hour, Mom walked into the room followed by grandma with feeble steps due to her arthritic knees. Their glance met mine; they nodded and smiled at each other...a smile of infinite understanding. Grandma sat on the edge of the bed and Mom pulled the desk chair and sat facing both of us. I walked toward Grandma and apologized for my behavior and back answers.

"I am really sorry for my rude behavior. It was wrong to speak with you in this manner," I said, in a remorseful tone.

Grandma looked at me and said, "Sometimes, I poured out the anger of Meera's struggle upon you. I had an underlying thought that because of you my daughter didn't start her new beginning of her life.. I never looked upon you as a reason for Meera's existence."

She wiped away her tears streaking from beneath her glasses.

Mom said to grandma, "Mother, Kalki is the perfect gift given to me. It was solely my decision not to remarry, please don't hold any grudge toward her. I rejected all the proposals for a second marriage. She was a just born baby at that time. What kind of anger are you holding against her? Had it not been for her, I could have got totally lost; broken, and emotionless suffering in the ongoing pain. Mom looked at me eagerly, pulling me closer to her, said proudly, "You are the reason, why I am here today - independent and self-reliant."

Crystal tears formed on the lower lashes of our eyes flowing down in perfect unison. We all looked at each another, finally, Mom spoke, "Come on, we have a guest arriving. Please all of you get cleaned up," She said in a high-spirited mood to cheer us.

"Kalki, change to something better. I am also, going to get ready," she got up from the chair to walk out when we both voiced together,

"Who is coming?"

"Watch out for yourself," she replied and slammed the door.

I and grandma hugged for a long time; it was truly a long-awaited reunion.

CHAPTER FOUR

THE FIRST LOOK

Far above, the sky is in a vibrant blue shade with a few white nebulous punching around to have fun. Taking inspiration from the ether, I dressed up in a sky-blue top knitted with a round neck and short sleeves and white trouser to look fresh as a tropical lagoon.

"Are you ready?" Mom snapped open the door and asked.

"Yep, ma," I replied.

"Wear your pearl earrings, and comb your hair, dear," she said opening the drawers to find comb and earring set.

"Mom, mom, I am getting ready, you please go," I tried to push Mom out of my room, but before I could, she had started opening my drawers and bursting things out of it.

"Mom," I said to stop her," She placed the earring box on my palm, and ripped open the lid signaling me to wear it on. I did as she wanted to make her happy. Before I realized what is happening, she untied my ponytail and rowed the comb through my straight waves. I breathed out the next puff that blew across her face. Seeing my response, she slightly smacked the comb on my shoulder. I slung my shoulder backward, giving her a frown.

"So, why are you dressed in a saree?" I asked Mom, moving my fingers across the large band on the edge of the pallu flanked with golden zari border with twill and minakari pattern. For the event, she wore a frost grey silk saree paired with a red color embroidered blouse. Her face was glowing with light make-up and the metallic luster of her golden studs radiating on her cheeks.

Mom remained silent and placed the comb in the drawer.

"Ok, I see a glow of your face, are you in love? Finally, are you officially divorcing your husband? The surprise guest is your 'would-be'? Tell me, I am anxious," I asked in a brave voice.

She didn't react at all; she didn't move a bit, she didn't reply to me, and walked out of the room leaving the suspense in the air.

I kept following her, pressing the topic to study her reaction. For seconds, she paused, then; looked up, her brown eyes penetrating my golden iris, and my heart skipped a beat. I quietly sat down on the sofa, psyching up for the surprise, and as our eyes did the talking.

"Mom, I am always there to support you in everything."

My mind just blurred as I scrolled through the Instagram but nothing seems to engross me.

Mom drifted from one room to another overseeing the

domestics. My anxiety drains away as she smoothed my hair away from my forehead and walked inside the kitchen.

At 6 o'clock, in the evening the doorbell rang. I held my breath and stood up as Vaishali opened the door.

A young male voice said, "Meera Ma'am," and before Vaishali could reply, Mom came racing out of the kitchen toward the entrance door,

"Come inside, Karthik. It's nice to see you after so long," she said in a happy voice. Mom laid her palms on his head as he bent down to touch her feet.

"Ma'am," he said in his own melodious, baritone voice as Mom gave him a light, tender embrace.

He looked and smiled at me; there was a mutual smoke in the room. There stood before me a young, tall man of radiant beauty wearing a neatly ironed red and blue checked shirt and black jeans. He had a clean-shaven face, wheatish complexion, sharp nose, light brown eyes, and a smile on his lips that could break fences. I secretly admired his well-built physique, muscular chest expanding in quiet breathing, his rolling six-pack abdominal muscles urging me to glide my hand over his wide and vast upper body.

I shyly walked up to Mom as she introduced me with pride," Karthik, meet my daughter - Kalki. I have spoken so much about her to you."

Karthik extended his hand toward me, and a dimple waved on his cheeks as he smiled "I am Karthik Kashyap, we spoke over the phone. Nice connecting with you in person." We shook hands and experienced something that never happened to me before - like an electric shock or something. When I retrieved my hand, it felt as if I know him and centuries had distanced us from each other. It took me some time to come out of his enchantment.

"Kalki," Mom held me in a close squeeze and said in a sarcastic tone, "Make our special guest comfortable, till I get some refreshments." Her words eased my mind as the wave of anxiety subdued down.

"Ma'am, please, don't be formal. Please sit down, we can all talk and share some stories. Let's hear a part of each other's lives, and connect with our talks," he said in a hearty voice that convinced Mom but she still insisted him to have some refreshments.

"Ma'am, you have invited me for dinner. Please, don't fill my stomach with snacks and beverages. I want to eat your hand-cooked meal and savor each bite," he said with a grin.

"I have cooked all your favorite recipes," Mom said with an extra affection.

"I hope your recipes are a good match for me, else, I will have to sleep hungry," I grinned and nestled up in the swivel barrel chair placed adjacent to his seating position.

"You won't, my princess," mom said with an answering beam.

"Ma'am, you have taught me to be receptive and open in life. So, definitely, I am willing to relish any item made by you," he said in a deep voice that showed his relationship with mom.

They talked a lot about active and engaging themes, Karthik updated Mom about his career roadmap and upcoming prospects. Mom spoke about a few other students, her career proposition, she also requested Karthik to digitally and socially enable me as a brand figure. The talks continued in exciting tones, a bit of whisper when Mom asked Karthik about his relationship status.

"Single, Ma'am." He blushed in front of me.

"Single?" I said aloud keeping my mobile aside.

Mom gave me a darting look as I said, "After break-up?"

"No, Kalki. I am seeking a long-term relationship in all aspects of my life. Family is very important for me because I have to rebuild it on a strong emotional foundation. A loving wife with health and sense, supportive in-laws, and a happy home to live in is enough for me." He sighed a deep breath. I was stunned by his commitment and made an abstract comparison between him and Abheer.

"Where are you planning to travel," Mom said to change the topic.

"Somewhere in Maharashtra, I have to shoot some videos for a documentary. Yet, finalizing the location," he said in a thoughtful voice.

"Good, we are planning to visit Kolhapur for darshan to our Kuldevi - Goddess Mahalakshmi," Mom said showing him the images of the temple on Google.

"Wow, Kolhapur is such a prominent historical place filled with knowledge, beauty, and traditions. Kolhapur is also called Uttarkashi for its grandeur and cultural significance. I can do the shoot there," Karthik exclaimed.

"When are you planning to go, Meera Ma'am," Karthik asked in a curious voice.

"I was checking the flight rates and also my class schedules for planning a leave - maybe next month," Mom replied in an assumptive tone. I heard their ongoing conversation and continued recording their talks on my mobile phone.

"Who would be accompanying you on the trip?" Karthik asked checking out few other details of the place.

"I checked with my brother, but he cannot take leave due to workload. His wife cannot join as the kids are having exams next month. So, I and Kalki, as usual," Mom said giving me a comforting smile.

"Ma'am," Karthik said in a soft pitch, "If you are okay, can I suggest something. You will be the final decision-maker, and please, be free in your decision," he pleaded politely.

"Is it ok, if I join you? I will manage my expenses and stay in a separate lodge. This will be your first visit to Kolhapur, and you can rely on me for making this trip a memorable one. I will arrange the best stay, best places to visit, and also try to arrange a nice darshan." He requested Mom waiting for her approval.

"Ma'am, I have traveled a lot for work but never with family. I want to be a part of this family experience. Believe me, I have always looked upon you as my own mother," He insisted desperately.

"I do have faith in you, Karthik. This trip is mostly from a religious (horoscope) perspective for Kalki. It will be a short 2-day trip," Mom tried to convince me, "You have to do your shooting work, it may take more time."

"I can do the shoot work after you leave Kolhapur, till then I can show you, people, Kolhapur at its best," He even turned to me to support him.

I saw the advantage of having him on this trip - photography.

My social account will be on a troll.

“Mom, let him join us,” she thought over it for a few minutes and agreed.

“Yes!” I and Karthik exclaimed in unison and did a hi-fi.

“Okay, enough, Karthik, I will communicate the dates to you and then we will do flight booking. And, now, get ready for dinner. Let me do the preparations,” she got up to get the dinner ready.

As he spoke to me about my website project, I could see the pain and agony in his eyes that had bounded him since childhood. He shared many ideas and concepts about how to establish a personal brand in the market and thrive. He showed me his idea about my website design and interface and asked me to mail the website content as soon as possible. Whatever he spoke, he said it from his heart and had a genuine outlook toward things and people. Very rare, in life, one gets to meet such a diamond in the rough.

Mom was arranging the table for dinner and Vaishali was helping her from the kitchen. She placed two serving bowls of Palak paneer and mixed vegetable curry, a pot of steamed white rice, and a dish filled with hot Rotis. Giving us a big smile, she put on our plates, a bowl of basundi sprinkled with almonds, saffron, and cardamon. In a jiffy, Vaishali served three hot Puris in our plates to relish with basundi.

“Ma’am, it is so delicious,” Karthik praised the food and continued to savor every bite. We were so busy in eating that we were not talking.

After a few minutes, she placed before us a platter of vegetable salad and hot pickle in a small bowl.

"Mom, when are you going to have your dinner?" I asked as she stood near us, watching us eat, and serving us more food in our plate. Karthik, also insisted her to have dinner with us.

"Please, you both eat first, else I will not be able to focus on my dinner," she argued and we agreed.

Mom was happy in serving us and also requested Karthik to mentor me to create my own brand as a content consultant. She was very supportive of my brand idea. Karthik shared some important tips to write and publish articles on Forbes India, High DA websites to gain exposure. He agreed to send me some sample writings and contact details of the website editors.

Our dinner was over and we gulped a spoonful of sweet candy-coated sauf that tasted intense.

Karthik was appreciating the food, efforts, and her affection. Mom was replying to him in big smiles and "mention not" slangs.

"Kalki, Karthik, till the time we clean up the table, and serve Grandma, why don't you both talk about your website project?" Mom signaled me to talk and make Karthik feel occupied.

"Would you like to see our home, Karthik?" His eyes were on my eyes, as I drove him around. "This is the living room, now, I will show you the interiors of our 2BHK flat."

We walked through the broad passage, and I showed him the kitchen, Mom's room from outside, and we walked into our room.

"Karthik, be seated and comfortable," I said and left the door open.

He looked around and said, "Your room is so vibrant and spacious with attached washroom."

Several potted plants and flowering plants were hanging at the top of the wide window. Though a monochrome palette, the shades of grey and white gave a placid and majestic look to my room. He saw my home office at a corner of the room - a shiny MacBook was parked on the desk with a few stationery items, a copper water bottle, iPod, and an Apple watch in a charging mode. A printer and several packets of printing paper were there on the lower shelves of the desk. Long rows of neatly arranged books lined the shelves of a bookcase against the office desk.

A queen-size bed with storage, a three-door wardrobe, a smart TV, a recliner and an elliptical cycle were the main constituents of the room.

"You live like a princess," he said in an enticing tone.

I shrugged and said, "No, my mom has struggled hard to give me the best in life."

"I envy you sometimes, Kalki," he said in a soft voice. "You have such a loving, wise, and amazing woman as a mom."

"Yes, I am lucky to have her as my mom." The leather work-chair squeaked as he sat down. I looked at him anxiously and sat on the edge of the bed. The coldness of the floors gave a chill to my bare feet. We had as silent exchanging going on, and we were locked in a suspended universe. We didn't discuss anything about the project; we were watching each other engaged in a supple contact. We were comfortable in the presence of each other, and the underlying emotion was trust. Despite our first meeting, we seem to be connected - as if a higher power had arranged this centuries-old reunion.

"Your website will be ready by next week. Do mail me the content once ready. Your social accounts are created; my team member will mail you the details. Do set up a professional banner, profile picture, and an excellent branding kit for an elegant and professional look. Also, start blogging and writing for top-tier websites to gain credibility in the market," he spoke only to break the sound of the bashing wind.

The sound of his deep bass voice was taking me by a storm; his rolling physique and beautiful features were arousing me like a waning moon to a full moon. He glowed like fire, and his fiery breaths merged in the air melting my skin.

"Look at me,
I will melt like a candle
Touch me and,
I will burn like a wood"

"No other sight could move me to this extent than the sight of seeing God's finest creation," he whispered, and I brushed a strand of hair from my face. Gazes and voices were heard, but there was no verbal comprehension.

"No, don't do this to Abheer," a voice echoed in my mind. There was stillness in the room as Abheer's thoughts fluttered in my mind in brief flashes and pauses.

Mom's entry brought a disruptive end to my dreamy wanderings.

"Have you discussed the project?" Mom asked us, and we nodded our heads in a mutual rhythm.

"Grandma and I had dinner. So why don't you both join us in the living room for our continued talks?" Mom looked at our quiet faces waiting for an intriguing reply.

But before I could respond, Karthik spoke, "Mam, it is already 10 pm. Even you people need rest, so please let me take your leave now," he said with thankfulness.

Mom smiled and said in a persuading tone, "I hope you enjoyed the dinner. I have prepared your favorite dessert. Have a bite of it."

"Nopes, Mam. I cannot take one more morsel of anything. I am full and really thankful for such a delicious dinner and beautiful moments. Also, Kalki's website will be completed next week. I will guide her to publish articles in Forbes India; and other top-tier websites. Very soon, her content consultancy will be peaking out." His voice was assuring and he sounded trustworthy.

"I am grateful, Karthik," Mom said with a big smile giving him a tender hug as we walked out of my room.

In a moist voice, he said, "Mam, I am here in life because of your grace and efforts to inspire me to live. I owe my every breath to you. This is the least; I can do for you. Anytime, call me if you need any help, and I will be here for you," and waved us good-bye and walked his way toward the elevator. We went inside the balcony to wave him a final good-bye as he got into his car and drove off.

"Kalki, I have a lot of mess to clear in the kitchen. Vaishali has left for the day. You can carry on with your work. I will change and start with the work." Mom hurried into her room and came out wearing an apron upon a black gown.

"You need any help?" I asked, but she just chuckled; "No, please take some rest."

Though Karthik was gone, he was not gone from my mind. I was under the subduing influence of his winning charms, silent conversations, and perfect confidence. For a time, I forgot about the registered paranormal activities happening around me as my heart blossomed in the refreshing oasis of tenderness.

The slow glow of moonlight instigated me to outline his beautiful lips, then his nose, and then up to his eyebrows, knitting his face in my imagery canvas. The distant sound of his beating heartbeat lulled me to sleep.

" From stones to paper to stories to books to library,
I am pulling together your authentic weaves
It takes incarnations to study a cosmos like you,
I continue to connect all the pieces in each life"

I woke up early in the morning after a tiring journey of gathering stardust from the night sky. After the bath, I got dressed up in a white T-shirt and denim blue jeans entering the kitchen to brew a cup of ultimate coffee for myself.

While I was in the process of brewing and percolating, Mom entered the kitchen and eyed me astonishingly, "You made coffee?"

"Hmm," I replied with a small smile.

Mom stared right through me as I sat down at the dining table to sip my coffee. She gently patted my back and sat next to me, "Kalki, how are you feeling today?"

"Mom, I had such a good sleep, feeling reenergized," I said with a good laugh.

Mom started to make breakfast, and the delicious aroma made my stomach grumble. I grabbed a plate and was about to pick up a hot paratha my phone beeped. It was Abheer's message. However, the message didn't excite me like usual. Somewhere, I was awaiting a message from someone else.

"What is it?" Mom asked as her fingers flipped the hot piping parathas, pouring ghee over it.

I read Abheer's message," Can we meet today at your Vi-Mall?"

Mom murmured something about being late and switched off the stove. She kept the dish of parathas on the table and sat down beside me to eat.

"When are you going to meet him?" she asked with a raised eyebrow.

"He is on leave today. He has some personal work, after he finishes that task, we will be meeting," I said in an uncertain voice, not sure, if he will be able to make it or not.

"Keep your location tracker on, just for safety purpose," Mom said and kept her finger on my shoulder to notify me that her breakfast was done and she needs to get ready to go to work. She swiftly vanished from the kitchen. The moment, she was gone, I did a swift search on social media about Karthik. She came out of her room in a floral straight beige kurta set and a laptop bag hung on her left shoulder. She waved me a bye and walked out of the house.

Though, Grandma's Ramayana recitals lacked a visual component, the audio waves were looming in the room.

My mind warred with my rational mind and said, "If you need to know a person then check his social activities thoroughly." I presumed the role of Sherlock Holmes in full swing and started scrolling through his social posts, apps and pictures. The more I dived in his bright, shining and churning world, I got lost inside it. Down, down and down, I galloped into the world like a pearl slipping off in the dark abyss of wildness. At this moment, social media seemed to be like a blue genie giving out all the information I wanted to know about Karthik. I didn't unroll my eyes from the screen even for a minute not bothering about the environment around me. It was Abheer's beep that brought my buried soul out of the mystic scrolls of Karthik.

"Meet me at 5 pm at Vi-Mall."

"Yep, Abheer." I replied quickly, coming out of the wanderings.

It was 3.30 pm but it still looked like 6 am in the morning. I saw through the window; the outside was growing quieter. It was the perfect time to complete few of the pending work and get ready for the date.

I picked up the perfect combination to look chic, a white color tunic with geometrical prints of orange and blue blocks. I unwrapped my new jeans dazzling in a bright blue hue and wore it to make a stunning style statement. I finished my makeup, loaded my wallet with essentials and was walking down the hallway while typing a message to Mom. I kept the location tracker on and shared it with Mom as per her instructions. I waved bye to Vaishali and Grandma as they gazed me in amazement. I picked up the car keys, stepped out of the front door and walked straight to the car.

I opened the front door of the parked car, got inside and turned my key in the ignition to make a whirring sound. Catching a front view and back view, I applied force to the clutch and gear to drive off on the road. Generally, I hate to be in the driver's seat but Mom says every survival skill needs to be mastered; and driving is one of them.

I drove off in a calm mood, revolving the steering, taping on the music to set the happy ambiance and heading to the destination. I could feel the wind in my hair, and the car moving ahead somewhere motivating me to move forward in life. After thirty minutes of exciting drive, I reached the mall, and parked my car in the outside section instead of underground parking provision. I entered the mall through the main entrance reached the central atrium and went to the second floor using the escalator on the left side.

I called up Abheer, and he replied instantly, "I am at the food court waiting for you."

I raced in the direction of food court to see after a long time. There he was, decked in white silky shirt that glistened in the lights and colors. His slim black trousers positively hugged his waist as it was in a great shape. Seeing each other, we both rushed and fell in a deep embrace. It activated my senses in incredible ways. A poet rediscovered lost words, a lover met the lovely moon, and a heart heard its beat in another heart. Countless stars fell from the infinite sky upon us at that moment. His skin brushed against mine and I felt a fire of passion from within. He was the joy of life, my first love, my soul's desire and the man I want to do romance with him forever. If here in this embrace is the love of my life, then who is Karthik for me? Why did I think so sinfully about Karthik? Why my heart got pulled to him as if I know him since ages?

I asked myself repeatedly and the voice of mind said, 'Karthik is the object of your infatuation but Abheer is your cosmic constant,"

"Hey, where are you lost? Come on, people are looking at us," He said in his usual soft voice and courteous accent, brushing his brown hair backwards. He was a perfect gentleman in every sense, even my mom agreed about this point. He leaned forward and close to me; I melted in the spark of his eyes as our grudges and differences reduced to ashes. He gazed deep into my amber eyes, eclipsing them with his thunderous clouds of rains.

I smiled, and he responded with a broader smile. We flew along like two poisoned birds toward the beautiful studded sky. He wrapped his arms around my shoulders and steered our way to the seating enclosure at the food mall.

Abheer questioned me as we sat in a quiet corner at the food court, "How is your mom? How have you been?"

"Mom is doing well," I replied, feeling glad that he cared about my mother.

"She is a professor, right," he frowned.

'Yeah," I smiled and asked about his family, their latest business goal, and his recent profile enrichment at work.

"Well, the job is becoming more interesting. I am never into the family business, so no comments on anything, but some new projects are in the queue. I have read a lot on Zen, Ikigai, MA - Minimalism concepts and have discovered the value of simple and small things, and the true essence of life is not accumulating but understanding. Kalki, I will be happy to live in Bhutan than in the crowded metropolis of top-ranking cities. Something changed; as you said, I introspected deep and swept away all the cobwebs that were blocking my way to a cleaner, calmer, and comfortable life."

He paused, and I picked up from there, "I am happy for you, Abheer."

"So now, can we have a new beginning, with a new definition," he said in a solid voice. A moment later, the waiter came to take our order, but Abheer asked him to come later as we wanted to focus on our talks.

"In your absence, I realized your true presence in my life. The GAP idea really worked," he said with a smile and continued, "I always ignored your story and focused on me and my world. I was wrong, and I apologize for this behavior. Believe me, from now; it will be a mutual relationship based on respect and trust; a better us. Also, I respect your mom's journey and struggle. Her path was tougher than my mom's struggle of facing internal conflicts at home."

"Abheer, we are not comparing our mother's pain, and let's not benchmark it. They faced what they were capable of facing in life. Grief is destiny gifted, so let's not dive inside it. I just wanted to make you understand that my mother has devoted her entire life to me. No one can outrank her position in my heart, and my mother will always be my priority in life. This doesn't mean; I have less respect for your mother. God knows; Kalki has the same regards in her heart for every mother. My life had only a mother figure to worship." I sighed out.

There was a momentary silence between us. We then talked about how life is taking shape, unexpected things that happened; there were high and low musical notes in our talks. We took deep breaths in unison as darkness turned in the sky. At this moment, we created the sun and moon with our unconsciousness. We were hungry to speak out our souls. To sing songs of love, and create our own realm of imagined future. We were so lost in each other that we ignored every message beep and incoming ringtone. The sky changed its hue from brilliant blue to springing black, but we remained absorbed in our love talks.

I checked my watch; it was close to 11 o'clock. It was late and we decided to leave for the day. We walked down the mall exchanging words of inspiration and goodness. We stood close at the parking lot holding each other's hand and talking of new possibilities to thrive. The clinging pressure of his lips said goodbye in the most creative way. I could see the moisture of my lips upon his lips and the moon secretly recording our play from his open gallery. We said goodnight discovering something amazing, something we had never found till now.

As I walked to the car, I checked the phone and realized that probably, I was going to be in deep trouble. There was a total of 5 unread messages and 10 missed calls from Mom.

I called up Mom, but she didn't pick up my call. So, I send a message, "I am reaching home soon. Just left from the mall now." Though she received and read the message, there was no reply. I drove in anticipation of this trouble.

I approached the front door, and was just about to ring the door bell, Mom opened the door. She didn't utter a single word but turned her head toward the clock hanging in the middle of the living room. It was 1 am, but I knew she was angrier about my non-responsiveness than the time lag. She locked the main door and walked into her room to avoid an ugly situation. I dared not to speak with her and went inside my room to sleep in a blended atmosphere of forgiveness and happiness.

But I could not sleep after upsetting the primary God of my life. I knocked at her door, but she didn't answer.

"Mom?" I entered the room, fearing her reaction. She sat at the edge of the bed in an upright position, reading a novel. I walked slowly, fearing her reaction, and stood beside her quietly for some time. "Mom, I am sorry. Things were going so well that I lost the track of time. Abheer was so different and changed, you wouldn't believe me. He was so concerned about you."

I said with watery eyes and my lips trembled with words, "I know; I should have reverted to your messages, and I am sorry for everything. But we both were so engrossed in talking...Please, forgive me and talk to me," I held her wrist and begged her for forgiveness, but she didn't melt.

Mom really cared for me a lot, and I could understand her anger toward me. I glared at Mom and said in a moist tone, "I think; I should get a punishment. I will give myself the best punishment."

I was about to walk out of her room when Mom said, "So, why don't you sleep here and tell me about your day?"

"Did you forgive me?" I asked bumping joyfully on the bed.

"For the first and last time. Next time, you will have it from me," she said in a strict voice. I kissed on her cheeks in an attempt to cool her down and said, "Trust me, mom, never again in this lifetime."

"Really," she said and drummed her fingers to tickle me.

Thankful, the night settled in with laughs, talks, and hope.

"The planets in their orbit may change,
The color of skies can turn pale from blue
Lone hills in the storms filled weather may crumble,
But, you mother, will always be with me, in every season."

CHAPTER FIVE

In Search of Blessings

As days flew, the weather of my life got perfect. Work progressed, so did my affection and trust for Karthik. I had gained wide visibility and exposure by distributing my content to multiple social networks and integrating a blog on my website. Also, I had mailed out a few articles and stories to newspaper editors, and top-tier magazines to establish notability for Wikipedia. Karthik had trained me on how to drive traffic to your website and capture new clients using easy SEO tools and tactics. As my website gained a lot of impressions in Google Analytics and links from social media virality, Karthik suggested that we should sustain the flow by adding cool content, infographics, content writing tips, and some visual art on regular basis. He even extended his full-time social marketing team resource to guide and support for an initial period of three months. This was his complimentary gift given to me at Mom's request, and I gratefully accepted the benefit.

For me and Abheer, love was rigged with video calls, voice calls, and fewer in-person meetings due to his new role and responsibilities at work. But I could see his face before me. I could feel his touch on my skin, I could hear his voice in my ears, it was like a boundless expression of love energies and I was willing to immerse in it.

Abheer was thrilled at his promotion, but found himself in the sea again due to the stormy market conditions. Thanks to his experience and penetrating insights, he was able to strategize a strong defense and lead his team.

"We will be leaving for Kolhapur next Friday," Mom said as she watched TV and keeping her hands busy painting ceramic pieces. I was watching her seated in a cross-legged posture on the floor mat and blending vivid hues to create delicate objects of art.

"You didn't tell me when you booked the air-tickets and made the plan. Just because I am a freelancer doesn't mean my office is portable." There was no reaction from her and she continued to hum and brush.

"I can manage work," I said in a mild tone, and she interrupted me saying, "Well, I knew it. Your Mamaji will come to stay with Grandma in our absence. Karthik is joining us and he was available on those dates, hence I confirmed the booking."

"Karthik..." my mouth opened wide in amazement. I thought, he was kidding when he asked about joining us. Also, he didn't tell me while we were working.

"Kalki," mom said in a relaxed accent, "Karthik followed my instructions. He is really a very good, cultured and supportive boy. He will be a great asset to you in the future."

"Asset, huh, Professor, come out of your accounting lectures." I said with a smile smearing some drops of paint on her cheek. She got very irritated and warned me not to touch her paints anymore or else I would be deprived of dinner.

"Are you witnessing any more paranormal happenings around you? I want to know the truth," she said raising the topic with concern. I paused for a minute and then spoke candidly, "What I can say that I do see bizarre dreams, strange visions, and faces of unknown dead people."

"You never told me that these things are still happening," Mom pointed out angrily.

"But I feel safe when I sleep beside you like a baby. So, I didn't bother you," I said though the reply didn't convince her.

"Well, let's hope, this visit to our Kuldevi, our lineage goddess, will relieve all our pain and burdens," she said assertively.

I nodded my head.

'Kalki, do you want to pursue a Masters' degree. Your father is willing to fund your experience abroad. You would be completing 1-year graduation anniversary soon," she asked and continued to paint with passion and her point of view.

I drew her close and said in a firm voice that sounded threatening to her, "Mom, I repeat that no one funds any of my requirements except you. If you ever cheat me then I swear the consequences will not be good."

"Kiddo, relax, it's okay," she said, kissing my fuming, invisible third eye on the forehead with tenderness.

"As of now, I don't want to enroll in any course. Give me

some time to create my brand in the market. In the end, only practical experience counts not theory lessons," I said and sank down onto the couch listening to mamma's stories and perspectives about many and few things. She talks really wise and some elements of talk are in common. I love to be her learning sponge; absorb her knowledge, concepts, insights, and create my own personal belief system.

A few days of the same routine passed. It seemed as if life has inflated some hidden power inside me to face all the paranormal events without a pause. For the first time, life was more colorful and challenging to me than the shades of grey, black, and white. The social marketing push had made my career from good to great. Life was filling up with more people of different shapes, sizes, thoughts, and clusters, enriching my insights and learnings on the job. I streamlined my working processes to be more agile and more aligned to give a better outcome. Pondering, thinking, brainstorming, disrupting, all these tools did wonders to my success roadmap. Articles got published, editors of famous magazines started reverting to my pitches and my clients list got extended to famous companies and celebrities. Seeing me gain recognition made mom happy but the most important motivation for me was to make her feel proud and redefine the status quo.

It was early Friday morning. Mom had an excellent knack for organizing things and had packed her baggage with essentials yesterday. I sat down on the bed wondering how to start when Mom entered,

"Kalki, what are you doing sitting here in Yogasana posture. Get up, you have to do your packing, withdraw cash from the ATM, and check grandma's medicines. I will go to college and come back after finishing 2 or 3 lectures. Till then, you have to be ready with everything. Daughter, this is my order," she commanded loud. In a second, I jumped in the shower, bathed, and came into my room to get dressed in a yellow T-shirt and red color relaxed pants.

Mom entered the living room dressed in a traditional teal colour cotton saree with batik print design and an indigo-colored boat neck sequined blouse. Her grace looked timeless as the sunlight reflected the glimmer of her pearl studs. The scent of her sandalwood perfume lingering in the air left behind a trail of inspiration. She had tied up her waist-long hair into a tight bun as she never let it fly freely.

Maybe, like her hair, she had also tied up her desires and expectations. When I was a kid, it was my favorite activity to untie her meticulously freshly tied up bun. Sometimes she would get angry, sometimes smile, sometimes tickle me, and sometimes give a whack with her wide teeth comb. Her reaction depended on her personal climate and my mischief on mood.

Mom hurried to rush to work, skipping breakfast, and grabbing an apple to eat on the way. "Come on time," I said, grinning, as she zoomed out of the door waving at me.

"Kalki, don't withdraw any cash from ATM machine. I will do it," I heard her distant voice. "Ok, Mom," I shouted loud and short.

I took a deep breath and placed the unopened baggage before me. Turning to the other end, I glanced at the massive walnut-colored wardrobe with apprehension. Knowing there was no point in prolonging the inevitable, I took another breath and moved forward to start the task.

I opened my massive walnut-colored wardrobe with curiosity. A pleasant scent of lavender rose and apple cinnamon was released from the potpourri's pouches placed inside. The beautiful fragrance complemented the vibrant colors and musical wind chimes in my room. I started picking and packing my clothes in the duffel bag. I selected two pairs of casual tops, two T-shirts – jeans and a pair of leggings and Arabic style long kurta. I packed my lingerie in a small travel organizer bag and placed it in a corner in the duffel bag. I loaded the government proof of identity in my backpack compartment. Happy with the progress, I asked Vaishali to brew a hot coffee for me.

'Now, I need to pack all the digital accessories, make-up kit, and a full kit of toiletries,' I rubbed my hands in the excitement of finishing the task. Believe it or not, I was looking forward to this trip with Mom to a new place.

After completing the cumbersome task of packing, I sat on the sofa in the living room to watch an intriguing thriller series on Netflix. Vaishali was commenting now and then on social topics, and Grandma uttered her emotional tweets in between to spice up their conversations. I left a message on Abheer's mobile about our trip and asked him to call when free. The heightening suspense and undeniably powerful diabolical moves in the episodes grabbed my total interest. Suddenly, the ringing of the doorbell diverted my attention. Vaishali opened the door and Mom entered with an exhausted look. She was sweating more than ever and panting heavily. Vaishali got her a big glass of water filled with ice-cubes and she chugged it down trying to be cool.

"Kalki is everything ready? We have to leave before 11 am. Our flight is scheduled at 1.30 pm."

She reached for the remote and turned off the TV. My initial reaction was to snag the remote and turn it on. However, her efforts mellowed down.

"Yep, Mom," I said with a bang.

Mom gave a few instructions to Vaishali. She requested her to wait here with Grandma till Mamaji arrives. Turning her head to me, she said," I need twenty minutes to fresh up. Get our luggage outside. Once; I am done, we are leaving immediately."

"Ok," I said following her inside. I went into our rooms, grabbed the pieces of baggage kept in a corner, and brought them out in the living room. After feeling a breeze, I came into the bathroom. I washed my face with glycerin soap and looked in the mirror. After the cleanse, I felt vibrant. I wore a printed grey T-shirt under a black jacket and black ripped jeans. I placed the Air pods in my ears and shoved the mobile in the pocket of my jeans. Here, I was all set to go...

When I came into the living room, Mom was giving Vaishali a list of instructions about Grandma's medicines, diet, and contact details of people to be contacted in an emergency. She then went into the puja room to take blessings from Ganpati Bappa. Grandma pulled me close to give me a comforting hug as Mom watched from behind. I felt so happy. Grandma was giving some spiritual tips to Mom about oracles, and she pretended to listen out of respect.

Mom turned around and asked me to book a cab from Uber to airport. I confirmed the pickup and kept a tab on the driver's movements toward our location.

"Mom, the cab will arrive in 5 mins, should we wait down?"

I waited for her opinion.

"Kay, call the watchman to help us to put the luggage in the cab." Hearing that, Vaishali opened the door and shouted out his name in her irony voice, "Oh, Dipubabu, Dipubabu, come up to help us with bags."

He arrived fast, and after saluting Mom, he picked up the bags and walked down the stairs. As we stayed on the first floor, there was much less dependency on the escalator. Vaishali also accompanied us as we walked down the building. Mom had great trust in Vaishali and she was eager to prove her loyalty and capability, especially now. The Uber cab arrived, making its way slowly toward us through the entrance gate. Dipu, our Nepalese watchman loaded the luggage in the trunk of the cab and wished us Bon Voyage in his hilly accent. Vaishali waved us a good-bye till we were invisible to her eyes.

We sat in the backseat of the car as the young driver sped up to complete a distance of 26.9 km. I looked out, luckily there was no sign of rain. The sun was shining and the entire city seemed literally glittering. The highway was on heels flashing with blue and red lights, and the filtered winds tousled my hair.

Mom was busy thumbing through messages on her smartphone. I looked at her and asked, "Will Karthik be comfortable with us? I know Abheer would have loved a family trip." She paused for a minute, then with a smile started thumbing through pics.

"I am not comparing the two boys. Kalki, don't create an A versus B scenario. I know them as talented, hard-working, and honest human beings except Abheer is more tender and delicate in nature. Karthik's feet are exposed to the rough greetings of life that got hardened as he grew. Abheer was born with a silver spoon in his life and is eating with a set of golden cutleries. Mere differences with his father are not the kind of curriculum experiences that will mold him to fit in the survival race and be a life warrior. The designer is done with Karthik but is yet to give a finishing touch to Abheer." She turned her head slightly so that she could glance outside.

"So, does it mean Karthik is a better choice as he is an updated version?" I said with a frown.

"No, both are evolving. I can't comment on who is better.
"No, both are evolving. I can't comment on who is better.
Each person has their own individual story, they design the artistic cover page, expose their own courageous spine, unleash their own capabilities, and create a powerful emblem of inspiration." She sighed a breath.

I carefully asked her in slight hesitation, "If you had to choose one of them for the rest of your life, whom would you prefer?"

She stared at me for a moment. "Daughter, though you are a piece of my heart, our perspectives will always be different. My choice may not be your preferred answer."

"Still, just for fun...or just like that," I put my hand on her shoulder to convince her more.

"It depends on the roots of the relationship and conversations, how authentic and enriching is the whole spectrum for you. Don't expect to create your own distinct position in their story; try to be a gardener and create evergreen experiences of landscapes for them." She said, cleaning the sediments from the glasses of her spectacles.

"Mom, this is a too complex answer, and I don't want to keep grinding my intelligence on it. Whom would you choose as your life-partner between Karthik and Abheer?" I asked impatiently.

"Meera in her twenties probably would have opted for Abheer – first emotional connection. Seeing life from a higher peak, Karthik would be a reliable choice. He wants a family; he wants love; he wants to offer his gift of life to someone. He is a wolf-man, will go to any extent to be a good husband, father, and protect his home. If your paranormal activities are a life-long legacy, then Karthik will be a safer choice. Abheer is unable to deal with tangible things and people in life; will he face intangible forces? Her voices echoed deep in my head, provoking deeper insights.

"To some extent, she was correct. I can't think of Abheer dealing with such scary and unusual stuff. He is miles away from watching horror movies; imagine the possibilities if he knows that I am seeing dead people," I thought to myself.

"Kalki," Mom distracted me from the exploration of thoughts. "This is the time to focus on your career and professional education. You are just 22 years now; there are two more years in your bank. Live, explore, and discover your wings," she stroked my hair and calmed my thoughts.

"Kalki, stay in the present moment, focus on taking energy from nature, don't worry about the future. Believe it or not, destiny is the greatest mystery." There was a touch of water in her eyes and rain in my mind.

The driver entered the airport premises, driving the car at a slow speed as it passed by the Mumbai airport terminal gates. He stopped the car at Terminal 2 entry point and kept his hands on his thighs, relaxed his knees and legs, then pushed his buttocks back and leaned slightly forward with the torso to stretch his hamstring. It was a kind of exercise and relief for him. He helped us to get down our luggage. We paid his fare through the Uber app and left him a tip with positive feedback.

I loaded our bags on a creaking metal-wheeled cart and pushed it toward the security checkpoint. The flight attendant checked our air-tickets and government proof and allowed us inside through a metallic security gate. Mom had completed the web check-in that made our process smooth and quick. The flight check-in counter representatives greeted us courteously and checked our web check-in slips, weighed our luggage bags, and handed us boarding passes with a friendly smile.

Mom and I walked together toward the lounge discussing some emotional topics. We reached a security checkpoint and deposited our handbags, mobiles, and backpack on a rolling flank passing through the monitoring base. Simultaneously, we had to get a physical check done as per the security protocols. After the completion of the security check, we headed toward the lounge of our departure gate.

Here, we were at the Terminal-2, the journey from this point is a cutting edge start to a new frontier of innovation and history. Our eyes dazzled seeing the spectacular art, grand mosaic artwork, grand pavilion reflecting the green luxury and spaciousness of the brand. The entire terminal is depicted to be a living museum taking us to different centuries and places from one common platform. Even, Mom couldn't resist her temptation and started clicking pictures and videos from her iPhone. The 'Jaya He GVK Museum' was a spectacular narrative of the diverse cultural shorelines that create glorious beauty in our nation. A global fusion of technology, innovation, and ideas has infused a memorable story and sensibility in this airport. Every artwork be it paintings, kinetic installations, intricate designs, and exquisite sculptures was a masterpiece in itself, so complete, so artistic. At dusk, the entire stadium blooms like a glowing, sculpted lotus flower. We captured our true essence in the global spirit of this Terminal-2.

The retail hub at the airport interconnects with the leading global and Indian brands in every consumer segment. I had an urge to visit most of these glamorous shops but kept it for the return journey. We finally sat at our departure lounge. Mom picked up an English newspaper and got engaged in reading the headlines. We still have a good amount of time at our disposal.

When everything around was getting boring, I spotted Karthik dressed in a royal blue shirt, black trousers, and a large duffel bag. He smiled and waved at me with happiness.

"Here is your perfect gentleman," I said to Mom. She slid her head out of the newspaper and gave a wide smile the moment she saw Karthik. He walked up to her and said in a thankful voice, "Thanks for making me a passenger in your journey."

"Uh...so dramatic, Karthik," I said to him, and he replied with a grin. Mom gave me a stare from behind that conveyed to me the unspoken message.

When Mom and Karthik were talking, Abheer called me on my cell phone. I excused myself from the ongoing conversation and picked up Abheer's call.

"Hello," I said in an accent of romance.

"Hi, Baby, I thought of speaking with you before the flight takes off. Take care, and do send me your pictures. I have a presentation in 1-hour, so I may not talk with you for a long time. I love you, and we will speak in the moonlight.

His lovely and caring words brought me to my senses, and I swallowed the moment of love in a single breath. And the flight announcement made all of us queue up in a line to get our final passes checked before we board the plane.

The departure gates opened, and I joined the queue standing ahead of mom. Karthik humbly stood behind my mom; if she needed any help. Our boarding pass got stamped and we followed the queue on the air bridge guided by flight attendants to reach our flight. The big plane was drawing closer and now in view.

We arrived at the stairs of the flight and walked on the top of the mobile stairs. An alluring air hostess dressed in her modern blue uniform politely greeted her arriving passengers. I smiled back at her and greeted her as a tribute to the girls walking on the skies. We walked down the aisle to our seats. Karthik helped me load my backpack in the upper compartment. Mom and Karthik gifted me the window seat - F. We took our seats in the fifth row. Mom was in the middle seat next to me, and Karthik in the aisle seat both conversing with each other on cultural, lifestyle and spiritual topics.

I started sharing my pictures with Abheer and pinging him with emoticons before his presentation starts. The flight attendant was doing her demonstration and I was expressing my conversation to Abheer.

From all the topics in the world Mom was talking about Abheer to Karthik. "He is Kalki's close friend and they met at an FMCG project work. His design capabilities and her striking content became a good match for repetitive works, and they have a good bond." She said, giving me a sarcastic smile. I signaled her through my eyes to stop.

Then, from strengths to weakness, she was charting out his SWOT Analysis to Karthik. She turned to me in between, asking my opinion on his design insights; and future potential as a Product Development Head.

I didn't reply to her though she was going on and on. The cabin door was shut but her conversations were opening my relationship diaries to Karthik. The flight started to vibrate and headed toward the runway for takeoff. I looked out of the window at other flights, little vehicles, and the airport stadium buzzing with people and emotions. My mind was so filled with love and poetic thoughts of Abheer that the thudding and tremors of the airplane seemed soothing.

Now, Karthik was talking about his adventures at Mt. Everest; the laughter and thrill continued in the background as I looked out of the window at the billowing clouds. No wonder, but I am always in awe of cloud formations. They are so intriguing; I simply cannot take my eyes off them. It is as if they are spilling out some secrets with me and asking me to decode them.

As the plane rose higher and higher, I could see different cloud formations playing in God's light. These formations are telling me that an opportunity will enter and fleet your life very soon. You have to be attentive and quick to respond to it. I clicked pictures of these awe-inspiring formations dipped in colors of white and yellow with my mobile phone.

Some passengers were busy on their laptops or mobiles, some chatting with each other, and others had fallen asleep.

I looked below at the scenery. The impenetrable cluster of the wilderness was so vast; it seems anyone could get lost in it. Karthik continued to talk about places to visit in Kolhapur, and Mom nodded.

"Kalki, do you want to visit any place?" he bent forward and asked me.

I stared at him for less than a second. It was hard to ignore his dimpled-cheek and a gigantic smile. There was a life in his eyes that was eager to explore everything.

"Let's see." I gave a neutral reply to avoid more conversations with him.

The air hostess pulled back the curtain across the aisle and brought out their trolley filled with food and beverages. Another airhostess joined her to ease the task of distribution and collecting payments.

Mom brought three sandwiches and Coke, one for each one of us. I opened the wrapper and started eating the sandwich. Mom pulled out a few currency notes from her purse to make the payment. Karthik's mobile beeped, engaging him into a conversation. I opened up the lid of the can and watched the mesmerizing beauty while sipping the Coke.

The airplane took slow radius turns as it approached the opening premises of Kolhapur. The airplane soared in few turns and then the captain announced that the plane was ready to land. An air hostess announced to the passengers to switch off electronics assets, fasten their seat belts and straighten up the seats.

The plane circled the runway to come into the headwind for landing. We felt a few bumps due to the braking effects. The flaps lowered a bit and the plane leveled off from the glide path so that the main landing gears could contact the ground surface. The plane made few bounces to balance the grip and then settled rolling at a lower speed to reach the parking ramp. The pilot cut off the fuel supply and turned off the ignition to stop the engine. The head of the crew walked to the rear end and opened the doors after the exit setup was ready.

"Here we are", Karthik said with a twinkle in his eye. He opened up the luggage compartment and took our stuff out. We stood in the departure queue, which was not so long, and quickly collected our baggage from the luggage carousel. I pinged Abheer that we had arrived at the city known to be the most outstanding storyteller of our iconic culture. As soon as we stepped outside the airport, Karthik was geared for action. He was busy responding to the cab-drivers chasing the passengers coming out of the airport. Karthik finalized a cab and signaled us to come to the Etios car parked a few feet ahead. We reached at the car, Mom and I sat in the back seat. Karthik preferred to sit in the front seat for a complete view of the road scenery. The driver had a local accent, yet his voice sounded sweet to hear. He was also very law-abiding and strictly followed traffic rules, refusing to exceed the speed limits. He made friends with Karthik as he looked trustworthy and a promising fellow. Karthik pulled out his mobile phone and saved his contact number as Santosh Chandekar.

The driver raced through the Old Pune-Bangalore highway known to be the fastest route of 25-30 minutes. The wet wind blew as we passed through the legendary Shivaji University established in 1962, today more than 280 colleges and recognized institutes are affiliated with it. Karthik had made all arrangements as per Mom's suggestions and booked our stay in Treebo Trend Balaji Residence; a 3-star hotel with the best amenities for a budget-minded traveler. It feels good to go on a trip managed by someone else, here it is Karthik and mom. You are left to only enjoy the moments and create joyful experiences.

The driver swirled the car, moving on the Konda Oal Road, from where we saw the modern and minimalist building standing in stark contrast to the overcrowded market ambiance around it. When we reached at the destination, the driver stopped the car and I got out to take in the metamorphosing views surrounding me. The watchman had already opened the heavy, metallic gate calling out the porter to pick up our luggage. Karthik walked through the corridors toward the reception desk along with Mom. I stood outside in the sun for some time. Ten minutes later, I went inside and sat on the sofa beside Mom observing the cultural decor on the walls. Karthik completed the formalities, showed our government-approved proofs for verification, and handed over the register for our signatures. Soon, the process was done. A porter pocketing the keys; innocently smiled at us and showed us our way toward our rooms through the thick passages.

Karthik had opted for standard accommodation, the Oak room suited best to his needs. Mom preferred the Maple room that offered the deluxe type of accommodation.

The porter showed us our respective rooms and placed our luggage in the corner of the room. Karthik tipped the porter generously for the service. Mom and I were standing at the door of our room, discussing the way ahead when Karthik stepped in.

“Hi,” he said with a heavy accent.

“Mam, I suppose you would be taking rest now and from

tomorrow, i.e. - Saturday we can schedule our Temple Darshan and sightseeing," he paused as Mom nodded agreeing with him.

"I have one activity at hand, will complete it, and return by 5 pm. Then we can do some shopping," he said with a smile.

"Please, go ahead. Take care," Mom gave a big grin and gave him a gentle tap on his shoulder. He left to get started with his scheduled task.

When we entered the room, it was like a breath of clean air - large windows, comfortable seating furniture, a cozy bed, and an extremely friendly atmosphere. I went straight into the bathroom to get cleaned and fresh. The bathroom was extraordinarily clean, clean white towels were hanging on the racks, a fresh bar of lemon soap, milk moisturizer, and Aloe-Vera shampoo bottle was arranged on the sink. The bathroom mirror was spotless and shining giving me a radiant reflection of my own beauty. I turned on the shower and jumped under the trickle of water to shampoo my hair and rinse my sweaty skin. While bathing, I could hear the loud TV noise from other rooms, the noise of people talking, the noise of the marketplace but bathing is a meditation process that aligns my energies in a state of mindfulness. The cream-colored tiles glistened under my feet as huge mounds of bubbles and water droplets splashed on the floor bed. Soaking in the water made my energy level go up. The interiors were so finely furnished it inspired a wonderful showering experience. Never before, I had felt such a passion for water.

I switched off the shower and unfolding a neatly spread towel wrapped it around my body. I rotated the bathroom handle to open the door and came out in the main room. Thankfully, the curtains in the main room were closed. Mom was ordering something to eat as it was approximately 4 o'clock. I wore teal-colored jeans and a red T-shirt with a V-shaped collar. Now, it was Mom's turn to have a bath and she takes a long time to feel clean and fresh.

I laid on the bed, surfing the channels until there was a knock on the door. The in-house hotel staff had brought our food order - a thermos of hot tea and three veg grilled cheese sandwiches. I called up grandma and informed her that we had reached safely. Vaishali gave us her blessings and kept the phone. I poured the clove infused tea in a cup and sipped it standing beside the full-view window. I was mapping out the city when Abheer called me on my mobile. I picked up the call and said in a loving voice, "Hello."

There was a momentary silence. Abheer said, "Hello, Kay, can we speak now,"

"Sure, Abheer," I was concerned after hearing his tone

"Is someone with you?" he asked to ensure privacy while speaking.

"Mom is having her bath now. She may take a couple of minutes more. So, please speak and be comfortable," I assured him that I would give him my best attention.

"Well, then you should know, I have moved out of my parent's home due to increasing strain of differences and comparison," he continued with a small break.

I feel suffocated there, listening to only company profits, expansion plans, and competitors' rivalry strategies 24 by 7. Dad and Kabir only talk, eat, drink, and even breathe business. I tried speaking with Kabir but the flavor of success has eclipsed him completely," I urged him to go on though it was difficult for him to speak. He is emotional and many people do misread him at times.

"Mom is just a neglected living thing at home. She continues her own story as an optimistic person. I am not as tolerant as her and finally shifted to our 2 BHK flat at Powai. I really miss her because of these people," he cried and I waited patiently till he continued speaking.

"Mom will be missing me but at least, I have my peace of mind here," he stopped to catch his breath.

"Abheer, one way it is sad, you're away from your parents. But, it is better than living with estranged relationships and diluting them further. Good move, dear. I am proud of the fact that you dealt with this emotional issue practically. It pained, ripped your feelings but you managed it with your well. This is my Abheer, strong in mind, decisive even in exigencies, and has the power of persistence within him." I said in a bold voice to make him feel happy.

"No, Kay. I followed your words. Remember, you said, if some problem is not giving you a good night's sleep, then it needs to be eliminated urgently. Here, I have created a distance from these blood ties that have made a knot of problems in my mind." There was a sob in his voice and somewhere a sense of guilt overwhelmed me.

"Maybe after a few days, you can go back home," I said to make the mood positive.

"You really think so, Kalki. A line crossed is always crossed," he said with a thoughtful that reflected his strength.

He spoke in a soft voice, "But, it's okay, Ma comes to meet me at my house and sometimes stays with me for the weekend. For the rest of the days, I am most of the time in the office and come home to sleep. Also, Mom has deputed a family cook and a caretaker to take care of me and home." He stopped speaking introspecting upon my unsaid thoughts.

"But a cook and caretaker can never replace your family member," I murmured.

"Kalki, Mom says, I should think of getting married and settling down. As of now, I have not communicated anything to her," he waited for my reaction.

"Abheer, you are just 25 years old; 3 years elder to me. I think we can wait for 2 more years. Let's get to know each other better, spend time traveling, exploring, learning, and thriving together. We can think of marriage too but not so soon," I made my stance clear to him and he did agree on this.

"But, I support your action-oriented step. Sometimes, distances can make you come close. You make not be the successor of his business but will always be his son. Trust me, no one can deny your existence in his life. Even though, Kabir takes up the business on his shoulder, you will always be his eldest son and our scriptures have written the significance of the position of eldest son."

Abheer felt comforted and ended up the call on a see you soon note.

Looking out of the window, I uttered in a distinct voice,

"You told me the tales of your bright life,
Of deep dark clouds shadowing your face
I heard your pains, passions, and poison,
That gulped your nights with a powerful tide
While you cried and wailed like a bird in the storm,
My soul rushed to kiss your beautiful story."

CHAPTER SIX

COLORS, CHAOS AND CONNECTIONS

Mom came out of the bathroom with a beaming face. She dressed up in her green color sari with a matching printed blouse. She wore her diamond studs in her ears, a gold bracelet on her right wrist, a watch on her left wrist, and fastened a chain around her slim neck.

"What happened?" Mom asked me as she poured her a cup of tea. I projected my feelings to her about Abheer's recent move and shared that I am thinking of myself to be responsible for it.

Seeing my response, she dragged me to sit down with her and said in a firm tone, "Stop making yourself the center of everything. Abheer is intelligent enough to take his own decisions. How much you love anyone, never let any person transfer their guilt, frustration, or accusation upon you. You gave him a few suggestions; he blended and infused his own analysis in it and derived upon a conclusion. Did he consult you while taking this action? Did he seek your advice before moving out? The answer is NO, he moved out of his parents' home and a week later informed you about it. Where and how do you stand responsible in this situation? There were tremors in her voice that shook my frozen nerves.

Her explanation made sense to me and helped to keep my spirit rolling.

At 5 pm, there was a knock on the door. Mom opened up the door and smiled wide as he entered in. There he was decked out in full casual style, his eyes sparkled as he looked at me. There was an approachable passion for him in my heart. He looked irresistible in his freshly washed appearance, wearing a white rounded neck T-shirt and a red casual blazer upon his black jeans. His pair of Nike shoes and apple smart watch integrated a sense of sophistication in his demeanor.

Karthik said in a loud and excited tone, "I am sure you ladies will love to go shopping in Kolhapur. What do you say?"

He successfully made us get up and go out with him in the city. We sat in the car and Karthik showed us the nearby whereabouts. He then told the driver to wheel the car to the most popular marketplace.

In Kolhapur, fashion is uniquely amazing. Women dressed in traditional sarees with heavy embroidery and adorned in heavy jewelry looked graceful in their full elegance. The smiling faces of shopkeepers and their modesty approach motivated us to visit their shops for purchasing. Kolhapur is a place where the Goddess abides in her full Feminine energy hence the images of the goddess are placed on the banners, car windshields, building walls, signboards to create a mural representation of their belief and culture.

"Mahadwar road is one of the oldest and most crowded places in the city," Mom said looking out of the car window.

"This is the primordial location where your Family Goddess resides. You will find peace and solace in her divine shade," she stroked my hair pointing her finger to the shikhara of the temple.

I glanced at the landscape wandering in the mysticism that quietly thrives in their surroundings. Mom turned to me and said remembering the earlier years," I had visited this place twice - after my marriage and a month after your birth."

There was a lull in her conversation. She stared blindly toward the window as the driver drove along.

"Here we are," the driver broke the silence with his husky, local-accent. We got down from the car at the arched entrance gate of the Mahadwar road and from there walked inside the marketplace.

"Wow, this is a shopper's paradise, Mom," I yelled out in amazement seeing the local delights, shining pieces of jewelery, stunning artwork, designer sarees, remarkable Kolhapuri chappals, and lots of things to buy and bargain. For the first time, in excitement, I held Karthik's hand tightly, and thanked me umpteen times.

There were big shops, small shops, and local hawkers selling artistic items. Mom had already entered a jewelery shop and was checking an exclusive collection of Thusi necklace. I requested Mom to set me free to explore the marketplace on my own but she was reluctant. After repeated attempts from my end, she agreed and asked Karthik to accompany me.

"Karthik, please take care of her. I trust you. Once, you people are done give me a call and we will meet at this very spot," her voice was very firm and she let me go with him to the most overcrowded place in Kolhapur.

We walked close to avoid getting lost in the market rush. "Take care of your mobile," Karthik whispered in my ear. We strolled through the market visiting shops, hawkers, and even footpath sellers. Karthik was willing to buy every item liked by me, making the situation a bit awkward for him.

I requested, frowned, and even scolded him but he continued to do as he pleased. "You can repay me later," he tried to convince me but it would be a difficult time convincing mom about this matter. Finally, I had the last weapon for rescue and gave him my swear. Then, he stopped and didn't interfere in my shopping but only carried the shopping bags. Along with shopping, I did click a lot many pictures and recorded videos of this jazzy marketplace. We also ate the mouth-watering chat items from the street hawkers.

"The best spicy roadside cuisine," I exclaimed enjoying the taste of tamarind chutney inside the panipuri. There was a delight in Karthik's eyes watching me gulp the puris in a greedy manner.

Finally, Karthik actually dragged me outside the market promising that we will come later for more purchasing. Mom was waiting at the decided spot, and seeing my purchase bags, she scolded Karthik in a loving manner.

"Why did you let her buy so many things? How will we take it home, now what about the packaging, etc.? You should have been strict with her? There is no point speaking with Kalki but you also..." Mom was ranting on. Suddenly, I hugged her and said, "Thanks, Mom. I love you," and she melted like the Himalayan ice.

Karthik called the driver at the entrance door as we walked to reach there. The car arrived immediately and the driver placed the bags in the trunk. It was almost 7.30 pm and Mom thought we could finish off with dinner. Back in the resort, we could sleep and wake up early at 5 am for tomorrow's temple darshan. I and Karthik nodded mutually as the driver raced toward the main road.

Karthik was sharing the clicked images on Whatsapp and simultaneously posting on social media.

"Your energy and enthusiasm never end?" I asked him anticipating an equally energetic answer.

"I have seen more ends in life than beginnings. Hence, I promised myself that my energy, courage, hope, and enthusiasm will never evaporate however volcanically the sun blazes. I want to live not because I love life because I hate death more. I think this is the most powerful way to defeat death - by loving and living life." He growled like an angry wolf and the glow surrounded his aura. He plucked his earphone in his ears listening to soothing music. I was washed away by the crashing waves of his passion but didn't get wet. There was an urge deep inside to pull the string of my heart to sing his song.

Mom was looking at her new purchase – a gold necklace. I deliberately moved my attention to her from Karthik.

"Is this the traditional Thusi, the elegant necklace jewelery?"

I asked touching the shimmering piece.

"Hmm, isn't it beautiful?" She was holding the red color jewelery box and scanning the necklace that laid in the satin blue bed of the box. I continued to watch her action figuring her love for jewelery.

"You know what is beautiful about this moment?" she was quiet for a moment, then looked deeply into my amber eyes, and said in a thoughtful voice, "This wonderful feeling of returning to a familiar place with a new identity rooted inside you. Coming back to the same place to discover new insights and perspectives. When I visited this place 25 years ago, I was just a bride or to be clear; an unhappy bride. I was losing everything due to this confluence and didn't like anything that got introduced to me because of it - relations, things, places. But today, I love this feeling…this feeling of stability, the fear of known and unknown is no more present. The rise and the fall, the incoming and outgoing, the acceptance that everything is just a procession of life and it comes to us in stories else in lyrics," she looked deep in the shine of my amber eyes and held her attention.

"Kalki," she steeled herself and said," Here is a very simple secret; your eyes are a remarkable inheritance. The only thing you have taken from your father. Rest all is only me."

My eyebrows knitted a frown and I said," I know that. Does it remind you of him every moment?"

"No, it depends on what you want to be remembered. I have wiped him from my mind. The only good thing about him is he never turned back to ask or reconnect with us. He accepted my decision and only communicated when required," she said with a soft roar.

"He didn't want any accountability and maybe it was a better option than divorce. His social status was also safeguarded," I sighed with a wave of overwhelming anger.

"My equation with him should never tamper your equation with him," she scowled at me and then spoke in a loving voice, "Wandering in a life of isolation and uncertainty, the soft golden spark in your eyes inspired me to live. When I had forgotten to light a candle in the darkness, your angelic eyes beamed up to show me the upcoming way. There is something inexpressible about your eyes, some kind of power that can offer peace, contentment, confidence, and hope to the seeker. Your eyes will always be my daily companion and this is the reason why I cannot see tears in your eyes...the eyes that drew a sunrise for me every day." Her eyes smoldered with infinite emotions that could not be comprehended.

"Take the car to the best restaurant," Mom instructed the driver and he listened in obedience. Karthik had unplugged his earphone and checked the restaurant reviews on Google, and selected the best pick - Dehaati restaurant with an outstanding record of 4000 reviews and a ranking of 4.5 on a five-point scale. Tucked in a brightly lighted corner of Ayodhya Park, the restaurant with a rooftop attracts new visitors due to its marvelous architecture, design painted glass walls, and traditional makeover that assures the best hygienic standards and authentic Kolhapuri food.

As we waited at the restaurant porch for our turn, some of the local people began speaking with us. They asked us where we were from and our purpose to visit here. Mom got engaged in speaking with them about life in Mumbai, her job as a professor in the most reputed college in Mumbai. The women there enquired with Mom about the recent MBA admission process, career plans for their children, how to prepare for top entrance exams, etc. They saved Mom's contact number as they found the interaction to be insightful and an interactive experience for them. Karthik stood there listening to her talks, remembering how she skillfully molded him. This was the beginning of her idea on starting personalized counseling for students from other cities and rural areas about higher education and career prospects.

Finally, it was our turn. We walked inside the 60-seater restaurant which was filled with frenetic energy. The walls were adorned with brilliant paintings of doodle art and traditional bells made up of brass hung as wall mounting. It was a busy place and people were constantly coming in and out.

The seating arrangement was for four people with the provision to accommodate more. The restaurant manager greeted us with a big smile and took us to a quiet corner for dining. We placed our purse, wallets, and mobiles on the edge of the table and sat down to dine. The waiter served us cold water and noted our order of three Dehaati non-veg special thali, one plate of Akka masoor, and an extra plate of steamed plain rice. The specialty of the Thali is an authentic combination of Tambada Rassa and Pandhara Rassa along with Mutton Masala, Chicken Fry, Mutton Keema, Mutton Pulao, and Bhakri. The warm and friendly ambiance made us feel comfortable and at home.

As we waited for our food, we engaged in conversations about the latest events in life and shared urban legends and mythological stories. In between, Karthik posed his mobile to click our pictures and my fair skin would blush like a red rose. His presence was giving me warmth and my mind had blacked out most of the people shrinking the world to only me and him. I had some different type of feelings for him that could not be decoded now.

The server placed the Thali in front of each one of us and bowed down in gratitude. The food was just awesome delivery a spicy tinge to the eater and served in a spotlessly clean steel plate and bowl. We ate in full swing relishing every morsel with delight. We had the ultimate dining experience in a charmingly designed atmosphere. Caramel custard was a great finish to a great dinner in the top restaurant in Kolhapur. We generously tipped the waiter and left positive feedback for the restaurant that had created a beautiful impression in our minds.

We headed to our rental car and told him to drive us back to our resort. The driver took out the car from parking and drove ahead. I saw Karthik through the rear-mirror view and closed my eyes to see a smile on Abheer's face.

A piece of your heart is always tucked away for your first love. The raw love that showed you infinite joy in small things. No surprise was as splendid as the first gifted red rose withering away in the pages of your favorite book. It was your voice that splintered my bones with joy. No one else other than you could read me like an open book. You were the womb from where my dreams were born; the first dream of my soul. The first very moment when you held me and I was completely absorbed inside you." The car jerked backward several feet abruptly waking me from Abheer's abstract embrace.

"Sprinkle our memories and moments, tears and smiles
Engrave our depths and isolations, delights and pleasures
To make our story a kaleidoscopic gift from a nameless writer,
To ignite those hearts not knowing the manifestations of love
To reincarnate again to fill the other blank pages in the world"

After a drive of 15 minutes, we reached our resort. It was 10.30 pm and we were feeling sleepy after a heavy dinner. Karthik tipped the driver and reconfirmed his availability for tomorrow's plans. Mom herself spoke to the driver, "Please reach tomorrow by 7am to drop us at Goddess Mahalaxmi's temple." The driver nodded and drove away saying Good-Night.

"Now, both of you please sleep tight and set your alarm for an early rise." She said as we walked inside the resort. Karthik's always been an early riser and enjoys a solitary hour or so, puttering around the house or working during the waking hours. As a night owl, the sudden change in the sleeping pattern was going to be a challenge for me. Mom was accustomed to waking me up at Brahma Murta (the morning hours of God) and meditating in the silently springing dawn seeds. Thankfully, owing to the rise of creative tribes, coffee lovers, and the creative impulse at moonlight; night owls are no longer viewed as lazy, juvenile, or sick people.

When we reached, we spoke for a little time about tomorrow's temple visit at the reception lounge and went to our respective room wishing Karthik, Goodnight. The porter helped us carry our shopping bags to our room. Mom inserted the key cards and we entered our room giving each other brief smile. We cleaned up, combed our hair, and changed into our nightdress for a comfortable sleep. The shades on the windows were pulled down, I came out of the bathroom and looked over at Mom as she was now fast asleep in her bed. I softly snuggled up into my bed, switched off the lights, and before I knew it, I fell asleep. I was screaming as a hand reached out of nowhere and pushed me into the dark vortex. Sharp and shrill screams piercing the darkness were heard after short intervals. Some kinds of ghosts or apparitions were suspended in the mid-air, probably by some magnetic force, wailing out silent cries in the skies that shook the depths of the Underworld. In the first place, I was crying, panicking, and trying to get rid of these specters when a huge force pulled me in deeper and deeper into the abyss of darkness. I was unable to breathe; soaked in the cold waves that numbed my emotions. The blackness got darker, the voices got stronger, and the ghosts hanging like chandeliers above my head wrapped their tentacles around me suffocating me to death.

There was a light brighter than lights. As I walked toward the light, it grew brighter and brighter promising dark peace. Within, the light, I could remember the powers embedded in me from ages of incarnation. I am not what I am and the core purpose of my life is to be a catalyst for healing. I felt their pain. I felt their agony. I felt their anger, and the urge for revenge. Peace was what they longed for and I could heal them.

Suddenly, few figures rose from the earth to the sky, in a great spiral of strength and force. They pulled me in, spun me with great unfathomable speed, sucking me away from the ground. After a supernatural whirling, the gravitational forces collapsed and crashed me down on the earth. It was the same earth but a unique landscape setting never known to me. I stood up, overwhelmed with pain, confusion, and fear seeing the moonlight, black trees, the presence of negative emotions, and weak gasps of helplessness.

I saw ghosts of dead widows, hundreds of them, bald-headed and cladded in red sari without any blouse, their loud lamentation expresses sorrow and anger. Even, the bright moon could not pacify them with its presence, light, beauty, and imperfection. In the flashing on and off of the ghostly lights, I could see the scars left on their soul by the torturers. Their red eyes were glowing like embers and my golden eyes purifying the polluted aura surrounding them. Thoughts were exchanged; eyes spoke the language of the master soul. They howled; the earth shook with tremors and the surface cracked creating craters. I stood firm, and said in a voice of command, "Don't read the stories inked on your flesh. The body is gone and the soul is higher than all these earthly pains. Those who did wrong to you are now living as per their cycle of Karma. What is your grieving about? Whom are you crying for now? Those are gone; stop immersing in the same pain again and again. Only you are drowning, the deeper you drown, the more you are lost in the ocean of nothingness. You are only abusing your spirit, soul, and self. The only way out of this is to walk out. There is a new life waiting for you with new destiny, happiness, soul path, and purpose of life. You can recreate everything there in the new world, rather than digging up the past that will give you nothing. What have you got in these countless years? But, if you enlarge your heart, show forgiveness, and trust the spiritual power, you can regain another incarnation. Here, you have your stakes on, you want to be a designer of a new life or an invisible ghost wandering in dark?"

My spiritual oracles shattered their dark, revengeful consciousness into a thousand pieces and left them drenched with open empty arms to embrace hope. The wind lulled the moment. A golden circle arched over each ghostly specter. The spot from a vague ruin and emptiness now shone with calmness, peace, and glow. Hundreds of flickering lights lifted up to fly followed by a pause that marked the beginning of a story from grey to pure white.

A flash occurred in the sky to announce the homecoming. The earth embellished the sky with the beauty of the luminescent particles flickering from these shining soul flares. I heard the vibrations of the crazy dance of these souls together in the heavens. Their feet banged and hard-pressed the amorphous sky to zestfully pour down a rainfall of contentment. The rain could not wet my skin or fill in the pores of my body but it moistened my heart.

I jolted and soared 2-3 feet above the ground. Within a certain time, I swayed back in the airborne with arrays of light bursting in my eyes. I kept on going faster and faster speeding through inter-dimensions. Finally, my soul landed on a hardcore surface with a big bang. I could feel the bones in my body, beating in my heart and stress in my head.

I could feel someone shaking my body. The shaking jarred me from my sleep. I was awake but not in a state of awareness. Slowly, my amber eyes open up to give me a blurry view.

Mom was waking me up. "What?" I asked her in a sleepy voice.

"We have to get ready to go to the temple. It's 5.30 am,

please wake up," she said as I continued to sink in my pillow recollecting what actually happened to me. I tried to sleep again but in a vain attempt. My mind drifted toward the recent out-of-body experience witnessed by me and I opened my eyes wide open.

"Kalki, get ready fast," Mom exuded an icy impatience, and this time irritation leaked in her voice. I pulled off the covers and slid off the bed. Giving her a look, I went straight into the bathroom. I turned on the faucet and cupped my hands to splash water on my face intermittently. I looked in the mirror and tried to reconnect with the happenings in flashes.

I started with my morning routines. After a brief pause, I turned on the shower to draw some time for the water to warm up. The hot water rushed over my body and pelted my skin from cold to hot.

Squeezing the fluid out of the lavender shampoo bottle, I scrubbed my hair down to the roots. After a minute, I rinsed the lathered hair under the water to get the foam out. After the hair wash, I hurriedly completed the bathing rituals hearing Mom's calls. I wrapped a soft white towel around my wet body and wrung the excess hair out of the hair with another towel. The hot steam from the bath renewed my cells and made me refreshingly vibrant. I wore a grey slip-on black short and hovered my baggage to decide my costume for puja.

Mom enveloped herself in a dark green cotton sari bordered with red embroidery. She adorned her wrist with heavy bangles encrusted with gemstones, applied sandalwood scent on her body, stacked a pair of anklets around her second toe, and hung a southern sea pearl necklace around her neck.

"Dry your hair first," Mom said trying to adjust her sari.

Without replying to her, I removed the hair blower from my bag. I plowed the wire in a two-pin plug switch and pressed on the power button. I circulated the dryer around my hair and styled it straight.

"What are you planning to wear?" Mom asked keeping a mysterious smile on her face.

"Peach colored embroidered designer silk lehenga choli," I waited for her approval. We exchanged glances as she came closer to me that confirmed her approval.

I elegantly wore the long, flowing, glittering netted lehenga choli. Mom adorned me with gold dangles, a gold-plated bangle set, and a gold-toned necklace loaded with designer stones. She proudly watched me dress up. I preferred to wear solid wedge as they are more comfortable to walk in and provides better-relaxed support than heel shoes.

Mom adjusted the pallu of her sari, straightening, and restraightening it on her shoulder. I was staring at her remembering the past. I would leap on the bed as she brought her expensive saris out of the wardrobe to get aired. I would crumble it, wrap it like a ball and throw it at her. Then, she would refold them neatly, place them in neat layers on a white cotton cloth, put few cloves, a homemade potpourri pouch in it, and tie the knot tightly. While doing this task, I would irritate her a lot by asking many Why, why questions. She had the tact of making me discover the answers by quizzing me with the same questions. So, this is how my curiosity developed, the curiosity that molded me to challenge the status quo.

Mom called up Karthik and asked him to join us when he is ready. I remained silent thinking should I speak about the dream or hallucination with her. She looked busy collecting the puja material and believing this spiritual visit will eliminate every negative aspect. As I kept on contemplating it, there was a gentle knock on the door.

"It's Karthik," Mom said walking to unbolt the door.

"Looking awesome," Mom touched his hair slightly as he slowly stepped in. He was dressed in a knee-length sky blue printed Kurta and white crispy pyjama, a platinum Kada in his right hand, and his smart watch on his right wrist.

Karthik looked at me like a fairy tale princess, my beauty sparkling through the grace and luster of the designer dress flouncing upon me. I could read his lips, eyes, and even heart and breathe his musky scent arising from his chest. Like the shadow of clouds cannot block the shine of the sun, the moon cannot stop the pull of the oceanic tide, the wings of my heart wanted to fly toward the small piece of sky standing before me. I am very certain had Mom not been here, at this very moment, it would have been a moment of weakness for us. Our eyes locked for an interminable moment. The whole air was filled with a peculiar, intoxicating fragrance. He was totally absorbed in my brightening and glamorous look like a water-nymph. I wanted to taste the flavors of sweet, sour, spicy, tangy, salty, and even bitter. The morning light adorned our storyline to make it into a beautiful book.

Mom interrupted the alchemical flow of our quiet lives. She was intelligent enough to read our silence. Mom picked up her phone and clicked our images, some solo, and some together. We were just standing statues before her. Our hearts and bodies wanted to gravitate close to each other like a river toward waterfalls. We were divorced from the world, immersed in solitude yet in connection with each other. At this moment, we appeared inseparable only cut apart by the merest physical body.

Mom's eyes beamed as she observed us.

"Let's go down for breakfast and from there we can leave for the temple. We are getting late. Kids, it's already, 6.30 am. Sum up," she actually pushed us out of the room.

We walked up toward the terrace overlooking the city where the complimentary breakfast was served. It was spacious with a temporary structure to acting as a rooftop. I liked the idea of morning open breakfast. My eyes were downcast, my cheeks were crimson; and though his gaze was darted away from me, I could feel his tall shadow falling over me.

Many eyes followed us as we walked into the dining room, some admiring me, some envious, some staring at me and Karthik. We decided to sit at the small table in the last corner to avoid much attention. The manager welcomed us and requested the servers to offer us water immediately. The breakfast buffet had everything to need for a breakfast. The resort kitchen serves you with ample options and generous servings of Poha, Idli Sambhar, Cornflakes with milk, and the slices of bread, butter, and jam. The standout of the breakfast spread was ginger tea and strong espresso. Mom and Karthik went to the "all you can eat" buffet spread to get the breakfast dishes for us. When they were gone for some time, I shared my pictures with Abheer and started chatting with him to come out of the strengthening influence of Karthik.

The cross-pollination of our messages and emoticons continued till Mom and Karthik, one by one placed the breakfast trays on the table.

"Lots to eat," I said for the sake of saying something.

Mom kept a dish of Poha, a bowl of Cornflakes with milk, and two bread butter toast in front of me.

"Finish it, you need a lot of energy to stand in the long queue for long hours," she elaborated listening to the non-stop WhatsApp beeps coming from my mobile. A stare from her and I muted the phone. We were indulging in a sumptuous breakfast hoping the day will be fine.

Breakfast was over, and we boarded the black sedan waiting to drop us at the main entrance gate of the temple. The driver adjusted the mirrors, the engine whirred in action as he turned on the key. He pulled the car on the road and turned the car to run on Laxmi road.

Mom asked the driver when we will reach the temple. The driver looked at us through the screen rearview mirror and said in a polite tone," We will be there in 10-15 minutes via Bhausingji road."

Flipping through a few turns, he gunned down the distance within minutes. As he stomped on the brake, the car stopped at an entry point, and he showed us the entrance gate of the temple from a distance. We got down from the car and walked toward the monumental entrance gate made up of rock located on the western side. The driver drove the car to the parking area where he was supposed to wait for us.

We posed for photos before these intricately designed architectural walls and inside the inner dome of the temple. Karthik and I were walking together, suspended between two worlds gazing at each other through our fantastical frontiers. Our feet stepped inside the Mahadwara, infused with perspicacious insights of architecture and culture. While walking with the crowd, our bodies rubbed like stones illuminating the deepmalas, shikhara, Garuda mandap with innumerable lights. We entered the premises of the temple through the side door entry. The sculptures depicted the exemplary artwork of the artists during the 18th century. The horizontal moldings and the vertical offsets created a light and shade pattern. Even the auspicious Shree Yantra was engraved on one of these mural walls to invite good energies.

There were dozens of shops lined up with brightly colored garlands, flowers, shrine images, saris, brass items, sweets, etc. to be offered to the Goddess. We selected a shop with a meticulous display of items for our purchase point. Mom scanned through the garland strings and other items required for the offerings. After she was assured of the quality, she made the purchase. We kept our footwear in the shoe rack counter of the shop. It would be a tough challenge to walk through the heated verandah to enter the main sanctum of the temple. Following the bolstering crowd, shouting aloud, "Jai Ambe," we queued up for the darshan. The energy of the people was contagious and even we got infected with the indomitable spirit of devotion.

"This is a Shaktipeeth, the place where Goddess Sati's eyes fell. If you pray here with a true heart, no evil will fall upon you," Mom shared her mythological bytes to us. Outside the main chamber of the temple, there was Nandi, the bull of God Shiva in its usual sitting posture. As we moved further in the line, we could see three idols in the inner sanctum facing westwards. The center idol with Sheshnaag roofing over it, adorned with huge jewelry and dazzling in golden light is Goddess Mahalakshmi. The other two goddesses on either side are Mahalakshmi and Mahasaraswathi.

"Finally, here," Mom sighed with relief. She turned to Karthik asking him if the main pujari is in the Garbhagriha. Luckily, there was less rush as compared to other seasons in the temple. Karthik signaled her to wait and tried to take an inside peek.

Mom smiled at me and said, "On the top of the idol there is a shivlinga which cannot be seen as the idol is covered with lots of jewelery. There are many temples in the courtyard of Navagrahas, Surya, Mahishasuramardini, Vitthal-Rakhmai, Shiva, Vishnu, Tulja Bhavani, and others. Some of these images date back to the 11th century, while some are of recent origin. Also located in the courtyard is the temple tank Manikarnika Kund, on whose bank is a shrine to Visweshwar Mahadev."

From the entrance door of the sanctum till the Garbhagriha there were some Samadhi stones. After an hour's wait, we entered the queue of Garbhagriha. Several Brahmins were stationed near the goddess idol receiving multitudes of offerings, chanting shlokas and Vedic hymns. I saw a glimpse of the extraordinary idol radiating soft beams of exemplified feminine energy.

"Your divine mother," Mom softly whispered in my ears as we moved forward.

Like the moon shining bright high up in the sky, the idol made from lustrous black stone poured a torrent of mysterious rhapsody in my heart. Her sanctum was adorned with marigold garlands, coconuts, diyas, and sparkles. The four-armed goddess in a standing posture depicted the four divine attributes of the Sanatan Dharma. In her four hands, the deity of Goddess Mahalaxmi holds items that represent symbolic lessons. The lower right-hand holds a Mhalunga (a citrus fruit), in the upper right, a large mace (Koumodaki) with its head touching the ground, in the upper left a shield (Khetaka), and the lower left, a bowl (Panpatra). Unlike most Hindu sacred images, which face north or east, the image of this deity looks west (Pashchim). The idol is placed on a stone made podium wrapped in pure silver. There was a small open window on the western wall. On three specific days in a year, sunlight falls on the idol emitting resplendent brilliance. The lion is the vehicle of the goddess. The deity is adorned with many diamonds and gold jewelery. A stone lion (the vahana of the goddess), stands behind the statue.

Finally, after small steps, it was our turn to worship the goddess. Mom handed over a note, thali with the offerings to the pujari cladded in saffron robes and white dhoti. She said something like Devi Abhishek Puja to the pujari. The pujari made us stand in a separate corner and started chanting powerful mantras in loud voice, another pujari played the cymbal, conch and started rotating the puja thali before the idol. The puja continued for the next 20 minutes and then, the pujari gave us some sweet, coconut, flowers, and kumkum as prasad (blessings from goddess). He placed his right hand on my hand, chanted shlokas, and sprinkled droplets upon me. He touched the colored forehead of the idol, smeared the red color on my forehead, and tied a red thread on my wrist. The puja was over and we walked out of the enclosure to the exit point. Mom asked us to wait at a spot and went to the temple office to inquire about online puja and donation. After she was done with distributing money, we walked back. I looked at the shikhara standing tall and alone in the heights of endless skies, listening to the howling of air and for ages watching the incoming and outcoming of people.

Maybe, it must be wondering when we would return again. And exactly, what would be our story at that time of life.

By the time, we reached our resort it was 12 pm. We were tired, dehydrated and our blistered feet were in pain due to the prolonged waiting. Karthik went into his room to rest. Mom had made clear she wanted to lie down and sleep after this tedious exercise of walking and waiting. I agreed with her as the long exposure of sunrays had drained us physically. We entered our room and sipped a full bottle of Bisleri water to quench our thirst. At this hour, we wanted to rest than anything else, even lunch. We fell into a gentle slumber the moment we lay down on the bed.

We woke up around 4 pm after feeling pretty good because of healthy REM sleep. Mom ordered an afternoon tea and toasted snacks as a private affair between us. We talked about the journey, Mom forced me to have cookies and my mind was reeling toward Karthik.

"Mom, should we call Karthik for tea?" I asked, anticipating a quick yes.

"Kay, he will be joining us at 5.30 pm and then we will go to Rankala lake. You can get ready in your casual wears."

"Yeah," I nodded and finished off my snacks in the excitement of meeting Karthik.

We felt warmed up after having the hot and crispy snacks. Mom went her way to the washroom to get freshened up. She then dressed up in a polka printed white kurta, red palazzo, and a multi-colored designed dupatta. I, too, speeded up to get ready in my blue jeans and an embellished black color top with a round shimmering neckline.

At around 5.15 pm, Karthik knocked on the door. Mom unbolted and unlocked the door handle.

Mom welcomed him with a big smile, and he entered like a prince with the gait of a lion.

My heart meandered like a yarn searching for a pattern. The wind blew his beautiful voice toward me and inked it on my neck.

"There are lots to see in Kolhapur - palace, museum, temples, and gallery but let us pick the best for you," he paused gazing into the depths of my eyes.

"A landscape of calm water and sailing boats to unbound ourselves. Please, let me gift you a forever memory in these numbered days," he breathed out his unspoken love. I was sensed with his passion, and aroused by his looming love. I needed rains, I needed storms, and I needed anything and everything that could pluck out his poisoning charm from each cell of my body.

"Can we leave now?" Karthik asked in a polite voice.

Mom was about to reply but then her phone rang. She received the call and spoke but the voice on the other side was inaudible due to traffic noise and network issues. Mom went out of the room; she was trying to reconnect with the call.

I stood in front of Karthik tearing the abstract manuscript of love penned by the whimsical winds. He knew about Abheer and didn't want to be a love breaker; hence he never spoke anything.

"We will be very good friends," I said breaking the suffocating silence.

"Always," he said in a bold voice. "Kalki, call me anything, anywhere, for any reason, I will be there for you." His voice had a strong tinge of honesty and truth. These words meant the world to me as I never had a male guardian in my life. Abheer had never uttered any such words of care. You need people with another organ of speech and heart for such unconditional commitments.

Though there was no light, the smoke was still tumbling out.

Meanwhile, Mom entered the room with a tense expression. She said in a worried tone, "Kalki, the pujari called me now. He is a bit concerned about some facts and wants to discuss them with me."

"Mam, we can cancel the boating plan, if this is more important," Karthik suggested as the silence lingered in the room.

"No," Mom said in a firm voice. "Karthik, take Kalki with you and let her see Kolhapur. This is her first visit, so please, make it interesting for her. On your way, drop me till the temple entrance gate, and then you kids have your fun."

"Mom, I want to come with you. I also want to know," I proposed my thought to her and she gave a deadly stare. She melted after a few moments. We walked out locked in the perimeter of our individual thoughts.

"Kalki, please enjoy the trip. The pujari wants to speak about some horoscope issue and their remedies," she finally spoke seeing the blank expression on my face.

"Are you speaking the truth?" I asked knitting a frown on my forehead.

“I never lie, you should know that,” Mom replied to make me feel relaxed.

We sat in the car very quietly as the vehicle headed to the respective locations. The driver stopped the car at the temple’s entrance gate. Mom pulled me close to her giving me a small hug. She smiled at Karthik and got out of the car waving us back. I saw her go and for the first time she looked less of a feminist and more of her feminism shone outward. Karthik was still seated in the front seat of the car. I didn’t ask him to join me in the backseat.

The driver pointed at different places, turns, and statues telling us the historic significance. I heard him but did not listen attentively. I kept my fingers busy tapping on messages, social updates, and emails to keep my mind busy.

“This place is Shalini palace and ahead of it is Rankala Lake and boating club. You can walk from here. I will park the car in this spot. Call me, Sahib, when you are done.” The driver spoke warmly to Karthik.

The palace stands on the west bank of the lake and it is at a distance of 2 minutes’ walk. We posed outside the majestic Shalini palace made up of black stones and Italian marble. We requested the people walking by to click our photographs together. We also, did the crazy sort of selfies thing and posted it on Instagram. The palace is surrounded by lush green gardens, towering palm trees opening the way for soft breezy air. We walked the stretch from Shalini palace to Rankala Lake. It seemed to be a light walk with a breeze, peace, and beautiful ambiance.

"Rankala," he said in a breathing voice as we walked toward.

"This resembles the Marine Drive of Mumbai," he pointed toward the vast water body reflecting the everlasting fervor of life. I imagined Abheer but Karthik's presence was flying across my heart and mind like the sky that darkens the Sun during an eclipse.

The banks of the Rankala Lake were clean to serve as a perfect seating arrangement for visitors. Boating is the primal enjoyment means along with horse-riding for equestrian lovers. We clicked pictures of people and landscapes. I desired to write a long poem to express the joy of the moment.

Karthik took me on a tour of something spicy, crunchy, chilly, and full of awesomeness; the roots of all of us - Chaat. We went to the stall to have crackling pani-puri, spicy bhel, and something of everything. Together we were savoring each bite, whipping up scrumptious tastes that were kindling our senses. Once we were finished, we would pause, glance in each other's eyes, and slow down.

I never had these kinds of liberating experiences with Abheer. For dating, we met only in the best concrete buildings with metallic stairwells and jagged pipes looming on the ceilings. Abheer's perspective was aristocratic, he was designed to live in this way. Still, he had an empathetic approach that manifested in a compassionate and humble persona.

"Time to go for boating," Karthik exclaimed as we caught each other's glimpse. He held my hand in purity and the imprint was pasted on my vibrating soul. He serenely arranged himself and showed me the glamorous show that the birds had set up in the waters. Some were standing on the small rise, a few were performing distraction actions, and somewhere love was blossoming between two birds.

We reached the boating club loaded with different types and sizes of boats. I had been in paddle boats and electric boats and wanted to try something new. So, I requested the club manager for a Shikara boat with ancient velvet curtains and calligraphic signboards. It would be an awesome Dal-lake boating type of experience. Karthik smiled, as he watched my excitement, emotions, and expressions.

"The Shikara," I shouted as the colorful boat vessel approached near us. I clicked many images of the boat enhancing the features until Karthik took my mobile and clicked one photograph of the beautiful boat in the twilight settings that summed up everything.

"Ma'am, the four-seater boat is waiting for you. I have paid the fare of four passengers. The Shikara is exclusively reserved for you," he said in a modest tone with a tinge of shyness.

I stepped on the deep velvety cushion covering the traditional floor of the colorful Shikara boat. We sat in the ferry boat loaded with designer soft cushions, silk awnings soaring to the musical beats of winds, and the beautiful songs played on the Saregama Caravan radio. The oarsman slowly pulled the oars and the boat moved an inch forward to lead us in deeper water. I looked out at the waters, and secretly Karthik was looking at me. I had an urge to play the trumpet in his head to wake up his senses. His gaze made me drown in the deepest center of the lake. Amidst the deep silence, only the soft chanting of music, soft rambling of birds, and mid-air noises were heard.

Twilight fell; accepting all the shades of orange, blue, purple, and red to enhance the heart of every artist. As Shikara scaled into the depths, the soft slaps of the oars against the water got louder. Everything else remained the same. Though it was quiet, the romance exploding in our hearts was volcanically powerful. In the exquisite background of the twilight, we had an intimate and deep talk even without talking. Karthik was so gentle, respectful, and attractive that he had become a threat to my love. For the first time, I got to know the pain of getting burned.

At certain times in certain places with certain people, destiny conveys some messages that are never said at other times. The oarsman extended the rowing of the Shikara across the lake for some more time, sunrays swayed, circled, and embraced the water for a goodbye. The passion of the twilight dissolved in the blue waters diluting it into a dark blue hue. No one knew how many times I have smashed my heart to stop stirring for him. Karthik leaned a bit forward; I got a nearer view of him. He was perfect - neither fair nor dark, a man born to be wild and free. He knows the art of being still and ever bright; a trusted companion loyal till death and beyond. You can stop someone from hurting you, abusing you, killing you but how can you stop anyone from loving you. I looked out of the small window at the watery twilight, soft waves, and stars in the sky; everything at the moment seemed to be a tender, little drawing of the infinite.

I was so engrossed in thoughts; that I missed noticing that the Shikara had approached near the bay. Our Shikara ride was over, but the chemistry was still sparking inside us. I offered my heartfelt gratitude to the widespread Rankala Lake drawing influence from the water element for soothing our mind with many beautiful themes. Before sitting in the car, we saw a neat and tidy sandwich hawker selling grilled sandwiches. There were no seating arrangements, but the surroundings were clean to stand and eat. We got two veg cheese grilled sandwiches and finished them while conversing about the origin of Rankala Lake. The sandwiches were yum, especially the filling of the green chutney.

We sat in the car, intoxicated by the presence of each other. The driver rode the car; toward the resort. I stared at the sky as the twilight meditation was deepening into moonlight passion. The moon was growing a little stronger as it slowly crawled in the enigmatic dimensions. Our car passed through dark and crowded roads, but I could only hear the howling of our hearts.

We arrived at the resort lobby. I called up Mom to check if she was in the room. She had reached an hour before us. We took some time to camouflage our emotions and make our expressions undetectable from mom. I wanted to tell Karthik what was deep inside me to reach out to him for another new experience without fear. While I was connecting the dots, Karthik walked ahead of me and waited near his door.

I looked into his eyes, and for a moment, nothing else mattered to me. Life is a collection of zillions of tiny and big moments woven like beads to create beautiful patterns. Some patterns are artistic, some are exemplary, some are fabulous, and few may be less than ordinary. But this is still an incomplete pattern, and I am curious to see it in the most striking design.

There was a light pain in leaving him behind as I knocked on my door room. Some pain makes you stronger, some pain makes you wise, but either way, every pain is a reminder of a story.

Mom opened the door and greeted Karthik with a welcome

smile. She asked us if we enjoyed the outing and should we go to have dinner. We replied to her questions one by one.

"The boating at Rankala Lake was an awesome experience. And, mom, we ate a lot of chaat items and sandwiches. I don't want to eat anything more." I pleaded to her.

"Yes, Mam. Same here. I ate two sandwiches on the way. If I need anything, then I will order late at night from the restaurant kitchen. You both, please carry on, I have to revert to official mails," he said convincingly.

We wished him goodnight and walked into our room. I cleaned my face, hands, legs, and dressed up in nightwear. Mom ordered vegetable biryani for her, insisting me to join. I dived into the bed playing the repeat telecast of the Rankala Lake episode in my mind. The winds came upon me from the open window putting me to sleep. I could feel Mom enveloping me in a soft blanket, and gently patting my back.

I was feeling a familiar nudge - in my dreams.

The morning sun was glittering to my right side. I yawned wide and rubbed the sleep out of my eyes. Mom was engaged in reading the newspaper headlines. It was Sunday morning and we had a return flight booked in the afternoon. I slipped out of the bed and hurried to complete the morning routines. Dressed up, I sat down to have a jolt of caffeine with her.

"Mom, how was your temple visit?" I asked her with curiosity.

"Kalki, I don't want to lie or give you any false assurances." she straightened up her voice.

"Speak up, Mom," I kept the coffee cup aside.

"The Pandit analyzed your Kundli (horoscope) in depth. You

have a unique planetary combination or yoga in your 12th house. This yoga gives you the power to see, hear, and heal the dead spirits." She paused for a second as my legs shook in apprehension.

"Kalki," Mom said, comforting my thighs with her soothing press.

"You are destined to be a healer. If this superpower is gifted to you by destiny then take it as a blessing. Prepare for it, as now onwards life will be different. Time will show you the light. You are the chosen one to do this by God. Trust the supreme power, awaken your soul, and learn to unleash your powers by meditation. I cried to him for a remedy but there is nothing. How can you change destiny? How can you change the purpose of your birth? How can you wipe out your inner soul?

The dead will come to you again and again because they know you as their healer. I will walk with you always but you have to define the journey ahead. Face it, Fear it, Fight it but remember you can't delete it," her voice stormed me.

"Is it a blessing to be a healer of dead?" I questioned her loudly.

She remained calm and said in a deep voice, "God has written your destiny. Remember, it is given to you because only you can carry it."

I couldn't move a muscle. Mom continued to speak, I heard a few of her lines. Is this a joke? To speak with dead people and do their counseling. In the entire world, there was no other scapegoat except me. My trust in God was deeply shattered and it would take time to rebuild. In the waltz of leaves, drifting of playful clouds, and the fast ticking of the clock, I was lost in thoughts. We packed our bags and left from there leaving a trail of suspense.

Karthik wondered what had happened to me. He wanted to know if he had done something wrong but I assured him it had nothing to do with him. I told him, the low feeling and irritation is because of my periods. He tried hard to believe me but kept on thinking about it. Mom was quiet but was making things normal for Karthik. Both of them bonded over talks, shopping, and making me happy. I didn't respond to Abheer's calls thinking will he accept me with such a paranormal background. There were many thoughts pouring in, and no answers to any questions. The airplane arrived, picked us and transported us back home but I was thinking of my future. It seemed to be a dead-end for me.

I didn't want to have a sixth sense activated in my life. Mom motivated me with her wisdom and promised to find out an answer.

"Kay, The Universe has many more secrets and possibilities than what we have explored and acknowledged. There must be a hidden answer somewhere, and I will get to the roots if you promise to support me." She said with a strong voice of confidence that strengthened my willpower.

We reached home but I feel the journey is still on...

"I am lost in a maze of destiny,
In the early bloom of a colorful life,
I am on a verge of complete doom
I have to find my way through the corridors,
Where there is no hope of a candle to throw light"

CHAPTER SEVEN

Way To Go

Nothing out of ordinary happened to me from the day we returned from Kolhapur. Mom believed the blessings of the Feminine energy are swirling around me like divine armor. It was at the break of daylight; I could hear a bawling cacophony permeating in the air.

" Here, another day for your thought experiment," I murmured and scrolled my photos to change my profile picture.

I continued rolling over in the bed as the sheets were rising and falling with my twists. Finally, I slid out of the bed to get ready for the day. The aroma of good food drew me in before I knew it. Mom had finished cooking breakfast for both of us - eggs, toast, orange juice, and cheese chutney sandwich.

"How's work?" Mom asked sipping a glass of orange juice.

"Yeah, I forget to tell you. I have got a proposal from the most reputed real estate group - Ambika & Group to create content for their upcoming project, Amravati to be constructed in

North Mumbai." I slowed down for a bit.

"So, finally your website has started paying off," she chuckled while eating her sandwich.

"And even Abheer's mentoring - he taught me Design Thinking skills, UI/UX, Innovation," I replied in a sarcastic tone.

"Wait, wait..." Mom exclaimed. "If I am not wrong Ambika Real Estate Developers are the best and brightest competitor of Suryavanshi Real Estate Developers, Abheer's family company. Are you sure you want to pursue this proposal? Why go on a bitter note with Abheer's family?" She gave me a stare to withdraw from the project.

"Mom, we are professionals. Ambika & Group approached me for the content writing assignment after an extensive market search. I can't turn it down for no sensible reason. Why did the Suryavanshi group never think of me for any such writing job? Plus, the Ambika Group is nimble, invests heavily in people, and focuses on practical aspects, ready to blaze up history under the highly structured leadership of Ambika Rajput." I defended stronger.

"Why don't you speak with Abheer and consult with him on this matter? Not only, but they are competitors but there is a personal rivalry going on between them. This information is even local news. You continue with the assignment but keep Abheer informed about it. Don't let his brother or father bring it to his notice," After hearing her words, she made sense to me.

She curled her arms up behind my shoulders, gripping me lightly, and wishing me luck. I watched as she left for work.

I left a message telling Abheer to call me; I had to talk with him.

My mind was empty, so I sat down at my work desk and started playing with the magnets. I stared at the ceiling thinking about the project and the possible repercussions. To further calm my mind, I played Zen music on my computer. I grabbed a pen and took some rough points for the content writing of the Amravati project. I thought to myself, "Do I even have this potential inside me?" The music could connect with the rhythm of life.

Success was looking up and I was waiting for Abheer's call. If I win this project, it would be my first high-level corporate project. Ideas are endless, but opportunities are limited and time-oriented. Juggling in these thoughts, I turned on my MacBook and opened a PowerPoint template. The project head had asked me to prepare 3-4 slides to explain how my content can influence conversions.

"I think for this type of project, I should create UGC - user-generated content that can attract audiences and convert into calls to action." I said to myself and embarked on the mission. I referred to reports to analyze the consumer behavior of home buyers, their intention, their constraints, and decided to leverage these pointers in my presentation.

The main slide will be the opening slide, where I had decided to write a practical tagline for the Amravati project. In today's world, we can't guarantee happiness, it is a combination of internal and external factors.

So I scripted a perfect opening slide –

"Get alive in Amravati - the residence of wellness and peace"

The next three slides were based upon the three-pointers that matter to every purchaser.

1.) How can we reduce the EMI burden?

2.) How can we help them gain income from their purchases - rent/lease etc.?

3.) Why should they buy flats from Ambika Group? What is our unique value proposition to them?

The last slide would be a– thank you for your consideration slide.

Anything without a mission statement is like a boat without an anchor. I glanced up at my mission statement, rethinking the inner purpose of the creation and reflection of the line, "Enriching Thoughts."

I repeatedly dialed up Abheer's number but there was no response. Assuming he is busy, I got back to work. Though the slides were blank, the outline was well-defined. Now, I had to present it in words, figures, and impactful sentences to ensure a powerful delivery.

After a hard work of eight hours without any break, I completed the basic PowerPoint template. I still had to add images, links, text, and do the fine editing. I called up Abheer, he picked up my call and said in a low voice, "Hi, why are you calling me repeatedly?"

For a minute, his reply shunned me. I managed myself and said, "Abheer, I have got a content writing proposal from Ambika Developers. Before, I accept it, thought of checking with you," I said nervously.

"You want me to help you with the project," he said in a

wavering tone.

"No, I have done partly finished the proposal. I wanted to be sure, that you are okay with me working with them." I said with a tremble.

"Because they are our greatest rivals in professional and personal life. My dad and Ambika group chairman have a mutual hatred that has attained its greatest strength. They had a mutual dislike at the first sight," he said with a voice of firmness.

His words and tone bugged me.

"But recently, my mom met Ambika Group's chairman wife in a handloom exhibition and things turn up. They became friends, then best friends, and finally managed to bury the hatchet by a mutual alliance," he said in a slow voice.

"Ok, forming a relationship?" I asked.

"Don't worry, I will speak to you later. As of now, this is in the discussion stage," he replied in a hurry.

"Relationship means are they planning Kabeer's marriage with Ambika?" I said in a bewildered tone as Abheer was the eldest son in the family.

"Not now. It is something that is in decision mode," he was loud, upset about something. He hung up my call. I felt hurt but smoothed it out with a cup of filter coffee.

A couple of hours later, I continued the PowerPoint work to stop thinking of Abheer's tone of delivery. Maybe, his younger brother's marriage alliance must have made him insecure. The alliance match is more of a business conglomerate deal. Mom was back from work but my focus was undivided.

The atmosphere in the home was quiet, which enabled me to complete the PowerPoint presentation. I added a covering note in the email body and e-mailed it to the project head of Ambika Developers marking all other contacts in CC and BCC sections. Now, the decision is at their discretion.

I had few chances of winning the proposal and hence pinned all hopes on unlikely to happen. Ambika & Co. is into a diversified business - real estate, education, retail stores, and even an old-age charitable institution. They can afford and hire the best content writers from the globe, and I am just a novice name in the market.

Mom was in the living room, watching a black and white era movie. I spoke out my doubts to her. She smiled and spoke her theory to me, "Look, they can hire any content writer from the world but will these writers connect with the local consumers? Ambika & Co. is looking for a young and dynamic thoughtful voice to bring in new ideas, shape a new outlook, and also, limited budget. If they have a brand name and have spent lavishly to build the best project, they want to curb other expenses to a minimal level. Now, in the market, you are the latest voice on the uprise. I feel you will get the project. Let's bet it up on a Barbeque lunch," Mom geared me up and I took up the bet with her. Either situation; would be a WIN-WIN-WIN situation for us.

It was 8 pm and we watched the news. All the news channels were repeating the same headlines, warnings, happening over and over. As it was Friday night, I decided to watch late-night horror movies on lines like Conjuring, Insidious, Evil Dead but thought of checking social media accounts before that. I went into my room and turned-on multiple tabs to open Instagram, Facebook, and Twitter. Like crazy people were posting weekend newsfeed to show off their cool attitude. I was reading, responding, and scrolling to the newsfeed, shifting from one tab window to another. I got hooked to Twitter, reading the intellectually stimulating and super funny tweets.

Scrolling up and up, I read a recent viral tweet that was spreading fast to city news, business news, and newspaper. The tweet was read as #AMBER BEGINNINGS - there was a million-dollar photograph of Ambika Rajput's in her full charm proposed by the Suryavanshi group's handsome, brilliant, and rich scion. I was dumbstruck as I gazed at the photo and growing retweets and likes. My anger grew no bounds and I lifted my hand to push her away from the photograph. I moved to another social account to check if it is a piece of fake news circulating on social media. But it was true; 100% correct news, the scion of the Suryavanshi group had proposed to Ambika for marriage at a family party. Both families were happy with the alliance since both came from a similar business and social background.

Except, the young and brilliant scion was not Kabeer but Abheer Suryavanshi.

In a fraction of a second my entire world had collapsed. The write-up of the social newsfeed said, "The BIG celebration will last till the weekend. On Sunday, we will light up every principal street of the city that brings people to our mega-mansion, Tarangan for the engagement of Abheer with Ambika. Here, we are excited to turn the Sunday night into a dazzling brilliance of glory and love."

Was I so cheap, he didn't even want to speak and then have a breakup? He just discarded me like in the recycle bin. I took a deep breath and tried to hold the downpour of water that splashed from my eyes. I wanted to tear off that giggling, romantic photograph and break down every device that showed it to me. I was in complete chaos and silence, as my mind gave explanations that my heart rejected.

I was broken down and wanted to set the room on fire. Abheer had just cut off my pulse with his mistrust, not realizing the amount of pain he inflicted on me. We spoke this morning, and in the night, he is announcing his engagement date to the world. Who does this kind of a thing? Only because; I belong to a middle-class family; this is the way of treating me. Ambika is a beautiful and wealthy daughter of a business baron, so can she snatch my love? I can't let this happen, so I picked up my phone and called him multiple calls, but he didn't pick up the call. His act made everything clear and evident, but the heart still pleaded.

I ran my fingers over his image in the photograph, imagining it was me instead of Ambika. My dreams were unweaving, my vision was becoming faint and my lungs were collapsing down. I was completely blinded by anger, sorrow, and envy, suffocating beneath it all. I looked up at the sky; a grim swirl of greys, purples, and black were opening up their arms to embrace me. There was a depth of emptiness and loneliness, at the bay waiting for me to jump in. I yelled out, howled out loud, and delved deeper and deeper into the empty void. I was so enraged, angry - whatever you want to call it - that I wanted an end.

My mouth was like an erupting volcano; sending flames of anger in the open air. The fire (anger) spread as countless emotions continued to fan the embers. I could hear mom's voice and feel her touch but I was not much in my senses.

Mom was yelling loudly but I couldn't hear a single word. She tried to hold her hand over my mouth but it was of no use. It was getting very difficult for her to get a grip on the situation. I threw away and tore down everything in the room, it looked like a disaster room. Mom was yelling loudly but the impact was nil. Finally, my body got hot and tired, as my voice got down to a whisper and I fell down unconscious.

I woke up in my mom's room. There was some noise of repairs activities going on in my room.

"Omg, it means everything actually happened. It is no dream," I murmured trying to locate my phone. I was so nervous and scared, that I laid in bed waiting for my mother. She was definitely angry with me for my violent behavior and thoughts like revenge, destruction, and worse.

She came into the room and was glad to see me awake. Suddenly, she hardened her emotions. We stared at each other for a brief moment. She unzipped her purse, took some money out of it, and left without uttering a word. I tried to stand up but the sheer dizziness made me stumble in the bed again. The whole episode flashed before my eyes draining the light.

In the depths of my heart, a storm was brewing. Higher and higher winds rose as blackness coiled before me. I wanted action, wanted more action, and only ultimate action. I searched for my phone on the bed, among the things lying on the top of the table, and in the drawers of the side table beside the bed.

Hearing the noise of fiddling with things, Mom re-entered the room and sat in a composed manner on the edge of the bed. She didn't ask me if I am feeling better or why I am weeping. It was odd, she was silent. I looked at her and longed for a word or a yell or a blow, anything but something.

Mom, he proposed to Ambika Rajput. In the morning, he spoke with me, and in the night, he announced his proposal day to the world. What am...?" I cried like a baby until there was no tear left to fall.

Mom sat composed, I tried to speak some sunless words, but failed to open my mouth. I knew she was angry with me. Another storm was brewing within her and I knew it would be a tough one.

Gathering all my courage, I spoke in a soft voice, "I am sorry."

She chuckled, "No, don't be sorry. You have to pay one lakh rupees,"

"One lakh rupees?" I said with a startled look.

"Yes, the total bill amount for repairs. Curtains, pillows, foam, wooden chairs, and smashing your iPhone on the wall. Also, medical expenses and I have not added my one full week leave to it," she took the helm in her hand to steer my mind in the correct direction.

"He did what he had to do. Maybe, that step was in the best interest of him and his family. What have you done for yourself or your family?" She pounced like a wounded lioness upon me.

"Kalki is this how you should be reacting to things? What if I had behaved like this in each situation of my life? What if I had thought of ending up my life leaving you alone? Abheer did what he had to do. Why are you watering these soggy-foggy emotions and creating a mess for me to clean? Even, you live normally and show him that nothing ever happened. There is no market in this world for sorrow or losers. If you want to make him, feel the loss, then stand before him as a winner." she roared straight at me in a forceful voice. She kept repeating her words, making them clearer and stronger.

"I am not going to tolerate such kind behavior ever again. Is there any point in such aggressive behavior like breaking and tearing? Never, again. I had to rush behind doctors, carpenters, repairers, and the Apple service center. Who suffered? Did Abheer suffer? Did Ambika suffer? No, only you and I suffered, dear," Her words pierced me harder than the sharpest objects.

"Do you know you were unconscious with fever for two days? The doctor had insisted on admitting you to the hospital but I convinced him somehow. Do you have any idea of how much mental, physical, and financial strain I had to undergo in this period? My only fault - I am your mother, but who cares for me?" she spoke low as her eyes moistened with tears.

The few words I had said seemed to have smashed her into a frenzy of rage. Mom was striking hard with her sharp words. I had never received such an expert tongue lashing from her till now. Her contents turned into an inferno as her eyes shot with red flecks. I darted my eyes on the floor but she lifted my chin forcing me to look in her eyes and answer. I thought she would deliver a powerful blow across my face anytime but she didn't do so.

I stammered, forcing myself to exhale. With a breakdown, I fell to her and cried upon her breast. She held me tight as I cried out loud and long.

"Hey, baby, it's okay now. Leave it behind and move ahead," she asked, and lovingly stroked my back. I got carried away at the moment feeling like a kid in her embrace.

Grandma entered the room. She smiled at me and asked Mom if the room should be cleaned as the repairs are done. Mom turned to her and said in an irritated way, “Sssh! Ma, don’t disturb. Why can’t you manage these small things? Let me be with Kalki.”

Grandma said,” Ok, ok,” and walked away.

“Mom, I am sorry,” I said in a deep, apologetic tone. “Mom, you can go out and manage the work.”

She sighed and continued to pat my back affectionately, stroke my hair with tenderness, motivating me with positive affirmations and inspirational stories of women.

“Mom, my phone...” I asked her.

“Did you think of the phone while throwing it, stamping it, and breaking it?” she spoke in gentle words. I had no words to reply to her question. Mom felt sorry for me and said with a wistful smile spreading across my face.

“It is in the Maple service center for repair due to external damage. The backup is taken on iCloud,” she observed my expressions with her amused smiles as I tried to think how to be without a phone.

She walked to her cupboard, opened it, and searched for something. “Close your eyes,” she announced as her footsteps came closer to me. She placed a packed box in my shaking hands. Slowly, I unpacked it and there was a brand new sealed latest iPhone.

“Mom, I really don’t deserve it,” I said as she hugged me again, so tight I could feel her heart racing.

“Daughter, never ever do this again. You actually killed me,” she cuddled me and I think she knew what I was feeling inside.

Mom unsealed the box. She took the shiny red iPhone in her hand and placed it in my palm. I connected it to Wi-Fi and the retrieval process from iCloud commenced. I kept the phone aside and laid down on the bed. In the meanwhile, mom was administering my fever, medications, and energy intakes.

"Mom, I will repay the expenses in EMIs," I said in a voice filled with guilt and shame.

She didn't make a U-turn to look at me. After a few minutes, she came over to me with a dose of medicine and a glass of water.

"I will get you a glass of milk," Mom said and went into the kitchen.

The moment, Mom was out of the room, I peeked in the phone. Today is Sunday, it must be their engagement. I opened the Safari browser to log into my social accounts and check but Mom returned with a milk glass and a plate full of sliced apples.

""From yesterday, someone is helping me with all the tasks and things. The person comes in the morning, helps me with everything, and leaves in the night," she said with a sparkle in her eye.

"Mamaji..." I said loudly as he was the only paternal figure in my life.

"Nopes..." Mom chuckled, "You have another chance,"

"Your cousin sisters ...or is it your husband?" I narrowed my frown.

Mom looked at me and said, "No, Dumbo,"

She walked toward the door, peeked her head out from the jamb, and called out, "Come inside,"

I was anxious to see the person as Mom stood near me. I clung to her waist covered by her chiffon nightgown. We were momentarily quiet; until he entered the room with enthusiastic greetings and a beaming smile.

"How are you feeling now – the first and only born child of Ms. Meera?" He asked me in a polite tone. I looked up at mom's face as I didn't know what to reply. Karthik sat on a chair besides the edge of the bed.

"Karthik, she is better now and I have brought her back to her senses," Mom said as she pulled my ear teasingly.

Karthik spoke softly, "I know some background about it. Kalki, believe me, no one in life is more important than your parents. You can get another boyfriend, another husband, but you can never get a replacement for your mother. How many times did you meet? How many times did you speak on the phone or chat? I didn't see the color of his love upon your cheeks, it never was there. You were eclipsed."

"I am sorry if I have hurt you," he said after a short pause.

"Bygones are bygones, Karthik. She has realized it. The way it happened was an abrupt shock to her. Don't make her feel guiltier," Mom replied caressing my strands.

"Mam, she didn't see the way you cried for her. I couldn't see a woman so strong and bold as you in such a sorrowful pain," he said in a voice of concern and angry eyes darting toward me.

"Did you think of me for a moment before picking up a cutter?" he directly questioned me and then stammered, "I mean us."

"Karthik," Mom pacified me in a second.

"Now, let's cheer up our patient and make her well soon," Mom said rubbing me on the shoulder.

Grandma got us some food, fruits, and beverages. We all sat down with eyes and ears wide open as Mom sprinkled stories upon us. Karthik made us laugh with his hilarious jokes, puns, and riddles. We listened, we smiled, and we laughed at each other and ourselves. Seeing Mom and Karthik shower so much love and care upon me, I thought life is a long line of a fine story. For the first time, I was clear about my feelings for Karthik. We were making stars out of smiles and heaven was listening to Mom's stories.

It was after 9 o'clock that Karthik thought he should go to his home. Mom walked with him to the front door to thank him for his timely support. Later, mom walked into the room with an empty tray to clear up the empty plates, spoons, and cups. She helped me finish my dinner and clean my mouth.

"Tomorrow, you can shift to your room. Some minor repairs are pending. You can sleep in my room," she followed me to her room. I laid down on the bed as Mom checked my temperature and lulled me to sleep.

Over the next few weeks, I got better due to Mom's love and care. Also, Karthik visited me in between to spark up my mood and make his presence more prominent. Mom had introduced Karthik as my paternal cousin (father's sister's son) in society to avoid gossips. We visited public parks, malls and even looked forward for more.

CHAPTER EIGHT

The Comeback

As usual, I was checking my emails when a mail dropped in my inbox from Project Head - Ambika Developers. The team had apologized for the late response due to some internal issues. The Project Head had reviewed my concept, accepted my quote and awarded the content assignment to me. I had to accept the offer and visit their office for a formal review meeting and paperwork.

I immediately messaged the good news to Mom and Karthik. For a moment, I doubted in mind to take the assignment or not. Ambika Developers had an outstanding reputation in the Indian and overseas markets. An opportunity to work with them can open the doors to get affiliated with many top brands.

I replied to the mail with a thank you and acceptance of the offer. I confirmed my availability for the meeting date and shot it to the Project Head.

I had to prepare for this meeting on priority. I sidelined other gig activities and even, delayed the deadline of a few gigs. This gig was offering me a total of 1 lakh rupees for the content creation job, higher than every other gig at my disposal.

Data was crucial but as this was my first meeting with Ambika Rajput, I wanted to focus on my personality. I browsed the trending outfits for top editors, celebrities, stylists and shortlisted something new after reading the article on Wall Street Journal - The Most Powerful Women in Business Wear Dresses, Not Suits by Katharine K. Zarrella. This thought-provoking article breaks the stereotype of women wearing blazers and jackets mimicking the masculine patterns rather than creating their own strong, tailored power dresses" for the office.

I shortlisted a business dress paired with a fitted black blazer and trendy wedge sandals. I thought of wearing a gold chain with a sparkling blue crystal pave. A glittering bracelet on the right wrist and a smart watch clasped on the left wrist to complete the style statement. For carrying the MacBook, I had a brand new grey colored laptop sleek briefcase as a fine addition to my new and trendy makeover. After the collapse of my relationship with Abheer, I had pledged to break the winds of monotony in every sense.

It was 3 pm and the perfect time when the beauty parlor is unlikely to be too crowded. That's the real catch when the beauticians and hairdressers are free to give few offbeat and witty ideas to look unique and attractive.

There was a trendy and branded beauty parlour at the corner of our area. I use to visit this parlor since college days and my face was familiar to all of the employees working there. I went inside the parlor. The interiors were flocked with wallpapers of female models, crystal decors, and lampshades that gave a dynamic and healing mood. The moment I entered the lounge, Muskaan, my hair-stylist warmly greeted me. We chatted for twenty minutes to know each other's personal updates.

"So, what is the purpose of this new look?" she inquisitively asked me.

"A layered haircut followed by eyebrows and upper lips threading, pedicure, manicure, and waxing," I said, motioning towards the styling station.

"Madam, let's add facial also?" Muskaan commented as I sat on the styling chair.

A slim, dark lady attendant started threading my eyebrows to style them in a hill shape. Another attendant was waxing on my legs, and underarms. After that, attendants barked on the pedicure and manicure work. My favorite hairstylist was in the queue to start her handiwork on my hair once other tasks were finished.

"Should we do facial before a haircut?" an attendant enquired from the main attendant as she supervised the work done upon me.

"Yeah, facial can be done with manicure and pedicure," she agreed and instructed the beautician to do my facial analysis. She suggested a silver facial that would make my skin glow, remove impurities, and look lustrous. It was expensive but still, I agreed to it.

The esthetician was a hard-core professional lady with fair skin, long hair tied in a bun, and a slim waist making her look beautiful. She left me in the facial room to give me some privacy to change. I wrapped my body with a long towel underneath my arms and laid on the bed. She knocked, then came in and covered my head with a headband.

First, the esthetician double-cleansed my skin, placed a wrap on my eyes, and then directed a vapor of warm steam upon my face. After some time, she arrived in the room and extracted the blackheads located on the bridge of my nose. It was a challenge to tolerate pain. Once done, she again applied massage strokes on my face, placing cucumber peels on my eyes, guiding me on to heal the skin inside out. She shared beauty tips and parked pearl facial cream on my face and eyelids. After half an hour, I rinsed it off with warm water and dried my face with a clean towel. The facial did wonders to my skin, radiating a glow of smoothness and luster.

Then Muskaan, took me over for a deep shampoo hair wash. After the wash, we went back to our styling station to dry the hair under the dryer. I glanced down at my shiny nails while she combed my hair to start a haircut. She started to work on my straight hair with a scissor and comb. The hair fell in a feathered cut with layers till shoulders showcasing the thick volume of hair.

"Perfect, this beauty journey has filled me with magnificent happiness." I thanked all the staff at the parlor and went back home.

I returned home with a new and exciting look. I unlocked the main door with my spare key. There was no one in the home. Grandma had gone to visit a nearby temple.

As I walked through the passageway, I noticed the door of Mom's room was slightly open. My instinct told me something was happening there. Full of apprehension, I pushed the door open. Mom was seated there in front of the mirror weirdly combing her hair. I stared at her as she continued the combing slowly and softly. I heard someone unlocking the main door but my motion sensors were totally inactivated. It was only when a familiar touch tapped on my shoulder, I came to my senses.

"Mom, you are here?" I glared at her in disbelief.

"Yes, kiddo, check your watch it is 6.30 pm," she said in a happy mood. "I have got your favorite pastry, you can have it after dinner," she said with cuddling my cheek.

Though I pretended to be normal, the fresh paranormal episode brewed in my mind. I quietly crawled in my bed and put on the eye mask determined not to remove them till the first stroke of sunlight.

I was afraid to go to sleep but exhaustion drove me into sounder sleep.

The day dawned bright and full of sunshine, with no symptoms of rain. I was getting ready for the meeting - dressing, packing, collating, and memorizing. Mom forced me to have a hot and heavy breakfast. Grandma's head hung deep in the religious books.

"Mom," I said pressing her palm nervously.

"Be confident and smart. Leave a good impression on everyone," she repeated several times.

'Yeah," I said and filled the address of Ambika Developer's office in Google Maps for tracking the location.

I picked up the laptop bag, plucked the car key from the key hanger, and grabbed my sandals to put on.

"Please don't keep calling to check on me," I replied in a

louder tone while going down the stairs. I checked if all the essential items were in the laptop bag.

"Going for a meeting. Looking very smart," said Mrs. Bottlewala, senior resident member of the building, as she scanned me from top to bottom with her bespectacled eye. She was coming from the market.

"Yes, Aunty, I have been called for a presentation. Actually, I am in a hurry so can I talk later," I replied to her in a courteous voice.

"God bless you, my child. It feels good to see all of you doing so well," she blessed me and climbed the stairs blaming the watchman for not getting the elevator repaired.

I rushed to the parking area and pressed the button on the central lock key to unlock my car. I sat inside the car, put on the seatbelt, pushed the key to start the car. As the car moved forward, I plucked the earpods in my ears and played the music. Pressing on the accelerator, I lurched the vehicle a little forward and reversed the vehicle from the parking area to roll the wheels on the driveway. I drove down the narrow roads for 15 mins then screeched it on the Eastern express highway. The car got warm inside as there was traffic jam at short intervals. I adjusted the air-conditioner to feel more comfortable. From Eastern express highway, I had now switched to Santacruz-Chembur Link Road. On reaching BKC Junction, I had to drive straight and then twist right, drive further, and twist left to reach the BKC Complex.

Bandra Kurla Complex is the first prominent commercial hub in India. The amazing complex glistening with power and revenue has absorbed the corporate offices of major Indian and international MNCs, institutions, high-authority government offices, and sports complex. I parked my vehicle in the nearest open parking space zone. I took out my laptop bag from the back seat of the car and shouldered it on my left side.

As I strolled through the avenues of the most enthralling offices and modern side-cafes, a security guard waved at me. He showed me the building where the office of Ambika Developers was located. I thanked the guard and walked fast to reach the pioneering curtain-walled office building.

The moment I entered inside the galvanizing building I fell in love with its architectural creativity. The lobby area of the gigantic building is a catalyst for artistic stimulation. Majestically painted walls glistened in the abundance of sunlight bursting joy in the hearts of the botanicals. Impressive sculptures, fish aquariums were placed at the prime spot to attract the attention of visitors.

I greeted the well-mannered lady at the reception desk inquiring about the way ahead. I followed her directions and headed toward the sophisticated elevator.

The elevator went ding and the door opened. I walked inside the elevator after a few executives walked out. The door closed and the elevator began to ascend. The elevator stopped on each floor, some entered, some exited and some waited in the lift as the lighted number overhead. I watched the elevator lights scroll number by number through the floors. This time when the lift stopped, a fair, average-height gentleman with a highlighting personality and drop-dead gorgeous smile entered the lift. I stepped behind, gasping for air as he stood beside me.

The elevator rode to the eighth floor and stopped. I moved out of the elevator and heard a few more steps walking out. The passageway was quiet and the offices were behind a frosted glass door. My mobile beeped but I neglected to read a tall brown board that had the names of departments with the left or right arrow.

'Oh, the entire floor is owned by Ambika Developers, pretty cool, huh.' I said to myself.

I was struggling to find the co-ordinates, when the handsome guy in the lift approached me and asked, "Mam, can I help you?"

"I have a meeting with Ambika Developers Communication team. Just try to locate the respective office," I said looking straight eye to eye.

"Well, follow me. I work here," he walked with me around the office. The Corporate Communication Office, CEO office, and legal office are located on the ninth floor. The other offices like HR, Finance, and Marketing are on the eighth floor. We can go by the stairs," he sounded very cordial.

"Hi, I am Kalki Agastya, working as a Content Consultant. The communications team has shortlisted me as the content writer for their upcoming project in North Mumbai, I am here for the project meeting." I looked at him for his introduction as most of the talking was done by me.

He extended his hand and said with a warm smile, "I am Nakul Kumar and as told you, I work here."

"In the communications team?" I gladly asked.

"You think so…" he asked me with a smile.

"I do a bit of people analysis; your personality is more inclined toward communication." I raised an eyebrow awaiting a reply.

"Little close," he said and laughed opening the main office door. He asked me to sit in the lounge and asked the office boy to serve me tea/coffee and biscuit. He made me feel comfortable and said he will speak with his team. The office boy offered me Arabic coffee and crunchy cookies with a glass of water.

I sipped the coffee and dunked the cookies into the coffee to eat the soft bits. Almost twenty minutes passed by. Finally, a male trainee executive showed up and asked, "Ms. Kalki."

"Yes," I responded politely.

He smiled and in a lowered voice replied, "Please come. The team is waiting for you in the conference room."

"Yeah," I followed him where multiple conference rooms were lined up.

He knocked upon the last conference room and opened the door. He half-turned toward me and said, "Mam, you may take a seat inside." As I stepped inside, it seemed all eyes were parked upon me. The trainee smiled at the seated members, closed the door, and left.

I took a seat and placed my laptop on the table, the spectacular view of the campus across the window caught my sight. The room was spacious and the atmosphere was cheerful. The outer walls were giving out much light and brilliance in the room. There was a large table made up of stone in the center of the room surrounded by leathery executive chairs. A whiteboard was placed on the wall at one end of the table and a projection screen was dropped down on the other end of the wall. All the members were honing around the table presenting their views in a casual yet skilled manner. The population was overall young and few members were slightly above my age-group.

A pretty young lady in her late twenties dominated the meeting table. She extended her hand to me and said in a dignified tone, “Hi, I am Ambika.”

I smiled and replied, “Hi, Mam, I am Kalki, Content Consultant for Project Amravati.”

“Yeah…Yeah…” she replied staring at her beeping mobile phone. She typed some lines on her phone and looked up at me with a slight smile.

“Please, introduce yourself to the Marketing, Business Research, and Social Media team,” she leaned forward to read some papers on the table.

I felt the nervousness in my spirit as everyone paid attention to me. As I was about to begin, the door swung open with an amazing speed. Nakul entered the meeting in his own element and sat down beside Ambika. They both exchanged glances and communicated something to each other.

Nakul’s attention fell on me and he said loudly with a clap,” Welcome to our organization, Ms. Kalki. Here, the young lady is our content writer for our Amravati project. Let’s start the discussion without any more delay.”

I reverted with a smile and sat down so that they could get started with the meeting. Nakul had authority over the entire meeting and kept the whole meeting bounded together. He proclaimed his thinking over every idea, proposition, and plans presented by the congregation. Except for Ambika, he was beyond anyone’s control or comprehension. I browsed his name in the Google search and then it landed upon me that his true identity was Nakul Kumar Rajput - Ambika’s younger brother, approximatcly of my age, just joined the family business. I kept this information concealed as preferred by him.

The meeting started in full force. Ambika extended her left hand to explain some concepts when I saw the 5 carats round diamond ring on her finger. It was a true one-of-a-kind design that's simple, elegant, and timeless. During the meeting, she kept on twisting the engagement ring on her finger, turning it around and around. Somewhere, I was trying to take a residue of my love from that ring.

Nakul prided himself on being the best-qualified person in the meeting. Within an hour, she let everyone know that she was in control of the meeting. Soon, Nakul became less passive and his influence showed a decline. He restricted to slight smiles and head nods in between the meetings. Ambika spoke short, accurate, and only when needed. Her dominating views were immediately accepted by the members without any probing.

The brilliancy of ideas had started to sweep the conference room. The voice decibels increased from mild to loud, outpouring suggestions, and oppositions. It was not easy to make a way for myself in the crowded room but somehow, I had to take a position for myself.

Ambika was analyzing me, everything from my personality to DNA. I was thinking if she knew about me and Abheer. Mom's words rebooted my mind forcing me to refocus on work only. I took notes for my reference. The marketing team proposed slogans, taglines, and logos for the project. Ambika's silence was a clear indication of rejection. Next, was my turn to offer a thoughtful series of ideas.

I grabbed the HDMI cable wire and connect my laptop to

the projector to run the team through my presentation. I had loaded the presentation with user insights, 'How Might We' statements, customer analysis, and current trends - spiritual themes, Zen lifestyle, and minimalist ideology.

"Why Spirituality?" Ambika asked loosely twisting her pen between her fingertips.

"She spoke with me," I said in my mind.

"Spirituality impacts people and even things. It touches the very core within them. Do I need to explain here to anyone the importance of home? It is our own place; a sanctuary away from the rest of the world. If we embed spiritual concept in our project it will sell like never before," I paused for a second.

"How can you be so sure?" She asked me narrowing her frown.

"Anything in the market with spirituality or mystic powers sells easily. People want blessings and peace, they ought to find these in things instead of their mind. Why do they wear gemstones and rudraksha beads?" My voice echoed in the closed, darkroom.

I paused and continued, "They think gemstone has some mystic powers that can leverage peace, prosperity, success on us. We need to convince them that our homes are built and designed on the strong framework of numerology, Vaastu, Fengshui, Energy of Chi, and other spiritual principles. Our spiritual efforts will be a great catalyst to give them a life of wellness, peace, and contentment.

Ambika drew a long breath before continuing, "But these spiritual concepts should be profoundly incorporated in the project. If we are implementing this as a core concept then all the spiritual angles should be converged. The research tcam can start the consultation with the concerned practitioners. Also, create an observer pattern to track the effectiveness of the concept and evaluation metrics."

Ambika put her pen down on the planner and looked at me more intently. She looked beautiful with her elegant features and a touch up of confidence. She slightly pushed back her chair and exclaimed, "Make this experiment perfect."

Cups of tea and coffee frequently rotated on the table. The meeting stretched from aside whispers to full-blown team discussions. Teams blended and disintegrated, hostility blended with cohesion, maintaining the team chemistry got tougher, and the storming moved into norming when Ambika entered in the debate with her individual thoughts.

In the room, some people admired her leadership style, and few hated her controlling style. She was very much a one-woman army with her finger on the pulse of many things and everything. Ambika assigned the tasks to each time and concluded on the pending matters of the project. The meeting lasted longer than I assumed.

"Team, you may leave now," she commanded and people moved out swiftly.

Her secretary stood by her side. Ambika glanced at the whiteboard and tapping her finger on the table said, "Nafia, forward her details and get the paperwork and NDA signed. You will be the single point of contact for her. All the content should be forwarded to me for final approval with Nakul and the Project Head in the CC section."

Ambika glanced at Nafia and walked out after a cordial

handshaking with me. I turned towards Nafia with a smiling face. She was a sweet girl with dark, black eyes, and wavy hair. She had a short stature but was well-proportioned.

Nafia came closer to me and said, "So, astonishing, you could convince Ambika mam. She is really tough."

"Well, they say, only the tough get going," I replied to her with a light smile.

"Kalki, can you wait here for 5 mins. I will get your documents from the HR department. Also, should I order any working lunch for you?" she spoke politely.

"Thanks, Nafia. I am on intermittent fast today," I expressed my gratitude towards her. Nafia smiled and walked out of the conference room to get the job done.

I send an SMS to Mom to give her a brief update on the meeting. Nafia returned in half an hour with a welcome folder kit. Nafia shared with me all the important details - contact list, Intranet access user id, and password, images of the product prototypes, template drafts, sample content. I signed the No-disclosure agreement and the invoices requesting for 50% advance payment. Paperwork was completed. I thanked Nafia as she was incredibly helpful.

"Your payment will be processed by tomorrow through NEFT," Nafia gauged my calm expressions. She kept on explaining to me, the escalation matrix, the work culture, the expectations, future career scope, as she walked with me towards the main gate.

"Bye, Nafia," we extended our hands for goodbye. I left the building and walked towards my car. I sat in the car and slowly drove it out of the parking area.

Ambika's car stopped in front of me blocking my path. The driver got down to check the engine and gave me an apology signal. I reverted with a tender smile. Ambika was seated in the backseat dressed in a black, open-necked dress and besides her, was Abheer. His face flushed to the very collar of his shirt upon seeing me. I remained calm, showing him no response. The driver fixed the issue and rode away with the car but Abheer's face replayed in the background of my mind.

I reached home and repeatedly splashed water on my face to discard the running images from my mind. Feeling relaxed after a hot bath, I started working on the project to divert my thoughts from Abheer and realign my focus.

I heard a knock on my door, and in a few minutes, Vaishali entered the room.

"Madam has asked me to cook dinner for you and grandma. She will be coming late," she waited for my reply.

"Vaishali Mausi, please can you make a hot strong coffee for me. You can make anything for dinner," I requested her. She smiled and walked towards the kitchen.

She returned after twenty minutes with a hot mug of freshly brewed coffee, espresso-style. Feeling energetic, I called up many contacts to collate data required for User insights and then filled it up in an excel template to derivate conclusions. I opened the content template sheets to study the details. After long hours of work, I wanted to reboot myself. I slid the patio door and walked into the balcony. I rearranged the pots of bright flowers and herbs planted in the container. Sitting at the edge of the patio in the swinging hammock chair, I kept on staring at the colorful bloom of petals to invigorate my neurons. The scent of the flowers and the taste of fresh foliage recharged me with superabundant delight.

In the end, all the breathing things will get silent. The soul will perish away in the womb of the five infinite elements to live for another million leagues. I was lost in these thoughts when the sky changed from blue to dark black, each stroke making the impact deeper. The piercing moon rays through the little gaps on the ceiling made the obscure things a little visible.

I lifted my neck to look at the super moon blooming in full glory. I can never understand how the moonlight – the visible splendor of the sky takes my breath away. The flickering stars weaved different shapes and symmetric designs to set up the game of maze for the moon to play in the ethereal plains. My eyes rested upon the lunar dot as it got brighter and brighter. I closed my eyes to immerse in the mysterious expanse to sort out the chaos. The stillness made my doubts disappear in infinity.

I admired these delicate, illegible moments of nights that made a spectacle of my loneliness. Absorbed in the willpower of darkness, suddenly I felt a soothing touch. I turned toward the direction and looked on when a surge of cool currents fully drenched me. Someone was there, unseen by the naked eye but present from the other spectrum of the world. Someone touched my whole body, healing me with a mystic coolness, even without physically touching me. I forget all the hurt, pain, sorrow, and pursuits, the cool waves offered me deep healing.

My consciousness fell into some kind of an enchanted half-trance. Time seemed to slow down, and slowly the current waves began subsiding, leaving many unhinged questions rotating in my mind. The identity left but it was neither forgettable nor discoverable? A question for a lifetime - "Who was it?"

I heard the main door open and the jingling of keys. Mom's footsteps moved from the tiles of the living room to the carpet in her bedroom. She closed the door of her room and then I heard the sound of running water.

After an hour, she walked up to me dressed in her long nightdress with a robe. She gazed deep into my amber eyes and swung my chair to and fro, "What are you doing here so late? You will catch a cold. You ate your dinner?"

"Why did you come late?" I asked her.

"Baby, in between, my car had a flat tire and had to wait for the garage mechanic to come," she gripped the railing and leaned a bit to feel the air.

There was a momentary pause.

"What is it, Kalki?" she asked in a little firm voice.

"I saw my ex-boyfriend with his fiancée today. After the meeting, while I was driving out, Ambika's car blocked my way for some time. He was there with her in the car. They were talking, laughing, and seemed happy," I said in a sorrowful voice that sounded envious.

"Good for them," Mom exclaimed, "Kalki, just wait for some time. Then see the fun. Every new thing is attractive, fresh, and significant as per the theory of evolution. Let the iron of monotony strike it..."

I had a harmless evil smile on my face. We switched off the lights of the patio and moved into our respective rooms to kiss the bed.

I had fallen half-asleep but heard a few knocks on my room door and then mom's voice. I could feel mom seated at the edge of the bed, tapping on my shoulder.

"Kali, what is the new password of your MacBook?" she shook me repeatedly.

"Now Karthik@123," I closed my eyes and turned to the left side.

I could feel her gentle kiss on my cheek. Then I heard the clanking of laptop keys as she sat at my desk to do some work on my MacBook.

As the Amravati project reached close to its launch deadline, the workload terribly increased, and so, the frequency of my visits to the Corporate office. After investing weeks in the content creation of the project website, brochures, mailers, and branding the gig was over and accomplished.

All the efforts came to fruition when my payment got credited to my bank account. The highest amount to be ever deposited in my bank account – One Lakh rupees with conveyance charges extra. I immediately forwarded the SMS to Mom and she reverted with an appreciation and emojis line.

The project made me more confident than ever before. I received many offers for other corporate offices and even advertising firms.

After two-three days, I received a call from Nafia. She congratulated me on the successful launch of the project. The customer response was 20% higher compared to the previous projects. Also, the customers appreciated the spiritual element leveraged in the project for blessings and goodness.

"It was the enthusiasm, openness, and brilliance of people at Ambika Developers that made it a wonderful opportunity to work," I responded with gratitude.

"Ambika Group is looking forward to work with you on the next forthcoming project," she assured me.

She asked me to check Ambika's congratulations mail and revert to it. I was highly ecstatic; an indescribable, incommunicable, inexpressible experience.

I messaged Mom to come home as early as possible to celebrate the occasion with a delightful dining experience. Deliberately, I didn't ask any of her relatives, or friends, or Karthik to join us to keep this an exclusive mother-daughter affair. Her support and encouragement about the project inspired me during the long hours of writing, researching, and then, rewriting again. I spoke with friends on phone to pique their interest in gigging jobs, and they wished me super luck. Even mom's colleagues and friends congratulated me on the shining success. It was a refreshing experience to share the joy and happiness on social media. I learned the value of authentic connections and had a deep desire to share this journey with readers and other aspirers, so I wrote about the experience on my online blog and also shared it with other editorial websites. There were a good amount of views, likes, shares, and comments within a short span of time.

When the doorbell rang, I rushed to open the door, it was Mom, and she looked happy; the real happy expression. She hugged me in the front yard itself. Something like this not always happens. I will always savor this moment throughout my life.

It was 7 pm and we preferred to take an auto-rickshaw for easy whizzing to avoid traffic rush. We went to our reputed, all-time favorite jewelery brand for a small purchase. A stunning piece of jewelery can be an elegant way of saying thank you to your loved ones. I purchased one shimmering yellow gold bangle crusted with ruby stones that complimented her skin tone. I leaned forward to offer the gift to the center of my life. Around her my existence revolves, the pure and powerful rays of her motherhood kindle my spirit, ultimately blending us from where our journey started. Somewhere in our minds, there was a slow and endless drizzle, and we didn't open the umbrella to avoid getting wet.

We walked down the sweeping curve of the main stairs to come out of the wonderful glory of shine. After walking a few lengths on the sidewalk, we took an auto to reach Barbeque for dinner. The best about Barbeque is that you get the royal treatment in every corner. We talked over the simple, sizzling, and scrumptious platter of seafood, chicken, corn on the cob, roasted pineapple cubes, and mushroom. The beverages, appetizers, side dishes, a top-notch salad, and sweet counter tell us that BBQ knows there stuff very well. The best thing about BBQ is a huge buffet set-up for hot soup, veg and non-veg menu dishes in Indian culinary and Continental style, where everyone can have something. There were more than thirteen items lined up to ensure the customer's dining experience lives up to the occasion. We indulged in eating with an open heart and complete candor. It was a multi-sensory experience, as all the five senses were activated and appeased through seeing, hearing, smelling, touching, and tasting.

It was the best and fine barbeque timed perfectly to complete our personal celebration. We stuffed ourselves not only with food but moments and went back to our home.

I went to my room to sleep with happiness. As I sat cross-legged on the bed, I shared the photos of the celebration with Karthik. He was in a Skype meeting with a Ukrainian customer, hence replied with a line of happy emoji's. I shared the images of the event online and it got viral among friends' circle in a fraction of seconds. As most of my batch-mates and friends have just begun our career, we focused more on work than Friday meetups.

Mom knocked on the door and I turned off the phone and kept it aside. There was nothing to hide; it was more of a natural tendency. She sat beside me, looking serious but happy.

"Kalki, I know you are going through a tough phase. Though I was the stronger one, nowadays you seem to be more of a super-warrior struggling with unknown forces."

A big smile lighted my face as I heard the implied metaphor. She gave another breath and forged on.

"Kalki, if not your own biological mother then whom will you share all these paranormal happenings with? She said forcing an emotional response from me.

"I am not hiding anything. I want to scrub it from my memory. Don't take me wrong, Mom," I said softly.

"Whether you share or not, I will come to know everything. I read your diary. The purpose was not to invade your privacy but to keep you safe. To know what is exactly happening in your life, in your mind, and your heart," she wisely defended herself.

"You are a mom, not a tracker," I said, a little annoyed. "Mom, I don't want to bother you with all this weird stuff. You are busy and burdened, why should I overburden you. Also, if this is pre-written in my destiny, then what will I get by beating drums?" I contemplated her argument. We paused and kept on looking at each other's faces for a long time.

I could see a fiery determination in her eyes to end the presence of paranormal elements from my life. She rifled through the pockets of her Kimono robe, and two small velvety boxes with OM printed on it tumbled out. I could straightforward feel these are spiritual items for cleansing or energizing.

"You visited an astrologer, Mom?" I asked her with a harrowed look and continued blabbering, "Why are you wasting money and resources? Don't make me feel guilty?" I powered up.

"Not an astrologer but a very competent astrologer. He is a highly regarded honest man, till date he has not charged a single penny, he is well-settled in life practicing astrology only for helping people. In a time span of 10 minutes, he gave a detailed overview of your past life, personality, and future events." Her voice was still tight while speaking with me.

Gauging my softened expressions, she continued, "He mailed me your Janam Kundli and suggested remedies for your prosperity. He has recommended you to wear these two types of Astro rings in the index and ring finger of your left hand. This one is an energized coral gemstone ring." She picked one of the rings and placed it on my ring finger. We gazed at the ring and hoping it will open up more vistas of success.

The triangular red coral weighing 10 Ratti was mounted on a Copper ring, left open from the backside for rays to pass through and reach the finger properly.

"Remember to recite the Beej mantra of Mars planet (Mangal Grah) every morning to increase your boldness and willpower," she said in a calm voice.

She turned to another box and opened it. There laid on the velvety cushion a bold, rich and glamorous yellow sapphire ring. The ring was set in fine 18K pure yellow gold with an open backside for the sun rays to pass through.

Mom placed it in my index finger, admiring the yellow glitter. She handed over a piece of paper with the Beej mantra of Jupiter planet (Guru Grah) written upon it.

"Kalki," Mom said in a serious voice, "These are not just guardians or lucky rings but your spiritual partners for life."

"Trust them, they will protect you,

Worship them, they will bless you,

Love them, and they will surrender to you."

"Kalki, this is one way else we can also consult a psychologist. The process will be of analysis and interpretation; they will probe into the reasons for stress, sleep frequency cycle, and other multiple questioning patterns. The tools used for the process can be regression techniques, hypnosis, and casual conversations. We can even seek their consultation if you are willing."

"Not now, Mom," I said in partial defense, "Give me some time to understand these mystic happenings. There are no sound theories for us to believe; some say ghosts exist, or some it is a work of fiction. However, I know what I am seeing and visualizing in the broad nightlight. Let me sort it out on my own. If destiny is personalized for every human being, then how can the answers be universal and common?"

She was strangely calm. Both of us got engrossed in observing the tint, smoothness, and symmetry of the ring. Mom kept on pouring more love to comfort me.

"Answers will find a way to come to the surface, "Mom gently patted my back as I sank to sleep in the bed. I grabbed the blanket tighter around my shoulders as mom switched off the lights to make the ambiance dark and silent.

"In the middle of the nights,
I wake up to write timeless stories
That will be a light in the darkness,
To the hungry ghosts living in emptiness".

CHAPTER NINE

New Beginnings

The Amravati project helped me to break into the market. Not only did my revenue increase, but my clients were spread across diverse functions and portfolios. I had a knack for enabling creative and insightful solutions that made the blur visible. Education is never enough—never complete. It's a formidable challenge to keep on enriching, learning new skills, and updating with the current trends, but the process is vital if you wish to thrive in your profession. You have to be sharp as an ax to offer thoughtful solutions to the thorniest of problems. I hadn't created a success story yet, but I was, without question, on my way.

My new relationship with Karthik became fast-paced and action-packed. His attitude toward life was so inspiring, and his energy was always amazing. Karthik made a big impact on me, disrupting my common life with art, exotic cuisine, culture, and entertainment.

I sang a song, and Karthik whispered it back. I wrote a poem, and Karthik wove the rhyme. Abheer had eroded the emotional lining of my heart, and Karthik was working hard to transform it into a juicy vineyard for our growing love.

We were sunk in the radical, inspiring moments of infinite abstractness. Sometimes, moving and disturbing tiffs would occur between us, but these were just another mode of expression. Destiny was molding our love into a surreal and fabulous story for upcoming generations to cherish. Even the streetlights weren't as bright as the soft glow coming from his eyes. I could hear the blazing of fireworks and feel the smoke around when he folded me in his arms. It was a real challenge to keep contention at the bay when the tides had their full motion in the ocean. He was like artwork to me—soothing with his extravagant hues and striking with his effective black and white study in contrasts.

I submitted articles for publishing consideration to newspapers, magazines, and blogs to establish brand credibility and notability for Wikipedia. It was imperative to keep my brand under the spotlight at all times. I wanted to take a break before getting back to work, however, so I walked into the living room where mom was seated on a maroon recliner watching the latest release on Netflix. Slowly, thoughts seeped into my mind to disclose my relationship with Karthik to her.

I came close to her and perched on the arm of the recliner. She wrapped her left arm around my waist and whispered, "Tell me the secret."

"How do you know?" I asked, amazed, resting my head on her shoulder. Her earrings got tangled in the upper strands of my hair.

She lovingly patted my cheeks and said in a motherly voice,

"Tell me, though I know what you want to say. I want to hear from your mouth."

"Mum, it's Karthik," I said, feeling so shy that I was tempted to go back to my room.

Mom was quiet. There was no answer or response; it surprised me, as I thought she would approve of Karthik instantly.

I said in a nervous tone, "Karthik and I are . . . sort of seeing each other. We're not exactly in a relationship but exploring our compatibility. We will wait, and I promise you, Mom, your word will be final. We are getting along very well, and we make each other happy."

Her bland reaction made my heart flutter. There wasn't a trace of contentment on her face—no hint of a smile.

Speaking in a wet voice, I prodded her shoulder. "Mom, say something."

"Kalki, let me be frank with you. Karthik is good from the core of his heart. I know loyalty and trust are certainly important in a relationship, but there are other important things that also matter—status, family ranking, and qualifications, just to name a few."

"Mom, are you really saying this stuff?" I pulled away in shock, giving her a bewildered look and sitting cross-legged. My amber eyes refused to blink.

"Let me finish up," she said, sharpening her voice and pausing the movie on TV. She leaned toward me, her deep black, blazing eyes tapping into my deepest emotions. There was no trace of anger in her eyes, but some emotion was forming on her face. As she leaned in further, I lowered my pitch in simple respect.

"Kalki, my struggle to keep you alive was like living my life once again. During your birth, I was fighting a near-death experience, and I fought back only for you. There was no reason for me to hold on to this life except you. I raised you with my sweat, blood, and tears, but you don't belong to me alone."

There was a momentary silence. The blowing wind chimes were sounding an alarm; the usual musical tinkling was lost.

She spoke in a strong tone. "Your father didn't interfere in my life, but he was seeking reconciliation with me. I gave him a clear 'No,' and he continued to pester me until I got rid of him. However, I can't revoke his paternal rights. He does check with me about your education, career, and other aspirations. He has a tab on your activities though you didn't accept his requests on social media or speak with him. He will take your attitude; he will listen to your tantrums, and if you ask for anything, the sky is the limit because you're his only child. This was not his initial approach toward you. Seeing you grow, living alone, and watching other fathers, his paternal instincts gradually awoke. He wants to make up for everything, and that can be the potential issue. Your father has a narrow mindset when looking at things and people." She raised her eyebrows till her forehead was rigged with curved lines. "That person will never approve Karthik because he is an orphan without professional qualifications, a rich family background, social ranking, or NRI tags. He will always want someone like Abheer—young scion of a millionaire—for you. He may go to any extent to remove Karthik from your life. I could withstand him, but what about Karthik?" She sounded concerned.

"Mom, I know only two things. First, I am only your daughter till my last breath. Second, no millionaire will accept me after knowing the paranormal stuff about me. I want to have a wild partner, and this is the one. Also, I don't care about whatever your husband thinks because I don't owe him a thing. Karthik is brave, street-smart, and confident; he will take care of himself and create his empire someday. If his parents had been alive, he would have been a B. Tech student studying in a US university. Believe me, Mom, the classroom defines students, but life creates students." My timid eyes filled with liquid sweetness as I looked up at her and she agreed with my answer.

I held her hand and slowly said to her, "He is really the best choice for me—trustworthy, loyal, intelligent, and caring," I said, releasing a long breath. "The best part is that he is desperate to have his own family. Will you not stand up for your only daughter's happiness and secure future? Do you want me to marry a rich braggart who will divorce me after he discovers my paranormal secret? I'm not confirming anything on paper now; I've still got three or four years for settling down, so let's keep this aside."

"But you two are together?" Mom asked in a reassuring tone.

"We're together, and we're in love." I finally placed my finger on her lips to end the conversation.

We spent the rest of the day walking under the canopy of trees in the park, visiting the nearby temple, and sitting in solitude to contemplate our decisions. If I had to sum up the day, I'd say it was a happy one that ended on a lighter note.

***

It was a new day, with a brighter sheen, but I had a different agenda in mind. I wanted to explore the mysteries of consciousness, understand the soul's power, and find something in the infinite ocean of energy. So, for some time, I closed my Mac and put aside my gigs. I settled into a still, stable, and comfortable posture in a quiet room. I could feel the healing energies touch my body with warmth and love as I sunk deeper and deeper into another world—a world so colorful and joyous, I could hardly believe it.

There were more colors and wonderful flora than here on Earth. Happiness was like a sixth element embedded in this other world—a place I named the Happiness Sphere. I stretched my arms in the sky to take a panoramic picture of the galaxy. A huge cloud of soft, scented smoke filled up the air, and I could draw vivid designs in the smoke with my fingers. A calm green landscape filled with bright, towering flowers spoke of freedom. Enormous, crystalline rivers led to grand waterfalls. The base of each cascade was aglow with billowing mists where the water met with great golden rocks.

The hot, black gates to the self-destructive inferno—anger, lust, ego, and greed—were permanently closed. The people in the Happiness Sphere were teeming with wisdom, love, humor, satisfaction, and light-heartedness. They had no desire for material things. As I ventured further, I discover that this ethereal world operated in various dimensions. There was a world for living a happy life, a world of science, a world of music, a world of dance, a world of magic, a world of arts, a world of imagination—and countless other passionate worlds for passionate souls beyond.

The preview was only for a limited time, and soon, my connection was disrupted. I plummeted back to the earth like an apple falling from the tree. You can travel to this spirit world only via thoughts. You need to relax, disconnect from this world, meditate, awaken your consciousness, elevate your thoughts to the higher dimension, and connect to the realm by invitation only. I was lucky to see something out of the ordinary realms and unlucky because I couldn't frequently set my foot there with ease.

I learned the art of traveling without a physical body. The secret of the spirit world was opening up to me. Finally, my personal watch was on being fine-tuned.

In the evening, we had a girls' get-together at my place due to the complete privacy. Mom would be coming home late, as she had to attend a college-sponsored event. We spent some time playing charades, and I felt inventive, acting out each prompt easily. In between, we pooled our money and ordered Domino's pizza, pasta, chips, and cold drinks to satisfy our hunger. Asma had brought her guitar along and eventually removed it from the red-lined case, handling it with care, positioning it around her neck. She then struck the chords with a powerful touch, penetrating our hearts with good emotions. The doorbell rang when I looked through the door-hole; it was Dominos super delivery.

We collected our food and pounced upon the pizza like a pack of hungry wolves. After our initial hunger was satisfied, we shared spicy talk, funny facts, and harmless conversation about our boyfriends. Then, our talks graduated to drawing inspiration and finding new reserves of energy from each other. We all agreed on one thing: a fierce, feminine connection is all the push needed to identify our higher role in the cosmos. We really had a good time, and when it was time to go home, our goodbye was emotional. After a few friends, had left, I had a close chat with Asma and Neesha about my breakup with Abheer and how things turned up expectedly with Karthik. They could connect with my pain of transition as we passionately embraced each other to say goodbye.

It was 10.30 p.m., and I called Mom to check in. She didn't pick up my call and then there was a message beep. I slid the screen to read the message: "Home by 11:30."

My stomach was full of junk food, so I sipped a small amount of cold drink and drifted off to sleep. My eyes closed, and suddenly, I could hear Mom's pips and squeaks in my room. I opened my heavy eyes, and Mom was there standing beside my bed, smiling at me.

"I'm sorry, baby," Mom whispered. "The event went on for a long time. You had dinner?" Her sari was still crisp and starched even after thirteen hours of work.

I could feel it as she planted a soft, tender kiss on my forehead and snuggled me up in a blanket. She adjusted the thermostat settings, then walked out of the room; as I curled into a ball on the bed.

Darkness descended in the room, and there was no source of light. Only the thin curtains blew up, allowing in a fractured moonlight that seemed to dance to tinkling music audible only to the ears of mind. I felt a sacred presence all around the room—and within her. A strong wind blew from nowhere. A swarm of neon-colored butterflies fluttered in, puffing the air with a delightful scent. The butterflies were riding on the storm. They encircled me, buzzing, fluttering, and clapping their whirling wings to arouse a spiritual emotion inside me. Like the moon, these beautiful angels were wading in the night sky. There were falling crystals that gave full indulgence to the existing phenomena of life and beyond. The sun of this spiritual vision shone through the temporary walls of darkness. A passionate torrent burst its bounds, and I rushed to it like a parched traveler desperate to drink the divine waters. I couldn't taste a sip, however; I just wasn't ready yet. Only the sight of the light blue aqua liquid shimmering with the dust of crystals made me complete. Slowly, the waters evaporated in the moonlight, and the encircling butterflies escaped through the window, putting a spell of sleep upon me. My eyes closed of their own accord.

The ordinary morning started in an unusual way for me. I sat at the edge of the bed and paused for a few minutes, wondering if last night's event had been a dream. I was fully absorbed in thought when Mom opened the door with a bang. She looked super happy, and her face radiated a genial, joyous light wherever she went. Her smile was full of life. She sat next to me, pulled my chin up with her finger, forcing me to look into his eyes.

"Good morning, my sweetheart," she said in a high-pitched voice.

"What's the matter, Mom?" You're in full bloom," I said with a curious look.

She tilted her head down slightly as we made eye contact. She spoke with a breath. "Do we need a reason to be happy? Everything is going so fine; shouldn't we be happy about it?" Her eyebrows pushed together.

"Hard to believe." I got up from the bed and headed into the bathroom to start my morning routine. Seeing her enthusiastic spirit, I kept my personal stuff at bay.

"Kiddo, till the time, you're ready let me organize your clothes by category. It won't be long till everything is in disarray again." She hummed one of her favorite movie songs and got on the task.

In an hour, I had finished my morning routine and dressed in a yellow T-shirt and black cotton pants. I hung a black formal blazer over the back of the wooden chair. In case of a sudden online meeting notification, I could quickly fling it on.

Mom finished setting up my wardrobe. I looked through the meticulous setup closet and thanked her.

She glanced at me and said in a loving voice, "Kalki, yesterday your Mamaji called me. He wanted to know if Grandma can come back to her home for the Ganesha festival. This will be a good opportunity for her to connect with her relatives and neighbors."

"Hmm," I uttered, understanding that after Grandma was gone, most of the time, it will only be only me at home.

"Your grandma wants to go to the festival. She doesn't like living with your Mami, but she misses her grandsons. Here, the environment is boring for her. You're glued to the computer, and I'm at work, so she has the only TV as a companion. Also, our neighbor is based in Dubai and wants to keep the flat empty instead of renting it out." She stopped as she saw my facial expressions getting stressed.

"If you want grandma to stay here, you have to interact—make her feel at home. Give her your love and empathy; spend some time with her. Every day, I speak with her for one hour, irrespective of my busy schedule. She isn't your guardian; make her feel your own presence." Mom tapped my left shoulder.

"But she's leaving now," I said and sighed.

Mom gave me a wave of a smile and brushed her fingers through my hair, she said, "Give her a reason to return. Everyone needs a trusted system to thrive. She only wants attention and love from us. She will be leaving next week and will let us know her decision of staying with us or not."

"I see what you mean," I replied in an obedient way.

She spoke expressively. "Remember this in dealing with everyone you meet in life. You need to earn people like you earn money. And, people are more precious than money. Money can buy you things, and people can bring these things to life. Whenever you meet anyone treat them with love, kindness, and respect, including your dad. Your behavior, values, and personality represent my parenting, so demonstrate the best of it."

"I promise you," I said giving her a tender hug and squeezing tight.

"Will you be fine alone?" she asked, appreciating my nervousness.

"Mom, I think so. Let me give it a try. If anything goes wrong, I can still spend my time in the malls or We Work offices," I said in an uncertain voice.

"And waste money?" she said, making her opinion clear. You give it a try, or else I'll try to make some arrangement with Vaishali. And, if nothing works, then I'll take my leave." She sounded stress-free.

"Kalki, be natural with your grandma. Don't be excessive; keep it genuine," Mom continued, speaking to other values as we walked into the kitchen to eat our breakfast.

Something was different. She was so free and happy. I was amazed by her vibrant spirit.

While eating, I looked through the window. A flood of leaves blew through the greenery and perpetually shifting clouds amidst the unsettled sky.

"I'm going to work now. Take out some time for grandma, and do be good with her," said Mom, kissing me on my cheek, she walked through the main door.

After finishing breakfast, I went into the living room, switched on the TV, and settled on the sofa to watch an old-time silver screen classic. Hearing the old-timey sounds, grandma joined me on the couch to watch. She remembered her college days, and we had a blast talking, laughing, and eating popcorn. And sure enough, the fun was on, sharing photo albums and video chatting with her friends. We brought love back into our relationship. The path was cleared by simple conversation, and we were enraptured by each other. I looked up at the sky, and it was clear.

In the afternoon, Grandma went to sleep in Mom's room after eating a mild lunch. I switched on my MacBook and got back to work on content writing gigs. But I learned it's important to care for each other, as the home is where we have to live. Vaishali entered my room at around 4 p.m., yelling as she placed the mug upon a coaster on my table, "Coffee . . ."

"Thank you for taking care of me. Also, can I get another cup of coffee at 6 p.m.?" I asked her in a polite voice. She was awestruck, as she just couldn't believe what she was hearing.

Vaishali nodded her head and walked away, wondering if I was okay. For the next few hours, I really did a lot of hard work without playing music or succumbing to distractions.

Work is a source of mystical union whereby I blend with my inner-self and reach enlightenment.

At 6 p.m., the doorbell rang. I knew it was Mom, as I'd heard her pull the car into our parking zone. I saved my files on the computer and walked into the living room to greet her.

"Mom, I hope you had a good day at work," I said in a cheerful voice. She gave me a blank stare for a few minutes and then eased herself into the chair. I increased the AC temperature to make the room cool and comfortable. She wondered why I was behaving so differently today. She assumed that I wanted some favor from her. Vaishali set a tray of apple milkshakes and sandwiches on the round table in front of her, then completed her pending duties and left for the day.

Mom sipped her drink and went into her room to freshen up. She turned back, looked at me, and asked, "You want something?"

"Yes," I said and paced toward her.

"What?" she asked, knitting her eyebrows.

"Mom, I have you. Why should I be engaged in the pursuit of material things?" I said in a naughty voice as she slapped me playfully.

"You're impossible," she said, entering her room and lightly closing the door behind her. My sweet, maternal grandmother went into the kitchen to whip up her own spectacular dinner. I followed her to see how she artfully turned the market produce into a mouthwatering meal. While cooking, Grandma made judicious use of spices, herbs, and seasonings to achieve a perfect balance of flavors. She delved into the stories of how the classic Marathi recipes had originated, enriching the Deccan culture for ages. I kept my phone in recording mode to capture our moment on video. It was a walking, talking cookbook-meets-travelogue experience for me. I was enjoying myself in Grandma's kitchen, stirring and licking spoons when Mom walked in dressed in a floral cotton night suit.

"What's going between grandma and granddaughter?" she asked.

"Learning and recording her secret recipes," I replied, tasting the reddish-brown tamarinds' distinct sweet-and-sour taste.

"Cool," she replied stroking my back and tasting the pulp of tamarind. "What's for dinner?" She raised her eyebrow up and down at me.

We both looked at the spread of tamarinds and yelled, "Panipuri!"

Grandma agreed to prepare the authentic tamarind chutney and spicy water made up of mint, chilies, lemon, and cilantro. Mom arranged a mix of grams and mashed potatoes for filling. I called the watchman and asked him to get two packets of pani puri from the nearby store.

I could hear the resident chef whistle five-six times in the kitchen. Within minutes, Mom had assembled all the ingredients on the dining table. I was sitting at the table waiting to gobble the puris when the doorbell rang. The watchman had brought the packets of puris. I thanked him and paid him the money with an extra tip of ten rupees.

Now, we were all set to pounce upon the most super-rated food—pani puri. Within nano-seconds, we were lost in the agglomeration of tangy, sweet-spicy wonder that makes everyone fall head over heels. Pani puri is the best example to understand the greatness of simplicity. We filled the small, crispy puris with aloo and chana mix, dunking it in pudina-flavored water, sweet tamarind chutney, creating an unbelievable explosion of flavors. The pudina water soothed our nerves with a refreshed sensation. Our dinner was simply delicious, and we kept on gulping the puris to our heart's content. The pani puri left a lingering aftertaste of herbal and spicy notes on our taste buds.

I went into the bathroom to brush my teeth, get into my nightclothes, and pull my hair into a ponytail. Tonight, Mom wanted to talk with Grandma about her decision to stay in our home or her son's home. I heard their ongoing conversation in the kitchen while doing the dishes. It was a hard decision to make, but Grandma wished to go to her son's home for the most popular festival of Maharashtra, the Ganesh Chaturthi festival. She explained to Mom that the true spirit of these festivals is social interaction, reconnection, and the development of empathy for each other. She insisted Mom also join in and enjoy herself for a few days. Mom refused, and the talk ended. I heard their footsteps moving out of the kitchen and approaching their room. Mom shut her bedroom door, and darkness settled in.

In the middle of the night, I was mentally woken up. There was a drop of adventure flowing in the blood of a common person. I saw a vague figure approaching me. The hideous glare penetrated my closed eyelids, forcing me to rouse. My body was stiff and rigid as if tied by strings from head to toes. I was unable to move a single portion of my body; I couldn't even blink an eye. I wanted to scream but couldn't even part my lips. My body was completely dead—like an iron bar—and my eyes were sightless. I felt like someone was sitting on my chest, trying to strangle me to death. The crushing pressure was making it impossible for me to catch a breath. Somewhere, I was straddled between the boundaries of wakefulness and sleep. No one could help me, except myself, and here I was lying on the bed, unable to move even my little finger or wiggle a toe.

But despite nothing else working, my mind was functional. The ultimate powerful weapon of a human being is the MIND. In sleep paralysis, we "wake up" mentally, as our dreaming mind is operational but our body remains paralyzed. One thing is clear; the mind will always wake up before the body wakes up during sleep paralysis.

Reconnecting these dots, I finally gained control over my mind and tapped into it to repeat the divine mantra, "OM," to awaken the inner powers of Kundalini. In a fraction of a second, the pressure was off my chest, the strangling stopped, and the immobility was gone. I bolted upright in the bed and drank a full glass of water.

During my initial research, I had read a lot about sleep paralysis and other near-death experiences. The Internet is flooded with information and scientific data about sleep paralysis, but each individual has their own encounter leaving much for us to infer.

I recollected some important picks.

In sleep paralysis, the body remains paralyzed while the brain awakens. You are mentally alert and conscious but are unable to move voluntary muscles. This is often accompanied by a sensation of chest pressure; this is the reason why many people also wake up from sleep paralysis gasping for breath. It occurs in one of the two transitions—when you're falling asleep or waking up. The body must go into REM sleep mode and come out of it. Sleep paralysis happens when your body has trouble making this transition. If it happens when you're falling asleep, it's called "hypnagogic" sleep paralysis. Whereas if it happens while waking up, it's called "hypnopompic" sleep paralysis.

Remembering all this, I stretched languidly on the bed. I kept wondering how much I would have to face in a single lifetime. The atmosphere in the room was getting gloomy and spooky. Sensing this sent a chill down my spine, causing me to scramble under my blankets, wiggling my body deep under the covers, and settling in the blackness. There was no sound of any movement, but distant ruffling floated across the room. After a considerable time, I slowly peeked out from the blanket, and a man was standing at a distance of ten yards from me. Tall, white as snow, his distinct features outlined as he stood there silhouetted against the darkness. The apparition watched as I looked upon it with fear.

I wasn't able to utter a single word. I had never known or seen the person in my life. There was a lot of grief, and perhaps he wanted to spill out the ocean of his sadness. The soul looked tired of the constant sauntering in the darkness. Though it made me feel sad, I couldn't be a soul healer while awake. It was much easier in the subconscious mind while dreaming.

There was a soft moan, then grunting followed by groaning. The moans were from pain etched deeply into each of his pores. After a brief stunned silence, a loud wailing splintered the night air. The suffering of his wounds and desolate loneliness engulfed the man, transforming him within seconds from the picture of horror to one of sorrow.

In less than ten minutes, he taught me of the longest chapter of life—the afterlife.

The prospect of an afterlife where nothing can be predicted. No one knows how to survive and thrive in the afterlife. Such a significant transition without any guide . . . except your true companion: your soul.

With all my guts, I dared to put a smile on my lips, and his expressions faded into a grimace of despair. I wanted to heal his internal wounds and tormented soul with my healing art, but I had inadequate knowledge to do so while conscious. I failed to bring happiness, contentment, and karmic vision.

The apparition pointed his finger to the wall, and neon-lit alphabet letters began dancing to form the word WAITING. I stared at the message as the letters were swallowed by the wall one by one. I turned my head in the direction of the apparition, but it was gone—and so was the specter. The visitor left behind a code to be deciphered. Be it a serious study or a curiosity, I knew that my future was hidden in this enigmatic code. The remaining hours of the night, I spent beholding the silence of nature, wrapped in extreme darkness. Everything was on the verge of change. High up in the sky, the blackness was painted with streaks of orange, gold, and red, giving it a new and vibrant appearance. The sky is constant, but art is ever-evolving.

The first rays of the morning sun illuminated the earth. Glittering sun rays shone on my tired face to make me feel better. A bright Sunday morning had begun. The entire city seemed to be drawn in the illusion of a happy and resting day. I was awake, but not in a peaceful mind. The paranormal events were still fresh in my mind, and I tried to convince myself to think less about them. Getting upset, I went into the bathroom to take a strong shower—powerful enough to break the stones. At these times, the showerhead is full of more promise than the bathtub. Tears were coursing down my cheeks like little rivers eroding the greenery of heart and mind. I took more than an hour in the shower, the sensation of lukewarm water falling upon me, and washing over my skin was simply cathartic, and it refreshed me to some extent. After stepping out, I wrapped a towel around myself and walked out of the bathroom. Quickly, I dressed up in casual wear, combed my hair into a ponytail, and sat down on the recliner in a fully stretched position. I actually felt sleepy; both eyelids were so heavy, they closed on their own, and my breathing got even. The blue denim jeans and red turtleneck made a perfect grab for the cool weather. My nap became longer than imagined. Rays of the afternoon sun streamed through the window in oblique lines, falling upon me. I woke up from my afternoon nap feeling hungry. I bottled up all of my emotions, put a little makeup on my face, and pretended to be fine.

I inhaled the vaporous trail of an aroma coming from Mom's kitchen. It was filled with herbs, spices, seasonings, meaty bones, and smoky grilled pieces—everything that makes clear something rewarding is on the way. I went inside the kitchen, where Mom was busy, moving to and fro while preparing a real, heavy feast.

"Anything special?" I asked as such feasts are only occasional in our home.

"Yes, a special lunch for a special one?" she said, roasting the chicken pieces coated with aromatic seasonings such as thyme, rosemary, and paprika in a fry pan.

"Special person—any guest coming for lunch?" I asked in a low voice, thinking about how to avoid meetups.

"Yes, the most special person of my life," she chuckled and flipped the chicken pieces as the color changed to red.

I kept quiet and stood beside her watching her prepare the sundry items—sauce, roasted chicken, boneless biryani, and gravy. Some of our best conversations occurred in this very context.

"Where's Grandma? I don't hear any chanting of shlokas," I said with a giggle.

"Your uncle came in the early morning and took her to stay with them for just two days," she said as she repeatedly washed the grains with water.

"Cool!" I said dipping a finger in the chutney. "Mom, please tell Mamaji to keep her there. I can deal with a dozen ghosts but not your mother," I said jokingly, and a giggle landed upon her face. "Sometimes, I feel that Grandma loves her son more than you. From childhood, I could sense discrimination in her behavior toward you." I glanced at her expression.

She lit a flame of the stove and kept the rice cooker upon it to prepare puffy and tender rice.

"Daughter," Mom continued with a pause, "be thankful for her. She is the reason I became such a good mom. Of course, if you agree that I am a good mom," she said in a gentle voice.

"No, Mom. You are not a good mother." I stepped a bit close to her. "You had to go through a lot of hardships because of my personal issue. I know your childhood could have been more luxurious than the life you've been living." Her face fell as she spoke in her pale voice.

"Mom . . ." I held her hand, took a breath of cool air, and said, "You are not a good mother and never will be. Let me make it clear to you. The reason is that you are a great mother."

The cooker whistled thrice as we remained silent.

I spoke in a confident voice. "Luxury isn't everything in life. Circumstance is a better teacher. It taught me financial management, determination, planning—all the hard skills and soft skills required to thrive. Love is a natural conditioner in life. Without your love, I could have never become what I am today," I could see the gleaming tears creating a waterway on her cheeks. With extreme gentleness, I wiped her tears and spoke. "Mom, I swear on my creativity. If I had to take a million births on the earth, I want you to have as my mother every single time."

She didn't respond or speak a word. We were both quiet, our hearts swelling with a high tide. Mom picked up a few onions, peeled them layer by layer to well up tears in her eyes. Though she pretended to hide, I knew the tears were derived more from the reasons of the heart.

"Help me to prepare lunch for the guest. Don't stand and give me talks," she said loudly to hide her surging emotions.

I didn't move from my spot. She looked at me, analyzing my face, and asked, "You didn't sleep well in the night. Your bed said that to me." She raised her eyebrow, trying to search for the truth while having a love affair with cooking. I paused for a moment.

"Answer me," she said. "I have asked you something," she said.

"No, I didn't sleep in the night." There was a momentary

silence. She darted her angry eyes toward me. I bowed down my face and narrated the incident from the beginning with less dramatic effect. She listened carefully with her ears and hearts not only to my words but even the silence. It was hard for her to believe that these things were still happening even after the Kuldevi darshan. She set the spoon on the counter and peeled off the cooking gloves. I saw the heightened empathy on her face as she pulled me in for a hug.

"I'm sorry for scolding you. I don't think you should worry about sleep paralysis. Nearly 80% of the population experiences it at some point in their life. It's common. Even I went through it during my pregnancy. Generally, the causes are sleep disorders, fear, and general stress," she said, stroking me softly and gently.

"Mum, what about the apparition and the word waiting?" My voice trembled.

She smiled to show off her strength. Even so, I could make out the unsteadiness in her actions.

"Hey, why don't you arrange the dining table for our special guest?" Mom said and took a deep breath. I turned around when she called me,

"Kalki, some things in life are far more complicated than we imagine. We can't comprehend everything with mathematical precision or scientific reasoning. There are definite limits for our human brain to understand and analyze things. Let's quit the impossible of solving a one-word code. If these paranormal happenings are imbued with a purpose, then the universe will open your mystical powers to show the way. You shouldn't be thinking too much," she took a deep breath.

"And, what if these paranormal happenings are meant to harm

me," I asked innocently.

"I don't think so. Otherwise, why wait so long? They would have done it by now. Ghosts devour the human soul, but certain laws of nature apply even to them. We haven't done any wrong to anyone; there is nothing to fear. Not all snakes are poisonous; similarly, not all ghosts are vengeful soul-seeking spirits. Trust me, there is a larger role-play for you. You should be bold, wild, and spiritual enough to assimilate it," Mom said wisely. Her words were reassuring and uplifted my mood.

"When will I be ready to take up the role? How will the knowledge come to me?" I held Mom's left arm, and she looked at my penetrating gaze with eyes full of tenderness.

"Ask your soul, dear. You can consider the fruit-ripening biological phenomena as an example to understand it. As the sunlight secretly ripens the fruit, your inner light will show you the way," she said, putting on the gloves and placing the chicken pieces on the cutting board.

"How do I ask the soul?"

"Increase your knowledge, read or speak with a spiritual master. Stop running behind me," she said in an irritated voice.

I was hurt. She could see the cuteness fall from my face.

Feeling apologetic, she said in a soft voice, "Your inner light is connected to the source of all consciousness. But you need to find out the PLUG that can connect you to the flow of consciousness. I don't know where your plug is in this infinite universal field." She stopped as we gazed into each other's eyes for a moment.

"Thanks," I replied in a confused tone.

"Kalki, smile and make the arrangements on the dining table." Mom motivated me to be fine. I smiled back at her, walking toward the living room to take a break.

I looked out at the street, which was filled with life from the living room window. I couldn't relate to most of the things mentioned by Mom, however, two things made sense to me. Firstly, the paranormal beings didn't dare to hurt me, so hurting me or killing me wasn't their prime intention. They wanted to convey me a message. Secondly, let the Universe work upon me. I am very happy not to have this burden planted in my head.

Rethinking these lines, I opened up the window a little to get a clear view.

"The dining table, Kalki," Mom called out loud, reminding me to do the setup.

"I wonder who on the earth is coming for lunch?" I murmured indistinctly.

There were two dining tables in our home. A small dining table with a seating arrangement for only two people in the kitchen corner—the place where mom and I used to eat most of the time—and an extendable dining table in the high-end corner of our living room. It had the capacity to be a comfortable fit for six people.

I cleaned the extendable dining table to make it shine. I spread a black and white floral pattern cotton cover on the table. To give the dining table an elegant look, I placed round-shaped braided jute table mats in front of each seat with a jute runner in the center of the dining table, laid over the table cloth. Four table mats graced the opposite sides of the table and placed the other two at the table ends. I went into the kitchen to get a stack of serving dishes, bowls, and glasses. As taught by Mom, I placed everything on the table to make the presentation look beautiful.

"Done," I shouted so Mom could clearly hear.

After about ten minutes, she came out of the kitchen and intricately surveyed the settings.

Mom appreciated my efforts and said in a judging tone, "Good, but next time use your creativity. Don't follow my style."

I simply nodded my head. Adjusting the positioning of the table runner, she said, "Sweetheart, I think you should join some baking classes. You'd enjoy yourself."

"Mom, I'm seeing freshly baked ghosts every night, and you want me to learn baking," I said in an irritated tone.

"Negativity, negative thoughts, and a negative aura attract ghosts. Move forward in life," she commanded.

"Who is coming?" I repeated, trying to get an answer from Mom. She smiled and went back to the kitchen to finish making the lavish feast.

The lunch was ready. Mom was transferring the chicken biryani in the serving bowl to serve it along with chutney, gravy, grill roasted chicken pieces, and veggie salad.

"When are your guests coming?" I asked Mom as she walked from the dining table to the kitchen singing to herself.

The dining table was set for lunch as perfect as ever with flowers. Most of the table was filled with food. Mom took my hand and led me to the dining room.

"To the most precious guest in my life. This entire celebration is only for you," she said lovingly, patting the sleeve of my

T-shirt. I sat by the dining table, feeling extremely happy and flattered.

"Why did you make such an effort?" I asked, confused.

"It's ok to do something special for someone special. I wanted to grab this opportunity to express my love," said Mom, squeezing my shoulder.

"Don't think so much. Just enjoy the moment. I want us to create our own personalized memories," Mom smiled graciously and filled my plate with as much as food possible. The happiness drifted through the room like a rainbow floating in the sky. Mom's warmth radiated throughout the room, enveloping me as I immersed myself deeply in the flavors. For the rest of the meal, she gazed at my plate as we pulled lots of conversation, shared stories, and laughed in unison.

"Kalki, don't rush with Karthik. You just had your first graduation anniversary. If you're interested, we can plan your further studies abroad in the US or UK or Australia." She sounded enthusiastic.

I looked at her with a steely gaze, and when I spoke, my voice was filled with deep resolve. "No. If I want to do any studies, then I can do here in Mumbai. Right now, our prime focus is only a successful career."

She trusted my assurance, and I felt new energy coming from Mom's food. We talked for a long time without entertaining any mobile calls or other disturbances. It was one of the best times we ever spent. After lunch was over, I gave Mom a strong hug to express my gratitude. In reply, her eyes showed all her love for me.

"We weathered the storms of life,
Finding strength in our own intuitions
Our aim was always the same,
To slice out the ordinary and create an extraordinary example
That would inspire and galvanize others to rewrite the future."

CHAPTER TEN

DEEP ROOTS

Everything around us was beautiful. The long grass swayed joyfully, and the wind flowed like water. When Karthik and I were close, even small things meant the world to us. The emerald green beauty was connecting our emotions to natural sublimity. I had never seen such an awesome September sky before. I had never beheld such graceful rose blossoms. Karthik and I were in the park, overlooking the loveliness all around us.

Our hearts vibrated in the lush green oasis as the grass sang our names. The primeval freshness penetrated our souls like rays of sunlight.

"What is it that you're searching for here, Karthik?" I asked him, as he didn't make much eye contact with me today.

"Nothing. I want to expand." He fetched a blade of grass from the ground and twisted it with his fingers. "Kalki, after the death of my parents, my life changed. From Dad's champ, I became a poor chap. People began to treat me with sympathy that I didn't want. They started to look at me differently, regarding me with a disgusted countenance. I want to achieve something great in life and show them my true potential—the potential of an orphan."

"I know it hurts," I said with a pause as some quiet exchanges happened between us. "Many people looked at me with pity. Poor girl, she has a single parent." I paused and gently pressed his shoulder. "We can't stop anyone from saying these things, but we can change their attitude. After my success, the same circle of friends and relatives looked upon me and my mom differently. But our story is different from your story. Your pain is too deep, and your anger is also justified. Just . . . don't fixate on revenge. Why are you aspiring to show your capabilities to a bunch of unconcerned relatives?"

He nodded again as he listened intently to my words.

"Think larger, Karthik. Be great. Be extraordinary. When you create your own amazing story filled with grit and passion, I want it to be an inspiration to every struggling orphan in this world. Leave a trail of hope and determination behind. Don't try to settle any scores. Focus on your happiness and make others happy. I don't want a mansion, page-three publicity, a Swiss bank account, or any justice from my paternal side. My ultimate goal in life is to make my mom proud and happy." I looked up, staring at him to see if I could read his expression.

He was the picture of confusion, shaking his head to replace the old thoughts. My words flooded his entire system with surges of positivity, wisdom, and inspiration. The chaotic bin of disbelief, revenge, fear, and anger was getting emptied from his mind.

"Thinker larger. Think from a higher level," he murmured repeatedly, clapping softly for a second.

After a deep introspection—nearly fifteen minutes—he spoke. "Kalki, you are awesome. Sometimes, you just speak like your mom. So sensible, so wise. Damn, you changed my entire perspective in less than five minutes. Imagine, what will happen if you're with me for a lifetime." He raised his mischievous eyebrow, expecting an answer.

I gently tapped on his head and laughingly said, "Nothing. You will become a cook, driver, and an ATM." His head sprang up immediately, and there was an expression of happiness and surprise on his face.

"I'm a good fit for these roles." He blinked his eyes to tease me.

"Karthik, I haven't yet decided on this aspect. Mom wants me to focus on my career and if interested then pursue higher studies overseas. I'm keen on planning my future. However, there are some reasons why I'm avoiding it." I spoke with caution, not wishing to divulge the increasing frequency of my strange experiences.

"Kalki, the paranormal happenings are cutting down your interest and desire," he said, voice laced with concern.

"Mom told you about it?" I asked with soulful eyes.

"Everything. The entire version. I know all of it, and yet, I am here with you because I really love you. I could never express my love with expensive gifts or poetry or by throwing grand parties. Still, I swear on my mother's life that my love for you is unconditional. Whether you marry me or not, I'm there for you till the last beat of my heart—till the last breath draws out of my body." His words were true, and my eyes were blinded with tears.

"Karthik, I want you to promise me that if anything ever happens to me you will take care of my mother as your own mother." I raised my right hand, unclenched the fist, and turned my palm toward him to promise. "The universe is a witness to this promise."

"Anything for you. Whatever the shape of our relationship, if you're not here, I will take care of your mother as a biological son. There is no need for a promise . . . but only for your satisfaction." He placed his right palm upon mine, giving it a light press to assure me.

I felt light as if some heavyweight had been lifted from my head. Karthik's promise gave me an energetic power to fight with all the paranormal forces on the earth. Perhaps, this was the main reason that made me feeble.

"Kalki, nothing will happen to you. You can deal with anything that comes your way. I love you so much, I'd fight the Devil himself for you. When did you think I fell in love with you?" There was a twinkle in his eye as he expected an answer from me.

"When you saw me for the first time at my home?" I waited for his response, but he shook his head to give a clear no.

"You saw my profile pic . . ."

He rejected the answer. I tried every possible answer, but he rejected them all.

"I quit. Tell me. I'm anxious to know." I stood up, glaring.

His strong hands encircled my waist. Slowly, his finger slithered down as I stopped him to free myself from his overpowering grip. He moved closer to me, and I paused, feeling my heart in my throat as he bent closer. His beard line was touching my cheek, urging me to get closer to him as my heart soared. His lips curled up, and my skin went pale under the glory of his masculine beauty. He smiled and placed a tender kiss on my forehead. Abruptly, he sat on the bench with a bang.

"Oh blinking blimey! You will never know how much I love you. I have lots to tell but don't know in which order do I start." He gazed at me as I scooted closer to him.

"It seems there's going to be a mountain of unpackaging for me." He paused, recollecting the day. "I still remember the first time I saw you and fell in love with you," he said, his eyes sparkling with light.

"What? Love at first sight? When?" I cried with surprise.

"Yes." He paused for a minute.

Karthik's voice conveyed fleeting moods as he spoke. "Rains had drilled us down. The sky was battered with nimbostratus clouds, hauling stores of thunder and lightning. Most of the students were standing in the verandah, chatting and playing the usual pranks. I was also there in one of those groups. We were cracking jokes and betting to kill the time. We were looking at the main entrance gate, speculating on who the next person to arrive would be."

There was a momentary pause. We faced each other, and from the garden to an island, from the island to an ocean, from the ocean to different multiverses, we flowed into each other. I had never felt the calm delights of mutual affection with Abheer. Karthik glanced upward momentarily, savoring the nectar of my lips. The universe looked like an artist's heart. I lifted my hand to stop him.

"Please, let me hear the story. I can't wait to listen any longer," I requested, making him tell his own story.

Suddenly, you walk up with drops of rainwater drizzling from your head to your face. Dressed in a bright yellow top and denim jeans, it seemed the sunshine had washed you. A gust of wind sailed by, pushing your blue doodle-print umbrella inside out to soak you completely. There was a look of embarrassment on your face as you adjusted the umbrella layers. Then you hefted the straps of your backpack to hold it properly across your shoulders.

"The cold monsoon winds sent an instant shiver through you. No one noticed how you silently trembled and absorbed the cold currents. The wide red belt cinched around your waist made a loud style statement, and the latest iPhone model peeking from your front trouser pocket showed your trendiness."

"Wait," I yelled. "You mean to say the first time I visited Mom in her office, you saw and liked me? That day was my tenth standard (SSC) result day. Mom called me to her office to facilitate the certificates attestation for the upcoming college admission process. It was 2011, and I was sweet sixteen then."

He laughed a little. I continued to spin around him with interest.

"Yes, that was my final year in college. Meera Mam was not much into social media. Her Facebook and other accounts had limited posts like quotes, book reviews, nature images, and food photos. We knew she had a daughter but had never seen you before. In fact, she never posted any personal photos to avoid controversies."

He continued recollecting the moment passionately. “You walked onto the college verandah, asking other students for directions to reach Professor Meera’s office. As you stumbled across the group adjacent to our group, I noticed a rain droplet run from the outer edge of your eyebrow to your cheek. I’ll never forget that moment. It rests in my mind like a pearl in an oyster. The amber light glowing in your eyes sparked radiance around your face. You were so beautiful, shining like a damsel. That was the first time, after my parent’s death, that I really wanted something from life.”

He took a deep sigh, giving me a playful smile. There was an authentic tone in his voice that forced me to believe his every word.

“I knew I was in love—deep love with you. A longing love that was willing to wait for all eternity.” He stopped as tears filled his eyes—and my own.

Where were you all this while? I said in my mind.

He held my hand in his and said with a poetic accent . . .

“Oh, golden eyes that behold the sunrise,

How little of my love do you know?”

“Destiny had made my life a heated desert. Suddenly, you appeared like an oasis to quench the parched traveler.” His lips turned to me for some moisture, but I kept them dry on purpose.

“Tell me more,” I said, shaking his shoulder, insisting that he speak.

“You followed the directions and entered Meera Mam’s office. There was a queue of boys till the end of the passage to see you come out of the closed room. You were in your mom’s office for exactly forty-five minutes. We were counting the time on our watches," he said, giggling.

"Yes, Mom was extremely proud of me. She was in happy tears about my success. My father had called her to ask about my exam result; he wanted to congratulate me. I denied the request, feeling a bit sorry. Mom was trying to persuade me to speak with him. We had a bit of an argument over it. Then, both of them thought there was no point in making me unhappy today. My father told her that he would speak with me later. I was drying myself under the AC air while mom was reading the marksheet out to dad on phone. They were discussing my career plans. My dad assured Mom that he would bear my college expenses and tuition fees, even providing a chauffeur-driven car. I didn't want anything but finally, Mom told him to gift me a MacBook." I could clearly recollect the day as if I was living it again.

"Then, you came out with Meera Mam. On the way, Principal Sir and some other staff members came to congratulate you. You touched Principal Sir's feet, showing your traditional values, and other staff members appreciated you by hugging." He smiled with a blink in his eyes.

"I remember it. I had heard someone in the crowd saying, "Even we want to congratulate you."

Some of the boys were passing comments. "How did you score 93%? Please tell us. We aren't able to score even 39%." I remembered this, and we both laughed.

Karthik continued. "One of the students even shouted, "Mam, your daughter is very beautiful. We never knew. Now, we will attend your accounting classes every day."

He moved closer to me and spoke in a shy voice. "Eventually, the principal had to intervene as boys swarmed like flies around you. I was in the corner gazing at you. You were the star of the day. You followed your mom to the parking lot, still surrounded by loads of students to congratulate you. I saw you in the dawning light going away from me. Finally, you sat in the car, waving bye to everyone as Meera mam drove the car away. I didn't wave goodbye to you . . ."

The intensity of his words pierced my heart for undying manifestations.

Keeping aside the emotions, I pushed on. "You are five years elder than me. Did you not like any other girl in your college days? Also, I met you at the end of last year, and we started in a relationship this year—2019. In all these years, how come you never fell for anyone else?" I raised an eyebrow at him.

He spoke after another long pause. "Kalki, I was immersed in loneliness, guilt, and sadness. Meera Mam was working hard on bringing me out of the traumatic stress. I had fallen into a ridiculous hole dug by destiny. I was pulling myself up, clawing through the pit of darkness, when you loomed in front of me. It was the most brilliant and inspired moment of my life. For the first time, I heard the rhythm of my own heartbeat, and it desired you."

I attentively listening to his trusting voice, muting all the beeps and rings of my phone. I was simply amazed, not understanding how to react.

Reaching out, he tucked my wavering tresses behind one ear. He smoothly traced the curve of my face with his thumb, and his eyes sparkled like a diamond in the sunshine. He whispered, "I was loving you in silence. In loneliness. In dreams. I was praying hard to every force in this universe to bring you into my life."

I stared at the deepening blue sky as the wind unfolded every secret. His love for me was greater and purer than mine; it put me to shame. Feeling annoyed with myself, I said, "You were so close to Meera Mam, how come you never knew about me?"

He let out another sigh and said, "Ask your mom. We knew she had a daughter, but there were no pictures anywhere on social media. Some students may have seen you two together but not me. Also, I was away from social media due to my own insecurities. Mam, spoke about you many times, and I heard your voice on her phone but never saw you. The first time, when you visited Meera Mam in college, I came to know you were her daughter. It was a cherry on the cake for me. I thought God was giving me a second family as compensation."

His words rung true. Mom never changed the God Ganapati wallpaper on her phone or her profile picture on messenger. There was no purpose for him to create a false story when we were in a relationship.

"Were you stalking me?" I said as suspicion grew in my mind.

"No. Stalking is different. I was only loving you. I never thought we would be together. I deeply prayed for this union. I kept track through social media out of curiosity," he said, defending himself.

"My motive was clean, Kalki," he said in a humble tone.

"How did you feel when I was in a relationship with Abheer?" I asked as my eyes roved in the park.

"It made me sad, but my intuition kept telling me that you belonged to me. I prayed for a miracle to happen and here it is." He smiled and pulled me closer. We sat quietly in the park, listening to the birds, trees, and the breeze as our souls revived in the lush peace. I gazed into his dark brown eyes to see an ocean of emotions surging up and down, creating a tide-like situation. He leaned forward to kiss me goodbye. I saw his love with each goodbye kiss, knowing he didn't want me to go. We held each other in a strong embrace for the longest time possible.

***

On the way back home, I was high in spirits awakened by a sense of air being perfumed. Karthik's soft kiss was still impressed upon my glossy lips. The watchman opened the iron gate of the building, noticing me. I ran inside, speeded up the stairs, and slid the key inside to open up the door. I entered, pulled apart the curtains, and lit up all of the rooms.

Something wasn't right. I tried to suppress this feeling and poured positive thoughts into my mind. I was certain this wasn't a simple, ordinary night. To eliminate the cold feelings, I switched on the TV and increased the volume to max. Feeling secured, I went into the bathroom to refresh. I finished the process fast and changed into solid wide-track pants and a printed maroon tank top.

The sun had long gone down, and I was starving. Within seconds, my stomach began to rumble. I strode into the kitchen to make an apple milkshake. I sliced a few almonds and cashews to sprinkle on top.

I comfortably sat on the couch in the family room in front of a big Ultra HD Smart LED TV to relish the milkshake. Soon, I was stuffed, considering the last few drops at the bottom of the tall glass. I washed the empty glass in the kitchen basin with liquid detergent and kept it on the shelf.

I heard a rustling and went to the window to see the moonlight. There was no one at home. Mom had gone to Mamaji's place for a family get-together dinner. They'd pestered me to join, but I deliberately refused, wishing for some private time.

The dim lights in the room shook my heart. A wail of soft, refreshing air passed by. I sensed the inertia and wondered where the energy was coming from. I sat still until I heard something moving toward me. This was a clear indication that something supernatural was about to happen.

In a trembling voice, I asked, "Who's there? What do you want?"

I had seen many things happen in this house, but this seemed to be the strangest. I picked up my cellphone, as talking with someone else might break the spell. The network bars slowly disappeared, confirming the presence of . . . something. The landline phone was in Mom's room, but I lacked the guts to walk across the hallway. It could complicate things more if the apparition wanted to attack me. I sat still in a meditative pose, chanting "OM" but failing to concentrate fully. The TV was on, but it was making no sense. I switched to a spiritual channel to play bhajans and divine mantras. Still, the entity was present in the room. There was a chase going on between us, and I wasn't competitive enough.

There was a specter in the room; and despite all my efforts to create a positive ambiance, I wasn't able to find where it was hiding. There was no one in front of me or beside me or above me or beneath the sofa. I searched everywhere but couldn't find. Finally, I stood calm for a second and rotated my thumb on the third eye to unlock the psychic abilities embedded inside me. My eyes open wider, and my heart became stronger.

Suddenly, I noticed my backpack lying in a corner of the room. My eyes gleamed with a spark as I got the answer: BACK.

I abruptly stepped back, walking toward the mirror, downcast eyes riveted. I slowly lifted my eyes, peering into the mirror to see the apparition strapped on my back. Nothing showed up. I turned my back to the mirror, walked two steps straight ahead, and scrolled through the pictures on my phone. Minutes passed; then, I quickly opened the camera in selfie mode and held it in front of me.

"Got you," I said in a victorious tone. The apparition was a boy of 10–12 years. He was a cancer victim and had suffered more pain than his age.

"This isn't your age to be a ghost. Don't trap yourself in this dark world of ghouls and ghosts. Why play here, when you can play high up in the sky among the stars? Look there, at the shining gems. Don't you want to hold them in your palm and wear them on your crown? See the vast blue sky, for it belongs to you. The hovering clouds will take you on a free ride, and you can see the earth from there. Come back, whenever you're done playing there. See, the magical world calling you!" I pointed my finger toward the big window to show him the sky.

The ghost boy was leaping around, looking at the magnificent sky. He was yelping, and there was an excitement in his eyes—seemingly wanting to be there. He smiled at me, set on his destination. I extended my hand to touch him, and from the window, a neon-lit butterfly appeared alighted on my finger. The butterfly flew and started revolving around him, opening and closing its wings. The butterfly created a cyclonic vortex, tossing him into an upward spiral, seeking a portal to another world.

They said, in early Christianity, the butterfly was a symbol of the soul, representing the never-ending cycle of life.

I murmured as the wind swept the dust and presence. "Maybe an angel has come in disguise to heal him with its goodness."

I still wondered how I had encountered this spirit with so much boldness, courage, and power. These questions continued to revolve in my head when I heard the noise of the key being turned in the keyhole. Before I could get up to open the door, Mom entered with a gasping breath.

"Sorry, I'm so late. Even Vaishali had to leave early today. Hey, are you okay?" she asked, tapping my shoulder, awaiting an answer.

I didn't mention anything to her. Let her freshen up and rest. I was slightly trembling, remembering what had happened.

"You're hungry. Shall I make something for you to eat? Are you feeling cold?" she asked with concern. "Everyone was missing you. Your aunt wanted to pack a dinner. Grandma wanted to see you, too."

"Next time, Mom. Going to sleep now. Good night," I replied and went into my room, giving her time to settle down.

I laid on the bed, dreamlessly thinking of what had happened and connecting the dots. I was googling to find more information. It was becoming an endless puzzle for me. I wanted more information and true insights to fill the gap. Immersed in deep thought, my eyelids closed to put me to sleep.

I woke up in the morning with an urge to lie in bed all day and think. Mom knocked on the door, and after two or three minutes, slid inside.

After the paranormal happenings, I didn't lock the room out of fear.

Mom came and sat on the edge of the bed. I sat upright and said, "Good morning," politely. She caressed my hair and said coaxingly, "Kalki, tomorrow is Ganesh Chaturthi, the arrival day of God Ganapati as per our Hindu Vedic calendar. I want you to come with me to Grandma's house, dressed in a traditional outfit, and participate joyfully."

"No, Mom. I'm not going anywhere."

Her expression hardened upon hearing my straightforward reply.

I tried convincing her with a gentler voice. "After what happened last night, believe me, this is the last thing, I want to do. Please let me be alone. If you want, I'll visit a temple or any place that feeds me silence and solitude. Don't make me go over there."

"Okay, tomorrow there's a holiday. From the morning, I'll be at Grandma's place for the function. But let me make myself clear: I don't want you to be alone in the house. Go out with your friends and come back when I message you. I should be home by 10 p.m., but still, if you want to come, you're welcome," she said, stroking my hair.

I nodded my head respectfully. "Mom, sometimes in isolation we feel so rejuvenated. It's a nice way to connect with our inner soul. No book has a definite answer in black and white to my questions. It's important for me to self-introspect. I have no intention to hurt you, but please excuse me."

Hearing my request, she gave me a gentle hug. Then, Mom left the room and I walked into the bathroom to clean up. I stretched in the bathtub, which was filled with lukewarm water and lavender oil. The water felt incredible on my trembling limbs. I inhaled the scent of the lavender essence, and after a soothing wash, I walked out of the tub and got dressed in a casual outfit. It was today that I understood how a hot bath and clean pair of clothes could bring calmness to the mind. I headed to my workplace and switched on the laptop to occupy myself. Though I pretended to be busy at work, my neurons were getting confused and losing ground.

I was disturbed by the loud, irritating noise of utensils and various types of equipment in the background, but I felt safe knowing there was someone with me in the home. While working, I opened an incognito Google tab about parapsychology and pasted some excerpts in a Word document. The operating model on parapsychology is based on a variable cause and effect model. Parapsychology teaches us about ESP powers, which open the theater of our mind's eye. The most original and penetrating ESP thinkers open up about how to see the life of dead people when our senses are spinning. Speaking about ghosts and ghouls, parapsychologists teach us how to partner with such entities and develop a powerful bond with each type of ghost. Still, much of the information is yet to be comprehended by anyone.

With renewed inspiration, I spent the entire afternoon creating social posts for my social accounts, writing an article to be published on the High DA website, applying to new gig offers, and organizing the disrupted work calendar. By 5 p.m., I was pretty tired and went out on the terrace of the building to get the pure air of heaven. To pass the time, I called up Grandma and then my besties, Nisha and Asma, to get an update on their life. While sharing our social stories, I gazed at the different hues of orange, red, and gold that congregated together on the horizon, creating a perfect twilight story. As the beauty of twilight darkened, I sent the video recording to Karthik to instigate him with sensual delights. He replied with emojis because he couldn't find words to express his feelings.

I saw Mom's car sliding through the road toward the parking area of our society.

"She's back," I murmured to myself. I was on my way back home when the phone rang. It was Abheer's call echoing out loud. I didn't know how to respond to the incoming call. Every memory of him came with pain and sadness. I thought for a while, wondering if I should pick up or ignore his call. Remembering how he had treated me, I finally got my voice back. I ignored his call and put the phone in my pocket. The phone rang for the fourth time and then a fifth, and I peeped at the ID to ascertain if it was him again. Sure enough.

I lost my patience, typed my two sentences as tears swelled in my eyes. "I can forgive you, but I can't forget how you treated me. For God's sake, never contact me again."

After a few minutes, the silence remained. The phone stopped ringing, and there were no beeps. I stood there as an emotional cascade ebbed and flowed around me. The sky turned dark blue, inviting stars to grace the dusky stage. I stayed there for a while longer as my face looked gray and drawn. To change the tempo, I scrolled through the videos of Karthik and me, and soon, my mood called for laughter and rhythm.

***

I was at home at 7 p.m., and Mom was preparing dinner in the kitchen. I decided not to tell her about Abheer's call, as it would only worry her more. After the paranormal happenings, I decided to shield her from any unnecessary worry. I walked into the bathroom, splashed my face with water, and cleaned my hands and feet. Feeling clean, I sat down at my desk to check emails.

Just as I finished up my work, I heard Mom's call for dinner.

The dining room table was set for dinner. The aroma of good food wafted through the air greeting me as I entered the kitchen. We were seated at the dining table, and empty words were filling the empty space.

I looked at my mom. She was as beautiful as a white tulip—bright and warm on the outside, sacred within. She was filling my lunch plate with all of her love, persuading me to eat more.

"Kalki, listen to my advice," she said in a confident voice.

"Hmm?" I replied.

"Never disclose your finances to Karthik or any of your friends. Some matters should always be confidential. Never trust anyone with money or financial details. You never know. Money is a very strong motive in today's world. Remember, money is equivalent to the sixth element. Do read Chanakyanithi whenever you have time," she said, and her keen, wise eyes studied my expression very carefully.

"I agree. I will keep my finances confidential," I said in an obedient tone. The point she had made was definitely a valid one.

Dinner was over. We did the after-dinner chores together. The work is completed in half of the time, and doing it together is twice the fun. I went into my room and switched on the MacBook to back up my work. Mom entered to say "Good night" and assign important tasks for the next day.

I was seated on my work chair. She walked toward me and asked, "Is your work going alright? You need any monetary support?"

"Thanks, Ma. All is fine as of now," I assured her, saying that everything was alright.

"Do share your investment portfolio and income sheet with me. Also, please pay the utility bills for this month tomorrow," she said in a clear, commanding voice.

I made a note for myself on a blank Post-it Note lying on the desk. "Yes, Mom. Anything more?" I asked smilingly, rocking my chair.

Mom hugged me tightly. I wrapped my hands around her waist and buried my head in her concave stomach. She tousled my hair a little, rubbing my back with the palm of her hand to make me feel loved.

I looked down at the tiles for a moment, then moved my gaze upward to see her soothing but exhausted face. Her face depicted the ups and downs of her journey—the struggles and challenges have molded her resilience to weather the storm. I lost myself in a multitude of emotions as she said goodnight and made her way to her bedroom.

***

It was the morning of a great day. It was the first day of the Ganesh festival known as Bhadrapada Chaturthi. Mom and I woke up early, all ready to celebrate the arrival of Ganesha, the harbinger of new beginnings, prosperity, and luck. In

Maharashtra, the Ganesh festival is celebrated on a grand scale with love and the utmost devotion. Mumbai could hardly suppress its joy, and the city was spruced up with fairy lights, floral decorations, and vibrant colors to welcome God. For the devotees of Ganpati, the festival had a deeper significance than what met the eyes.

We looked out from the balcony at the bright street, which was filled with processions of God Ganpati. The processions consisted of two groups—family processions and Sarvajanik (public) processions representing each street, each market, or specific community. The spirits were high, and the day seemed uniquely bright. Crowds were dancing to the drumbeats, and whoops of "Ganpati Bappa Morya" were tearing the breast of the skies, which dripped rains. It was so amazing to see women decked out traditionally, thrusting their hips to the music. I took out my phone to record the live performance of women rotating in circles, playing the game of Phugadi. The music, dance, colors, and fireworks melded in a wild display of joint enthusiasm.

The high-voltage energy of the crowds made the concrete walls of buildings palpitate. It felt as though the processions would wrap up everything and take it along with them on the journey. Many families had gathered in their balconies to ardently welcome the lining processions. Everyone was immersed in the gusto of the festivity, and many were capturing the moments in their DLSR and mobile cameras. Our home was on the first floor of the building, giving us an opportunity to get a close view of the celebrations. The raucous men smeared red gulal in the air and maximized the explosion of fireworks to give us an adrenaline hit. The crowds sprinted faster, bellowing loud slogans into the air as the smoke and sound slowly pervaded every nook and corner of the nearby area. Idols of different sizes and shapes made for a glorious widescreen presentation. Out of respect, we folded our hands to the passing idols of Ganesha, seeking his blessings.

Seeing the vigor of the people, Mom talked about how a city full of contrasts, open to infinite possibilities of change, was growing to be a central hub. As we were engaged in an interesting mom-daughter conversation, my ringtone rang amidst the chaos of celebrations and conversations.

Due to the celebration noise, I couldn't hear anything. I sent a message to Karthik, asking him to speak on messenger. He asked me to meet him around 11 a.m. near the end road of our street to visit the pandals and see the big processions. I shared Karthik's plan with Mom, and she permitted me to see the city, especially during Ganeshotsav.

Mom reminded me that she would be going to her brother's home to be a part of the Ganesh festival there. She wanted to be there for the ritual of Pranpratishtha (breathing energies into the idol) performed by the priests—and other rituals like the prasad preparation. She also reminded me to cross-check with her before entering the home.

Karthik and I were loafing around the city. It was exciting to watch large processions bringing in big majestic idols and installing them in beautifully decked pandals teeming with dance and music. Karthik was recording the colorful vibes, spectacular views, and the robust energy of people to prepare a video documentary, MUMBAI 2019: GANESHOTSAV.

He also clicked the photos and videos to use them in his future web design projects and photo exhibitions. I loved the freedom; at least, it pulled me out of the momentary deadlock.

The fierce spirit of people from every class and category were rejoicing in the festivities, forgetting their pain, motivating me to choose life, career, and family, and leave behind the companionship of dead people.

The streets of Mumbai wore a bridal look decked with sparkles, colorful flowers, and bright colors. There was a line of kiosks playing the old festival songs and selling sweets and puja items to its customers.

As it was the first day of the Ganeshotsav, the queues were relatively small. Still, crowds thronged at every other pandal. Karthik and I visited the smaller and larger pandals to take the blessings of Ganesha. It was a fantastic to see the glorious idol of Ganesha, appreciate the decorations, taste the sweet prasad, and soak up a new energy. Karthik joined some processions for a dance, shrieking, “Ganpati Bappa Morya!” all the while. He even pulled me into the crowd to dance. I resisted at first but later turned up on the beats. We weren’t even hungry, simply roaming since morning, gathering enthusiasm and vigor from the atmosphere.

On the other side of the road, there was a petrol pump. I signaled Karthik, and he understood the rest. We walked to the petrol pump to purchase mineral water and a packet of chips. I gestured to Karthik and went the ladies’ washroom to pee. After coming out from there, I sanitized myself thoroughly.

We continued having the best time of our lives. I found myself getting in touch with my inner child. I had missed enjoying so many simple occasions that craft the essence of a contented life.

Karthik’s excited voice fell on my ears, overshadowing my thoughts. “Come sit in this taxi. Guess where I’m taking you.”

We sat in the taxi beside each other wordlessly. For some time, we both wanted space to check our phones and take a rest. I just remembered about the payment of utility bills and exclaimed loudly, "Bill payments. I forgot yaar."

"Do it now. There are a dozen of online apps for bill payments," Karthik responded. His voice was parched from yelling, and he was in desperate need of water.

"Drink some water, and please be quiet till your voice returns to normal," I said and opened up an app to do the online payment of all the utility bills. In less than ten minutes the task was done. I forwarded the generated receipts to Mom for her reference.

Karthik was sipping water, viewing the running street beyond the window. I saw the banners placed on the road and got a hint of Karthik's surprise.

"Lalbaugcha Raja," I said in a fairly confident voice. Hearing my reply, he chuckled and spoke in a tender voice he used with no one else. "I brought you here for a reason. This is the place where I prayed for years to have you in my life."

"Karthik, I haven't made any decision about the future of our relationship." I spoke in a humble voice to make him feel better.

"Kalki, your presence is enough. I didn't even believe you would be my girlfriend. Even these moments are precious for me. It's your life, and your decision will be respected." I sat astonished, listening to his words as he drew nearer and nearer with outstretched hands, beaming eyes, and a mild voice.

His love was unconditional. Like an overwhelming magnet-like force, he kept on pulling me toward him. We got down from the taxi, walking toward the Lalbaug market to reach the Lalbaugcha Raja Sarvajanik Mandal for the darshan of Mumbai's most iconic God.

We reached the entrance of the pandal. There were throngs of people queued in a series of parallel lines, and we joined them. Following the volunteers' instructions, we passed through a multitude of lanes to reach the final destination. Karthik engrossed me in talk as the line moved at a limited pace. We were in the queue for Mukh darshan, so the waiting period was less compared to Navas (Charan Sparsh) darshan. There was palpable excitement in the air. We entered the main pandal, which was decorated with artistic grandeur and replete with the strong aroma of incense sticks diffusing in every corner. The background of the pandal was covered with colored curtains, and the floor wore a skin of red carpeting. The entire arrangement was alluring and attractive, and the celebrations were thunderous. After standing in the line for an hour, we were fortunate enough to get a glimpse of God. The twenty-foot idol of Ganpati was embellished with gold ornaments and shining jewelry to attract maximum attention. Enthusiastic devotees were cheering and shouting "Ganapati Bappa Morya" to revive the festival with greater gusto. The spirit of the ever-expanding crowd was contagious, kindling a small flame in my massive heart.

As I folded my hands in front of the magnificent idol, peace and harmony reigned inside me. At that moment, I discovered an oasis of positive thoughts and strength. I felt like a pillar of light coming from the stage and entering my head. The realization dawned upon me that some things and moments come back in our life in some or another form. With all the things that had happened up to this point, I felt this Ganesh festival was a big reset for me.

After the grand darshan, we walked out of the over-crowding pandal by 7 p.m. Karthik purchased three boxes of prasad, red-colored threads, and a small picture frame of Lalbaugcha Raja to place on my work desk.

"I'll drop you off at home," Karthik said and started hunting for a taxi as we reached the main street. The roads were brightly lit up, people were freely roaming the streets without any fear, and the colors were filling every face with hope. Mumbai is a city that never sleeps, and during festivals, it's nothing short of explosive.

We sat in the taxi, peeking out at the dark, intimidating indigo sky. We talked, shared our photos, and craned our necks out of the taxi window to yell. The taxi stopped at the adjacent road across from my building. Karthik paid the fare as I called up Mom to check if she was home.

"Hello, Mom. Where are you?" I asked in a hurry as soon as she picked up the call.

"Kalki, I'm at home. You can come now. Did you enjoy yourselves?" Mom asked in a loving voice.

"Yes, we visited Lalbaugcha Raja. It was such an amazing day," I exclaimed as Karthik stood beside me to hear.

"Is Karthik there with you now?" she asked.

"Yes, you want to speak with him?" I asked.

"No, bring him along. I want to speak to you both about something," she said and ended the call.

"Mom has invited you in. Come," I said to him. We were anticipating the reason for this meeting.

"Did anyone complain to her about our dance on the street?" Karthik asked in an anxious voice.

"I don't know, Karthik. It's a special occasion. We don't do it every day," I said in a defensive voice.

Keeping silent, we walked into our building. Mom had kept the door open, so we entered and saw Mom seated cross-legged on the sofa reading some notes.

"Ma'am, good eve," said Karthik nervously.

I went inside to clean up a bit and change too. I made it super quick, sensing Mom's mood. When I came back, Karthik was settled in a chair and Mom was still reading something.

"Sit down," Mom said, gazing up at me. "I need to speak with both of you." Mom firmed up her voice.

"Ma'am, we were only watching the Ganesh pandals . . ." Karthik politely interrupted her. She turned toward him and gave him a look to be quiet.

"I met our family Panditji today during Ganesh Puja. In utmost confidence, I discussed your matter. I am sharing his explanation with you." She paused to see our expressions.

I moved a bit closer to her, and there was a sigh of relief on Karthik's face. Mom kept her eyes fixed on mine; then, she tilted her head slightly and sharply spoke. "It is mentioned in holy texts that the vast emptiness in the universe is Shiva. It is from this emptiness and darkness that everything was born, and everything will return at someday to the womb of Shiva. Maybe in this place of exceptional divine powers, we will find a suitable way."

We listened to her as she continued speaking with a force that made us believe her.

She went on to explain the significance of Shiva to us,

"Shiva is the principal deity of even the Tamas Gunas (darkness, destruction, chaos), and Bhutagaṇa means 'troupe of goblins and ghosts.' So, you need to worship Shiva and seek his blessings. Through Shiva's meditation, you will learn to awaken and internalize a few of these properties. I can't clarify the properties, as you need someone higher than me to guide you. Shiva is Bhoothnath. Bhoot means 'past,' and Nath means 'Swami.' Shiva has control of time, happening, and impact—hence known as Mahakaal (Timekeeper). So, only the God Shiva knows the climax of your story."

She stopped to drink a glass of water. Karthik looked at her and requested to say something. "Ma'am, will this definitely work?" he asked in a curious voice.

Mom raised her eyebrow. She looked at him and said, "Where is your trust? Ask a farmer who sows a seed in the field trusting in God for the rain. Ask a mother who bears her child in her womb for nine months. Not everything is a result-oriented experiment. Some things in life are based on a model of trust."

I looked at Karthik's face, his golden tan, long dark eyelashes, and strong lean features were absorbing the mythological talks.

Mom re-emphasized her thoughts. "Shiva is unknown because he is without a beginning or an end. As his name implies, he is infinite light and is contained within all dualities and contradictions. Therefore, there is no certainty or uncertainty. Even today, can you speak about a single thing with absolute confidence? We can experiment, but the outcome is never guaranteed. That is the only difference between science and spirituality," she said, smiling with a thin line.

Reading the apprehension in my eyes, she continued. "We all know Mount Kailash, the divine abode of Shiva and twelve Jyotirlinga temples in India, which collectively represent the body of Shiva. According to the sacred scriptures, these temples are awake and auspicious. Shiva appeared here in the form of an eternal light column. Out of these places, we selected Kashi (Varanasi) due to its spiritual significance."

Karthik interrupted. "After my parents died, my grandfather visited Kashi several times to discover peace and the eternal truth of life. I had been there for shooting documentaries on Varanasi, Ganges and Shiva, unraveling the truth of life. I have good contacts with local people there, especially the guides and the boatman." It seemed that he agreed with and supported Mom's decision.

Karthik began summarizing his opinion about Kashi. "No one can explore Varanasi in one trip. Even one lifetime isn't enough to do the synthesis of the city of temples, Ghats, and the ancient seat of mystic knowledge."

Mom thoughtfully said, "Panditji explained to me the significance of Kashi. I had some insight about the place but never deep-dived into it. Thanks to Kal, I got this opportunity also."

Mom recollected her conversation with Panditji and said, "Kashi is said to be older than tradition; it is the oldest living city on the planet Earth. It is said that the city rests on the trident of Shiva and never faces tremors. It is here in the holy place of Kashi that Shiva was set free from the curse of Brahamhatya."

She stared at us. The discussion was generating more excitement; we were experiencing a subtle flow of energy.

Mom showed us a sketch of the mandala and kept her index finger on the circle said, "A mandala is a sacred circle that represents the entire universe, its powers, its connections, and grounding centers of energy. Kashi is viewed as a Mandal through the mythical lens with mysticism in the temples and stupas that are a part of an ordered world. Hence, it is said that the energy in Kashi is powerful, the place is an energy center, and it is an energy source that can enlighten souls.

"Besides the mythological significance, there is a lot of science and mathematical logic prevailing in the ancient books found in Varanasi. Some 2,500 years ago, Pythagoras went from Samos to the Ganga (Ganges) to learn geometry." She browsed Kashi and shared the information with us.

Surprised, Karthik said, "France's greatest thinker, Voltaire, scripted, 'I am convinced that everything has come down to us from the banks of the Ganga (Ganges)—astronomy, astrology, metempsychosis, etc.' I wonder how it's possible." His curious eyes searched Mom's wise face for a revelation.

Looking at his eyes, which were clouded with unseen emotions, Mom said clearly, "I don't know, but give me some time to find an answer to your question. Like Mark Twain said, 'Benares is older than history, older than tradition, older even than legend, and looks twice as old as all of them put together.' Goswami Tulsi Das composed the *Ramcharitmanas* and the *Hanuman Chalisa* here, thereby changing Hinduism forever."

She stopped to sip few ounces of water. As the conversation intensified, I got up from the sofa and sat down on the patterned carpet by my mom's side. Seeing me, even Karthik sat by her right side to engage more deeply in the conversation.

"Mom." A thought immediately passed through my mind, and I placed my questions before her. "This is a place like other holy places in India. Who will give answers to our questions? A place cannot speak to us. How will we discover the solution without a map or a code or a book? Who can devise an apparatus to protect me from these paranormal forces? Who can show me the way?"

Mom returned her steady gaze upon me. She then spoke. "I am your mother. This is the exact question, I asked Panditji."

Karthik and I spoke together loud in unison—as one voice. "What did he say?"

Mom took a pause and said in a fearless voice that hammered our senses. "Aghori.

"AGHORI!" Karthik exclaimed in a louder voice, making my eyebrow go up.

He stood and spoke aloud. "Ma'am, they are dangerous. There is no doubt, they are powerful, full of ancient wisdom, well-versed in tantra-mantra, and worshippers of the Tamas-Gunas. They live in the cremation ground filled with ghosts, ghouls, dead, and disembodied powers. The Aghori even eat human flesh. They roam naked in the heat and the cold—so mystic and so powerful, they can break the walls between the limited and the infinite. But what if there is some kind of danger there? What if they want to take undue advantage of her ESP? Is this the only solution given by your so-called Panditji?"

"You have any other option to set my daughter free?" Mom spoke with powerful reasoning. They looked at each other, and Karthik's eyes conveyed a silent endorsement of Mom's bold decision.

Mom stood up and walked around the sofa to straighten the pillows. She was still for a moment. I got up from the carpet and walked around a bit.

Mom spoke with a thick accent. "Our Panditji feels only an Aghori can decipher this mystical puzzle. Since his grandfather's time, they would go to visit Kumbh Mela every year."

"Kumbh Mela, the largest religious gatherings on the earth backed by millions of sadhus, Aghoris, and akharas . . ." Words tumbled from my mouth.

"Yes," Mom said, willing me to be quiet till she finished speaking. My eyes sank under her glance. Then, she continued. "Panditji knows a few Aghoris that stay in the Varanasi jungles and visit the Ghats of Ganges at nighttime for meditation and for collecting the food. He has shared a contact list of some people who can help us to connect with them. These people are in regular touch with Aghoris for spiritual guidance and other activities."

Her eyes fixed anxiously on Karthik. He got a hint of what was expected to be done. He walked a few steps forward, took the paper from Mom's hands, and read it carefully.

"I know how to get things done. I will speak with these people and try to do get a favored setting for the meeting. Also, I will be contacting my known people there to help us meet any other equivalent Aghori if the ones mentioned by Panditji aren't available. But, mostly, I will emphasize meeting the recommended Aghori," he said with an undeniable passion.

"Okay, but when should we go to Varanasi? I mean, we need to do the airplane bookings," I said to Mom but stared at Karthik.

Mom opened the calendar app on her iPhone and checked few dates. After a couple of minutes, she announced, “These dates are best suited for me. We will arrive on Tuesday, October 1, 2019, in Varanasi, and our departure will be on Saturday, October 5, 2019. I will have a Sunday to rest and refresh before resuming work. Let me know if it works for both of you.”

“Ma’am, even I will be joining?” Karthik asked in an unbelievable tone.

“No, no, why would you join? You have to coordinate with Aghoris through Skype or Zoom. Are you serious, Karthik?” Mom rebuked him. “Don’t you understand you would be very much needed? Is this not your family? Leave me, at least to think of Kalki,” she admonished him lovingly.

Mom’s words instilled in him a sense of love and acceptance. He gently hugged Mom and said in a high-spirited voice, “Ma’am, I’m the CEO of my web development company. I’m available whenever you command.”

“What about you, Kalki? Do I need to mail any invite to you?” Mom asked in a sharp voice.

“Mom, I’m a freelancer. You know my office moves with me,” I replied impatiently to avert her anger. She was on the verge of losing her composure.

“So, done. Karthik, you can do the bookings. I will mail you our identity proofs and transfer our flight booking amount to your account number,” she said with finality.

“Ma’am, assume the task is done,” he said in a high-spirited voice.

"Karthik, don't think I'm taking advantage of you. If I had a son, he would be doing this instead of you," Mom said, rubbing his hair.

"Ma'am, I'm your son. Please, don't ever repeat what you just said now. You have my promise." Karthik's hand gently pressed my mom's hand.

"Karthik, have dinner with us, and then go home. You must be very hungry. First, I will get beet soup for both of you," she insisted.

"Ma'am, today is my fast," Karthik smiled and spoke.

"Okay, then have an orange juice. No more arguments," Mom commanded more sternly. She went into the kitchen to prepare the orange juice. Years of preparation had so perfected her routine that the best juice was made in the span of minutes. She came out of the kitchen, carrying three glasses of juice in a ceramic tray. We picked up our glasses from the tray, and Mom placed the empty tray on the dining table, sitting down with us to drink the juice. I just was raising my glass to drink when Karthik showed me breaking news of our city.

CLASHES BETWEEN AMBIKA AND ABHEER, WEDDING BELLS ON HOLD?

ENGAGEMENT ON FALLOUT FOR RAJPUTS AND SURYAWANSHI

"Leave it, Karthik. I'm not interested to read it. I have tremendous respect for Ambika—as my client and as a woman on the rise," I said, suppressing my desire to know the true story.

"Okay, sorry, Kal," Karthik said, forwarding me the news link on my messenger.

Eyeing me, Mom set her empty glass on the center table and said in a deep pitch, "Please, stop empathizing with him. The man was born to whine. If ever whining was a sport, then he would win an Olympic gold medal. A man should know to rule with an iron fist and love with a golden heart."

I made no comments on her statement.

"Do you agree with Ma'am?" Karthik asked, gazing at me, compelling me to speak.

"The sea is washed-out now. I can't swim inside it." I spoke in a remarkably strong voice.

While leaving, Karthik handed over the box of prasad and a small-sized Ganpati photo frame to Mom. He assured her that all of the arrangements would soon be made.

Mom said, "Karthik, do your best. But, at any cost, finalize the meeting with the Aghori. We have no other option now."

Karthik hunched toward her and confidently said, "Ma'am, believe me. I will manage everything. Leave it to me. If I fail, then I will never show you my face again."

"Thank you, my son," Mom said affectionately as he walked down the stairs, waving back at us till he disappeared.

"Let's see how our trip to Varanasi turns out," Mom said as we locked the main door of our home. "Kal, I'm very tired and going to sleep now. You can cook whatever you want and go to bed. Good night!" she said, looking brighter than ever before.

Mom held me close for a minute, her eyes curiously wide and eyebrows raised. "I hope we're on the right track. Trust me. Everything will be okay." Her words symbolized hope for survival—coming to understand all of those thoughts of origin.

I stared at the lunar beauty. The genuine poetry. The rhythm of its sacred flow to all of those who looked upon it. The beautiful Zira (moonlight) gives power to the emotions that are experienced in isolation. The night is a wonderful meeting spot—for opening up the conversations hidden by the harsh sunlight.

The quiet fears erode and flames of anxiety cool down as we sail under the starry skies in the night boat . . .

"I share some pieces and stories of life,
When the night curtains fall, exposing all
I know there is something deep inside me,
Is that fear? Uncertainty? Is that old anxiety?
That's cutting out a bit of my smile every day."

CHAPTER ELEVEN

THE MYSTIC ODYSSEY

After a few weeks, we flew to Varanasi, the epoch of mysticism and the place of spiritual quest. Here, at this place, the vigorous energy of God Shiva merges with the water element to take the form of the river Ganges. It is rightly said, this liquid energy of Shiva has secretly guarded the ancient secrets constructed under the cosmic Mandala layout of this city.

Call it Kashi, call it Benares, call it Varanasi; it has a veritable mind of its own. This supreme platform of Hindu Dharma is an interesting jumble of contradictions; spirituality versus dark science, sanctity versus filth, purity versus deceit, culture versus unevenness, wisdom versus superstitions, that will always remain and never be harmonized. Kashi has a cosmic linkage; the city is above the normal ground level, a part of an imagined landscape where mythology and topography are intrinsically interlinked.

Benares is timeless, stilled rooted in rites and rituals. This place is far abstract than other places embedded in a complex contextual frame. To linger in Benares is to be in an unknown era where the old is juxtaposed with the modern.

As per the texts of Sanatan Dharma, "Blessed is the soul of human being that is captivated in the breathing wisdom of Varanasi."

Maybe, I am not ripe enough to absorb the mysticism and mythological narratives of Kashi. Seeing through the lens of Benares, it is clearly evident, the entire spectrum of Hindu religion is represented in a microcosmic symbolism.

As the taxi drove us, I fell in love with the chaotic, disorienting timelessness of the place that lives in the past. The beautiful color-changing theme of the city depicts dynamism in the cosmos – the movements happening in the universe that change the pages on the earth. I inhaled the countless fragrances at every breath as the simplicity resonated within me.

The beauty of the narrow lanes surging with life in Varanasi is proverbial. I was inspired to get off from the car and wander in the narrow tapering lanes of Varanasi. Even Karthik, and Mom were taking a closer look at the local life residing in the holy city. Karthik was looking for the quintessential pictures that would complete his life photography album. Though the lanes were behind as we stride ahead, the insights of the lifestyle and culture of the people were engraved in our travel experiences. I was wowed by the driving skills of our chauffeur as he rolled in and out of the twisting, narrow, and overcrowded lanes. The streets were full of noise; ringing bells of rickshaws, animals moving leisurely on the roads, people conversing in groups standing on the edges, and shops extending their premises on the pedestrian walk. The local people glanced up from their newspapers to look at us with great interest, some young men did a whistling and giggling at me, however, I showed no response to their symptoms. The driver took the car ahead as soon as possible to avoid any drama.

"Death is woven in the fabric of Varanasi. Everything ends here," the driver said as we heard distant chants of Ram Naam Satya hai.

"Kashi Mriti Moksh Nirnaya - a new journey begins from here," Mom replied insightfully. (Kashi is not just about death but is a path to Moksha.)

It was taking a long time for the driver to reach the Old city. However, it didn't matter to us. We were adept in discovering the mythological presence everywhere and observing the various aspects of human life as psychological research.

The people living here know how to make a loud and bold statement that displays their eccentric personality, and extraordinary wisdom that is refreshing even in the global age. The place seemed to be supercharged, as our car moved forwards, we could feel the high voltage of energy transmitted to us. There was a roaring sound of bikes, the loud humming of cattle while crossing the roads, crumbling sound of some architectural piece, hissing sound of wires made by the jumping monkeys, and cries of children scuttling around to play. A lot was happening in a small amount of time.

For a minute, I thought of how Abheer, an inherent designer, would have reacted to this place - a bursting kaleidoscope of art and architecture. Kashi is a sanctuary for the spirituals and a heaven for the creative folks. The entire city is a manifesto of an old parchment that never deteriorates with age. The writings on the parchments are ineradicable, and the old layers are clearly visible through the fibers.

"Varanasi is older than history, if a city can preserve and thrive on its ancient past and heritage then it is obvious if my heart sometimes rekindles embers of my first love," I convinced myself for thinking of my ex-boyfriend.

The noises of the people brought me back to the present. Mom was settled by the window watching the whirring scenery - an endless, beautiful canvas of art. Karthik was clicking the photos of architectural pieces, people, and scenery. I admired the driver's precision as he rode the vehicle in the maze of street alleys. The city of lights was like a kaleidoscope, full of colors, symmetry, and connecting to open the third eye of Shiva located in our mind.

"I believe, Varanasi is blessed with a boon of virginity; no matter how many times you explore, it is forever pure and new."

Leave aside humans; every place is its own innovative stage, inventive scriptwriter, and imaginative storyteller. Find a place that has not yet shared its story either through excavations or topography. Why will Varanasi be an exception in this storytelling contest?

The dripping aesthetics, the confluence of mythology and history, and the powerful vortex of energy are intricately embedded in the way of living. As the vehicle rolled further, I wondered if this place will script the climax of my paranormal trauma. Will the indestructible and immortal city of Kashi end up the horrors that are rambling my nights? The place that hoards more than 23000 temples and the largest number of religious books will discover a solution to my problem? Kashi engulfed in all the divine powers of the Universe and Codes of Metaphysics, will decode the haunting puzzle of my life? On the mystic Ghats of Kashi, will these extrasensory powers die away, and I will be reborn as an ordinary human being?

A flood of emotional thoughts surged through me. Suddenly, the driver pressed the brakes, and I bounced back to the present. It was clear we reached the shore of our travel. Karthik was speaking with the driver about the trail ahead. The chauffeur parked the car in a corner that was not supposed to be used for parking. We got down from the car and followed a helper person deputed by the hotel for our pickup. We got down from the car and walked down a few steps to arrive at a meeting point on the Bhaisasur Ghats.

This is the first time; I placed my feet on the historical Ghats of Varanasi, and my mind swung open. I turn to see a strange shore never seen before. The sky above is another grand spectacle after the Ganges. The long, endless, winding sky appeared to be a lifetime mirror of the Ganges across all the lifetimes. They say the sky is the purest element that has an akashic record of every breathing being. I even extended my hand toward the sky to fetch my record from its vault. Mom thought I was pointing out something to her and she also scanned the sky for an answer.

The road toward the hotel was ahead. As we walked, the smoke, ashes, and dust blew to welcome us along with the salt wind. Two porters dressed in blue kurta and grey trousers came in front of us. First, they welcomed us with a benignant smile and then greeted us with a "Namaste" with their local dialect. They bent to pick up our luggage and deposited it in the motorboat. Boating is a family sport that excites everyone, and this boat ride had brought me to a stage of exhilaration.

"Our palace hotel sends a private motorboat to pick up and drop every guest. The main motto is to make our guests feel special and deliver them an awesome travel experience," the boat attendant said watching my joyous face.

One by one, we hopped up in the motorboat to embark on our mission ahead. We sat on the planks to get a better view of the ghats. The driver started the boat with a sputtering noise and off we went slicing through the Ganges waters. I touched the blue water to transfer the water energies in me. Our boats passed few ghats as we watched the activities of the people on the ghats. Be it on the backstreets or the ghats, the people of Varanasi are vibrant and alive. We were mesmerized seeing the splendor of the ghats. It didn't give me the answer to the question that brought me here. Standing before the massively lined up ghats in silent admiration, made me remember that I am an infinitesimally small piece of this infinity.

The attendants of Brijrama Palace on the boat offered us a welcome drink and mineral water to be hydrated. One of the attendants explained the history of each passing ghats, but I was infatuated by the ravishing beauty of the uniquely structured panoramic view.

On the banks of the river Ganges more than 100 ghats are lined up capturing the timelessness of the faith-scape. It was afternoon yet windy and the ghats were still filled with local people, sadhus, animals, and tourists. Each ghat has its own aesthetic identity unchanged from eternity and a story hiding behind every sundial. We had a short drive in the water and reached the shore of our palace resort in a span of twenty minutes.

As we reached the palace, we received a very warm traditional welcome from the Brijrama team, a spacious, royal palace resort located at a magnificent spot.

An elevator installed back in 1918 through the ghats carried us upstairs to our room. It was indeed a fun ride. Karthik had specifically booked the Varuna Burj room for mom and me on the high floor. The Burj is a semi-circular extension of the Palace wall with a turret that throws up a 180-degree view of the Ganges River. He booked the Nadidhara (Deluxe room) with a lit bit of Ganga River view from the window for himself. He had visited the place often and was not so keen like a first-time traveler. The only interesting thing about his room is that it opens to the gorgeous corridors of the palace along with the courtyard.

"Karthik," I whispered as we walked inside the palace hotel viewing the Maratha dynasty architecture in the palace. He looked at the small frown knitted upon my crown and asked, "What happened?"

I softly asked, "Why are you not booking the Maharaja suite for yourself?"

He paused for a second and said, "Not required. I will not be utilizing the room to this extent. We have come here to hunt for the Aghori baba. These people are really hard to find. They have no fixed place of residence or any contact number to connect. I need to go on a lookout with my guide and few trusted people."

"So, you will not be coming with us?" I asked in a sharp voice that was overheard by the passing members of the hotel.

"We are not here for a picnic. Meera mam has financed the entire trip with a clear purpose. I have to fulfill my obligations. I have only four days in my hands to get this thing done. Today is 30th Sep 2019, the day is almost gone, and we are departing on 5th Oct 2019," he gently shook me, speaking a firm hand that demanded no arguments.

"I promise you. As and when possible, I will devote my maximum time to you," he spoke in a little mild tone seeing my face turned pale.

I gave him a comforting smile knowing all his efforts were only for me. Karthik went to Mom and spoke something confidential. Both seemed to be determined to bring the matter to an end. He called out for another porter to carry his luggage and made his way to his cozy room.

The resort porter and a dedicated staff member accompanied us to our Varuna Bhuj room. The moment, I stepped in, I was spellbound on the spot. The sheer splendor and magnanimity of the room were beyond words. My eyes dazzled seeing the original artwork and precious antique pieces neatly arranged in the room to give it an elegant and traditional look.

Mom turned to the staff member and applauded them,"It really takes skills to add antiques in the contemporary mix. I appreciate the keen sense of your designer."

The staff member was delighted with the applause and left with a cheerful disposition. As soon as the person left, I sunk backward to toss upon the soft, luxurious mattress and glanced at the most iconic pieces in the room. Mom clicked the photos of the interesting stuff and designing patterns in the room to implement similar ideas in our home.

"I am totally intrigued by the palace, the royal experience, the artistic cavern, and the full open view of the Ganges from this turret," my voice was so very happy that I jumped out of the bed racing toward the turret.

"Isn't it expensive?" I asked with concern. She kept quiet and went on observing the artworks in the room.

"Mom, I am willing to contribute to the expenses," I spoke and then felt a bit guilty.

"Once in a while it is okay. Now, you stop asking me questions and quickly refresh yourself. I will take long to refreshen up," she said pointing her DSLR lens to a broad painting hung on the wall.

"It's 3 pm. I will be out by 3.30 pm," I said and entered the royal bathroom. A marble bathroom was built with classic antiquity and the best fittings inside to give you an immersive experience. I soaked in the hot water for a longer time than estimated. Finally, mom tapped on the door and called me, "Kalki, come out fast even I need to refresh."

"Yes, Mom. Only 5 minutes more," I replied and quickly finished my bath routine. I came out and Mom entered the bathroom. I wore denim jeans and a white top with peacock prints and a halter neck design.

Around 5 pm, we were settled in our room. I parked my laptop on a desk in a corner of the room to check urgent incoming mails. Mom spoke with grandma and her brother to ensure them that we have reached.

"Kalki," Mom called me. I walked toward her, gazing at her and wondering what she wanted to speak.

"You can have Hi-tea at the terrace with Karthik. I have scheduled a visit to listen to the live classical music at the main atrium. After the musical feat, I will go to the Panaya boutique shopping center located in the resort palace," she said with a hearty delight.

"You can do shopping later," I suggested to her. She pulled me to sit beside her and calmly spoke," Let me complete these minor tasks of buying gifts for friends, relatives, and colleagues today. From tomorrow we will be occupied with sight-seeing and visits to temples."

Kamalaya terrace offers a sense of intimacy despite an al-fresco seating arrangement that opens up to the panoramic views of the Ganges River and an endless horizon. Karthik was there gravitating toward the porch to feel the open air.

The Ganges wind was blowing his white denim shirt away from the skin. While looking at him, I saw his beautiful nature, willingness to do anything for me and my family. What more do you expect from your partner? Karthik has never given a "No" to any of our requests. He was always there when we called him and needed him. Like a farmer, he plowed love, care, and trust in our relationship to reap an abundant harvest of relationships.

On the other hand, Abheer had never practically done anything for me. Abheer was an expert in milling words and a master of only long conversations. He had never visited my home or invited me to his home. My relationship with Abheer was only a dark hole, where only I fell deep down in the pit. How come I was so blindfolded that I could not sense the absence of reciprocal love?

Karthik was in my life at this very moment. He has taken efforts to build bridges to come closer, he prayed to God for me, and more than everything, he waited for me to come into his life. His love is equivalent to pure meditation.

I looked at the sky above him. I looked at the Ganges in front of him. I looked at the wind playing upon him. He isn't affluent like Karthik. He isn't rich like Karthik. He isn't a spotlight like Karthik. But, he made me realize that all these things and materials are minuscule and temporary in comparison to the real human emotions of love and trust. Conversely, he has sunned up my darkening life with his brilliance and love.

He lies in my heart, I can feel him under my skin each time, he comes closer and closer. I am reborn every time his breath falls upon me like a diamond reflecting on crystals. My life with Abheer consisted of silence, discipline, the all-good approach, the high-energy work discussions, the appraisals can never be fired the embers of love. It never had a spark to create fire, a wildness to savage upon one other, to taste the nectar that spilled from our lips, or to lay outstretched in each other's arms contemplating each other's body art.

Karthik stood there looking at the birds flying high in the sky. His physique spills a magical charm to change my mood from lovelessness to deep love. I walked toward him, standing next to him, to smell his musky cologne mixed with his own sweet masculine body scent. I glanced up at him wanting him more than ever but still holding on to myself. Karthik ran his hand upon my back slightly down till spine and then hugging me close.

"Everything will be fine, I will get you out of this mess," he said lovingly. The desire of pure lust shone on his face.

"Be seated," I purred softly, drawing him close to a seating arrangement sectioned for two people. I called out the concerned person stationed at the Hi-tea arrangement for the tea and snacks servings. He sat and cast his eyes down to resist his kindling desire. I trusted him even at such tender moments, knowing he will never betray my mom.

He pretended to scroll the messages on his mobile and said, "I am calling up all my contacts to find the whereabouts of Aghori. During the night, I will personally go out in the forests with Raghav (my guide) to search for him. It will be a long dark travel."

I heard him out and we continued to sip tea and munch on the tasty finger chips.

"Will you be safe? Do you want me to join you in this exploration?" I asked knowing he will never agree.

At the first reaction, he barked upon me, "Are you crazy?" Then he rephrased in a mature tone, "We will be roaming in the forests, not in the waterpark. You are brave but I am accountable for you. If anything happens to you, I will not have the guts to face Meera Mam. Please have some empathy for me."

He pressed his finger firmly against my pulse. "Listen, Kalki, I am not new to this place. I know it in and out and also, I know many people here. But it will be difficult to go on a search with you around. Once, I meet the Aghori Baba, I will speak about you and get you to see him." He said with a monotone but firm voice.

"I understand but keep messaging me," I said as we glimpsed into each other's eyes to come on fire.

"I cannot assure you. It is important to save the battery to use a flashlight in the thickets and also for urgent communication. I will carry my power bank but still the reserve is for exigencies. Please don't call me also. I may not be able to come for sightseeing in the morning if the search continues for long in the night." Karthik convinced me to set him free and simply trust whatever he was doing.

I asked still more pressingly than before, “What about your dinner? We can have dinner together and then you can go ahead with the search?” I literally prayed for a positive reply from him.

He remained mum for a moment and spoke gently,” Isn’t it important to have dinner with my local friends, create an atmosphere of unison and then go out with them for finding the Aghori Baba. You tell me?” His eyes darted at me for an understanding answer.

There was a pause. I didn’t speak and he didn’t ask. At such times, touch is more effective than the yarn of words.

He leaned close, gently touched my cheekbones, and rubbed his thumb on my chin. I could see my reflection falling in his hazel eyes, desiring to be in his skin. As a result of the desirous gazing between us, he opened his mouth to divert our attention, “You should take rest today, and from tomorrow you can explore these ghats, temples, alleys, and the Ganges aarti in the evening,”

I nodded while checking a few beeps coming from my phone. He continued speaking, “I will leave at 8 pm to meet my friends, have dinner at their home, and then around 10 pm we will embark on our search journey,” he explained his entire schedule and then took me in his warm embrace.

A waft of wind passed between us, calling us to join on a wider expanse. His heart whistled to my heart as we held each other a bit closer. Our emotions were incomprehensible, how can our finite set of words define our infinite longing. I let my heart winked its eye to express the fullness of joy beholding inside me. Karthik changed my definition of first love. He is a miraculous being flooding me with love that percolates through my pores as radiant rays.

His steady footsteps pursued their way out of the terrace. Slowly, I watched as his silhouette disappeared in the darkening twilight. At this moment, I would have loved to sink deep in his arms, leaving behind the chaos of life.

I heard the musical symphony of birds as they warbled high in the summit of heights. The voices of birds blended harmoniously with the other sounds in nature. The chirping of the birds increased as they flew north. Above them, there was a loud boom noise though it brought no rains. The twilight transformed into the grey light, bringing the ghats back to their quickened pace and active mode for the preparations of the Ganges aarti.

Take me away from the stress, sounds, and sources; make me a glistening drop in the Ganges. Make me a stripe in an infinite sky, let me tear open the fiery wounds of my heart to pour down in form of the cooling rain.

I went back into my room and sat at the turret watching the silently rising waters. Sometimes it wept, sometimes it moved rapidly, sometimes it leveled up and sometimes parted away from the other waves knowing this was the last meeting of life. That's how I think life is made up of simple and ordinary emotions, sometimes a slight or a big disruption happens that sweeps the entire coast to recreate a new pattern.

Mom walked into the room with bags filled with big and small gift boxes. I pretended to be excited over the gifts as she shared the photos of the items. After a general discussion on the total expenditure on gifts, and the allocation of gifts, she kept the gifts in the closet. It was already 8:30 pm, and we decided to have an early dinner as we had not eaten lunch.

Mom and I strolled in the palace resort. We had a stellar gastronomical dining experience that is more than just about the food served on the plate. Every morsel of food had a way of keeping intact with our origin, our culture, and traditions that weave us together in a common palette of taste. I added tags and shared the spectacular image of food dishes on social media to seek social applause. Somewhere, in the deep cavern, my heart was tracking Karthik's whereabouts.

"Is he fine?" I asked Mom raising my eyebrow.

"Oh, come on. This place is his second home. He has a number of official and unofficial contacts here. Many of his contacts are the grassroots people that are important and influential to execute such tasks. Always remember, I care for Karthik more than you," she said patting my left cheek.

"Do you want to walk on the ghats?" Mom asked to get me out of Karthik's thoughts.

I didn't speak anything except walked up to my bed feeling guilty for Karthik.

Mom pulled me near and said, "Kal, you have come to such a beautiful palace, don't be a moving and breathing statue. Take care, Good night." She replied stroking me on my back.

Darkness was deepening in the skies. I wore my nightwear dress and put on a smiling face before going to sleep. A message notification buzzed on my mobile. I read the message banner and kept the mobile down.

"Hear him out once," Mom said eyeing me from another corner.

"I am accessing your MacBook to check some urgent office

mail," she said and walked toward the desk where I had set up the Mac.

"Hear, who?" I asked her what she meant.

"The one who messaged you," she said with a kind of sarcasm.

"Do you know who messaged me?" I said with an agitation that was so strong I could say no more.

"It's Abheer's message. Your facial expressions already spoke to me," Mom said to make her point.

"The truth is that I cannot swim in a washed-out sea," I screamed in an angry voice.

Mom spoke calmly, "I am not telling you to reconcile with him. Listen to what he has to say and accept his answers with all your heart. It's all written in destiny, sometimes, things fall apart so that more amazing things can blend together. Just speak and finish the matter."

She walked up to me and rubbing my hair said," Speak with him with a happy voice, keep your head high, and show him there are lots to be happy about in life. Don't show him that you were affected by him."

I reflected on her words. The more I thought, I was internally convinced about her logic. I went out of the room for introspection.

With great guts, I picked up my phone and called me up instead of conversing on messages. He picked up my call and said, "Hi," but my heartbeat didn't shoot up this time.

"Abheer, I hope you are fine?" I asked him in a voice so loving he had never heard before ever.

He was quiet like absorbing some type of shock. After a

pause, he said in a faint voice, "I know there is no point in apologizing to you. I will not ask for forgiveness. Let's focus on our future and give up everything that weighs us down," I interrupted while he was speaking.

"Fair enough," he gave a long sigh as it came from the very beneath of his feet.

"Now, please let me speak. My dad called me to attend the party and declared my engagement proposal with Ambika. It was an unexpected turn of events for me. For the sake of family reputation, I couldn't back out before the Rajput's, media community, and high profile guests. It took me so long to accept the fact that Ambika is my fiancée. I visited her office many times to speak but couldn't do it. She is a very dominating character, and I am totally lost with no one trying to understand me," his voice shook along with the words. I heard a very faint hushed sound of crying.

"Abheer, I don't know how a normal person will find a way out of it but you have a powerful creative outlet. You are an ace designer; you are a pro in creating your own expressions. This is your testing time, and you have to creatively craft a way to come out of it. For years, you have designed the best products and ideas. Now, design your own future - that connects, builds a chain of trust, and takes ownership of your relationships," I consoled him not thinking if he spoke the truth or lied.

"One more thing, Abheer, please take care of Ambika. Don't worry about me. I have found a loving and caring partner. Our roads have diverged but we are friends for life," I spoke in a voice that understands the musical lyrics of life.

"Kalki, thank you for giving me the best always," he said

realizing that we have drifted apart. His voice echoed in the darkness.

I felt lighter after speaking with Abheer. I had loved him for years but now, I am drowning in the ocean before the storm. Holding on to these thoughts, I went inside my room and laid down on the bed to unwind.

The past doesn't impact me and I am not keen on settling scores or holding on to grudges. I am intoxicated in Karthik's love, wrapped in his ecstatic charm as he shackled down my ordinary life to recreate a marvelous living experience - where there are no more walls.

CHAPTER TWELVE

THE INNATE DISCOVERY

A mystical aura lingers across the waters of the Ganges River. It is wrapped with the faith of innumerable devotees, echoes the sounds of tinkling bells, and sends the fluttering prayer flags to the sky. The myriad waters are laced with religious life spilled out since the making of history. Even the Gods in heaven with all their might cannot erase the divine and purifying powers of the Ganges River that have mothered living souls without any discrimination.

There is an unspoken passion that pulls us to the enchanting melody of the wave stirring the discreet impulses of the soul. The quietest spot sprang out of a recess in the river Ganges where we discover a longing of our voices pouring through the sunbeams, waters, stars, and tiny blades of grass. Here, at the edge of the Ganges, my perplexed soul roams in a playful extravagance searching for its purpose as well as its perils, its visions as well as its ruins.

I learned in Geography; a large number of tributaries join the Ganges to create the world's largest river delta and then change the course to continue their aqua exploration. People are also river-like, ingenious and intelligent; they know when to join and when exactly to leave.

The greatest rivers on the Earth – Ganges, Nile, Mississippi, Yangtze, Mekong, and many more have widened and deepened as they coursed through the thicks of nature. Do you know how they grew into mighty rivers? These rivers are always on the move; sometimes surging, sometimes flooding, sometimes breaking the boundaries, sometimes creating a tsunami, and sometimes, eddying on its back to kiss the sky.

A damn freshness that blows off the waters, cleansed my face. I bent near the water to see my reflection in the gleam of the water, an opulent thought diverted the melancholic storm.

"Why am I not like a river?" I asked my inner mind.

"Why did I allow these emotions, pain, and fear to deteriorate the spirit of my mind? Sometimes, I had these hot impulses of quitting, sometimes, I had uncontrollable gusts of sorrow and strained each nerve to the greatest possible effort."

I bend further in the water; its pristine beauty soothed me. I had an innate desire to encircle in her physical warmth like an infant seeking cradling.

I heard a soft voice speaking to me, "Instead of admiring these incoming and outgoing tributaries, isn't more imperative to empower a powerful personal shift that enriches my wisdom and fighting spirit. Why am I allowing some dead souls to make me a canal that can irrigate their afterlife goals and aspirations? No one can decide what I want to be and do in my life without my permission except my mother."

I had pulled myself out of the bed in the early dawn to experience another boat-ride with Karthik. The last time, we sailed together across the Rankala Lake, and now we are on another boat-ride amidst the Ganges River unfolding a very tender moment of our romantic life.

The rowing boats were in readiness on the Ganges. Seeing the magical-looking bioluminescent waves, I had the emotional urge to dissolve in the foreground skin that was a picturesque scene of a fresh, reposing, and calm beauty. The sun scattered its tangy golden rays around the landscape to repaint it with a lovelier and prettier look. These subtle batteries of nature inhale a delirium of delight that intoxicates our senses.

We gazed into each other's eyes blending in the beauties that lie far outside the domain of articulation and expression. The birds were singing sweet songs, the winds were playing stirring music, bringing every strand to life. Our heart was filled with delicious musings that were sweeter than the flowers tinkling at our side. The basket of wild roses on the boat, with their dark coloring and strong perfume, clustered desire of intimacy inside us. I touched the raw flesh of his earlobes pinning down my wilderness.

The strong, tanned hands of Kissan, our oarsman sweated as he pulled the oars in a pendulum stroke, in reassuringly perfect synchronicity. The oarsman was known to Karthik, and he was engrossed in telling us adepts of the past that created this holy city and the structured linings on the ghats. An awful and sublime mystery drenched me as I stood on the bridge of the boat staring at the most geomantic architecture ever made on the Earth.

The soft bellowing of chants, walloping of bells, hustling of peoples converged a harmonic background to the scenery on the Ghats. There were eighty-eight ghats on the banks of river Ganga.

Kissan was taking us through these spiraling structures explaining in short stories their distinctive and timeless character. Listening to the heartbeat, I longed to embrace the breathtaking beauty of the intricate structure of Ghats. This is a very deep love - a whole new way of loving and relishing love without a slight touch.

Our body steered forward to witness the end of the wide spectrum. Compared to the turbulence of noise, movement, and sound playing on the other ghats; Manikarnika Ghat is consumed in grief, silence, and smoke. This is the place where the ultimate scheme of the Universe is executed with great sanctity. Manikarnika Ghat is called Mahasmashan, the Greatest Smashan which speaks of life and death in the same breath. At this burning ghat - the gateway to heaven, we have a non-stop celebration of death. My ears imported the remorseful chants that are sung every hour.

"Not a single day passes when dead bodies are not cremated here. On an average 2-300 cremations happen here every day. Come and watch from here the unusual and never seen anywhere - Tourism of death," Kissan spoke with a full and unwavering faith.

"Hindus from all over the country bring their dead near and dear ones to cremate them here and free them from the cycle of liberation," Karthik said and pointed his finger to the engulfing smoke and blazing embers spiraling upwards from the burning pyres.

As our boat inched closer to the ghat, we heard the chants of "Ram Naam Satya Hai, "and smoke blending in the air leaving behind a trail of faint echoes and booming cries. It is only here in Kashi, the cremation ground in the navel of the city.

Kissan moored the boat and got a cutting tea for all of us. Looking at the flaming embers, he spoke in a local accent, "The southern end of the ghat is loaded with huge stacks of woods that are used in the cremation. You will find Dom workers and Purohits working here to meet their livelihood."

I clicked images of the monumental relics that narrated stories of a more prosperous past. Though, these looked worn and faded standing at the same place since centuries, they are still active and full of radiance.

"Ma'am," Kissan called me.

I turned to him. He seemed excited to show me something. He lifted his finger showing a spot at the ghat and said in a joyous voice, "A fire burns here twenty-four hours. You will not believe but the fire has never extinguished even in the toughest storms and strongest floods."

I glared in half-belief and half-disbelief, capturing the spot on the lens of my mobile.

"Some facts here are to be believed with faith," Karthik said with a smile seeing the doubting expression of my face. He continued saying, 'Legends say that this is the eternal abode of God Shiva. He roams here in the nights; surrounded by ghouls, ghosts, and dregs as they dance and meditate in the darkness. In the day, God Shiva lingers in form of energy charging the vitality of the mankind."

Karthik seemed to be far more knowledgeable than I had

anticipated. My mind was jogging through the deep dust, looking into the far away shores of the Ganges with a quenching thirst for wisdom.

The burning pyres chewed and puffed out, clouds of volcanic ashes enveloping the top-most sights of Manikarnika Ghats. Loud chants of Shlokas and Sanskrit mantras echoed, bursting the stones into flames. I inhaled deeply to filter the energies of aura encompassing around me. The three-color bands of charcoal, red and yellow highlighted the full premises of Manikarnika Ghat.

At one place, we saw a group of people breaking out a loud lamentation. In between at regular intervals, there was an uproar of grieves and mourning from the crowd. A corpse wrapped in white cloth was lying at the edge of the river, waiting to be thrown out to the Ganges.

"Why is this corpse deposited in the waters instead of lighting it on the pyre?" I asked Kissan the reason, he looked at the aggravated waters and said in a tone of pity, "Ma'am, not everyone is cremated as per our Hindu religion. There are exceptions: the dead bodies of holy saints who have renounced the material world, children below five years of age are considered to be sinless, people died of snakebites, leprosy, and smallpox are buried or taken to the middle of the Ganges and dropped to the bottom of the river with a weighed stone."

"But why so?" I asked out of curiosity, not able to understand the spiritual logic governing these cremation laws.

"Ma'am, these practices are based on the fundamental tenets of Hinduism - it depends on the transmigration of soul and reincarnation," he said in a voice that spoke the quoted texts.

"Sometimes, even the corpses of suicide, murder, and other

victims drown in the river, it is believed that these souls will not gain liberation," Karthik said and then, hummed a popular tune under his breath.

I watched as the river took the corpse in her bosom, cradling it with love, singing a soft lullaby in its ears, and taking it along with her on a higher journey. Some of the people in the other boats shrieked with fear or made gruesome faces and requested the boat to be driven off from the spot. I remained calm, running away from any place or question is not the solution. The oarsman steered back, as I bade goodbye to the thickening clouds of ashes that hung over the ghats of Manikarnika. The embers cast huge flames on the throngs like fireworks celebrating the eternal feast of death.

River Ganges braids strands of life in all the things that flow. Known to be a divine figure as per the Vedic Hindu scriptures, it is also a bed for the poor, income livelihood for the boatmen community, a refreshing point for backpackers, and a source of life for the entire community.

The three-hour boat ride was a thrilling experience, and more than that it was an awakening call. Though a skilled content writer, it is not possible to write down everything across the line on the blank pages. I have heard the slang, "Make it Large," but Varanasi taught me, "Make it alive," and I am focused on it like a laser beam.

After the boat ride, we debarked and spanned across the Ghats to get an insight into daily life. Karthik shooed away the beggars and children selling various tiny items consisting of marigolds, shells, and candles for money. There were clusters of people on the ghats engrossed in networking or doing their routine activities. I watched with amazement as men and women dipped in the water to cleanse without any shyness or sexual harassment. The oarsmen had stationed the boats in line at the river-banks to do brisk business. The season was on and the demand was high to fetch customers toward them. I ran up and down on the ghats, spun around the interiors of the ghats in complete freedom making Karthik more nervous than angry.

"Kalki, this isn't funny. Please stop, why you are behaving like a kid?" he started shouting and searching for me in the winding alleys. Ignoring him, I continued to roam and hide in the winding alleys, sky-reaching minarets, and amidst the ruins of constructs. I could see the fear on his face, the way his eyes began to blaze over.

I could hear his continued shouts, "Stop, enough, Kalki. Come out, or I will leave and go."

The flowers blossoming on the trees were taking my breath away. The white birds spreading their wings glided across the air, setting my spirit to soar high with fond delight. Karthik followed, breathless without hesitation, pleading me to stop. He even warned me about complaining to my mom. I ignored his futile threats with peals of laughter.

I was racing around a very narrow ravine caring for nothing. Suddenly, a wild-haired, matted long-bearded sadhu in their trademark orange robes and rudraksha beads garland came and stood in front of me. He had a strange look on his ash-smeared face, but in the dark hollows of his eyes, a fire had begun to rise. Frightened at this fierce looks, I nestled my glance down at his feet. His bare, calloused, and cracked feet showcased his wayfaring lifestyle that scorched to reach the ends of the earth.

"Bam Bhole!" he exclaimed in a hoarse voice of ungovernable rage.

I stepped an inch backward. He lifted his right hand in a blessing posture and fumbled indistinctly. His black-stained teeth flooded with a disgusting trickle of red saliva produced from his betel chewing, which he jetted out at regular intervals. Every moment increased my fear and disgust, but I was under a trance of his solemn, stern, and unearthly glare.

He drew a weird smile on his face and spoke in a low but confident voice, "Where will you hide from them? They will follow you everywhere?" and then he spurred into loud laughter that sounded more grotesque and frightening than the roaring blast furnace.

I stammered for words, for sentences but could barely get any word out of my mouth. I stood in a jumbled state of mind; the sadhu was still monstrously laughed on.

Karthik grabbed my arm from behind, interrupting my stuttering. Every nerve and fiber of my body quivered like a leaf shaken in the storms. I clung close to Karthik's chest, unaware of the proximity. The sadhu stepped forward and put his hand in a metallic vessel. He took out some ash which he held in the palm of his hand. Karthik didn't stop him for reasons best known to him. The sadhu leaned close, pasted the ash on my forehead, and uttered few mantras. Scalding tears were flowing from my eyes, and my whole body was shaking with fear. My feet wanted to be transported in his manly arms. His one hand encircled my waist, and his other hand wrapped my back. For the first time, I felt a kind of love in his embrace that I had always longed for since childhood. I sobbed hard on his chest. He wiped my tears with his handkerchief and tenderly stroked my back with another hand.

The sadhu smiled in a villain style. I pressed closer to Karthik. The sadhu scared the hell out of me by removing a human skull from his bag and bringing it in front of me. I had a fearful reaction seeing the skull. Karthik yelled at him and asked him to leave immediately.

The sadhu laughed more powerfully and said, "This is our place, you leave, travelers. You will not find for what you have come here." The face of the sadhu was fearless, he observed me and said, "This is your abode. Discover yourself here."

Karthik was a lot enraged. He pulled me closer, taking me along, and he started walking away from that spot. My fingers were tightly clutching his shirt. We walked past the alleys, and narrow lanes lined up with sweet shops, souvenirs shops, and Kiosks selling puja items. Thankfully, people were busy in their works and were not dotting on us.

We reached the front of the gateway of the most sacred temple - Kashi Viswanath temple. Tears profusely sprang from my eyes as the images of the sadhu's red saliva, ash, and skull replayed in a slideshow before my eyes. Karthik tenderly moved me aside and glanced through the crowd. In a blur vision, I could see him speaking with someone on the phone and guiding with directions.

The words of sadhu echoed in my ears like an explosion. I trembled like a leaf in the hurricane. I could see Mom hurriedly coming out of the temple's gate toward me from a distance. Karthik swiftly passed through the distance to explain everything. She gave the yellow-colored puja bag filled with garland, idols, a bottle of Ganges water, and sweets to Karthik. In a fraction of seconds, she stood before me like a

Mommy range, stretched out like a huge fence to protect me.

Karthik was giving information to Mom about the incident. Mom asked him to be quiet. She caressed my hair and said in a soothing tone, "Kal, have you not seen more monstrous, dreadful, and deadly ghosts then how can a sadhu impact you to this extent. I am here, and stop crying like a baby. Come on, be a grown-up, there is more to life than such small incidents."

Mom turned to Karthik and asked him in a strict voice." So, why did you not take good care of my daughter?" She even pulled his ear playfully to make me laugh.

"You have to be stronger than the bolt, girl," Mom said and pulled me in her maternal shade. She held me in her warmth giving me some time to settle down. Karthik got a cold bottle of mineral water. Mom made me drink it to calm down. After a long outcry, I was physically exhausted and requested Mom to take me in the room for some time.

Mom agreed and we walked toward the palace resort through the ghats.

"How was the boat ride?" Mom asked us. Karthik didn't give any reply.

"So, no one is telling me how the Ganges cruise was?" Mom asked again waiting to hear my voice. I remained silent, thinking and analyzing the words spoken by the sadhu.

We walked on the steps of the ghats to reach Brijrama Palace resort. There was a good distance to be covered and we walked in small paces.

"Karthik, you tell me how the boat ride was?" Mom looked at Karthik hoping it will help me open up. Karthik gave short answers to Mom's questions.

"I think both of you should visit the Kashi Vishwanath temple tomorrow early morning. Both of you can read the legendary story of this temple on Google," Mom said, waiting for my audible voice to fall on her longing ears.

The words of the sadhu seemed to have pierced not only my ears and mind but every fiber of my frame. Mom's words fell upon my ears. I looked at the sky promising a heavenly trust, and the sweet murmurs of the Ganges moved the tenderest chords of my heart. From the vibes of the air, the immense creative energy in the waters, and the sunshine, I swung back in optimism.

We sat on the steps of the ghats for a momentary pause. I closed my eyes for a minute and experienced the supreme expression of Shiva-Shakti.

"Mom," I awakened myself the black chasms and said in a concrete voice, "Every tattva produced on the earth is present in Kashi. In this place, where rhythms, rituals, and rites blend, the Great God of cosmic order surveys the entire domain of creation. This is the omnipresent Shiva, present in the divine amalgamation of five elements - water, fire, air, earth, and ether."

Both, Mom and Karthik gave me a blank stare.

"Did you google all this stuff?" Karthik asked in amazement.

"No, sometimes, these thoughts just weave in my mind. It just a bit of reading and logically connecting," I casually replied.

"Well, then, that is very smart of you," he applauded my skill of applying theory in a practical framework.

"Karthik, she is my daughter after all. I have taught her how to learn, think, experiment, rethink, and relearn," Mom said taking pride in herself. I gave a smile acknowledging her natural talent in teaching.

"Continue, dear," Mom said, gently tapping my shoulder.

I took a deep sigh, breathing in the essence of life, and spoke in a strong tone, "These five elements reignite the creative force in the Universe. The energies of these elements are both exoteric and esoteric, permeating and purifying our body, mind, and soul."

I paused and then drew a conceptual image in my mind.

"Mom, if we leave behind the physical boundaries then we can see the fundamental truth of Shiva in his outward appearance. Shiva exists in nothingness, in darkness, and in the wilderness. If these paranormal creations happen out of darkness, then only Shiva energy can answer this quest," I concluded with a joyful note.

Happiness beamed on their faces, as I explained the Shiva rationale to them. After a moment, I had a radiant glow on my face, as an idea emerged in my consciousness. I pointed my index finger toward the panoramic view of the ghats and Ganges and said, "I think this is the most powerful, unique, and abstract Shiva lingam residing in the womb of nature (Prakriti) that supplements the life-force."

"Wow! What an amazing spiritual interpretation. You should write on this idea," Mom appreciated me, and pulled me up to walk. Slowly, we all trudged to reach our resort room, after freshening up we met in the dining room to have our lunch.

We ate lunch in a luxurious way putting together an incredible stimulation of talks. Each of us shared our discoveries with a keener zest. With a light discussion on places and way of living, we nudged on to our traditional culinary dishes full of delicious nutriment.

After lunch, we retreated into our bunkers to lay down for a while before we set out on another venture. As a newly minted entrepreneur, I kept a track of incoming communications and notifications to not lose any big clients. Content writing is a hard sell; we have to make and sell the most natural product in the market. I was glued on the MacBook, pretty focused. The art of being a successful entrepreneur lies in selecting the best picks. I rejected few gigs though there were not many in my hands. There is no use in doing work that is not enriching you.

"Kalki, enjoy your vacations. Please don't be a nerd," Mom sarcastically smiled.

"Mom, it's over. Only 10 minutes more," I replied in a smiling voice.

"It means an hour to go," Mom joked back at me. She came near me and pushed my chair a bit, "I think you should lie down for one hour. You must be severely dehydrated, roaming on the ghats and then crying for long."

"Mom," I said in a long exclamation and turned the rotating chair toward her. I looked up at her, as she raised an eyebrow demanding an answer. Feeling a bit guilty, I hugged her around the waist and buried my head in her concave stomach.

"Why did my brave daughter behave this way? What will Karthik think about you? Are you a timid girl?" Mom asked in a firm voice, caressing my hair.

"I don't know," I said politely.

Mom gazed at me for a moment thinking how to react, "But, learn to control your emotions. The next time you are afraid of anything or someone, imagine your beloved person next to you. It will keep a tab on your volatility. Believe me, the trick works," she said giving me a tight squeeze as we released each other.

"Hey, girl, it is 3 pm. Do you want to take a nap?" Mom asked again.

"I want to roam freely on the ghats," I replied walking toward the turret to feel the breeze that rejuvenates us.

"Let me call and check if Karthik is free. Then, both of you can visit the Kashi Vishwanath temple. Are you okay with the plan?" She asked and I nodded my approval.

Karthik agreed upon Mom's request and informed me to be at the hotel reception at around 3.30 pm. He instructed me not to carry any purse or wallet for the possibility of theft or loss. I dressed up in a teal color kalidar suit with golden prints on the sleeves and hemlines with matching churidar. The main highlight of this dress was the netted, embroidered dupatta which is giving a gorgeous contrast match to the teal-colored suit set. I dug my feet in a shimmery pair of heels that finally hit the mark. I preferred a natural, no-makeup look to visit the Shiva temple. In a short period, I was ready to leave. My mom was standing by the door, she hugged me strongly and said, "Goodbye. Please take care of yourself. I am here in the room completing some office work. Bye, and be good."

We reached the Kashi Vishwanath temple premise and stood in the long queue that waited for hours. The energy source of the people was contagious and impressive. They rented loud cries of "Har Har Mahadev," in the air. Thankfully, the security arrangements were tight and abreast to the converging queues of devotees who thronged through different lanes surrounding the temple. Though the line was long, it was moving at a reasonable speed.

Karthik purchased a basket of flowers and offering from the local shop selling puja items. We kept our mobile phones and shoes in the lockers at the shop. Slowly the queue inched forward and we entered the Goddess Annapurna temple. The atmosphere inside the temple was soothing and peaceful. A strong flow of energy with the strength of a tidal wave revolved inside the temple. We prayed to the Goddess for her blessings of abundance and vitality. From here, we again stood in the queue for visiting the Golden Kashi Vishwanath temple.

I stared at him; he was unaware gazing at the surroundings.

"Karthik, will you always be the same," I said in a low decibel to avoid anyone from overhearing our audio exchanges.

He paused not understand the connection of my words with the current situation.

"Kalki, what do you want to say?" He looked at mc for a long time as the queue stood stagnant.

"I have no plans of settling down for the next two years. I am in the age bracket of 23-24 years. Are you ready to wait till then? Also, my mom has sacrificed her life for me. I know her very well, she will never come to stay with us, are you willing to move in with us without any ego issues? Third, if ever our relationship changes, will you still be my friend?"

Karthik looked straight into my eyes for about half a minute. There was a pump in my heart anticipating his response. His eyes stared with wonder. He smiled in a significant way as though he was waiting to hear something like this for years.

"You pierced my soul. I have loved none except you and there is no one constant in my life except you," He sounded truthful.

"Karthik, answer my questions. I want practical action, not purple prose," I brought him back on track.

He leaned closer so that only I could hear his words. His breath exhaled a fire that ruffled my moon dangle earrings and blew a million dreams in my eyes. The surrounding trapped us in a bond, and scattered love spells upon us. He came closer, I felt his bold outline enveloping me. My eyes fixed on the clusters of blossoms decking the trees.

"Kalki, I will wait for you till my last breath. And even after death, I will watch from the darkness that you live your life to the fullest. When we will see each other again in some other reincarnation, we will have so much to talk about again," his voice impregnated my soul.

It was a perfect moment for a French kiss but we just snuggled closer. I tapped my emotional outburst and said in a balanced voice, "My second question - will you come to stay with us?"

Karthik smiled as men smile when they have no choice left. Gathering guts he said, "The year you say will be our year of a union. The place you decide will be our home. Your word will be the command. Give me the feel of a family man in your way."

He stopped for a moment. We were moving in the line, creating visuals of our future together.

"I have a question to ask?" he spoke with hesitation.

"Kalki, you are gorgeously beautiful, intelligent, well-qualified, and the only daughter of your parents. Will you not leave me for someone wealthy and educated than me? In the end, I am an orphan, graduate, web-developer."

Initially, there was an angry expression on my face that melted down understanding his dilemma. I had thought about an effective solution on this point when Mom had objected to my and Karthik's relationship.

"Karthik, once you are a part of our family, you are no longer an orphan. I want you to enroll in a full-time or part-time MBA course, considering your business priorities. It's only a two-year investment that will benefit you to take our business to a new level. So, you will no longer be only a graduate. We can transform our web developer agency into an Infotech Company," I said in a voice that showed the farsighted vision.

"An Infotech company?" he exclaimed in an unbelievable voice. "Will it happen? I am afraid of dreaming, Kalki," he held my hand tight and said, "Will this be a reality?"

"Yeah, but first, get your MBA degree from a patronized management institute. Then, we can start the blueprint of our startup project," I spoke in a cool voice.

"Yes," He yelled so loud that people stared at him. I giggled and walked inside the holy sanctum. Our heartbeats thumped in unison as we stepped together before the God of cosmic order. The Shivlinga stands in the middle of the platform. I took the garland out of the basket in Karthik's hand and placed it around the lingam. The rush was high and there was a pushing factor but Karthik covered me well. I could sense the energy swirling from the watered lingam that moved me across eons of the past, where the galaxies whirled in the great universal field. The pandit worshipping the lingam statue looked up at me and sprinkled some drops of the puja water on me. The drops splashed upon me like the waves of time opening up their scripts.

It was an awakening moment. I felt that Shiva - The Mahakaal (infinite timekeeper) is revealing the secrets of the time cycle to me. I came out engulfed in a trance of timelessness and mystery.

'I look to discover the micro-worlds inside you,
Unravel layer by layer thousands of mysteries
Interesting to know your biology and heredity,
By curiously zooming in the pieces of your history.'

CHAPTER THIRTEEN

THE ZEST FOR QUEST

The sun was setting, changing its beautiful streaks of color from ice blue to golden and slowly, settling down for indigo to paint the sky. Finally, we came out of the maze and reached the ghat.

As dusk descends every evening, the most powerful and insightful ritual is celebrated in a highly flamboyant style. This is the most magnificent event that is celebrated on the earth every evening irrespective of any happenings.

People and priests were preparing for the ceremonial Ganges aarti. Seven wooden platforms were installed on the ghats covered with saffron cloths, a rod with electric lamp tied on each platform, and all the pooja items like copper pot, flowers, diyas, large brass lamps, peacocks' feathers, conch shell, and musical instruments placed on the board. Platforms lit with oil lamps teleported you in some other celestial space.

" Look, as the last sun rays bade goodbye to the earth, here walks the fire to worship the persistence and energy of water,"

I murmured to myself seeing the zest of the population.

A lot of devotees and tourists gathered to watch the forty-five minutes solemn affair of the Ganga aarti at the famous Dashashwamedh Ghat. With sheer excitement, I boarded on the rowboat with Karthik to watch the evening Ganga aarti. Karthik was negotiating hard with the boatman to give us a clear view of the aarti. People from steps of the ghats, floating riverboats, and standing below the raised platforms, rooftops, and terrace tops were jostling to get a good view to watch the greatest synchronization of rituals, culture, and colors.

Seven good looking, young priests dressed in cream-colored dhotis, red kurta woven in silk arrived at the platforms. After few minutes of performing some hymns rituals, they blew the conch shell in the dark sky to announce the commencement of the Ganga aarti. I started recording the entire event to upload on social media and spread the buzz. After conch shells, the priests waved the fuming incense sticks in a clockwise direction while ringing the prayer bell with their left hand.

In the next round, the priests used huge lamps lit with flames and camphor to wave and circle them on a rhythmic soundtrack of Vedic hymns. The smoke coming out of these lamps was creating unknown patterns in the sky. Live music was played in the background with the sound of people clapping and singing adding to the backdrop. At the end of the aarti, the priests flapped the peacock feathers fan in a well-choreographed style.

After the completion of the Ganga aarti, priests poured the divine water in the river, offering flowers to the holy waters honoring her existence in their lives. For people, the event marks a devotional ritual or cultural affair but for me, it was a balanced combination of five elements – sound, water, air, earth, and ether. I want to be here again and again, in the multitude of divine gatherings celebrating their eternal gusto. Seeing the Ganges aarti celebrated in a wild gusto, I sensed the divine presence that showed me the divinity in the whole world. If you celebrate every moment of life, then you have pleased the Creator.

The Ganges aarti resonated deeply with everyone, whether the old or young, modern or orthodox. The shining beacon of devotion and bliss is filled with direct transcripts that decode the universal message scripted for every individual. The aarti ceremony was an awe-inspiring moment coupled with evocative chants, billowing flames, spectacular patterns, and high energy that moved our core.

I completely immersed my soul in this ancient ritual, promising to revisit tomorrow. Let me witness the majestic worship of Mother Ganges in the presence of my beloved mother.

Today was 3rd Oct, our third day in Varanasi and there were no signs of connecting with Aghori Baba. Mom looked tensed but somewhere, she believed all will happen as expected. She was calling up the Panditji to establish some sort of communication with the Aghori. On conversing with Mom, I got to know that Karthik had left at 5 pm to search for the Aghori in the nearby jungles.

Seeing the grand guilty look on my face, Mom tried to make me smile to peel off the gloomy mood.

"Hey, come on, get ready for sightseeing," Mom said cheerfully but it sounded like an order.

"What sightseeing? We are seeing the ghats, Ganges aarti," I replied in a lousy mood.

"Darling, this is Varanasi. You can't explore it in one life-time. What you have seen is the most important and influential constitution of Hindu Dharma. There are other spots also of equal magnitude and historic luster," she said in a tone that wished to venture out.

"Even she needs a break after following up with so many people for my well-being," I murmured to myself, dusted an excitement on my face, and got up to explore the famous spots.

We walked on the narrow streets where shops, hotels, and old buildings were racked up. Traffic, noise, and population were flowing through the congested roads where even the cows walked as if they were the elite of the city.

Tourist's cars were lined up at the end of the road to receive passengers. Mom called up the local driver referred to us by Karthik and the car zoomed in at the other side of the road. We crossed the road to avoid a drive through the U-turn.

She positioned herself upright in the backseat of the car and instructed the chauffeur to drive us through the city to the prominent locations. The quiet country lanes gave us happiness and freedom from the chaotic mess. Nature had a pleasing symmetry that super unified our body and spirit. Perfect silence fell upon us as we grazed on many moments in the boisterous car ride.

We sliced into the heart of the city to start our sightseeing.

The driver parked the car by the sidewalk and waited for us to visit the Sankat Mochan Hanuman temple at the banks of river Assi. This temple has a lot of mythological and historical references as the most revered Hindu sadhu, Kalidasa, had a divine vision from Shree Rama at this very place. We were served a prasad of Besan laddoo made in pure ghee that had an awesome taste of the local cultural milieu. Colors, stories, and a feeling of stepping back into the old millennium are a perfect introduction to the city. Our driver drove us to the most famous and jammed alleys where the centuries-old temple and monasteries breathed. The facades of the temples were embellished with architectural carvings that were worth an immeasurable photogenic beauty. On the walls of the temple, there were hand-painted images that narrated the spiritual stories of Vedas and other scriptures.

"Ma'am, in Varanasi, there is a temple in every home," he said in a boastful voice as we rolled ahead to an authentic handicraft and handloom center. It was a big shop where local artisans were weaving from natural resources and some were working on the primitive rural craft. Mom was taking a delight in seeing the yarn, candles, soaps, wool, paints, resin, and antiques. She was recording the activities to learn from weaving, spinning, molding, brushing, stroking, and even sculpting. The shopkeeper was a kind-hearted gentleman and offered us a glass of lassi to drink. She strolled through the priceless hand-crafted marvels of art and craft, appreciating the owner for sustaining the authentic science of artistry. He shared with Mom how his local business was now entering into the global market through digital platforms. We almost spend 2 hours in the shop, learning the way art thrives as a source of income in rural places. More than the time spent, Mom had made a purchase worth sixty thousand rupees from the shop. The items were sent for immediate packaging and outstation courier dispatch. We had given our home address for delivery of the items, worrying about the fragility of few items. However, in case of any damage, there was a refund or replacement option provided by the owner. The shopkeeper was very happy with our purchasing power. He gave us his visiting card and product brochures that tell the complete details of each product for seasonal purchase.

I wondered, what happened to my mother's budget-conscious temperament but dared not to question her out of fear. The shopkeeper waved us goodbye as we sat in the car to embark on a further journey.

We missed our lunch as we roamed through the crammed bazaars to purchase pure silk material and Benares saris that depicted the unique creation of our Indian cultural heritage. After another hot money blowing purchase of Benares saris, we decided to visit the Benares Hindu University (BHU). Being a professor herself, Mom was very keen to see the oldest and largest residential university in Asia with five institutes, sixteen faculties, and 140 departments located in a huge campus. Among all the places of national importance, BHU is top-ranked as it symbolizes progress through revivalism. The University embodies the dream of its founder, Mahamana Malaviyaji, a great modernizer and religious scholar. It was his brilliant idea to have a Hindu University defined through the colors, time, architecture, lifestyle which even imparts western knowledge.

The lush greenery in the sprawling concrete building is an oasis of tranquility. In the grove of nature, there nestles the magnificent Old Viswanath temple showing reverence toward our Sanatan Dharma. Breathe deep, meditate here, and your soul will elevate to merge with magnanimous cosmic energy operating in the Universe. We prayed to the God of the Universe for abundant positive energy that will reap us happiness and contentment. It was not easy walking away from that place, it was a feeling of leaving one's home behind.

Besides, the complex mythological significance, prodigious display of geometric structures, rituals of life and death, voluminous Vedic literature, Varanasi is also known for Jantar Mantar, an observatory that is a perfect epitome of astronomy and cosmology.

The driver aroused our interest by sharing the immersive experience of his previous visitors at Jantar Mantar. While he was speaking, I was posting my pics of Varanasi and replying to my friend's comments on social media.

The driver cum guide looked at us through the rear-view mirror and said in a thick local accent, "Our Maharaja Jai Singh II designed and built the strange but intriguing structure of the observatory in 1724, and even today, it can tell you the perfect answers of any astronomical question - time, distance, altitudes, or eclipses. It knows how to read the sky!" He said with a grin.

We reached the open-aired place, partly in shambles, depicting the fine blend of Rajput-Mughal architecture on the walls made up of stones. Once inside the observatory, Mom selected a good English-speaking guide to make us understand the different types of equipment and their working.

I was moving into the scientific playground in a thoughtful mood. The guide was explaining the intricacies of the scientific pieces of equipment with interesting names like Shankhayantra, Samratyantra, Chakrayantra, Naadiyantra, etc.; and I kept on nodding cluelessly. Mom as usual recorded the talks for her analysis as to how these instruments precisely facilitated the study of motion, speed, and properties of stars and planets. We walked out of the observatory trying to understand the working of many instruments.

We sat in the car, praising the driver, for showing us this larger-than-life astronomical laboratory.

"Ma'am, now I will show you a part of Nepal in Varanasi," the guide's eyes beamed as he spoke.

"Nepal in Varanasi?" I exclaimed loudly, sitting bolt upright in an instant.

There are thousands of temples bolstering the spiritual faith of the devotees. The driver parked the car in a corner of the road and accompanied us to show the way to the Pashupatinath Temple at the Lalitha Ghat. We passed through a few windings and reached the temple premises. The temple is also called the Kanthwala Temple; "Kanthwala" means "wooden temple". Even though it is made out of wood, the structure is termite-free and not prone to decay.

The moment you stand in front of the Pashupatinath temple, it is obvious that your brow rises with curiosity. This place is a hotspot attraction for visitors to click photos or shoot videos. There are a lot of idols piled up in the adjoining sanctums of the temple. Mom sat on the long wooden bench adjoining the outer structure of the temple to rest for a while. She was feeling tired and the fresh breeze was rejuvenating her coolness. I caressed the cows that roamed in the outer court of the temple. Holy men sit at the entrance of the temple and the open yard to bless the devotees with divine remedies for their problems. There was a quite good number of incoming and outgoing people. After a while, we visited the temple for divine blessings and also surveyed the exquisite Nepali architectural style embedded in the interiors of this deep-rooted sanctuary.

The vivid afternoon sky morphed into a shimmering twilight beauty. There was a riot going on in the sky between the multiple hues and streaks of light. The evening lights passionately ignited the entire city. We had a long day, and decided to recede back to our resort.

The porter carried our shopping bags to our room. I tried Karthik's number several times but it was switched off. Mom was not worried about Karthik, trusting that he was absolutely fine. She was speaking with her mother, then brother and his wife on the phone. Mom shared her travel stories with them, and even forwarded the images of her purchases with her sister-in-law.

"Kalki, I am going for a bath. Don't mess with these bags," she said smiling and walked in the bathroom.

I played music tracks on my phone, raw emotions slipping from my heart to feel the song. Mom came out of the bathroom wrapped in a dark blue bathrobe around her thin frame.

"Now, it's your turn to have a bath. Go fast and stop your musical concert. I have to make official calls," She gave me a gentle nudge and I went in the bathroom for a quick shower.

We had a sumptuous dinner at 8.30 pm in the lavish dining room of the Brijrama Palace. Mom was calling Karthik but his mobile was still switched off so we decided to go for a walk on the Ghats to soak in spirituality. A walk on the ghats is a spiritual session that communicates with the inherent meanings and messages of the place. It fulfills our spiritual quest to understand the secret principles operating the cosmos.

There was something beautiful about the ghats in the deep abysses of darkness. I closed my eyes for a moment and surrendered to the darkness and nothingness that purged the creation of the Universe. A strong wind, heavy with synergies, tussled my face, to share the symphony of cosmic notes in the form of rough poetry. I imagined myself to be a staggering part of Shiva channelized on the earth to converge on beatific inception. The profound thoughts set my spirit as an eagle with golden plumage soaring high up in the skies, as I had never dived before!

We walked in dark ghats, filled with a scent of burnt wood, incense sticks, and dried floral fragrance. The sacred Ganges seemed to have a private conversation with the ghats that desired to pick her up in their massive arms. In the last few days, I had seen that the ghats never go to sleep. From the first golden streak of the sun till the last dark ray, the ghats are awake to serve the constant flow of devotion, traditions, and survival.

As we walked, we saw boatsmen repairing and fixing up their boats. Tantriks and Babas wander with their weird stuff and attract some desperate people needing divine intervention. The engulfing thickets of smoke showed us that Manikarnika and Harishchandra Ghats burn relentlessly day and night.

"Does it ever stop?" I asked Mom, she was engrossed in seeing the beauty of the waters that churned the vitality of life.

"This is an endless procession... a celebration of death in a unique style," she sounded insightful.

"Someday, even you will have to cremate me here," her words cut me deep.

"Mom, this is the first and last time. If you ever speak something like this then I don't know what I will do," I answered strongly in a heat of anger.

Realizing how much it hurt, Mom held me close.

"You are not a quitter. Keep it in mind," she said as we walked forward to explore the nocturnal view of the Ganges.

The glowing embers under the broody sky consumed an ethereal experience as they mounted toward the high skies. For some time, we sat on the steps of the ghats as the cool breeze ruffled our hair. The moonlight reflected on the rippling water like numerous gleaming pieces of a broken mirror. Through the signs and constellations, the night sky drenched us in calming energy that vanished the dense pain of our life.

For the first time, Mom shared her life stories with me. As she peeled the picture of her life before me, she looked even more beautiful than before. She opened up the deep conversations of terrible moments, lost aspirations, sinking desires, and battles of hope by drawing a miniature version of her life. I plunged into her story to take inspiration from her real-life insights and merge them into a stunning and powerful literature to be read as a family legend.

We talked deep and free that night. The stars were out to participate in our talks. As we walked away from the grandeur of heavenly art, it was just like leaving another home - somewhere in a parallel life, we had already settled there forever.

The next day, I woke up when the sky illuminated a pearly glow. Due to the late-night walk and talk, I had difficulty waking up early in the morning. Standing by the turret, I sipped a cup of green tea, checking the messages over mobile. I looked up at the beautiful background of pale blue and white clouds that added a luster to the sky. Leaning a little, I saw the deck of the ghats filled with bolstering crowds and non-stops activities happening at the ghats.

Mom was busy fishing in her gargantuan purse. She had tagged the gift items for gifting.

“Any info about Karthik?” I asked in a worried tone.

“Yeah, I forget to tell you. He had come in the morning and left after an hour for a documentary shoot. You were sound asleep, so we discussed it on the patio. He will be coming to the resort at around 9 pm. He is trying very hard and we can expect something positive response. Also, he is busy in shooting for a video documentary,” she said it in such a way it made me feel lighter.

“Great news,” I exclaimed as the thought of seeing him took away my breath.

“Mom, I am going for a bath. Don’t order breakfast for me. It is already 10 am. We will directly go for lunch,” I sounded enthusiastic and bubbly. Mom smiled at me, partly knowing, the shy and enchanting expression floating on my lips.

Nesting my eyes on the floor, I walked into the bathroom and turned on the shower. I stood under the shower, thinking of Karthik’s favorite poem and song. I immersed my body in an aromatic bath, not only to inhale scented vapors but to thoroughly cleanse my body and mind. I methodically moved my hands slowly in a parallel motion - up and down - left and right to scrub my body. While bathing, I remembered with fondness how Mom would splash the bucket to rinse off the soap and we would clap and laugh together.

Listening to the continuous music of water my thoughts swayed to Karthik. I closed my eyes, visualizing me and Karthik frantically bathing under a small waterfall creating a chaotic atmosphere of love.

I came out of the bathroom after having a fantasy bath. Wrapped in a white towel, I sat on the edge of the bed to check my phone. I slid the bar on the phone to see Karthik's messages waiting for me. He had apologized for not being able to contact me and giving me the deserved time. He had to do an urgent shoot for an international documentary. Also, catching Aghori is becoming a difficult task for him. He also promised to make up for this later.

Well, I am a hard-wired professional and do understand such critical moments. He was doing so much for us I had no words to thank him. From the message box, I scrolled to the recent photo gallery to see the most majestic scenes, the quaintest towns, the most influential historical sites, and the architectural splendors. I reimagined the people and places in these images as people and places of good vibes and diverse colors. The series of photos sparked my interest as I again scrolled through them to redefine my most meaningful life experience. I rubbed my finger on Karthik's photo taken during the boat ride. My eyes fixed on his flaming eyes and his handsome face engrossed in watching the glistening sun rays. After looking at him, there was no thought of ever thinking of having someone else in life. He was more dangerous than the ghosts for he had fully possessed me. In a full tide of poetic enthusiasm, my emotions outpoured from the very depths falling all over his image. I know my happiness is built upon him, out of my heart and life, endless chords of a musical dream. I kept on going through his photos, finding more of myself in him than in me. I was weaving a colorful future bringing in gorgeous colors and splendid patterns. I hung on the weaving threads, spurning around for a joyous dance and then falling to the ground as Mom called me out.

"Kalki, get ready. How long are you going to stay wrapped in that towel?" she raised an eyebrow expecting an answer.

"Yeah, Mom," I jumped from the edge of the bed and went to the wardrobe. Mom's eyes were surveying me as I unpacked a pair of jeans, a cobalt red sleeveless top with a white shrug to wear.

"Mom, I am starving. Let's try something new - street food of Varanasi instead of the traditional and royal dishes," I coaxed her to come out and taste the culinary treats of the Varanasi lanes. Willing or unwillingly, it is really hard for Mom to say "No" to me. After all, I am the apple of her brilliant eyes.

Mom's eyes were full of happy and quiet light, her lips were about to say a "YES" but she held them tight for some time.

"Please, Ma," I pleaded to make her feel important as the final approver.

"Ok, girl. Give me 10-15 minutes. Let's taste the local chat and sweets made in pure ghee," she agreed with my idea.

"Kalki, call the driver and ask him to wait at the rear of the hotel," she handed over the phone to me.

"Yes, doing it now," I immediately called and passed on Mom's instructions to our driver.

From our resort room, we were transported to the busy streets of Varanasi in half an hour. The culinary delight of Varanasi is as popular as the historically significant landmarks. A trip to Varanasi is not complete without trying the lip-smacking delicacies served here in desi ghee. Food is the most common expression of any culture that unravels the mysteries of the civilization.

Banaras or Varanasi is richly embedded with diverse cultures and spiritual forces. Buddha crossed the river here to teach his first sermon at Sarnath. The Buddhist traveller, Hieun Tsang, scripted his greatest documentary on enlightenment here. At the Hanuman Temple on the banks of Tulsi Ghat, Tulsidas wrote the most read magnum opus of the world - Ramayana in 1500 AD. On the banks of Panchganga Ghat, the renowned saint, Kabir experienced a strange gush of energy flowing inside him that marked the beginning of his Kabir Panth. Varanasi was the native place to the seventh and 23rd Jain Tirthankara.

The Mughal Emperor, Akbar facilitated the building of temples here while Aurangzeb not only destroyed them but also named the city - "Muhammadabad".

Attracted to this place of splendor and secular power in the 18th century, Maratha, Bengali, Rajasthani, and Bihari elites made the pukka Ghats, palaces, and temples upon them. The womb of Varanasi has delivered endless pilgrimages but still the waters haven't dried up.

From snacks to the main course to healthy beverages, the streets of Varanasi were filled with numerous shops serving soulful food with bold and rustic flavors. Where a soul's inward quest for wisdom is fulfilled here, the yearning for food cravings is also satisfied at the same place. Scriptures say, Varanasi is not attached to any earth, it is hanging in the air much above the ground level, balanced by the trident of God Shiva. Mythologists say, "Varanasi is the universal answer to all the appetites and faculties of our soul, mind, and body."

We meandered through the lanes to reach the Kachori Gali tucked behind the popular Kashi Vishwanath temple. The entire lane brims with the vaporous aroma of Kachoris frying in blackened cauldrons.

On the outer edge of the tiny shop, stands a makeshift kitchen, where a cook squats before a large handi, filled with oil, bubbling over a big flame to prepare the snacks. There was a milling crowd before the cook for the tasty items. Though the seating arrangements were limited, the owner provided us a space to sit on a floating bench with a slate wall. The server brought us hot Kachoris with piping hot aloo-matar curry and imli chutney in leaf bowls. The taste was eclectic and tantalized our taste buds for more. I tore the Kachoris and their round shape collapsed completely. Inside the Kachoris, there was a respectable amount of filling that focused on the core of hunger - fullness.

As we chewed on the Kachoris with contentment, the sizzling sound of jalebis, frying in the other cauldrons distracted our attention. Jalebi is the love of the city - a sweet dish to be relished on every occasion. The treat of Jalebi is gifted to Varanasi by the Turkic invaders, Mughals, and for this reason, its popularity extended to North India.

Out of curiosity, I went to see how the overworked cook makes the Jalebis. He lifted a cone filled with a batter of maida, cornflour, baking soda, pure desi ghee, and other secret ingredients. With great precision and years of practice, he delicately creates concentric circles over the crackling oil. After initial heating, he stirs the oil and moves the steel ladle, till the Jalebis change color from white to glistening golden hue. The spiraled sweets are then dunked in sugar-infused syrup with saffron and fragrant herbs. The Jalebis are served in a betel-leaf bowl that adds up the essence. I took a bite of the crunchy Jalebi and the sweetness crystallizes over the surface. The sweetness and subtle beauty of this dish had the ultimate power to dissolve the storm.

I pointed out to Mom the expertise of the cook to determine the circumference of each spiral, the flavor of the batter, and syrup consistency - these are the success codes of Jalebis. Mom challenged that she would make razor-thin, crisp, and tasty Jalebi, once we were at home. The bet was on between us and the stake was high - pride.

We walked a little ahead to another storefront to feast on Dahi chutney golgappe. I was almost full but Mom insisted me to eat and not worry about my waistline. Small, crispy golgappe are stuffed with mashed potatoes and chickpeas, and overloaded with curd, sweet and spicy chutneys with a tangy twist. A final seasoning of sev, pudina, and pomegranate seeds are given to explode countless flavors in your mouth. I ate two golgappe from another site of the plate from where Mom was eating. This was awesome and filled me up completely giving Mom the pleasure of eating Malaiyyo the famous ice-cream street dessert of Varanasi.

We were both full and thought of walking under the glory of the afternoon sun. I requested Mom not to shop anymore, but it was in vain. She purchased a can of Ganga water for puja, every Hindu house must have Gangajal for rituals. As we turned to go back to our car, an intricately decorated elephant, peacock, and box caught her surveying glance. Before the blink of my eye, Mom was in the small shop, and the shopkeeper was showing her the Gulabi Minakari or the work in pink color that is done only in Varanasi. For some items, the cost exceeded even lakhs, however, Mom looked for items in an affordable range like decorative boxes, showpiece items, and crystals.

Coming out of the shop, I saw a street vendor selling colorful wooden toys - keychains, pencils with caps, birds, animals, wooden bangles, handmade diaries, and human figurines. Mom was not so keen on purchasing these items but I pulled her to the cart and insisted to buy. Though, unwilling at me, she also got interested after seeing my childlike enthusiasm. She purchased a set of three diaries for her writing purpose, leaving with me the absolute freedom to buy anything that I wanted.

It was a long walk and the shopping made us more exhausted. The afternoon was lingering on our heads and we walked to the end of the lane where the car was parked. Seeing the extreme weakness on our faces our driver suggested having the special Garam Kadak Varanasi tea that will make us feel vigorous. Tea is an integral part of our daily lives interwoven in our social fabric; it is more of a philosophy than just a drink. Indeed, Mom nodded her head in approving his idea and he drove to land us at a side of a busy road.

We followed him in the narrow lanes near the Dashwamedh Ghat. I could easily guess the place as the entire lane was filled with painted artistic signboards to guide the way. The owner, Vishnu was a trustworthy, generous, and creative human being making everyone feels at home. He was telling us the recipe on how to brew the perfect tea, he spoke with Mom about the other tourists' spots to visit here and even shared some exciting travel stories. He had a lot to speak about a good network source and a prompt service attitude toward each customer. He had extensive knowledge on every subject that made his Vishnu Tea Emporium an intellectual hub to enrich people in small ways and simple methods.

We had an interesting conversation while sipping his masala

tea. The strong brew revived our stooping energy reserves. With a renewed mind, we got up to get going after spending almost forty minutes at this cool cafe. Mom bought the chai masala packets, the specialty of the emporium for gifting to her colleagues and seniors.

"What to do next?" Mom turned and generously asked me as we sat in the car.

"I want to watch the Ganges aarti," I leaned at the backseat, and said in a requesting tone.

The driver patiently held the steering, listening to music, and awaiting our instructions.

"You already saw it with Karthik," Mom raised her eyebrow as I gently pressed her palm.

I spoke in a slow but insightful voice, "Mom, it will make better sense if I watch the worshipping of Mother Ganges with my mother.

I was created in your amniotic field, from there I gathered courage, learned the act of survival, nourished on your love, dreams, pieces, and bytes. For nine months, I floated in your amniotic bliss, free from the effects of gravity or light. It is impossible to resonate with anyone else more than the body that labored in pain to give me birth."

As Mom's eyes brimmed, I drew a long breath and lovingly said, "You are my source of life like Mother Ganges is the nourishing center of the earth. Though I am precipitated out of your womb, I shall forever be an inseparable part of you. My process of creation happened in your amniotic ocean, I can sense the essence, the breaths, and the energy. I want to see the worship of the Ganges River as a tribute to you."

There was a momentary pause. Tears gleamed in her eyes and I picked up a few glistening beads to apply on my head as blessings.

"Mom, there is nothing as powerful and addictive as first love. Abheer was the love of my life in between our bond, there were many words and margins, but no amount of scrubbing could plug him out of me," I spoke in a tone of sadness that broke Mom's heart more than mine.

I continued with a deep pause, "But, Mom, practically I know, Abheer is a limited man, happy to live a life of limited challenges, limited responsibilities, and limited risk. Whereas Karthik is a forceful personality, he can go to any limits for his love and family. And, in this scenario of a paranormal mess, I need a volatile and agile personality to be a part of my future."

"I agree with you, love," Mom said holding me close.

"Mom, I want to have Karthik as a partner because I know he respects, loves, and cares a great deal for you - and you are the first love of my life."

Hearing my heart out, she hugged me tight and instructed the driver to drop us at the backside of the Dashwamedha Ghat. As the driver rode off, I looked at the changing sky from azure to coral. Somewhere, the platinum moon was taking its position to anchor the playful constellations. In this moment of a makeover, everything is amplified by the metallic streaks that shone in bold and colorful sequins. In this time, everything seems to be divine and intimate; switching off from outside and entering the inner world.

As darkness outlined above the ancient temple, we watched the six priests perform the Ganges aarti with bells, conch, and other sacred instruments. A loud pre-recorded music is played from the ghats that reaches the other end of the shore. While facing the river, the priests use six-layered lamps that are circled in a clockwise manner, accompanied by chants or songs in praise of Mother Ganga. There was a huge and enthusiastic crowd of people participating and recording the event. The locals' people had assembled on the banks of the ghats while tourists preferred to see the panoramic view from the boats anchored in the Ganges River. The vibrant atmosphere was an alluring mélange of culture, colors, and creative chaos.

As the well-synchronized aarti comes to a concluding part, the priests offer flowers, milk, and floating diyas to the Ganges. Worshippers released shallow clay dishes filled with oil and lit with wicks on the floating waters that create an impression that stars are shining on the ripples. There was a deep silence when the pre-recorded music stopped and the aarti finished.

Mom pulled me closer to her and gave me a contented smile. I knew this gesture of her, it was her style of saying thank you.

From there we walked back to our resort. The driver pinged his total charge to Mom on WhatsApp messenger. Mom transferred the money to him through the payment app and waited for the payment confirmation. It was then when Karthik called her up. They both had a small conversation that brought relief to Mom's face and curiosity on my face.

Turning to me, Mom said in an ecstatic tone, "We better hurry up. Karthik was successful in tracking the Aghori's whereabouts. He spoke with him and has requested the Aghori to meet you. I hope we will find a solution to this problem. Karthik will be coming to pick us at 11 pm. Let's go to the room, get refreshed, and then have a good dinner. You may need to be awake for the entire night."

I nodded, with an outpour of questions in my mind.

"Come on Kalki, fast," I heard Mom call me from a few feet distance.

I raced toward her. After that, we completed the activities at such a light speed that around 10.30 pm we were at the reception desk waiting for Karthik. Luckily, my power bank was fully charged and I had kept it in Mom's purse.

We looked at each other, groping for words but finding none to speak out. I was delighted but not sure if the Aghori will resolve our paranormal issue. Mom's confident attitude installed fresh vigor inside me.

Barging the entrance door, Karthik entered the room like a storm. His face simply refreshed the boring regime of the wait. He smiled at me and proceeded to update the details to Mom. I overheard some parts of the conversation but just hooked on to his masculine beauty. He wore a casual black shirt and rebellious denim jeans that reflected his rough and tough personality.

"Let's leave," he asked us to follow him as fast as possible.

"You ate dinner?" I asked him. He smiled and said, "The best dinner cooked by my friend's mother. Don't worry about me. I am doing great," he replied with a smile that peeled the layers of romanticism.

"Come fast," he made us walk even faster than before.

Walking on the ghats at the midnight was a sublime and seductive experience. The black expanse of water was cloaked in quietness. The boatmen were sleeping in their boat with a quilt and a cushion. Some professional photographers were delving into their lenses to capture the black expanse of water. Devotees were grouped in a corner of the ghats practicing tantra-mantra under the guidance of seers and sadhus. The poor and destitute were sleeping under the open sky as they had no place to live.

A pack of stray dogs followed us hungrily uncowed by my gestures. The cacophony of nocturnal birds and frogs were singing out the pain of the homeless people as they sank into sleep. Even in the darkness, the Varanasi Ghats maintained its out of ordinary demeanor and humble attitude to serve.

Thick grey smoke and red flames were engulfing the upper strata. The smell of the endless pyres swallowing the burning body indicated that we were close to the Manikarnika Ghat – Maha Shamshana. It is rightly said that Manikarnika and Harishchandra Ghat never sleep. The glinting ripples of the Ganges River whispered death stories in our ears and then the leaping flames danced rhythmically sending pulsating waves to space.

I looked up at the starry black sky imaging a vision of God Shiva encircled in flames dancing on the beats of a symbolic damru composing his eternal dance.

A moist wind ruffled the water and cooled my forehead. Slowly, I exhaled the clouds of doubts and darkness. Under the blessings of infinite cosmic energy, I opened a new chapter in my life, now that everything was falling in place, I needed more words and fewer margins…

CHAPTER FOURTEEN

DECODE THE DEAD

The spooky naked fashion statement made it easy for me to recognize them in a second. I noticed an Aghori doing a bizarre ritual on the banks of the Ganges River. Somewhere at the other end, loud drums were being beaten and a faint trail of voices could be heard.

"What's going on there?" I asked Karthik.

"Why do you want to be Sherlock Holmes? Just mind your business," Mom snapped at me.

"Please, I need to know," I said, trembling and considering my retreat from the mysterious hamlet.

"Hey, Kalki, relax. They're performing certain penances to gain supernatural powers," said Karthik, trying to make me feel more comfortable.

"What kind of penances?" I asked, knowing he was hiding certain facts.

"Kalki, why are you fluctuating?" asked Mom, having noted

my tremulousness. "You had read about their extreme lifestyle that incorporates nudity, a love for skull jewelry, strange sexual practices with corpses, and cannibalism." After taking a pause, she continued in a milder tone. "Aghoris believe that Lord Shiva manifests in three forms - omniscient, omnipotent, and omnipresent. According to them, whatever happens in this universe happens as per the will of Shiva. They have untold supernatural powers and even extensive knowledge of medicines that can cure the deadliest diseases . . . but the information isn't shared outside their ambit."

I saw an Aghori dancing in the cremation ground in an explosive manner that pierced the heart of the viewers. He danced in a trance, stepping over slow flames and smoking hashish. Some members of his cult clanged the metallic instruments in a high-pitched range to produce volcanic music. In his powerful steps, there was a revelation of the joy of being. These Aghoris spend their nights doing the Tandava Nritya, eating corpses found floating in the Ganges River, or collecting the firewood from the funeral pyres to use in their rituals.

My heart was beating fast, seeing their topsy-turvy postures on top of dead bodies. The taboo-bursting universe crawled with vile gastronomic habits, necrophilia, and esoteric practices. Somewhere along the way, my hope of receiving a solution from these Shiva-worshipping mystics had gotten bleak. Mom knew exactly what was going on in my head, and she was waiting to clear the clouding darkness.

"Ask a social scientist, and they will tell you: the Aghoris are eccentric but true to their original selves. They're openly practicing their beliefs rather than dealing with hypocrisy, corruption, and greed." Mom spoke the truth, and it made sense to me.

She scanned the dark ghats, and then her eyes returned to me. The light in her eyes shone in the depths, and she sounded wise. "All of these are people but we are evaluating them from a different perspective. The universe in all of its diversity, maintains a delicate balance of all the complex and diverse forces . . . but we micro-analyze it to draw out meaningful contrasts."

"The mystery of the dark energy that strangulates you in darkness can only be decoded by these mystic worshippers of the dark. Gather your guts. You have to interact with them for several hours but Karthik and I are with you." She tried to cheer and strengthen me, giving me a gentle pat on my back.

We walked through the maze of funeral pyres. The thick black smoke hovered high above us, displaying the ultimate truth of life.

From a great height, I could see the magnificent sweep of ghats and the river traced a black outline. I asked myself, "What is darkness? An absence of light. And what is light? An absence of darkness."

We passed through an uncharted lane and reached an open backside space mostly filled with firewood. We went to a very dark place. A strange odor surrounded us, but it was faint and thus bearable.

There in a corner, an Aghori covered in black clothing was seated in cross-legged on the ground. A huge bonfire was piled up before him, and the smoke ascended in a vertical column, conveying with the breeze to reach the low-hanging clouds.

We went a bit closer to get a proper look at him. His long, matted tresses pulled up on the top of the head, giving it a pyramidal edge. He wore heavy rudraksha necklaces around his neck and drank water from a human skull, which seemed to be his prized possession.

Locals were seated before him, prepared to address grievances that required miraculous intervention. I turned to Mom and Karthik, vibes of timidity and apprehension revolving around me.

"What is the difference between them and us?" I asked, a frown knitting my forehead.

"Faith is common," Mom replied in a sharp voice. "Look at the few Westerners seated there in the crowd. Why are they attracted to the tantric yoga of our culture? Why are these people running away from the increased materialism toward the confines of peace? All of them are finding tools to awaken their intelligence system. Let's see if your tool can be found here," she said, asking me to stand quietly and conceal my lack of trust.

Karthik went to the Aghori, whispered something in his ear, and pointed his finger toward me. The Aghori vigorously shook his head, stood up on one leg, and raised his skull in the sky, performing an acrobatic feat. Immediately, the crowd reacted to his agility and balancing skill with wild applause. Then, the Aghori grunted a few chants, added wood and other ingredients to the fire, and sat down in his yogic posture.

He signaled the crowd to disperse, and the entire ground was empty within minutes. The Aghori rapidly rotated his upper body from left to right and then turned his face toward the sky. There was no sign of shiver as the wind ravenously buffeted his body, which was only covered in the thinnest of clothing. He continued to smoke weed relentlessly as if he were invincible.

The Aghori craned his loaded neck to look at me with heavily intoxicated eyes and waved his bony hand toward me. He gave Karthik a ferocious glance that made him retreat to another end.

Mom followed me as I moved toward the roaring flames. The man extended his palm toward, Mom asking her to stop there. Mom was reluctant to let me go alone in front of a wild Aghori. I assured her there was nothing to worry about. I trusted Karthik, and in his presence, I'd be safe.

There, I finally stood before him, after a series of tiresome efforts. I wanted to have some dialogue with him, but his face was expressionless, and his painted forehead lines rolling as he cried, "Bam Bhole!" The tall nest of matted locks on his head was aspiring to break into the mystical realms of the stratosphere. Though he was a symbol of mystical powers and abundant divine strength, his physique was extremely skinny. He had long fingernails, and a bony, wide frame.

We were face to face, and the fire in the furnace was heating between us. From the front, he changed his seating direction to the right side and asked me to sit in the front. Mom was unable to see us, as the bonfire had blocked most of the view. Karthik was standing next to Mom, assuring her that everything would be alright. I caught a glimpse of her in between the gaps, but red flames kept shooting out like torches. She was agitated, looking more frightened than I'd ever seen her before.

There was no tract of the moon in the sky, and the aqueous vapor had diffused, leaving a glow in the sky. In a fashion, for a while, all was silent—no sound breaking the silence except the creaking embers. No words could describe the wonder, terror, or other infinite emotions flickering within me. He sat and stared at me as if pythons of silence had coiled around him. The breeze died away, and the Ganges was in a perfect stage of rest. There was a need for a subtle sound to bind us together.

"Baba . . ." I attempted to speak but couldn't take the conversation ahead.

"What do you want from one you don't trust?" He spoke in a hoarse voice that almost sounded like a hymn.

I had no words with which to reply. Not all answers are taught in school. I decided to sidetrack the redundant and focus on the core.

"Baba, I have been seeing a lot of things from the other world—dead people—and having out-of-body experiences. I want to live a simple, common life. If you could guidc me out of this mess," I pleaded with folded hands, hoping to draw his sympathy out.

He coated his thumb with ashes and whispered a few chants. Then, he extended his protruding hand toward me and placed the greased thumb on my third eye. He smiled, giving me a devilish look. Closing his eyes, he took a deep breath and firmly pressed the spot of esoteric wisdom. I felt the world around me was spinning, and I quickly closed my eyes.

"Your eyes . . . your wolf eyes." He laughed a long and bitter laugh as he leaned toward me scornfully. "Your eyes say it all." He laughed on in a strange, pathetic way. Rolling his eyes, he said, "Eyes are the window to the soul."

"I have read it," I interjected, but the Aghori neglected my words.

"You people know only texts. The practical context is zero. Eyes are the window to the soul. You have heard it, but do you know the logic behind it?" he screamed as loud as he could, practically bursting my eardrums.

I replied defensively. "There's a scientific explanation to it. The optic nerve is also called the 'second pair' of cranial nerves; it's the means of communication between the eyes and brain, creating our emotional responses. Also, in simpler language, it is through eyes that the soul sees the world."

He marked the rage in my eyes and immediately stopped the topic.

"You are unaware of what you have received from the universe. These amber eyes are a gift that's been in the making for millions of years—ever since mankind first walked on the planet. Only 5% of the population have amber eyes. It is a well-known myth that amber-eyed women have supernatural powers." For the first time since we spoke, there was an intellectual exertion in his voice.

"Are these eyes the root cause of all the happenings? I have seen many movies that depict the stories with such themes," I said in a curious voice.

He smiled a simple smile that broke the barrier between us.

He rubbed his palms with ash and said in a decent voice, "It is said that amber eyes are embedded with mystic powers. It doesn't come to everyone. In the same sense that you don't get to choose your parents, it's given to you as per your Punyakarma or karmic cycles. You inherit these eyes through your past incarnations or cosmic deviations. This is bestowed upon you by the Creator because you are worth it."

"Baba, I have a query. Can I ask you?" I spoke in a humble voice as our rapport had been established. "Even, my father has amber eyes, but he never had any such experiences," I said.

"Does he have a good and honest heart? Has he ever expanded and elevated his mind to think about anyone else except himself? Does he possess anything more than money and position? Inner awakening happens. Everyone has a dormant psychic energy center . . . but not all leverage it. You are a refined, sensitive, spiritual, and blessed soul chosen for it. Accept it, for it is the universal role given to you." He paused to consider my expression.

"Why this universal role? Why not something better?" I asked him if he had anything to say about it.

The universe has your akashic records. It knows what to entrust to whom. Keep your trust. They will show you the way," he said, humming a mantra under his breath.

"I don't want these supernatural powers. I want to live a simple and common life like everyone. Please eliminate these powers from my mind." I spoke loud and clear, thinking he could help me out.

"Sure, before you please answer my questions. If you give the correct answers, then I will give you an appropriate solution." His voice was more compelling than before.

I didn't like this question-and-answer forum, but there was no other choice. We had taken so much effort for this moment, and I couldn't let it go.

"Answer, if you want to come out of the maze," he said in an indistinct voice, with a sardonic smile, mocking me.

"These questions have no recorded answers. However, you can answer them based on your intuition. Your answers will be a personal barometer of your spiritual awareness. "His words had a peremptory notion that commanded instant attention from me.

"Okay, Baba. Give me five minutes to refocus. Once you think I'm ready, you can ask me," I said in a slow rhythm, closing my eyes. Meditating upon the word OM, I disconnected from the outer world and reflected upon the representation of space—the real world, imaginary worlds, parallel worlds, hybrid worlds, galaxies . . . reality.

As I expanded, my face transformed to a full-length ethereal sky, and my body slithered like a meandering river toward the ultimate destination: Blue. Pure blue.

I heard the opening question asked by Baba. "Who is a ghost?"

Great energy in all its authentic strength overpowered me. Words like a river flooded within me. I wanted to ensure my answers were unbiased and rooted in warmth, rationality, and empathy.

"Who is a ghost?" he asked again, and my deeply engrossed subconscious mind placed emotions and feelings on top and replied in a calm tone filled with neutrality.

"A soul that needs healing."

He didn't reply to my answer. My eyes were closed, but I could see his plain expression through the eyes of my mind. He asked the second question in a solemn tone. "How do you know if a spirit is good or bad or evil?"

I juggled as fierce and calm thoughts simultaneously beat the walls of my mind. The Aghori repeated the question with a serious import.

The answer came like a flash. "To know if a spirit is bad or good, we need to sense the energies when they are present. A spirit can misguide those that see it, but energies never deceive."

The Aghori Baba fired another question in rapid succession. As he asked the third question, a smile broke in his eyes. "What does it mean when you see a ghost crying?"

In my full somatic awareness, the answer came like a wail from my lips. "The ghost wants to kill you to seek revenge."

There was a silence between us. He leaned a little closer and posed another question to me. "What does it mean when a ghost shows you its back?"

I wielded my mind to extract divination skills from the stratosphere. His question echoed in my mind, and I replied in a torrent of confidence. "The ghost hated you when it was a human and has carried that bitterness to the grave. But, it cannot be said with certainty if the ghost will hurt you or not."

Then he quickly asked another question. "If you see a ghost smiling then?"

I replied with boldness that surprised him. "The ghost wants to convey something—a message or a warning—or unveil a hidden fact."

After waiting for a while, he asked me, "If you see a ghost sitting on a chair?"

"The ghost has assumed ownership of something at that place," I replied in a cold, black and white tone.

The Aghori paused for a while as if mental combat was going on inside his head. He resumed asking a question with a smile curled on his lips. "A ghost points its finger somewhere?"

In a gentle voice, I said, "It's misleading you." The answer seemed to amaze him. With burning eyes, he fired off another question at me. "A ghost is fiddling with hair."

I opened my eyes, but our gaze was fixed and expressions rigid. The Aghori sat stupefied, and perspiration started to form on his brow.

"It's of evil origin. Get rid of it as fast as you can before it swallows you." I'd given a remarkably powerful answer.

He stared deep into my eyes and asked with shivering rage, "You see a ghost eating?"

"The ghost is of an evil origin and wants to feed on a soul," I said with a strong impulse.

The Aghori threw another question, and I was prepared to gulp it down. "A ghost whispers in your ear. What does it mean?" His gaze loomed over me.

I said in a deeply moving voice, "The soul wants to use you as a medium to fulfill a pending task."

He smeared ash on his face and made an awkward sound. He then looked up at me with a sound of amazement and asked, "What does a ghost standing near a window mean?"

"The soul is waiting for something or someone," I said.

He asked me more and more pointed questions which began to evolve into a parapsychology seminar. His questions didn't stop and neither did my answers.

Finally, he labored through a long breath as the moonlight fell on his white face. His thick eyebrows knitted into a frown, and there was a display of conflicting expressions on his face. I couldn't decipher the meanings behind these and wondered if my answers had angered him. Suddenly, his eyes darkened, and the dilating pupils expanded to his rising emotions. He expanded himself in the dark caverns and spoke to me with such strength that it shook me from inside.

"There is no scripture or book where we can evaluate your answers as right or wrong. However, a wise man or a Tantrik has enough reasoning powers to know the worth of what you have said." He took a skull in his hand, poured some water from a tin vessel, and drank of the contents.

The Aghori wiped his wet lips with his palms and continued speaking. "You didn't know about it, but when perfectly focused, you answered all of the questions with ease. It was like these answers were treasured in your dormant brain. Softly, unperceived layers of time fell upon this unopened box, covering it with its grains."

I listened to him very carefully, with respect, to understand his derivations. His rationale seemed to be true, and he said, "I can't touch the part installed by the source. How can anyone, even the Aghori or Nagasadhus eliminate something that is implanted by the universe? We are mere mortal forms of Shiva, and this is beyond the spectrum of finitude. Take this as a blessing, and it will bless you. Take it as a curse, and it will ruin you. The choice is yours . . ." The Aghori smiled at me in such a way that made the blood in my veins run cold.

"Did I come here to listen to this?" I murmured to myself bitterly.

His lustrous eyes glanced about for my mother. He waved

at her over, asking her to join our much-coveted talk. Mom walked toward him, followed by Karthik. She touched his feet and sat down beside me, casting her eyes upon my expression, seeking to understand.

She looked at him in amazement. In her creative lens, he was just a pile of bones seated upright.

"You have fulfilled your responsibilities with tremendous strength and endurance. Your enormous vibrations of optimism bestow great creative and spiritual potential upon your child. Your prayers are her complete armor." His words brought triumph to Mom's face.

She spoke in a low voice with a well in her eyes. "Baba, you know everything. I have no one in my life except my daughter. And now, her life is in danger. Can you free her from the paranormal forces hounding her every night?"

The night wind moaned, working its way through the place. After moments of uninterrupted silence, his voice broke in. "The sheer amount of content seen in this interactive universe is nothing short of overwhelming. The universe is arranged in a very complicated manner—68% dark energy, 27% dark matter, and 5% is the residue where normal energy thrives. The same formula is applicable here on the earth. We only understand a small percentage of the matter—and the rest is the stuff of mystery. Sadhus and seers have been meditating for ages, trying to decipher the dark matter, dark energy, and the darkness prevailing around us."

He paused to consider the peaceful expressions on our faces.

Mom folded her hands before him and asked humbly, "Baba, how is this related to my daughter's problem?"

The Aghori unfurled a smile and decided to speak straight rather than leading us through the maze. He said in an unflinching tone, "This knowledge is embedded in her subconscious. Sometimes, due to the activation of the third eye—or the opening of Chakra—the subconscious mind gets awoken and relays the information to the conscious mind. Whatever is happening with your daughter is the doing of her active subconscious mind."

The expressions on my mom's face hardened, as it was getting more serious than she had imagined.

"What's the way out? How to make the subconscious mind inactive again?" she asked hastily.

The Aghori realized a savvy generation of words would make no sense to a mother. It's better to refresh our minds with a pause and rephrase the concept with a brush of virtue and higher good.

He sang a short verse, but no onc responded, as if it had fallen on deaf ears. The Aghori sensed the concern and spoke in an applauding and attention-seeking tone. "Oh, Mother! Your daughter has brought with her to life the mystic knowledge of her past incarnations. She knows the answers to the unknown domain. Isn't it astonishing?"

The Aghori stopped speaking to see if the look on Mom's face had changed. He continued milling his words, "Look, Mother, how she has downloaded the mystic powers from the Akashic library in the Universe. This is the rarest of the rare cases."

There wasn't a single trace of pride or happiness on Mom's face as he spoke. The Aghori spoke with a twisted style. "Congrats, Mother. Your daughter is born to be a soul healer. To heal the pain of the dead and if needed to destroy the evil rooted in dead souls. Here is the reliever of the ghosts. The soul world was waiting for this moment of awakening. Someone to free them from ages of wandering and searching."

Before the Aghori could complete his lines, Mom exploded. "Why can't anything be normal in our life? I had seen only common dreams—a happy married life—but it never happened. I was okay with it and thought my destiny was ill-fated." She let out a few sobs, and I tried to calm her down, but still, she reacted. "I poured my sweat and blood to raise my daughter. For this day that she heals dead people who are suffering because of their deeds? To be a doctor or a counselor to the ghosts? Thesc are ghosts because of their karma, and now my daughter will strive, sacrifice, and suffer to erase their pain?"

There was a confused look on the face of the Aghori. His lips moved to speak, but Mom was on and on, expressing her anger. Finally, he gave a loud grunt to clear his throat and spoke in a gruff voice. "So, Mother, tell me: do humans not fall ill because of their eating habits or lifestyle or addiction or negligence? It is okay to treat them because they are humans? Do counselors not treat patients with depression or bipolar disorder? Do they not treat alcoholics, abusers, and criminals? Ghosts are no different. They are also like them, Mother." He tried to cajole her to empathize with the dead.

"Mother," the Aghori continued to draw her attention to the plight of the roaming souls. "These poor souls couldn't get this healing when they were alive, and hence, after death, they are stuck in the hollow darkness. They need someone to free them from the cycle of revenge and pain, so a soul healer is born after a specific timeframe and is sent to address their grievances. Your daughter has been given this role in the universe; this is her purpose, and she should fulfill it as a universal obligation."

Mom turned her face toward me and gazed into my wolf eyes. For a moment, fear crept over me while anticipating her next move. She cuddled my tresses, moved her hand over my face, and spoke in broken accents. "I am a mother and have only lived as a mother. Don't tell me of these heavy universal roles, purposes, and obligations. I have strived to bring up my daughter and give her all that she deserves."

Mom folded her hands before him and said in a drenched voice, "For the first time, when I laid my eyes upon her, a burst of wild laughter rang through my deserted life. When I pressed my cheeks against her velvet red cheeks, peace kindled in my heart. I glanced at my daughter, noticing the tears fall as she cried, and I decided to walk out of this abusive marriage to give her a happy upbringing. This decision wasn't easy; I struggled a lot at home, in the office, and in society to reach at this position—this pinnacle. I lived for the sake of my daughter, for her happiness and secure future. I swear on the banks of the Ganges that every word is true, or may Hell fall upon me. My daughter is my life's only creation and aspiration. Save her," she pled.

The Aghori listened her every word with great attention and speeded up to speak in an ordinary tone. "A stone will light a fire anywhere. Her subconscious brain has retrieved these mystic powers, and sooner or later, time will rekindle the passions from the past. It can't be eradicated or destroyed on the whole."

Mom was shaking upon facing the cold facts. She was caught up in grief and anger, but after a moment of crying, she gathered her courage and said in a blazing voice, "Baba, instead of making my daughter see these ghostly specters and apparitions every night, instead of leaving her with the fear of being possessed or killed by a ghost, and instead of looking out for a solution at every doorstep, put an end to this mess. If not a life of peace, then let my daughter at least die in peace. I will live in an old age home with her memories. Aghori Baba, you need a corpse to eat and meditate upon, take this: take my daughter, for sooner or later she is going to end up like a corpse." She broke out in a wail loud enough to be heard at the other edge of the shore.

For a moment, the Aghori was blank as she manifested her feelings so intensely.

He spoke in a soft voice to calm her down. "Oh, Mother, one day, some of us will be on the other side of the fence, a silhouette in the darkness, waiting to tell our story to a soul healer."

His emotional words had no impact on Mom. The Aghori saw moonlight reflecting in Mom's eyes like shining quarters. She repeated her previous lines. "Relieve my daughter from the pain. You are an Aghori. What do emotions matter to you? Take out your weapon and slit her throat. Bring an end to this perpetual torture and free all of us. At least, this is something that an omnipotent devotee of Mahakaal can do with ease," she said with eyes dark with anger and a voice ringing like a death knell.

The Aghori gazed at my mother as if his very mother was in that gaze. Mom's wet eyes repeated the requests, and her sad tone pierced a corner of his encased heart, shattering it completely. He stared at her for a minute, perhaps, connecting to the maternal feeling swelling inside her. There was a tug of kinship that he reconnected with instantly. Maybe he remembered his mother for a moment.

The Aghori rotated his neck, from side to side and then upwards and downwards. He swallowed up the silence in the darkness and slowly said, "There is one way."

In this moment of complete chaos, complexity, and confusion, his words shifted my winds, pushing me to fly toward the northeastern sky to find the star of new beginning, at last.

"What way?" Mom asked, raising her eyebrow, impatient to hear him speak.

The Aghori saw Mom's anxiety and spoke in a thoughtful voice. "We cannot eliminate or transfer this psychic power possessed by your daughter. So, let's experiment. We can attempt to suppress it like a dam on a river."

"Suppress it?" I repeated with a quiet emphasis.

"Yes, you heard it right, child." The Aghori evoked a sense of warmth and curiosity with his words.

"Suppress something when it becomes too powerful. You must have studied that in your history classes." He gave a small laugh and continued detailing the plan. "You will have to suppress them," he said, pointing his index finger toward me and said in a commanding voice. "For the sake of your family and future, you will have to suppress their presence. Only you can do it. Remember, it's not so easy to pull off."

"Baba, please explain it to me," I said.

"If you see a ghost, however fearful or sorrowful it looks to be, don't react or respond to it. You should behave as if you haven't seen it. These souls will manipulate objects, create frightening illusions, or try to entertain you by showing words on the walls, but don't react. Over the years, seeing your no-response, the paranormal energies will leave you to search for another soul-healer."

"Another soul healer?" I asked, surprised.

"Yes, child. You are not the only one. Another soul healer will be born after a particular duration. It can be ten years, twenty, or even after your existence on the earth. Only the universe knows the timing." He sounded very prophetic at that moment.

"It's difficult to execute, Baba." My golden eyes pierced his black, sunken, hollow eyes and moonless face.

"Difficult but not impossible. If you can heal them, then only you can command them. Never forget, only the person who holds the key has the option to lock or unlock the doorway at hand. You need only avoid them, avoiding anything that may arouse your powers—like reacting or responding or reverting to the dead souls. They will cause a lot of drama around you, but you shouldn't fall prey to them," he said in a merciless voice.

He looked at my mother and calmly said, "I know the efforts taken by you to raise the kid. Mother, now, there is an additional test you need to pass. If you want this ghostly distraction out of her life, then listen to what I say." He looked at my mom's soft beaming face. "These ethereal creatures of the dark lookout to make a connection when an individual is alone or isolated or low or unwell. Science explains these phenomena with big and complex names. Let me make it simple for all of you to understand. Did your daughter witness anything paranormal here in Varanasi?"

I shook my head to say no. There was an impish smile on his

face, and he said in a pressing voice, "There are two choices—live your normal life and neglect the paranormal stuff, or heal the dead souls and live a life full of restrictions."

The Aghori turned his face toward my mother and said with his queer fierceness, "Mother, fill your home with positive energy. Light aromatic incense sticks or sage; play instrumental music or classical ragas; ensure she is never left alone at home. Give her happiness, love, and good vibes."

I was trying hard to connect the dots when the Aghori's bones began quivering with excitement. The Aghori glanced at the studded night sky and said in a solemn voice, "From the day you reach your home, remember the concept of selectively selective or conscious experience. You have to decide what to define, see, and explore from both spectrums—conscious and subconscious."

I exchanged glances with my mother and put my doubt before him. "Baba, how is it possible not to react to a ghost? However hard I try to follow your instructions, a stimulus-response behavior is bound to happen. How can I work on this aspect?"

My question gathered his brows in deep thought. He scanned the space, squinting to get a better view of the surroundings, and then replied in a profound voice, "Practice. Keep practicing because this is the only answer—your love for your mother."

There was an awkward silence. Karthik was playing the role of a dutiful audience, listening to our conversations. There were many pauses in between.

"Baba," I said, "as you know there are good ghosts and evil ghosts. How do I protect myself from evil spirits? What if I'm not able to recognize an evil spirit in disguise?" My voice stirred the silence of the night.

The Aghori saw the puzzled, scared, and confused look on my face. Contemplating, he said, "Your intuition is connected with something greater—the mystic wisdom. Meditate on, trust, and listen to your intuition. Ensure that it is always in an activated mode—like a north star, follow its directions, and you won't be lost in the sea of infinite energy.

"I agree with your thoughts," I interjected and then paused after realizing my mistake. The Aghori baba signaled for me to continue, and I pled him desperately. "I understand all about intuition, but something tangible like a compass can be of use when the sky is eclipsed. Please, Baba, give me something tangible rather than a metaphysical barometer."

Agreeing with what I had said, Mom and Karthik also requested the Aghori Baba to give us a totem or a protection crystal. Mom extended him a monetary favor, but he refused, as materialism didn't mean anything in their extreme, wild lifestyle.

The Baba placed his hand in his saffron-colored jhola bag, which was lying nearby. He chanted a divine mantra in an unknown language and then fished out something from the bag. A beautiful fragrance emanated from the thing he had touched, soothing our nerves. We were awestruck by the singular spectacle that depicted miraculous power.

The Aghori baba gazed at me before handing it over. There was an emotional note in his voice as he whispered to me, "This Ek-Mukhi Rudraksha bead was given to me by my Guruji. This totem will protect you from all evil energies. Always keep it with you, for as long as you wear this Rudraksha, no one can harm you. If any malicious spirit comes near you, this Rudraksha will change its color from brown to black, and it will emit a foul smell till the energy is around you. Once the evil spirit is gone, the Rudraksha will regain its original color. On every full moon and new moon day, cleanse the Rudraksha, worship it and re-energize it, so that its spiritual energies are recharged. Remember, never keep this Rudraksha away from your body for more than an hour."

The tone of his warning echoed in my ears.

After a moment's pause, he resumed. "It takes the collective energy of meditation, austerity, and prayer to create a totem like this one. This Rudraksha has been passed down for seven generations, and it draws its power from the ancestral energies. Please tie it on your right wrist with a religious red cotton thread. My guruji handed over this powerful bead to me and said, 'the Rudraksha will choose its own wearer."

"But did your guruji ever tell you how you would identify the wearer?" I asked curiously, desirous to know the answer.

"Intuition . . . my guruji had told me. You will identify the wearer of the Rudraksha with a single glance. The wearer will be bestowed with the powers of Shiva's dark energy," he said and gently placed the Ek-Mukhi Rudraksha bead in my palm.

I could feel a divine power flowing from the palm to my third eye. The sweet, faint smell of sandal emitted from the Rudraksha, signifying its divine properties.

"I should go now," The Aghori said, marveling at the sky, which was sparkling with stars.

We prostrated before him and repeatedly thanked him for his guidance.

Before leaving, Mom turned to him and said with folded palms, "guruji, can I have your contact number, in case, there are any exigencies?"

The Aghori laughed aloud with a tinge of mockery and said, "Mother, we don't have a home, and you are asking for a contact number. Shiva is the protector of your daughter. Trust him, he will send the medium. But still, if you need me, leave a message with the corpse-burner at Manikarnika Ghat. I will connect through them on their phone." He smiled, looking at Karthik.

Once again, we got up, touched his feet, and walked away. There were still thousands of probable destinations waiting to be explored. Still, as I walked back from the magnificent ghats of Kashi built in an amphitheatric style, I felt as if I had left a piece of my heart there.

Beware, you may find it lying on the wooden plank of a boat gazing at the shimmering waters under the spreading sun of dawn or on the banks of the Dashashwamedh Ghat, waiting for the ceremonial Ganges aarti to commence at sunset or rejoicing in the vibrant atmosphere of peace and purity. Please, be careful. Don't walk over it in the milling crowd, for the heart is still beating.

CHAPTER FIFTEEN

MOVING FORWARD

Nothing connects you better than a pause. Today was our last day in the ancient and timeless city of Varanasi.

It was 10 am and I was laying in the bed harboring many thoughts over yesterday night's meeting with the Aghori. The session had so much spirituality and rationality, that the boundaries of reality and supernatural were slowly dissolving. I was wandering all over the transcendental terrain to search for answers to the questions raging in my mind. From the borders of the human and divine, heaven and Gaia, I created higher connections with the vestiges and fragments of diverse interpretations.

I felt my consciousness is limited within the bandwidth of the infinite mind to board the gigantic questions of existence. Upgrading my knowledge seems to be the only viable route to understand the mysticism and mysteries of creation.

Mom was sorting through and packing up our things for the departure. I looked at her with sacredness; she had galvanized the ups and downs in her life with tremendous resilience and persistence. She had the guts to forge a trailblazing path and map out her journey while being responsible for me. Her inspiration was the foundation for enabling and empowering me throughout the years.

"Mom, why did you overreact before the Aghori?" I sat on the edge of the bed and asked her in an amplifying tone.

She continued to gaze at me for a minute and then, remarked, "The end-result matters; means make no difference."

The entire room was silent... except for the rhythmic beats of the winds that lulled our apprehensions, preparing us for a wild breakthrough.

I heard her words, she made sense. Sometimes, her intelligence is indefinable, the way she draws on it, converts it into an influential tool, to create an embodied experience from it.

There on the center table, the Rudraksha bead was kept in a glass bowl filled with the holy water of Ganga. With an emotional softness, I saw my ultimate savior hoping it will make the change happen.

After a year of draining and logging in difficulties, I could get in touch with my dreams, my inner self, and my emotions. The battle was not over but at least, I am armed to strike in a never-before-done style. Imagining the best possible future, I headed to the bathroom to purify and revitalize my body and soul in the rejuvenating properties of the water element. The sacred bathing of the body evokes new proverbs that can inspire you to wipe a storm.

I bathed slowly as my head was clear and thoughts settled. I filled and refilled myself with the healing energies of water and fusion of rose, lavender, and rosemary scent. I bathed and dressed slowly to feel the gap in between the activities. For the first time, I fell in love with the pause...

I wore color-washed denim jeans, a multi-color halter top, and clinched my waist with a belt. I put on an off-white-colored front open shrug to reflect my style statement.

The insights in this trip have taught me to find a balance between the good and the bad, the dark and the light, the yin and the yang.

I have so much love for this special place, such a strong connection, it entices me, again and again, to look back more enthusiastically than forward.

Peeping into the lives of people around me, I have understood that the algorithms of the problem will exist forever. There is never going to be a perfect state with flowers, with nature, with the blooming of the spring in many ways. What are sorrows? What are obstacles? nothing; but an infinite loop ready to crush our spirit and taint our aspirations. But now, I have learned the art of trampling down such iron thorns and thrive in the complex and fascinating moon phases.

Mom had ordered breakfast for me. The waiter brought a tray with piping hot seasoned parathas, a bowl of pickle, and hot coffee in an insulated mug.

"Here, Kalki, eat your breakfast," Mom said spooning pickle from the bowl and placing it on my plate of hot parathas.

With a pleasant and cheerful tone, Mom said, "In the afternoon, we will fly away from this place, obviously it will be a very emotional moment for us. But definitely, this is not the last time, we will be coming back again. Let's take these wonderful memories with us to make a lifetime memory."

Mom cut the yellow-red spiritual thread in the size of a bracelet and stung the Ek-Mukhi Rudraksha bead in it. She tied the Rudraksha bracelet around my right wrist with multiple knots and chanted the Maha-Mritunjay mantra. I felt the life-force energy that makes the Ganges flow, streaming in my body and spirit. I could sense the Shakti of Shiva armoring me with a vivaciousness. There was an expression of joy and victory on my face as if, for the second time in history, the man had discovered fire. Believe me, it was nothing other than magnificent - I had mastered winds, waves, tides, storms, and energies but now, I had learned to tap the greatest renewable power source - Shiva.

I felt the warmth of her hand as she stroked my back tenderly. She sat beside me, circling my coffee, and said, "Karthik is not in the resort. He has gone to do some purchasing, complete his final shots for the documentary, and say goodbye to his friends."

"Hmmm" I nodded sipping on the coffee.

Though crafted with doubts and hopes, there was illuminating parallel energy running between us. Keeping her eyes fixed on me, she said in a selfless voice, "I think that a pause will be good for me. For the last so many years, I have been working as a professor, maybe, I can opt for the voluntary retirement scheme. Let me focus on the second innings of life - I can spend more time with you, we can travel, we can work on a start-up, we can do everything we missed in all these years before you get married and go."

She stopped but the outburst of her tender emotions and expressions was continued. Her unsaid words lingered in the air, seeping through her mind. I proudly looked at her and said, "Whatever decision you take will be acceptable to me. I know you love your job very much, so don't leave it just for me. Also, I don't want the upcoming generations of students to miss the opportunity of learning from you."

She smiled, got up from the sofa, and walked toward the turret. After a moment of fresh air, she turned to me and said in a determined voice, "What made me such a skilled teacher? You... were the catalyst that evolved me to my true form. My experience as a mother and life-circumstances made me a better teacher. If you are not in my life, then I will collapse down. So, don't convince me to change my decision. I can continue teaching as a private tutor. Let me decide how to chalk out my roadmap ahead."

"Ok," I answered.

"We were running on an emotional roller-coaster and maybe, after reaching home, she will reconsider her decision. And, even if she wanted to slow down and take a pause, I think, she deserved it. She had toiled from the utmost depths for these years. Let her live her life as he desired from now on," I concluded in my mind and gave her an embrace as an acceptance.

"Mom, I would love to have you with me," I softly kissed her forehead.

She saw the slanting sunrays fall inside from the casement windows of the turret. She sounded excited as she spoke, "Hey, you are a creative genius, so let us rattle our brain to make our life more interesting and happier. I want to be with you when these paranormal attacks befall on you. I want to simplify these cosmic mysteries to ease your journey. I want to sit in one place like a tree and make my roots deeper and stronger to support you. I want to rebond, restart, and redesign our moments together in perfect synchronicity."

Hearing her out, I couldn't stop myself from gathering in her arms and crying like a baby. Mom consoled me with her high-spirited talks and asked me to gear up as she was ready to steer our boat in another direction to reach the new destination - "LIFE 2.0"

I reached out for my iPhone; we clicked few selfies in the total Nirvana settings to later post it on the social media with the caption - LIFE 2.0.

Mom was still packaging the stuff and I joined her to complete the task fast. We spoke about our travel plans to Everest base camp, Mansarovar, Nepal, Bhutan, and African safari. After all the bags and baggage were done, Mom sat on the imperial couch. I sat down on the carpet by her side, placing my head on her lap, forgetting everything around me.

"Mom, I have asked Karthik to do a full-time MBA to upgrade his skills and concepts. Till the time, we can help him by managing his web development agency. After he completes his MBA, we are thinking of starting an Infotech company - conceptualizing the idea," I said in an optimistic voice.

"That's good," Mom lightly pressed my shoulder.

"Mom, I realized my mistake. Problems, odds, obstacles are a part and parcel of life. There is no point in waiting for a perfect climate. Life should move on ...we don't stop breathing because of problems then why should thriving?" I roared out, looking up at my mother as she grazed through my hair.

"Tell me, baby," Mom insisted me to speak out my heart.

I tried to overcome the momentary shyness and said in a deeply moving voice, "Mom, I want to engrave a significant memory in the upcoming year - 2020. If you approve, I and Karthik can get engaged," I said and my heart skipped a beat. I didn't dare to look up at her recollecting her previous conversation and kept my head bowed.

There was a stillness in the air and silence between us. I assumed the answer was a NO, due to her delay in replying. I was in a dilemmatic mode when she lifted my face and drew a happy smile with her beautiful lips. She pulled me up and hugged me so tight that I felt we are inseparable.

During lunch, we spend a lot of time talking about the anticipated event discussing everything as if it was happening before our eyes. We talked about the venue, food, visitors, costumes, jewelery, and budget until we were mentally exhausted. Her spirits were on a surge, ready to create a tide of celebration. It took me a lot of nerve to eventually calm her down.

"Mom, please keep it a secret till we officially announce it. Also, we have to speak with Karthik's grandfather and relatives. We can't take them for granted." I discussed as we walked back to our room. These lines were effective to bottle up her enthusiasm.

There was still a gap of two hours for us to leave. I took Mom's permission to wander off on the ghats alone. I captured many images in my DSLR camera lens. Some images were of people basking in sunlight, some images were of people seeking spiritual experiences on the ghats, some images of local people struggling to meet their end, but every single image had a story to be shared. It was not an easy task, focusing on the angle of the shot and controlling the thoughts warring in my mind. In between, the mobile rang. It was Abheer's call and without a moment's delay or any confusion in mind, I disconnected the call. I never felt so certain ever before.

I shot videos of the wandering ascetics on the ghats to tell the story of how some people swoop to the higher dimensions of life. The ghats, narrow streets, ancient temples, architectural charms, people, tourists, Ganges, and other infinite things merge up to create a unique essence, I see all of this as an anatomical form of Shiva.

Varanasi's waterfront, the panoramic stretch of ghats, represents his long, dark black and matted hair. On top of his head, the tresses circle up in a knot form creating a valve for the sacred Ganges to flow. The narrow alleys are his infinite veins breathing life-energy in the cosmos. Both the Manikarnika and Harishchandra Ghats are powerful tools that ignite the breathing process again in the dissolved atoms. Varanasi is just the physical body of God Shiva; he has taken this form to come closer to you.

Zoom your lens, expand your thinking power beyond the dimensions of life and time, and it will highlight you with the greatest truth ever-prevailing in the Universe. Varanasi shows you the whirlpools and eddies of the magnificent cosmos in the final few breaths of life. The solace and peace in the place draw your mind, body, and spirit in complete synch to manifest the earth.

I glanced at the pure ether where air breathes. The infinite energies that arouse our earth to live, billions of minuscule particles scattering in the air like ashes, and the moonlight rejuvenates the weary earth with milk and love. Starring in the depths, I saw the grandeur of the beautiful sky, and how it is interconnected with the omnipresent Universe to create a breathing pattern that rekindles the fire of life-energy.

The whispering Ganges spoke in my ears an indefinable and sacred truth of enlightenment. My golden eyes stared at the mysterious elements singing their hymns to the benevolence of nature. I stood firmly between the strands and ripples, the passage of opening and closing to see the greatest power of the Universe touching every sea and every soil.

As my heart throbbed louder and louder, I could feel the veins and energetic trails of Varanasi settling within me. I was in oneness with the creative energy of the universe, the matrix of life-force. I could breathe, digest, and reproduce the higher vibrations of the cosmos, joining forces with the Creator.

Varanasi was nothing less than a sip of ambrosia that transformed me into an alchemist. At the feet of Ganges, embracing the breathing ghats, I could feel a meta-nostalgia of emotions and expressions creating a culture of Shiva inside me...to purify everything that comes in my touch.

I felt the confidence that Shiva's alchemy will filter and purify all the evil and malefic elements on my way. I know, this is not sounding science or medicine but spirituality - unventured science for many scholars.

In some places, saying good-bye is easy with a mere shake of hand but to a place like Kashi, it is emotional turbulence. As our airplane jostled to take us back to our home in Mumbai; my eyes overflowed with tears. I tightly pressed the Ek-Mukhi Rudraksha tied on my left wrist with red thread woven like a bracelet. Closing both my eyes, I chanted the Shiva Gayatri Mantra, focusing only on divine consciousness. In a fraction of a second, it uplifted me and activated higher powers to interpret the universe in a series of intuitive visions.

I know these visions, intuitions, and mystic understandings cannot combine to transmit the sacred lineage of Buddha in my veins. Still, I want to merge all these spiritual units into a kaleidoscope and manifest it in form of a colossal galaxy orbiting on a spiritual axis.

Sensing the beautiful sky loaded with fleecy clouds, my mind began to draw a wonderful image of the future. Life is ready to be loaded with immense love and care from Mom and Karthik. Instead of feeling sculpture in life, it is the time to feel the clay – moments that mold life.

Instead of straight lines, I felt the impulse to write in curly, doodled, freehand lines that signify freedom and passion. The pages ahead are to be filled with explorations about rediscovering self in people and places. Hopes are high in the air, and the desire to glide is larger than life. Some challenges need to be tackled but let me try to write triumph instead of giving up.

Bright things lie ahead, be it engagement with Karthik, new friends, career on shine, or restart 2.0 with Mom. Thinking about my psychic abilities, I resonated, "Actually, do I have a superpower? Isn't it cool to have a superpower?"

Do people know the risks and accountability of owning a superpower? Anything more than a necessity, higher in quantity, even elements like water, heat, light, and fire cause the only destruction. Imagine if the gravity was a little in excess or less - guess the consequences.

Mom is right, even ordinary powers like courage, laughter, and willpower is a superpower and at times, more powerful than even the superpowers. This is how ordinary man has progressed to this level with his ordinary powers loaded with extraordinary attributes of determination, intelligence, curiosity, and skills. It is a noble task to help someone but not at the cost of my life, safety, and peace. I am not God but a medium of God.

It is an art to heal a lifeless, emotionless soul. I am blessed that nature chose me for this artwork. When the light comes, darkness follows, if I start healing souls, then good souls will be followed by bad souls, and bad souls will be trailed by evil souls. In the pursuit of healing them, my life will come in danger.

Yes, it sounds selfish but it is not selfish when our life and family are at stake. So, in the end, I am a selfish artist renouncing my ability of healing for the larger good of my family and happiness. Dark energy is everywhere even in the universe; like ghosts and other dark entities roam freely in our terrestrial zone. We can't see them but a kind of presence is felt in the late nights when something bumps.

There are unlimited doors for paranormal identities to invade my life but no lock and key with me to stop their entry. It is in my best interest to stay away from these dark energies and not burn my night oil to light them up. One thing is clear, I am no saint or monastery to conduct spiritual offerings and sacrifices. I am an ordinary girl; my mom's daughter, this identity is enough for me in this lifetime.

There are many Shamans with superpowers to explore and heal the consciousness of the dark dimensional world. If not me, these souls will find someone else, stronger or weaker than me.

During revolutions, certain species are supported to survive but then these species turn out to be the new oppressors and the cycle continues. Connecting this concept, what if the poor spirit healed by me turns out to be an evil spirit desirous to hound upon me or wants to possess my physical body to fulfill their greed?

Bhagavad-Geeta emphasizes that "Life, living and human incarnation are of significance and difficult to attain than anything else."

It makes sense to be away rather than get trapped in this endless game that may continue even when I die. What is the guarantee that these spirits will not follow my spirit after my physical release from the earth?

As the airplane moves closer to my new territory of happiness, I am gearing up to walk away from certain things and embrace some things. I have already tossed the previous book of my life in the high altitudes and am now, I am all excited to open the pages of a new beginning.

My energy is bursting to break the orbits and float in the infinite expanse without thinking of anything else. I have found and stirred the courage lying dormant inside me. I am now, someone new with the same body but a new mindset, new spirit, and new attributes including an erased past.

Be it a ghost or a paranormal evil, no one can mess with me. This is the promise I have made to myself. I will honor it with everything possible. Not only my life is at stake now, but mom, Karthik, and someday, of our offspring.

I will not allow them to haunt the rest of my life; a struggle will soon begin between me and the forces of the paranormal world. However, fierce this battle be, I will not give up the joy of living; positive waters of Ganges are now distilled in my arteries. I will not drain the efforts of my mother to raise me into a beautiful and talented woman.

Walking away from the night of fear, I am moving closer to every moment of my new beginning. As the plane passed through the Equator of the Sun, I assured myself to make all things right and ensure my willpower is strong enough to deal with everything. The time has come for me to wear my mom's shoes. I am her daughter; her strong lineage of courage and power runs in my veins.

Glaring back at the glimmering light of the sun, I crossed my fingers and whispered to myself, 'From Good Night to Good Morning!'

The future is clear before me; a happy family with Mom and Karthik. But there is a fear, life is never predictable, you never know when you are forced to take a sudden U-TURN on a straightway. Until now, I am determined not to pause and give a thought about intersecting on another curve. Let's see when the time comes. Why worry now?

"Carpe-diem" is my life-motto and I am ambitious to live it to the fullest – good food, exciting trips, late-night dance parties, lots of books to read, listening to stories from mom, meeting new people, and loving Karthik like I never loved anyone before.

What a cup of life to sip on.

Varanasi was the catalyst for my self-discovery. The Universe is a powerful observer and teacher. When I was falling in life, it brought me on the ghats of Kashi and turned my life upside down.

For, in the end, there is nothing more precious than life, and I want to safeguard mine. I am going to apply the same force in living a passionate life as it took me to swim and emerge out of the dark womb. I left something behind in the dark chasms of Varanasi and evolve out in a new form – a happy human being. Life goes on, death goes on but the essence of the Universe lies in thriving.

I may get hurt, defeated, bleed but I will not give up the breath that was gifted to me by Shiva, the cosmic energy that purifies everything and anything.

I am sure, this is the time to thrive not die. Do you agree, with me, Life?

"Good night, dark and evil forces in the Universe. I am ready to live my life on my terms and conditions. See you never again…"

This is not a perfect ending. It is a pause as I move on to a new beginning of life. Endings should always be perfect but it is in stories not in real-life excerpts. In any personal story, the ending will be made of clay – imperfect, full of blemishes, dissolvable if not made up of strong cement, and fragile.

It is similar to my interim climax – if I don't stand up strong then the dark waters can drown me away. In this process of churning and changing, with an extra ounce of courage, I am ready to leap to a new transition that marks a glorious season of intoxicating Cherry blossom – an enduring experience of renewal and survival. I know, in the upcoming beginning, more splendor awaiting to meet my golden eyes.

"For what is life but a fleeting moment of experiences,
Untie from the themes of mortality and materiality,
And leave behind a timeless reminder for the world to relish".

Here, the pause marks the beginning of a new season in our life!